Kirov Saga:

Altered States

Volume I

By

John Schettler

Discover other titles by John Schettler:
The Kirov Saga: *(Military Fiction)*
Kirov - Kirov Series - Volume I
Cauldron Of Fire - Kirov Series - Volume II
Pacific Storm - Kirov Series - Volume III
Men Of War - Kirov Series - Volume IV
Nine Days Falling - Kirov Series - Volume V
Fallen Angels - Kirov Series - Volume VI
Devil's Garden - Kirov Series - Volume VII
Armageddon – Kirov Series – Volume VIII
Altered States– Kirov Series – Volume IX

Award Winning Science Fiction:
Meridian - Meridian Series - Volume I
Nexus Point - Meridian Series - Volume II
Touchstone - Meridian Series - Volume III
Anvil of Fate - Meridian Series - Volume IV
Golem 7 - Meridian Series - Volume V

Classic Science Fiction:
Wild Zone - Dharman Series - Volume I
Mother Heart - Dharman Series - Volume II

Historical Fiction:
Taklamakan - Silk Road Series - Volume I
Khan Tengri - Silk Road Series - Volume II
Dream Reaper – Mythic Horror Mystery

Mailto: john@writingshop.ws
http://www.writingshop.ws ~ http://www.dharma6.com

Kirov Saga:

Altered States

Volume I

By

John Schettler

"Mother Time is a dressmaker specializing in alterations."

— Faith Baldwin

Kirov Saga:

Altered States

By
John Schettler

Foreword:

At the end of Book 8 in the *Kirov Saga* five new novels were proposed as put to a vote by the readers. It was not surprising that this continuation of the *Kirov Saga* in a 9th volume entitled *Altered States* ranked #1 in the reader poll, and was also the #1 vote getter in all the many emails I received, which constituted the bulk of the voting. The #2 proposal was the alternate history of the WWII naval campaign in the North Atlantic that was entitled *Hindenburg* and predicated on the assumption that in 1936 Germany initiates an aggressive naval building program to produce ship designs conceived under the code name "Plan Z."

As *Altered States* was to present the world that was born as a consequence of *Kirov's* many interventions in the past history, it seemed plausible to me that the Plan Z alternative could have easily been one of the many things that changed. I therefore decided to please as many readers as possible by combining those two top proposals into one new story here under the title *Altered States.* In so doing I will present all the historical material for the *Hindenburg / Plan Z* story, as integral to the continuation of the ongoing trials and travails of the mighty *Kirov.*

Though this story is a fiction, I have made every effort to underpin it with sound research concerning ships that fought this campaign and the men who led them to sea and served on them. All the old characters you have come to know aboard *Kirov* are here, along with several new historical characters I will be developing as this portion of the saga both continues the story from where it last ended while also beginning a new series that will take you through the naval campaign in the West.

Historical characters are real persons who lived, fought, and sometimes died in the actions described…and some fated to die live here in my story when fate or chance changes their personal destiny. LtC. Christopher Wells, for example, died aboard HMS *Glorious* on that ill fated day in June of 1940 when she was caught by *Scharnhorst* and *Gneisenau.* Yet here I have given him a new life, with all respect to those that knew and loved him, and I sincerely hope my fictional depiction is deemed worthy of the man he truly was.

The *Kirov Series* itself has gone through many evolutions, and though I have thought to bring it to a conclusion several times, it keeps finding a way to carry on. At present it is structured as a set of trilogies linked by what I call "bridge novels." The opening trilogy comes to some satisfying end at the conclusion of Book III, *Pacific Storm* when Karpov spares the *Key West.* It was then that I wondered how their contemporaries would have received them upon their return to Vladivostok, and how they would explain their strange disappearance and unexpected return. This gave birth to *Men Of War*, where Fedorov hatches his plan to go and find Orlov, thinking it was essential that they leave no unfinished business from their jaunt through time.

The second trilogy was born from *Men Of War*, beginning with *9 Days Falling* and extending through *Devil's Garden*. I could have left Karpov in 1908 at the end of that volume, simply sending *Kirov* back to 2021 and then showing the consequences of Karpov's intervention. This would have been another point of possible ending for the story, but Fedorov again refuses to permit the contamination, thinking he can somehow still preserve the time line and the history he so loves. The plan he hatches this time became *Armageddon*, another "bridge novel" which served not only as a sequel extending the *9 Days Falling* trilogy, but a prelude to what is now before you—*Altered States*.

I conceive this part of the saga as extending at least through three books, at which point I will see if anything remains unsaid in this long tale that would compel me to continue it. I realize that it is more a long episodic story within its own world now, much like the never ending *Star Trek* saga which saw so many rebirths. In some ways the main characters on the ship are as familiar to me as Kirk, Spock, Sulu,

Scotty and McCoy, or the all new cast that I also came to know and love in the "Next Generation."

Here now is the next generation of the long *Kirov Saga,* and I hope you will enjoy it as much as I enjoyed writing it. There is so much more to come.

~ *John Schettler*

Part I

Altered States

*"Things alter for the worse spontaneously
if they be not altered for the better designedly."*

— Francis Bacon

Chapter 1

It was over…finally done, or so they thought. They stood on the bridge with heavy hearts, each man silent with the inner weight of his own conscience. Then Admiral Volsky closed the book he had been reading from, slipping it slowly into his uniform breast pocket. The poem he had read carried a dour sentiment, and an equal burden of guilt. He knew that the ship had been responsible for much harm, fighting in three wars across two centuries. The damage they had inflicted on the mirror of time was easily seen, the cracks webbing out through the months and years to change the reflection of history. Yet there was no way to fully understand exactly what they had done, or so they thought…

We have been blundering about with good intentions for the most part, thought Volsky, yet blundering still. Fedorov launched his mission to find Orlov for every good reason, yet he could not control the outcome. It seems that every mark we have left on the days of the past must inevitably work its way forward in time to some resolution, some consequence, and we cannot hope to measure or even know the whole of what we may have done.

This was what he had tried to convey with his words. Yes, they could not measure it, could not hold it, yet it was nonetheless theirs. They had to own it and accept the responsibility for what they did, for whatever reason—to preserve the ship, to save their own lives, or to embark on the bolder agendas that grew in the Devil's Garden of Karpov's mind.

What had happened to the Captain? Volsky saw the blood, still wet on the gunwale of the weather bridge. Rodenko had told him they heard gunshots, yet no body was found. Could he have fallen from that high place and careened into the ocean? If that were so he would have been pulled into the void right along with the ship. Did that mean his body was out there somewhere, adrift on the heartless sea?

"Well now," he said. "Time to grieve it all later. At the moment we must determine where we are, and look to the safety of the ship and crew. He turned to Rodenko to ask about *Kirov's* overall condition and the *Starpom* gave his report.

"Chief Byko is working below decks on the situation in the bow, sir. We struck a mine and there was a minor hull breach. Three compartments flooded but they have been contained and the pumps are working now. I'm afraid we have lost the Horse Jaw sonar dome, and we will need to make repairs to the bow."

"That means no active sonar from that system…Well, we will have to rely on *Kazan*. Their systems were completely operational, so I will be sure Nikolin establishes a direct communications link and monitors it at all times."

"That would be prudent, sir."

"And how are the men here?"

"We are fine, Admiral. The situation we just faced was difficult, but I think the men can continue this watch and we can make regular relief rotations as scheduled. Facing the Captain in his rage was no easy task, but it is certainly better than what we were facing in that impending battle."

"Yes, Armageddon, you fought it here on this bridge and saved Admiral Togo and his lot for another day. It must have been very difficult indeed. Thank God no one else was hurt. All things considered, the crisis resolved itself fairly well. Yet I cannot help but wonder what happened to Karpov. Was a search made for the body?"

"Yes sir. Byko put divers in the water to inspect the damage while you were touring the ship. I gave those men orders to have a look around, but nothing was found. Just a few fishing boats off near the island that I hope belong to this day and time."

"Very strange," said Volsky, still very disturbed by what had happened. "We will arrange for a sea burial ceremony at an appropriate time," he said heavily. "We owe the man our lives many times over and, in spite of what he became in the end, we owe him at least that respect."

"I agree, sir," Rodenko said solemnly.

Volsky shrugged, looking about the bridge and seeing the men smartly at their stations again, which gave him heart "A fine day," he said looking out the viewports at the sea. "This damage to the bow—will our speed be affected?"

"Byko has asked that we do not attempt to exceed 20 knots."

"Is it repairable while we are underway?

"The flooding can be controlled, but to adequately repair the outer hull we will need to be in a stable environment. Dry dock would be best, but that is impossible. He thinks the divers could do something, but we would need to be anchored."

"Well," said Volsky, "until we know just where we are, I think it best to maintain a modest cruising speed. What is the status of our radars and electronics?"

"The *Fregat* system is returning out to a 50 kilometer radius at the moment. That seems to be gradually extending, almost as if we were in some kind of expanding bubble, sir. I think we should have normal coverage in about an hour."

"What is our course?"

"We are hovering just off that island, Admiral."

"Then let us set a course for Vladivostok at sixteen knots until we know where this time displacement has sent us. I think I would feel better in familiar surroundings."

"I'll get the ship moving , sir." Rodenko moved off to instruct the helmsman.

As always, Fedorov huddled with Nikolin first, and the two men were monitoring signals all through the radio band. At first they had heard nothing more than the backwash of static, but now the garbled sounds of voice transmissions were picked up, though they could not make anything out yet. Like the radar systems, the radio was slowly recovering as the effects of the time shift wore off by degrees.

Oddly, it was the lookout on the main mast that Rodenko posted above the bridge that saw it first. There was something in the sky, a gleam of sunlight on a sleek surface, the yellow glint of light on metal. Just as the sighting was sent down to the bridge radar reported the contact close in, the operator shocked to see something this close unnoticed.

"Someone is curious about us," said Volsky. "It must have been just launched from beyond those hills."

"Most likely, sir, or we would have certainly seen it this close on radar long ago." This was very unexpected, but Fedorov immediately realized they should be in range to communicate with the contact. He asked Nikolin to switch to standard AM bands to see if they were picking anything up and, sure enough, there was a stream of unintelligible language in his headset on a low dial position.

"It's Japanese," said Nikolin, handing off the headset to Chekov, who spoke the language.

"They are asking us to identify ourselves," said Chekov directly.

"Of course, what else," said Volsky. "Well if they have a good telescope or a pair of field glasses they will have already seen the naval ensign flying from the main mast. I think it best to strike those colors. We do not yet know what our situation is and for all we know Russia and Japan may have not healed the rift Karpov opened here in 1908."

"What do I tell them, Admiral?"

"Say nothing for the moment. I think we will just be on our way. Sixteen knots. No rush about it, but Mister Samsonov, if you would stand ready and see to the ship's defensive systems that would be prudent—just as a precaution."

"Aye, sir. Shall I come to condition two alert?"

"Not just yet. But be prepared in the event we run into anything unexpected."

So they eased away, leaving silence behind them like the thin foaming wake on the sea; leaving the island and everything that had happened there behind them as they went. Signals traffic soon convinced Fedorov that they had not been able to advance much more than twenty years into the future.

"I'm not sure why, sir," he explained to the Admiral. "It could be that the mass involved was too much to move. Remember that the test reactor in the Primorskiy Engineering center left a man behind. We were lucky that Rod-25 was able to move both *Kirov* and *Kazan*, but we're not home yet."

"Then we will try again," said Volsky.

Kamenski had come aboard the ship in the last hour and so the Admiral convened a meeting in the officer's stateroom to determine what to do. Chief Dobrynin had also come aboard to check on *Kirov's* reactors and was seated with them to provide technical advice.

The old ex-KGB man spoke first. "We could find ourselves hopping through the cold war next if Rod-25 can only nudge the two vessels a few decades at a time."

"That might be better than finding we are in another hot war," said Volsky. "What do you suggest?"

"We have three control rods—two that have never been tested for this application. We might try one of those here on *Kirov*, and then see what Rod-25 can do with *Kazan*."

"Chief?" The Admiral looked to his reactor engineer, giving him the floor.

"A couple things come to mind at once, Admiral," he said. "First, while we have three control rods, I cannot be in two places at once to monitor the shift. I could control one shift, but the other ship would be on its own."

"A good point. What are the dangers involved?"

"Perhaps none at all, sir. We could dip the rods and everything might work out just as we hope. Then again, given all that has happened, I tend to doubt that will be the case. The first problem we face is that the two rods may perform differently. Rod-25 is older, more weathered by continuous use, yet it has proven to be very reliable. It tends to pop into the 1940s every time it shifts, one direction or another, but it was able to get us home once, and it was also able to get us to 1908. One day soon, however, it will go the way of all spent control rods. There is a limit to the radiation it can absorb. It will have to be removed and retired."

"The other two rods—they are completely new, yes?"

"Yes sir, they have never been tested, as Mister Kamenski indicated. So they could perform in unexpected ways, or perhaps even fail to perform at all. This remains to be seen."

"What do you recommend, Chief? We must rely on your experience in these matters."

"Well, sir, Rod-25 is beginning to present some telltale decay signatures in the absorption spectrum data. I was just looking that over and comparing it to logs from our earlier shifts with the rod aboard *Kirov*. I would not suggest trying to move both ships again, even if *Kazan* was right beneath us now."

"I see… Then we must install one of the other control rods."

"If we do this I recommend we leave Rod-25 aboard *Kazan*. It is radioactive, and difficult to manage. The other two rods are still inert, and much easier to transport and install here aboard *Kirov*."

"You would use both rods?"

"No, just one at a time. But *Kirov* is a dual 24 rod reactor system. I could place these new control rods in the number 25 spot in each of those two reactors, so the second would be immediately available should it ever be needed. It takes several hours to install these rods, and we have been in situations where our displacement in time literally saved the ship from almost certain destruction."

"This is a good plan," said Kamenski. "But will the engineers aboard *Kazan* know what to do?"

"I have some well trained men over there. They can initiate the maintenance procedure easily enough, though controlling it is another matter. I think I would need to be here aboard *Kirov* when we attempt to use one of these new rods."

"So that leaves *Kazan's* shift to the roll of the dice," said Fedorov.

"Perhaps," said Dobrynin. "Yet this time *I* have a plan, Mister Fedorov. I thought that I might be able to use the recording of our last successful forward shift and extract that data. It will tell the engineers aboard *Kazan* what I did by way of adjustments to the reaction to produce a safe shift home. This is by no means a sure thing. They will not hear it as I do, but it would be like a template of a proper shift, telling them when to adjust the power, the speed, and how to respond to flux events. I cannot guarantee anything, but it may work."

Volsky sat with that, thinking. "So we give them a kind of road map home in the data and hope they get there. That is very risky, but I do not see any other alternative. Yes, I agree that you will be best placed here to break in these new control rods. Who knows where we will end up? Everything about this entire affair has been one surprise after another. Something tells me that fate may have a few more twists and turns ahead for us. That strange balloon was one thing. What do you make of it, Mister Fedorov?"

"It could have been a weather balloon, sir, or just a simple observation balloon."

"You are hearing radio signals now?"

"Yes sir, which means we have advanced beyond the era of simple telegraphy, though that is still in use in modern times. The presence of AM and FM signals is very telling."

"Well, where are we?"

"We have picked up Japanese and Chinese stations—a lot of ship to ship traffic, and some signals that could be coded messages on a military channel. Chekov has been on duty for the last two hours to translate as he can speak Japanese. Nikolin is listening for English. We have no firm dates yet, but I believe this is the early1940s."

"How can you know this?"

"We received a transmission with what appeared to be a news feed out of Russia. I thought I heard the announcer speak of June 1940, but we got interference at that point. It came back and spoke of Orenburg and the war on the Volga. Then we lost it until the station signed off as the Soviet States of Siberia."

"Very strange," said Volsky.

"Then there was another clue, sir—music. We picked up a station in Manila playing the music of an artist known as Tommy Dorsy, a song called 'I'll Never Smile Again.' It was announced as being in the number one spot this week and I checked that ship's library. It released in June of 1940 and was 12 weeks in the number one spot." He said that with a very disturbed look on his face, so obvious that it prompted the Admiral to prod him with humor.

"Don't look so glum, Mister Fedorov. If this music does not suit your taste, perhaps Nikolin can share his files with you."

"It's not that, sir. Don't you realize what this means?"

"Yes, yes, it means we are back in the soup again, and likely to run afoul of the Japanese Navy if we linger here."

"That is the least of my concerns at the moment, sir. If this is 1940 as I suspect, then we are all in grave danger here, mortal danger, though it may not be from the Japanese fleet."

"I don't understand. Japan did not enter the war until December of 1941, or August of that year after our meddling. That is fifteen to eighteen months from now. There is no reason to assume they would be hostile. They would probably assume we were a British warship out of Hong Kong."

"But sir…It's not that. This situation is very unusual. Until the journey to 1908 we have always shifted to the 1940s at a point *beyond* our last visit there. If this is mid 1940, then that has changed and we are now here before the time of our first arrival. A year from now what happens in the North Atlantic? We were supposed to appear there, and that would not be possible if we are already here. So we cannot remain here. It is imperative that we leave before the time we first displaced here in July of 1941. Otherwise...Well I think something will have to happen to us if we remain."

"Happen to us...That has a rather ominous tone to it, Mister Fedorov, but I believe I understand what you are saying now. There cannot be two ships, two crews, and heaven forbid two of me! So before the date of our first arrival here we must be elsewhere or suffer the consequences of that paradox."

"Correct, sir. Remember that list of names Volkov got his hands on? There were no records on any of those men when we arrived at Vladivostok. It was as if they never existed."

"And we could be added to that list if we remain here before the date of our first arrival."

Chapter 2

Kamenski had been listening closely and now he added his thought on the matter. "What you say is very interesting, Mister Fedorov, assuming this is the same meridian of time we were on before."

That gave Fedorov pause. "What do you mean, sir?"

"I mean that much has happened to the world, and most of it our doing. This message you say you received—the Soviet States of Siberia? I have never heard of such a place. If something happened in 1908 to change the history, then the 1940s we find ourselves in now may not be the same as those you visited earlier."

Fedorov took a moment to absorb that, but he realized Kamenski was on to something here. This was a time subject to the dictates of all the history that had come before it, and if Karpov did do something in 1908 to change the course of events…

"But I do not see how that is possible at the moment," he said. Wouldn't the history have to remain cohesive enough to give rise to the building of this ship? That would have to occur for us to even be here at this moment. It's maddening, sir."

"Yes it is," said Kamenski. "Other men *have* gone mad over it— the Siren's Song of time—yet we dare to sit here and listen, and it seems we have been bold enough to hum along as well! Remember that we remain loose variables at large in history until all these events reach some definite conclusion. We undertook the dangerous mission to try and reach the ship in 1908 and remove it from that time, and that we have done. But the job is not yet complete. We are still a needle in Mother Time's finger as she darns her dress, and as long as we are here the possibility of changing everything that follows this moment still exists. That said, we must not be surprised to find that all the days between 1908 and this moment may have *already* changed, and that the world we sail in now is not the same one we left. I do not know if we can untangle that knot just yet, but at least we have a year before we would ever have to face that paradox you raise, which is plenty of time to shift elsewhere."

"Try to verify that news feed you heard," said Volsky, "and nail down our exact position in time. That would help. You must be able to find out what band BBC was broadcasting on. See if you can listen in on that, Mister Fedorov."

"I've listened on shortwave 6195 and 9740, sir, but atmospheric conditions are not good at the moment. We are also detecting jamming. The Japanese naval facility at Sasebo is uncomfortably close, and if we were reported as an unidentified warship someone is likely to investigate." The implications were not lost on anyone present.

"Here we go again," said Volsky somewhat dejectedly. "They investigate, we try to remain silent and undetected, they get pushy and then we are forced to defend ourselves. The next thing we know we are at war with Japan. Well, I think we should contact *Kazan* at once and make arrangements to get those spare control rods over here. I believe we must put Chief Dobrynin's plan into action as soon as possible."

"Right sir, but there's one more thing."

"Yes, Mister Fedorov?"

"If this works, I very much doubt that we'll both end up shifting to the same place in time, sir. In fact, I would guess that the odds on that would be very slim. I believe the two rods will definitely perform differently as the Chief suggests."

"Then we may lose contact with *Kazan* altogether if we do this?" Volsky was obviously troubled.

"Yes sir, and *Kazan* may find itself adrift in time even as *Kirov* has been. Captain Gromyko is a good man from what I have seen, but *Kazan* is a powerful weapon, perhaps even more powerful than *Kirov* now. We have seen what a temptation that has posed."

"Yes, he will have to listen to the Siren Song just as we have. Well, I do not think I can put the wax back in his ears, Mister Fedorov. He already knows the truth, even if his crew remains oblivious of our real situation. Everything we propose here now is a grave gamble, and perilous to even contemplate, but we must decide. Either we stay together here, and that will mean we are the most powerful force in the sea if this is the 1940s again. Or else we part ways, and each of us vanishes into the ether again to points unknown."

Rodenko returned just as the Admiral was finishing, his face betraying news held in hand. "Whatever you decide, we must be quick about it, sir. Gromyko called to report fast screw noise off to the south and on a bearing to intercept our last reported position. We have no long range radar returns from the south yet, but *Kazan's* sonar can actually hear things at a much greater range than the Fregat system."

"Then the contacts are still well over the horizon?"

"Yes sir, but something is heading our way, and in somewhat of a hurry. I believe they may be fast destroyers or patrol boats. Their speed was estimated at just over 30 knots."

"How far away are they?"

"Their sonar man is still listening, but he thinks the range is at least 150 kilometers at the moment. Assuming they are gaining on us at 16 knots, then they could be in visual range in about four hours."

"We may not be ready to initiate another shift in that time."

Dobrynin spoke up, offering to do what he could to get things moving again. "It will take about three hours to install both rods. I see no reason why we cannot make an attempt shortly after that."

"Very well," said Volsky. "Do what you can, Chief. I will inform Gromyko of the plan."

* * *

Hours later Volsky was weary, though unwilling to take any rest, except for a brief time when he went below to the sick bay to visit with Doctor Zolkin. There the two men had spoken briefly of what they were now attempting to do, and as always, the Admiral sought the council of his close friend and long time confidant.

"So there you have it, Dmitri, we are about to pull the plug and go down the drain again. We hope to move forward this time, but we could slip into the past again. None of this has ever been certain, and we have never used these new control rods before."

"This has been some vacation," Zolkin joked.

"The problem is this...If I allow this, the two ships may be separated. One could end up in 2021, the other in 1990, or 1960. We just don't know. In fact, Fedorov is of the opinion that it is almost certain that the two ships will not shift to the same time period."

"He's a sharp young man. We owe him a great deal."

"We owe *you* a great deal, my friend. I have learned that it was you who gave Fedorov your ear when we were in the Atlantic and Karpov dismissed him from the bridge. You told him to return here for his prescription at 18:00 hours, and it was that happenstance that allowed us to get out of Karpov's little trap here."

"Ah, yes, I had forgotten that."

"So you see, if not for your open heart, siding with Fedorov that day, we may have never been able to take back the ship."

"Oh I think that the crew would have sided with you in the end, Leonid. Don't make me out to be a hero or saint. I have too many sins on my soul for either."

"Yet it was a matter of seconds in the balance there, and you were the lever on all of that. Then it all comes full circle and Karpov is again on the bridge ready to destroy the entire Japanese Navy in 1908—until you showed up."

"Now, now—"

"Yes, Dmitri, I *will* call you a hero. You stepped onto the bridge and faced Karpov down, the first good man to stand up and do something."

"Yes, and I might have died for it if his aim had been better."

"That said, fate saw you at the heart of both these events, and so your part in all this was very significant. Would Samsonov have stood up as he did without your words, or seeing what had happened to you? All I can do is thank you for what you did."

"Well I should have acted sooner. Rodenko came to me earlier with his reservations about what the Captain was doing. I told him I would back him up if need be, but I left the matter with him. In all truth, Leonid, I believed we were marooned in 1908 just as we all did. That control rod was not on the ship and I could see no volcanoes about, so there we were, and likely to remain there unless Karpov used another nuclear weapon. Still, I believed Rodenko should make the decision as *Starpom*. I wanted to give him that choice first."

"That was wise, Dmitri. Well…what do I do? Should I go forward with this plan, with the risk that we will be separated from *Kazan?*"

"What else is to be done?"

Volsky hesitated, thinking, his eyes searching, head inclined as if he were listening to something far away. "I know what Karpov was trying to do," he said at last. "He tried to argue it briefly when I called with the order to stand down here. The man believed he had the power to prevent the rise of the Japanese Empire that eventually led to the war in the Pacific. Fedorov tells me that war killed twenty million people, so this is a hard nut to chew on. I am sitting here with *Kirov* and *Kazan*. If we thought we were powerful before, with are twice as strong now. I realize that with these two ships I *could* do what Karpov was trying to accomplish. We now believe it is June of 1940. That means the Japanese have not yet launched their war plan, but I realized that, if I so desired it, I could stop them right here. I could make sure no Japanese troop ships ever reach their destinations, and there is nothing they could do to oppose me with the power at my command."

"So now the devil sits on your shoulder," said Zolkin. "Yes, I suppose you could do something, but it would mean you would have to sink quite a few ships and kill thousands of more in the process."

"To save millions," said Volsky. "Is that why we are here, I wondered? Is that why Rod-25 delivered us to this time and place?"

"Leonid…This same bird had been on our plate ever since that first accident with *Orel*. It has always been a question of whether we should intervene or not to shape the days ahead. Fedorov, god bless him, was trying to put the eggs back in the nest, but I think it is far too late for that now. Save twenty million lives? Yes, it sounds like a noble cause. But we never fought with any of that in mind. I think we just fought to save our own lives, as any man would."

Volsky nodded. "I said as much to the men on the bridge. We were here, then one thing led to another. War is war, so I am not surprised that the moment we were discovered the other side started taking shots at us. This will happen again unless—"

"Unless you go find your island, eh?"

"I suppose so. Yes, we need some mysterious island where I can hide *Kirov* and *Kazan* away from the woes of the world. I thought I had cut a deal with that British Admiral once, then we vanished again. It was Rod-25, of course, but we did not know that at the time."

"Well, do not waste your time looking for that, my friend." Zolkin shook his head now. "No matter where we go, the world will find us. We will stick out like a loose thread in a well hemmed dress. Yes, it will be obvious to anyone who encounters us that time has slipped a stitch. We can jump from one place to another with these control rods, but one day they will fail us, and leave us somewhere, and on that day we decide all this, for good or for ill. Now, however, if you can take us forward to our own time where we belong, then I think you must try."

"Of course....But I am not so sure that world will be the same, Dmitri. Fedorov has been hearing odd things on the radio here. He gathers that the history between 1908 and this time has played out quite differently."

"Oh? How so?"

"The revolution seems to have torn Russia apart. In the last hour he has heard radio transmissions from Russia and they call themselves the Soviet Siberian State. There was something about a war being fought on the Volga."

"On the Volga? Then the Germans have already invaded Russia?"

"We do not know yet. The news has been spotty. I have him trying to find a BBC broadcast now. In any case, I am thinking that if the china is cracked this badly here, what will the plate look like in another eighty-one years?"

"I see what you mean."

"Yes, and suppose we do try to go home, but it has happened that events were changed so radically that this ship was never built! After all, the original *Kirov* class missile cruisers were a product of the Cold War. That rests on the outcome of this war, World War Two, so if things change here..."

"I see what you mean. This is very puzzling, Leonid."

"Fedorov thinks that our very presence here is proof that *Kirov* is built, but Mister Kamenski has plopped another fish into the soup. He has intimated that this world, the air we breathe at this moment, may be a completely different meridian of time—an altered reality that is the product of all our meddling. In that case then we have shifted farther away from home than ever before, even if we are closer to 2021 than we were in 1908. If we have slipped through some indefinable barrier and entered a new reality here and the future that progresses from this point may not be the same as that which built this ship....Well it is frightening to think of this."

Zolkin had a grave look on his face. "I think we have been doing this all along," he said. "Remember when we first reached Vladivostok and Volkov got hold of that list of casualties?"

"Yes, I have discussed this with Fedorov and Kamenski. We found out those men were never born!"

"True, but there were other cases, Leonid. Remember the suicide we had aboard ship after we docked? Voloshin, that was the man's name. He had come to me with bad dreams after that nightmare when the Japanese ship went right through us while we were shifting."

"Yes, I think we all had nightmares after that."

"So I gave the man some pills to calm his nerves, but he hung himself—and not because of bad dreams. It seems he and his wife had moved to Vladivostok two weeks before we left Severomorsk for those live fire exercises. As soon as we reached port he and a few other crewmen went to the apartment, but now this is the strange thing— they said they could not find it! All the addresses on the street were changed and the building was not even there! At first I thought the men had simply gone to the wrong address, but they seemed adamant. The city was not the same. So I think we have been breathing the air of a different reality each time we have shifted. This is what I believe."

Volsky took a moment to let that sink in. "Then we cannot save it," he said softly. "We never could save it—put the eggs back in the nest as you say with Fedorov."

"Leonid, men have looked to the future for generations with the idea they could build it, shape it, save it for their old age or their children and grandchildren's sake, but they never could. Most of the time it was all they could do to try and hold it together in the moment they lived. That's all we can do, my friend. This moment, for most men without ships that travel in time, is the only place they are ever at liberty to be. They say they do things for a better tomorrow, but what they really do is live in the here and now, whether good, bad or ugly, and they try to make it just a little more sane, and a little more comfortable."

"But we *are* at liberty to be somewhere else. That is the mind-numbing thing about our situation. The train is off the tracks, and we no longer have to follow it. We can move to another time—I can order Dobrynin to start the procedure in half an hour, and the moment we do this air we breathe, this sacred moment we once called the here and now everyone else is stuck in, well it just vanishes!"

"So you get another here and now after the fog clears, yes? It's no different than going to sleep tonight. You close your eyes, your thoughts linger, images drift through your mind, then you let go and drift away. The next thing you know it is tomorrow, only that day is no longer something waiting to be, it is right there in the palm of your hand. So what do you do? You wake up, get out of bed, and walk into that new here and now. You see, Leonid, we are all time travelers. We get the present in little slices, like a loaf of bread, day by day."

Volsky smiled. "Give us this day our daily bread…"

"And forgive us our trespasses," said Zolkin.

"As we forgive those who have trespassed against us…" He took a long breath. "I suppose I had better get things moving. Dobrynin is waiting for the order."

"So what have you decided?"

"Time to go to sleep, Dmitri. We may soon wake up and find *Kazan* is no longer in bed with us, but I don't see that there is anything else we can do. If we stay here it will be a very long and sleepless night."

The Doctor nodded, smiling.

Chapter 3

Fedorov was on the bridge, finally hearing the news he had been searching for on the BBC. Nikolin was translating the English, and the picture of the world being painted was quite astonishing. When Admiral Volsky returned he came to the communications station to see what he had discovered. He saw his young ex-navigator sitting with a pad device, checking references as Nikolin fed him information, a perplexed look on his face.

"Mister Fedorov, you look as though you are having difficulty balancing your checkbook."

Fedorov looked up, scratching his head. "I'm afraid I have bad news, Admiral. We've been monitoring BBC as you have asked. The date is June 11, 1940, just as I suspected, but the news is very strange. Some of it makes perfect sense to me. The British have just evacuated Norway, the German Army is in France, Poland has been divided between Germany and the Soviet Union. The big news of the day is the declaration of war by Italy against Britain and France."

"And the Soviet Union? What was this business about a Siberian State you heard earlier?"

"That has also been confirmed, sir. From what I can gather, Russia has divided into numerous factions. One calls itself the Soviet Union in the west and the news from there is centered on Moscow. A second state seems to exist in the heartland of the Urals and south into Kazakhstan. News there came out of Orenburg on the shortwave, something about the 17th Airship Wing and Samara."

"Airship wing? That is very odd."

"Then we monitored that other source again, the Free Soviet Siberian State. But it wasn't broadcasting from Vladivostok. The signal signed off at Krasnoyarsk. In fact, we could hear nothing at all from Vladivostok, at least nothing identifiable in Russian. Nikolin says he has Japanese stations broadcasting on that vector, and the call sign is Urajio."

"What does this mean?"

"I looked it up, sir. It is the Japanese name for Vladivostok. Apparently the Japanese Empire has established itself there, and extends from Korea, through Manchukuo and into the Trans-Baikal and Amur region."

"This entire sector is occupied by Japan?"

"It appears so, Admiral."

"So Russia is divided. I cannot say this surprises me. It is a miracle that the nation survived the revolution in one piece after the Tsar fell."

"This would have to mean the civil war had a very different outcome. Perhaps the Bolshevik Reds were unable to completely defeat the Whites, and these other two states arose."

"That is a reasonable conclusion," said Volsky. "And what of this fighting on the Volga? Have the Germans invaded?"

"No sir. In fact, Soviet Russia is a declared neutral in the conflict. Instead there seems to be ongoing fighting between that state and the Orenburg Federation, and there is fighting in Samara, Saratov and the Don Basin along their common border."

"Well Mister Fedorov, the history did not survive Karpov's intervention after all. We did what we could, but *Kirov's* engagement there may have caused irreparable damage even before we snuck in with *Kazan*. Now the only question is what will happen if we try to shift again as planned? If the history is this badly fractured, I cannot imagine what the world might look like in 2021."

"It might heal, sir. History has proved to be very resilient. There could be ethnic and national forces at work that will eventually see Russia re-united, and the war now underway in the West will also affect the outcome and shape of the post-war world."

"So Stalin will be busy getting his house in order for a good long while. I wonder how this will affect the war?"

"Who can say, sir, though another odd thing is that there has been no mention of Stalin, at least not in the news we heard. We did here something else, a broadcast out of Volgograd."

"Volgograd? The city was not called that during the war, yes?"

"No sir. Before the war it was Tsaritsyn, and then it was renamed Stalingrad in 1925 and was called that until 1961 when it changed to Volgograd."

"What do you think about this, Mister Fedorov?"

"I cannot be certain without a good deal more information, sir, but it could mean Stalin failed to consolidate power in the Bolshevik faction."

"That would be welcome news." Volsky looked for a chair to get off his feet, sitting down next to Nikolin at his station. "The two of you have done well. Yet now we must decide on this shift. I have spoken to Doctor Zolkin and Rodenko, and they both feel we should try another shift. Chief Dobrynin says he has both control rods installed. What about those contacts Rodenko reported on? Are they still closing?"

"No sir, they broke off and turned back to Japanese territorial waters once we were well into the Sea of Japan."

"Good. Then we will have time to move north and sort ourselves out without being bothered, and we do not have to rush into this procedure yet." He looked at his watch, thinking how he never felt the same about it now. It was always a touchstone and reference point in the day, but now the time was never certain.

"Mister Fedorov, do you have any ideas concerning the deployment of *Kazan* relative to *Kirov* when we attempt this?"

"Well sir, given that the two vessels may not move together, perhaps they should stage at a very safe distance from one another.

We know Rod-25 has a radius that can affect things several kilometers away."

"Then you suggest *Kazan* be well outside that range. I suppose this is a good precaution. If we are poking holes in Mother Time's dress again, we might tear it apart if we shift too close to one another. Yet I have also wondered that if we do attempt a close coordinated shift, might it not increase the chances that we shift together? What do you think?"

"It is difficult to know, sir. My feeling is that these effects from the rods could interfere with one another. It may be very risky and we could open a much greater breach in time. Who knows what could happen then?"

"This is as I feared," said Volsky with a shrug. "Very well, we go our separate ways, but I am very nervous about this. We could be sending *Kazan* off to an uncertain future. It could appear anywhere and then Gromyko is trapped in the same nightmare we have been living in. I have briefed him on this, but what will he do? He is only now revealing the true nature of this mission to his crew."

"I have thought about that sir. Nikolin and I have set up a secure encrypted channel to *Kazan* on a special frequency. What we will do is immediately broadcast on that channel after the shift to determine the location of *Kazan* relative to *Kirov*, and they will do the same."

"Yet we would only be able to communicate if both ships arrive in the same time, which you yourself argue is most unlikely."

"That may be so, sir, but it must occur that one or another ship arrives first. The signal will then go out automatically. It might be heard even if the other ship arrives days or even months later."

"And if it arrives ten years later?"

Fedorov raised his eyebrows, knowing that they were again facing a great unknown. Volsky could see his frustration, and raised a hand. "We may never be able to sort this out, Fedorov. But this is a good idea. Yes. Set up your automatic signal beacon, and let us hope for the best. We have some time yet. I want to get well north before we shift, and find a safe place to see to our bloody nose in the bow. Any suggestions?"

"The Sea of Japan is likely to be busy if we linger here, sir. If we could time it for a night transit we might slip through the Soya Strait north of Hokkaido and get into the Sea of Okhotsk, but it would take us two days to get there at 16 knots."

"Plot that course. We have the time. But I have asked Gromyko for a little favor before we make the final decision."

"What is that, if I may ask, sir?"

"I consulted with Samsonov on the state of our remaining weapons inventory. It seems we have eighteen missiles, nine each of the *Moskit II* and *MOS III*. Considering that we have an uncanny knack of finding ourselves in hot soup when we shift, I have asked Gromyko to transfer over nine of his P-900s. That will still leave him six of those and sixteen *Onyx* missiles, and all his torpedoes, so his boat remains very strong. But I would feel just a little more comfortable with a few more missiles—not that I have any desire to use them. Rodenko also tells me Karpov had re-configured several SAMs for special use. I want those restored to normal operating status."

"I understand, sir."

"I also want to arrange a ceremony for Captain Karpov, and brief the crew on what is happening. Then we will give Byko and his divers a day for repairs before we shift."

* * *

Orlov watched the last of the missiles being carefully loaded into the silos. The Admiral had come to him and asked him to oversee the operation, and he made sure it was done quickly and efficiently. *Kazan's* teeth were a little smaller, by just a few centimeters, than the normal P-900s *Kirov* would carry. They also had a much smaller warhead at just 200 kilograms, though they had twice the range, out to 660 kilometers. Martinov checked them into inventory and set crews to see to their safe loading in the vertical silos. There was a modification kit that had to be installed for use on a surface ship, but otherwise they were soon lined up on the forward deck silos, and the hatches were slowly closing.

The Chief saw the lights wink farewell from the weather bridge on the sail of *Kazan*, and he raised his arm in return, hand making a fist. Then he watched as the men there scrambled below and the submarine slowly submerged. Gromyko, the Matador, was on his way to an unknown fate. Who knew if they would ever see the sub again?

With the missile silo hatches sealed and the forward deck cleared, he punched up a nearby intercom and reported the reload operation as completed. "Weapons secured in silos," he finished.

"Very good, Chief," came Rodenko's voice in return, and Orlov smiled. They are still calling me the Chief, he thought. This is a forgiving ship and crew. If they knew what really happened back in the Med, I suppose they might think otherwise, but we will let those sleeping dogs lie.

He reached into his pocket, able to light up a cigarette at last. So now what, he wondered? Where are we off to this time? I get my little slice of redemption here, just as Karpov had his. But a leopard does not change his spots easily. Karpov was back to his same old self the instant he thought he was beyond the reach of higher authority. And what about me? What have I become in all this? Molla got what was coming to him. I've settled that…unless the bastard is still alive now. They say it is 1940, two years before I paid a visit to Molla. One day I would like to go home to Georgia, but that day may never come.

He looked at his watch, seeing it was nearly 18:00 hours and time to assemble on the fantail for the ceremony for Karpov. An empty casket was being laid to rest there, beneath a Russian flag.

Hollow…That was how he felt about it, as hollow and empty as that casket. Karpov had tried to manipulate him to support his play for the ship, and positioned him to take the fall if things fell apart. Well, he felt my fist in his belly for that, so I will call things even and join the crew. I wasn't here when Karpov was given command of the ship, but the men spoke highly of him. I suppose we owe him a decent burial, though his body is probably rotting in the sea by now.

He went forward where most of the senior officers and a good number of the crew had gathered on the fantail near the helo bay. Orlov slipped into the group, staying on the fringe of the crowd as he watched. The Admiral was there, standing by the flag draped casket, and now he spoke.

"Fighting crew of the battlecruiser *Kirov*," he began, placing his hand on the casket. "Here we would lay your fighting Captain to rest. Yet he is not with us. His body was never found. So here we stand to pay our respects, and lay what we knew of this man to rest. He was a mystery to many of you, and yes, a man you may have feared. Yet when this ship was faced with certain danger, he fought, and saved us all on more than one occasion. I gave him command of the Red Banner Fleet because I knew he would do his best for us. It was only when he thought himself to be forever lost in time that his heart hardened again, and for that we can forgive him. Yes, we must forgive."

Now he turned and faced the casket, saluting slowly. "Vladimir Karpov, Captain of the First Rank, acting Commander of the Red Banner Pacific Fleet, may you rest in peace."

The boson raised his pipe and three long notes trilled out, cutting the silence. Then the Admiral nodded to Troyak where he stood with a squad of Marines in full dress uniforms. He unsheathed his ceremonial sword, raised it to his chin, and then turned his head, his voice sharp and clear as he ordered the squad to action. The Marines moved in well drilled unison, shouldering their rifles and firing once, twice, again. Then the boson's call sounded a second time and a solitary trumpet followed it playing the national anthem of the Russian Federation. The high notes echoed in the helo bay, and not a man there was unmoved to hear them. Even Orlov swallowed hard, tightening his jaw as the anthem concluded.

Then, with a final salute, the Admiral reached for the lever and pulled it solemnly. The casket slid down a chute and into the sea where Karpov had fought and presumably died. And it was over.

Over for you, thought Orlov, but not for the rest of us. He knew the ship was going to try to shift again, all the preparations were made, only this time the Admiral had ordered that the crew would come to full alert. They had no idea where they would turn up, and for Orlov it was somewhat unnerving.

I was all set to live out my life in the 1940s, he thought. I wrote that stupid journal to the ship and crew, asking them to be heroes, valiant men of war and defenders of the Rodina. Yet there is no unified Motherland now, or so the rumors have told it. I wonder if Karpov had something to do with that? I wonder if we go now to the world made by his black heart? Perhaps I choked the breath out of the wrong man after all. Well, rest in peace, Captain. You can do no more harm in your watery grave, and now it is for the living to sort out the mess you have made of the world. He turned and looked for a ladder down, wanting nothing more now than a little time alone and another cigarette.

An hour later Admiral Volsky ordered the engineers aboard *Kazan* to initiate the maintenance procedure with Rod-25. He determined to wait until they got definitive confirmation that the submarine had shifted, and it was not long before Tasarov, listening on passive sonar from the ship's horse tail hydrophones, was able to confirm that the signal was lost.

"I can no longer hear them, sir," he said. "*Kazan* is very quiet, and our sonar system is damaged at the bow, but I think he is gone."

Go with God, thought Volsky. "Very well, Mister Rodenko, please inform Chief Dobrynin that he may begin."

"Aye, sir."

They could all feel it again, that emptiness that weighed like a thousand kilos. They were alone.

Part II

The Spin

"Let the great world spin for ever down the ringing grooves of change."

— *Alfred Lord Tennyson: Locksley Hall*

Chapter 4

It was madness, it was mayhem. It was a mystery that none of them could even begin to sort out or understand. But the evidence of their senses soon told them something was amiss. The air around them was suddenly charged with static electricity and Tasarov's bushy hair began to flare out at odd angles beneath his headset. Volsky felt a strange tingling on his fingertips, and was surprised to see what looked like tiny sparks there. A peculiar light seemed to emanate from the very heart of the ship itself, deep below decks where the reactors labored behind their shield of 300mm armor. A dense mist surrounded the whole region, thick and impenetrable, and scored by streaks of glimmering green lightning. There was a tang of ozone in the air about them and a sudden chill, the cold draft of infinity as the hole in time began to open.

Then they heard it, that deep sound that quavered in the air, yet it seemed held in a restless suspension, neither climbing the scales or descending as it often did in the past. It was just a long, distended note, a breathless suspense, an interminable chord that hung in the air and would not abate or diminish. Finally the strange drone gradually faded to the barest whisper and then all was quiet. The light still glimmered around them, and they could see that they were on a sallow grey sea, the skies pale and wan all about the ship.

"We've moved again, sir." Fedorov stated the obvious, and Volsky nodded, feeling a bit dizzy as he sometimes did after the strange time displacement effects.

"Well, it appears our new control rod works. Signal Chief Dobrynin and ask him what he thinks."

Fedorov was still with Nikolin, but before they could send down the message there was a sighting alert from watchmen posted above the bridge on the radar mast. With ship's systems groggy after a shift, this was a precaution Rodenko had ordered as part of normal battle stations.

"Ship sighted, Admiral, bearing 150, but we have no radar yet. The system is rebooting now."

"Ship sighted?" Volsky swiveled his chair to have a look at the bearing. "My god," he breathed. "More than one ship, Mister Rodenko. Have a look, please."

Rodenko had been leaning over his old radar station watching the Fregat reboot, but now he stood, eyes searching the grey horizon through the viewports. Fedorov was also up, immediately looking for sun and moon position, though both were no more than diffused light behind the low sky.

"We're not where we should be," he said in a low voice, more to himself than anyone else. He was quickly to his navigation station, slipping into a chair and winking at Tovarich there. He was the ship's new navigator when Fedorov had been promoted up the chain of command.

"Tovarich, how is your system?"

"Rebooting is nearly complete, sir. I should have computer assistance momentarily."

"Then key in sun and moon data for our last reported position and find out what we should expect to see in 2021. I'll plot present sun and moon positions and we'll do a reverse calculation." In effect, he wanted to key the approximate positions of the sun and moon and ask the computer what date the two celestial bodies would be in those positions.

"I wish we could see the moon through this cloud."

"I have the data up now, sir. We should not be seeing much of any moon at all for 2021. It was a new moon on June 10th."

Fedorov looked over his shoulder to the place in the sky where the cold while light of a moon shone behind the clouds. That was clearly not a new moon, he knew. It was a least half full to make that much light, and the sun was still up as well, also lost behind the clouds, and low on the horizon.

"In 2021 that moon would have to be rising and virtually invisible," said Tovarich. "And given its position in the sky the sun would not still be up. It sets at 17:06 hours if the day remains the same."

"No…It can't be June 10th or 11th in 2021. We would still be at Severomorsk before we ever went to sea for those live fire exercises, and so we could not appear here as well. It would have to be later in the year, at another time to avoid any paradox. We'll have to reverse the calculation and find the date from this current sun and moon position," he concluded, but after keying the command he was not getting any good prospects. It was soon evident to him that the particular configuration of these relative sun and moon positions was not going to yield a convenient date close to their shift time in the year 2021. In fact, he was having difficulty getting any close match at all in that year, which led him to the conclusion that something was very wrong here.

"Admiral," said Nikolin, "I'm hearing Morse code—international call signs asking for identification."

"At least they are polite," said Volsky. "Look there, gentlemen." He pointed out the viewport and they could now see bright lights winking at them on the near horizon."

"Admiral," said Rodenko, an edge of trouble in his voice. "Radar is back up, very short range but enough to reveal a very large formation of surface contacts out there. Fifty discrete contacts, sir, and that close one in the van signaling with lights is quite substantial."

"Give me a Tin Man display. Let's see what we have here, and as a precaution, Mister Samsonov, please ready the forward deck guns."

"Aye, sir, guns reporting ready with manual backup and optical laser sighting. The ship's fire control radars are not yet operational."

"Very well, laser-optical will have to do."

What in the world could be up here in the Sea of Okhotsk? Fifty ships? It would be nothing from our old Red Banner Fleet, Volsky knew. If they had managed to shift to 2021, all that was left was the *Admiral Kuznetsov* battlegroup, just a handful of surface vessels. Something told him they were about to have a very unexpected encounter here, and the look of that distant ship on the Tin Man was soon enough to confirm his worst suspicions.

* * *

Convoy HX-49 was a fairly large assemblage of merchantmen, oilers and cargo vessels out of Halifax on the 9th of June, 1940. It was the largest convoy to make the crossing to Liverpool that month, with several tankers carrying oil and lubricants, an ammunition ship carrying aircraft munitions, ships with steel and scrap iron, and a mix of grain, paper, wheat, wool, lumber, cotton and other odd resources. Considering its value it was lightly escorted, as U-boats were mostly congregating in the Atlantic south of Ireland at this time and little trouble was expected in the first week of the long journey east.

To avoid the wolfpack area the convoy route saw it steering northeast to a point just off Cape Farewell, Greenland and then turning gradually east to pass beneath Iceland to eventually sail north of Ireland, taking the narrow strait to pass the Clyde. At this point the convoy would disperse, with ships heading to any number of destination ports in the UK.

Two small destroyers from the British-Canadian Halifax Escort Force, *Assiniboine* and *Saguenay,* led the convoy out, then returned to Halifax a day later when the sole trans-Atlantic escort HMS *Ausonia* arrived to take up the duty on June 10. Oddly, *Ausonia* was not a warship by trade, but a large 14,000 ton ocean escort liner originally built by the Cunard line in 1921 and requisitioned and fitted out as an armed merchant cruiser when the war broke out.

She was given eight 152mm guns, four on each side, and a pair of 76mm guns with one fore and aft. A slow ship at just 15 knots, *Ausonia* could waddle along with the large pack of merchantmen, but looking after 50 ships was a tall order for her Captain, Horace Norman of the Royal Navy. There wasn't anything he could do if they did encounter a submerged U-boat, and if a German raider were to come upon the convoy, the ship might try to look imposing with her size and give the impression that there was, indeed, a large British heavy cruiser present in escort.

This was just the dilemma Captain Norman found himself in on June 12th as he steamed in the van of the large 50 ship formation arrayed behind him in six wide rows of six to nine ships each. The sea was calm that day, the slate grey sky low, shrouding the horizon with clouds that made sighting potential threats a chancy affair. No one from the watch called the sighting, but the Captain had been watching the sea off his port bow when he saw what appeared to be a ripple of green lightning and a strange phosphorescent glow. Thinking he was seeing the onset of a sudden squall, his eye strayed to the nearby barometer, which raised an eyebrow. It read an even 30 millibars of pressure, approaching fair weather conditions, so he instinctively reached out and gave it a tap to see if the needle might be stuck, yet it remained unmoved.

"Have a look there, Mister Bates," he said quietly to his Executive Officer. "I thought we were to have even seas and quiet skies for another 48 hours."

Bates noted the odd light on the horizon. "Squall brewing up?" He raised his field glasses, taking a closer look without much concern. "It's very odd, sir. St. Elmo's fire?"

"More like ball or sheet lightning, yet no sound of any thunder, and the color is very strange."

"It is, sir. Should we signal LDI and MAC that there may be rough weather ahead?" He was referring to the two call signs for the convoy Commodore and Vice Commodore steaming in the first line behind them.

"They undoubtedly can see what's going on, but do note it for the log: 21:30 hours, sighted squall line on port horizon." He looked about as if to survey the conditions behind him, seeing the convoy steaming sedately in those long slow lines. In this northern latitude the sun would not set for another two hours and a half moon was already up, but glowing through the clouds on another heading. So that peculiar lighting wasn't a moonrise, he thought, and the sun was low to the west, and certainly not off our bow.

"Might it be an aurora, sir?" Bates was still watching through his field glasses.

"Never saw one so low on the horizon like that," said Norman.

"Well, sir. It doesn't look like anything to be concerned about." But the longer he watched the more that trouble on the horizon loomed as a possible threat in his mind, and he soon saw something there that finally alarmed him, an odd angular shadow in the light.

"Perhaps we should send up to the mainmast to see if the watch has anything, sir."

"Go ahead and call up, but we can see it as plain as day from here."

Bates indulged himself, walking to the voice pipe up and asking about the contact. A minute passed before he heard a voice calling back, and now he *was* concerned.

"Ship sighted, Captain! Right at the edge of that squall."

Now it was Captain Norman reaching for his field glasses, his eyes lost in the rubber cups as he squinted and adjusted the focus. Damn if it wasn't true, he thought. Damn my eyes, there's something there, a shadow crowned with lightning, and it looks big. He knew in his bones this was a warship.

"Mister Bates," he said quickly, "pipe the W/T and report ship sighted, a warship, identity unknown. Give our position and ask if we're getting a new escort. Otherwise I'm afraid we've an uninvited guest this evening. The ship will come to battle stations."

"Aye sir. Battle Stations, and piping to W/T now."

"Notify LDI and MAC and tell them we're investigating. The convoy may have to come twenty points to starboard. Helm, port ten and ahead full."

"Port ten, aye sir, and full on."

The ship's alarm was sounding and they could hear the scramble of heavy boots on the decks below. Men were already rushing to man the 76mm bow gun and he knew the same was happening on the larger 5.7 inch guns to port and starboard. Well, he thought, I hope to god you are not what you appear to be. They had heard nothing about any imminent threat from a German surface raider when they left port three days ago to link up with the convoy. The last information he had was that the British were busy with the final evacuation of Norway, and in fact, *Scharnhorst* and *Gneisenau* were reported off the Norwegian coast on the 9th of June, but there was no way those ships could be here today.

"Mister Bates, signal that ship by light and wireless. Request identification." The Captain knew that if this were a German raider he would likely get his answer with a salvo of 11-inch shells. In that event he had few options here. He would come about and present his broadside to the enemy, firing with four 152mm guns in the hope he might run the enemy off, but he did not think they would run, not when they did have better guns and a nice fat big target like *Ausonia*. Behind him the convoy would have to scatter, and he knew that even now the Commodore was tensely watching the situation, ready to give that order at the instant hostilities opened. Then it would be every man and ship on its own, like sheep scattering to flee from a prowling wolf.

That's what the shadow looked like now, large, dark and threatening as *Ausonia* came around to have a good look at the contact, her nose pointed at the threat and search lights flashing, lamps fluttering, the fingers on the wireless keys tapping out their fitful messages.

Bad weather was now the least of Captain Norman's worries.

Chapter 5

Fedorov stared at his data, clearly perplexed. They were not where they had hoped to be, in 2021. Chief Dobrynin had called up to the bridge, but in the business of all that was then underway, a *Mishman* was holding the line.

"Look there, Fedorov, what do you make of that?" The Admiral was pointing to the Tin Man Display, and when Fedorov looked up for the first time his eyes widened with surprise.

"My god, sir. Look! That ship is flying British colors!"

"That did not escape my notice," said Volsky.

"And it's a White Ensign, sir, which was used exclusively by the Royal Navy."

"So the next question is obvious. What is a Royal Navy ship doing here in the Sea of Okhotsk? And that certainly does not look like a modern warship. Could it be that our shift failed and we remain in the 1940s?"

Now Rodenko spoke to say the Fregat radar was recovering rapidly. "We have radar out to near maximum range sir. A very rapid recovery this time. The odd thing is that we should be getting landform returns from Kamchatka to the east, we were only about a hundred kilometers west of the peninsula when we initiated the shift. There are elevations there as high as 1900 meters and we should be seeing them clearly at this range. What we do have is landforms to our north, and I'm sending the data to navigation for a digital map match."

The Admiral immediately looked for Fedorov, who was already working on plotting their position in time. Now he called up the data Rodenko had sent him and the computer's response immediately gave him a sense of foreboding.

"This is impossible," he said aloud, "impossible!"

Hearing that, the Admiral knew enough to put caution at the forefront of his thinking. Yet he retained his composure, looking to the Helmsman and issuing a quiet order. "The ship will come full about and ahead two thirds."

"Aye, sir."

"Mister Nikolin, signal that ship in the same Morse code standard you received. Simply bid them farewell, please."

"Very well, sir."

"Now if you would be so kind, Mister Fedorov." Volsky swiveled his chair and looked to the navigation station, seeing Fedorov still looking at the screen map with a shocked expression.

"Sir," he said haltingly. The Admiral's last order to Nikolin rattled in his mind in an odd moment of serendipity just as he realized what he was looking at. "That is Cape Farewell! We're sitting about 220 kilometers south of Greenland! According to that radar plot our position is 57.51 by -45.24. Our longitude is identical to what it was at the time of our shift, but our latitude…Why we've move half way around the earth, a full 200 degrees to the west! We've moved in space!"

"Calm yourself, Mister Fedorov. I need you to think. How could this have occurred?"

Fedorov thought for a moment, his eyes still scanning the data he had been keying on sun and moon data. Now an idea occurred to him and he put his estimated sun and moon positions into the computer again for this new position in space and asked it to display all dates where those two bodies would be in this position. He soon saw what he feared.

"Admiral, the sun-moon configuration at this location would be valid for 1940—June 12 to be exact. We've shifted alright, but in *space* this time. It's as if the procedure simply picked us up on the 11th in the Pacific and then dropped us here a day later…Yes…" The light of a sudden discovery flashed in his eyes. "That it! The only thing that makes any sense here is the earth's rotation. It's as if we moved into some null zone in time, but only for a brief moment. In that interval the earth rotated and then we manifested again, on the exact same longitude but half way around the earth!"

"Good lord," said Volsky. "You mean to say we disappeared, but did not move in time?"

"No sir, it was as if we were simply suspended in time, then dropped into this present again when we just manifested. It's a wonder we made a safe landing here. Another few degrees to the west and we would be sitting in Canada on dry land!"

"Thankfully the surface of the earth is mostly water," said Volsky, but now we are in the pot again, and from the looks of this radar contact and that ship out there it is starting to heat up. Any further trouble, Mister Nikolin?"

"No sir. They just signaled farewell back."

"Mister Fedorov...Please open your history books and kindly find out what is going on here."

"Fifty ships in the Sea of Okhotsk did not make any sense in the world, sir, particularly with one of them flying a Royal Navy Ensign. But here they make perfect sense, on this day and in this year, if my calculations are accurate."

"Then what have we just encountered here?"

Fedorov smiled. "I'll have your answer in just one moment, sir." He pulled out a pad device and opened an application, poking at the screen briefly as he set up a search. Then he spoke into the pad's microphone. "Display convoy data for June of 1940." He waited, his eyes afire as he scanned the screen. "Let's see what we have... HG-33, Gibraltar to Liverpool...There! It has to be this one, HX-49 out of Halifax. I can even get the convoy route data from U-boat dot net. I've got their entire database here." He had that information soon after and smiled, looking at the Admiral with satisfaction.

"The route crosses our present position, sir. We've just shifted half way around the world and almost landed right in the middle of HX-49, Halifax to Liverpool. And that—" he pointed at the Tin Man where it was still tracking the ship that had been signaling them. "That is the auxiliary cruiser *Ausonia*. It was the only escort assigned to the convoy on this day according to my data." He put the pad down, folding his arms with a smile.

"Well our resident historian does not fail us," said Admiral Volsky, amazed at how Fedorov had quickly ascertained their position in time. "And it appears that your history has not failed to skip a beat either, at least not this segment. But apparently our new control rod needs a little remedial work. Did we hear from Dobrynin yet?"

"Sir," offered the *Mishman*, "I have him standing by."

"Put it on the overhead speaker please."

"Admiral?"

"Go ahead Chief."

"We have a bit of a problem, sir…"

* * *

"They're turning away, Captain," said Bates as he watched the distant contact through his field glasses. The odd lights at the edge of the sea had glimmered for a time, then faded away. Now the day looked much as it did before, with no sign of threatening weather and relatively calm seas. The only danger on their horizon was the shadow of that distant ship, which Captain Norman was fully prepared to challenge by putting *Ausonia* in harm's way. That was why he was there, the sole sheep dog guarding the flock should the wolves appear—and this one looked dangerous.

So it was with some relief that the W/T room sent up a message that the ship had sent them a single word: Farewell, as it turned away. He could have pressed the matter or even fired a warning shot to insist on a proper identification, but why tempt the devil, he thought? The ship obviously had a very good look at us, and I don't think they were at all fooled by our mass or intimidated by our challenge. *Ausonia* has but one single stack aft, and she doesn't present a silhouette anything like that of a real heavy cruiser. They will soon realize we are a sheep in wolves clothing, to switch things around. But why would they break off if this was an enemy ship? Could they be simply opening the range before engaging us?

Might they be biding their time to vector in a nearby wolfpack? It seemed unlikely that any German subs would be this far out, but it was not impossible. What was really going on here? Why didn't they send their call sign and ship ID if they were friendly? Could it be a Royal Navy ship on a special mission? If so they might not want their position or identity known. *Farewell...* Well here we are just south of that cape and ready to make our turn east. He looked at his Executive Officer.

"They appear to be moving off."

"Yes, sir, that they are. Shall we pursue?"

"What, at fifteen knots? No, mister Bates, I think we'll leave well enough alone for the moment. We've sent our sighting report, now I think it best if we make our turn east. If that is a German ship it may be passing the convoy heading and speed along as well. Signal the Commodore—twenty points to starboard and we'll come round to zero-six-zero. And tell them to be especially vigilant for the next several hours in case we get more unexpected visitors."

"Very good, sir. Right away."

If anything happens, thought Captain Norman, it will happen after sunset in the dark. That's when we'll have to keep a sharp eye. It's going to be a long and sleepless night.

* * *

Either there was nothing left of that world they were trying to reach in their own time, or else time had sullenly refused to let them leave without seeing the consequences of their misdeeds, but the ship had not moved but a few minutes in time. They were still marooned in the past, trapped in the web of the war where they had sailed and fought so many times. Yet the odd thing in Fedorov's mind was the ominous fact that they had come here at a time *before* that of their first arrival in the Norwegian sea so long ago. Then it had been late July of 1941, and now they were here a full year earlier in mid June of 1940. The realization that they had also obviously moved in space was most unsettling. In a meeting of the senior officers with Dobrynin they discussed the situation to determine what they might do.

"I do not know what happened, Admiral," said the Chief, "but this shift sounded nothing like any of the others. Clearly the rod does something, but the sound was all wrong. No matter what I did to try and control the shift, it held steady."

"It did move us in time," said Fedorov, "yet only for a brief moment. Then it returned us, and in that moment the earth had rotated 200 degrees. So it is that we find ourselves in the Atlantic, still a year before the time when we first moved here."

"Very odd," said Kamenski. "These control rods were even more enriched with the substances that we suspect as being responsible for these time displacements, yet the result is obviously quite different."

"And quite dangerous," said Volsky. "Fedorov says we might have landed on dry land! It appears only by chance that we were dropped into the sea again. What about *Kazan?*" They had been so busy with that initial contact that they completely forgot about the submarine.

"Our automated signal activated as planned, Admiral," said Nikolin. "We have not yet received a response."

"*Kazan* was using Rod-25," said Fedorov. "Old faithful."

"So where might it be? Could Tasarov hear them if they were close by?"

"Possibly, sir, but they would certainly hear us…Unless they are in the Sea of Okhotsk, which is where I fear they remain now. Rod-25 has never exhibited this behavior. It always shifted in time, but there was never a spatial variance."

"So I do not think we can expect to see Gromyko and *Kazan* any time soon," Volsky shrugged.

"No sir," Fedorov put it bluntly. "They could be half a world and decades away by now. Only a long range short wave transmission could possibly reach them now, just as we called the ship all the way from the Caspian before."

"I could try this, Admiral," Nikolin volunteered.

"Try, but I don't hold much hope for any result," said Volsky. "The question now is what do we do here? Should we try this procedure a third time?"

"Third time is a charm," said Kamenski.

"Indeed, we might just charm ourselves right into the middle of Siberia and come careening down on some mountain like Noah's ark after the flood. No, I think we must learn more about how this happened before we attempt to run the procedure again. See what you can determine from the data recording, Chief Dobrynin. In the meantime, gentlemen, we are here in June of 1940. What should we expect to find, Mister Fedorov, aside from another of these convoys?"

"It is likely that they reported a ship sighted, and we do look rather intimidating. That said, it was wise to simply break off as we did and signal them farewell. Perhaps they will conclude we were another Royal Navy or Canadian ship."

"The last time we were assumed to be a German raider. Their Admiralty will soon receive this sighting report, yes? What if they run down their list of ships and realize they had nothing out here?"

"Then they may get curious as before, sir. When we showed up last time we introduced our first variation in the history by diverting Wake-Walker's carrier force from the planned raid on Petsamo."

"Well we have just diverted that convoy," said Rodenko. "They made a twenty point turn to the east just as we broke off."

"That doesn't surprise me," said Fedorov. "The Germans had auxiliaries at sea that would often make sighting reports and vector in other raiders, be they surface ships or wolfpacks."

"What is the danger of encountering submarines here? Our Horse Jaw sonar is down and is not likely to be repairable, at least according to Byko. Tasarov says he can use the side hull sensors and the Horse Tail, but submarines are much less detectable now."

"We still have one KA-40, sir."

"Indeed. Well what is happening in your history books at this time, Fedorov?"

"As before, sir. It is a fairly momentous period. The Germans have already broken through to the coast and the British have evacuated at Dunkirk. That will continue at Le Havre, Cherbourg and other French ports for some days. The Royal Navy has also just concluded the evacuation of Norway, and they are about to lose one of their principle aircraft carriers in that withdrawal—HMS *Glorious*. She was found and sunk by the Twins, sir."

"The Twins?"

"The battlecruisers *Scharnhorst* and *Gneisenau*. That's what the British called them. They also called them Salmon and Gluckstein after a tobacconist firm in the UK, but those two battlecruisers were operating to interdict the British operation, and got very lucky."

"A hard time for Admiral Tovey," said Volsky.

"Oh, he should still be in the Med, sir. But yes, the Anglo French resistance on the continent was fairly well beaten. Italy has just entered the war. Marshall Petain sues for terms of Armistice in a week on the 17th and France formally capitulates on the 22nd, at least in the history I have on file—but that could have changed."

"It was remarkably consistent up until now," said Kamenski. "The Admiral tells me you were able to identify that convoy and its escort in a just a few minutes."

"It comes round to my cracked mirror theory," Fedorov explained. "Throw a stone at a mirror and it will not crack everywhere. There will be large segments that remain just as they were before, then a web of fissures and cracks where the damage occurred. This part of the history may not have cracked."

"But the damage may be elsewhere," said Kamenski. "Russia, for example, was fairly well fractured."

"I suppose that the closer you get to the source of the real damage the more broken things will seem. Something big obviously happened in Russia to produce all these separate states." Even as he said that Fedorov experienced a roll of misgiving and quiet inner guilt. Something big? Perhaps not. Maybe it was only that little errant whisper that cracked the mirror this time….Me and my big mouth.

"I suggest that you get those ears of yours to your station now, Mister Nikolin," said Volsky. "See what you can hear of the history. Try all the BBC channels and record anything of interest."

"Alright, sir. I'll get to work at once." Nikolin was up and to his station, back under his headset where he lived each day in the world of dots, dashes and radio waves.

"It's a pity Admiral Tovey is in the Med," said Volsky. " I think that before we are discovered again it might be good to arrange another little meeting."

"With Tovey, sir?"

"I think he is a man I can reason with."

"Well, yes sir, but he will have no knowledge or recollection of us at all. You met him in 1942, years from now."

"Yes, and that is a pity. We will have to begin all over here."

"And there's one other thing, Admiral. If we cannot use these control rods to shift again soon, I'm still worried about what happens to us a year from now when *Kirov* is supposed to arrive here for the first time."

Kamenski raised his heavy grey brows at that. "Well, Mister Fedorov. *This* is now the first time, isn't it? Something tells me this is not the same world you shifted into in July of 1941—certianly not with Russia divided as you believe. Something tells me that the mirror is already badly cracked, and the world we see reflected in it may be very different now, in spite of the near picture perfect replaying of the events concerning that convoy we stumbled upon."

"Well, gentlemen, the world took a spin and here we are." Volsky put his finger on the heart of the matter. "Now any suggestions on what we should do?"

Chapter 6

The world was indeed not the same. Kamenski's instinct had been correct. It had spun off its axis long ago, when Japan had decided to punish Russia for the losses they sustained in 1908 and invaded to seize all of Sakhalin Island and occupy Vladivostok. Karpov's dream was dashed, and instead of inhibiting Imperial Japan, *Kirov's* intervention only catalyzed the rise of that empire. Soon all of Manchukuo was re-occupied by Japanese troops, and all of Primorskiy and Amur province as well. Fedorov and Nikolin would now hear things on their radio that were quite shocking, and they all spent some time trying to determine what could have gone wrong.

Yet they knew in their hearts what the real reason was. Too many things had changed; too many transgressions and sins, repented or not. The fatal stroke, however, was not the work of the man named Karpov. It was not the heedless abandon with which he flung the might at his disposal against the world, shattering fate and time even as he broke and burned the armored hulls of so many ships he faced in combat. His bold appraisal, that he was the man Fate must bow to, was mere braggery, the boastful ambition of a broken soul.

Nor was it the work of Gennadi Orlov, who's self-centered vendetta had ended the life of Commissar Molla, and in so doing gave life to thousands who might have died under Molla's cruel regime, and tens of thousands more that would be born from those who escaped his malicious influence.

Men had died that might have lived, and other men stood alive who should be in their graves. Yet none among them, the living or the dead, had the power to really work the change either. They lived their humdrum lives, ate, played, married, worked and died, yet none had the power to shift the lever beneath the ponderous weight of history.

No, it was a quiet whisper on the upper landing of the back stairway at the railway inn of Ilanskiy. That was the final stroke, and it had been delivered by the a man who had set his mind and heart to the preservation of the past he had studied and so loved. There, in that wild, unexpected moment as he looked into Mironov's eyes, Anton Fedorov succumbed to the folly of an inner desire for justice and good.

He had tried to set things right in the long journey west along the Trans-Siberian rail, though he knew his intervention there had been useless. He sparred with the NKVD, standing up to relieve the harsh conditions imposed on innocent men and women who had been rounded up for the work camps. They had done nothing to deserve the fate that had befallen them, or so Fedorov believed, and he did his part that day to ease their suffering and chastise Lieutenant Surinov in the process.

He could not make an evil man good, he realized. All he could do was stand against him, though the futility of what he accomplished that day had been made plain to him when Sergeant Troyak reminded him they could not place clean straw and fresh water in every train heading east to the camps. The war would go on—Stalin's war—and there was little they could do to prevent that…until that quiet, desperate whisper that was powerful enough to change everything.

It came like thunder, heralding the storm, that fateful rumble in the night, an echo of the titanic explosion of a vagrant from the deeps of space. Then came that strange walk down those stairs and the encounter with Mironov. That interaction, and the curiosity of the man he knew to be Sergei Kirov, was the decisive moment of change.

It has been said that all that is necessary for evil to triumph is that good men to do nothing. In this case it was a good man who did something, for every good reason, and then the history he had so jealously thought to guard came tumbling down, brick by brick, hour by hour, day by day. When Anton Fedorov whispered his warning in Mironov's ear, he did so in an impulsive moment of hope—the hope to save the life of one good man who might stand against Stalin even as Fedorov had stood against Lieutenant Surinov, and it worked.

It would not be Stalin's war this time around. The world that Time built after that was altogether new, altered, a changeling doppelganger, a twisted image of the old history in the shattered image of time.

There, trapped in the reflection of that broken mirror, like a stone embedded in the glass, sat a ship, alone on a still and quiet sea. There sat *Kirov*, named for the man who listened to that whisper of fate, and took it upon himself to take the life of Josef Stalin on a cold dark night in the stony cell of Bayil prison in 1908. That one single act, the flexing of a finger in the night, would change the lives and fates of millions, redraw the borders of nations, and recast the entire political landscape of the world in decades to come. Was it born in Fedorov's plaintive and desperate whisper, or given life by Mironov's insatiable curiosity that day?

It did not matter. It was done. And by 1936 when another demon came to power in Germany, things were about to change yet again.

* * *

The Fuehrer looked at Admiral Raeder, his eyes dark and vacant, as if seeing visions of some apocalyptic future, compelling yet dreadful, an inner specter of chaos, war, and the triumph of his dream of Nazi supremacy.

"Yes, yes, yes, I know all about the cruisers, and the U-boats, and destroyers. The battleships, Raeder," he said. "What about the battleships?"

Grossadmiral Erich Raeder never forgot those eyes. Every time he thought on this meeting they seemed to brand his soul again, haunting him. There was a darkness and a void in them, as if the Fuhrer was some satanic Golem, animated only by the hidden inner energy of his vision. The admiral cleared his throat, expecting this question, ready for it, yet still finding these waters turbulent and fraught with an element of danger. How could he satisfy the seemingly insatiable desires of this man's blackened heart? He would offer him the moon, but the Fuhrer would reach for the stars.

"We have made considerable progress in our thinking on this issue, my Fuhrer."

"Progress in your thinking? It is actions I want, Raeder. Not more thinking and planning. Not more talk. Where are the plans? Are the keels being laid? Show me."

Raeder nodded, maintaining his professional composure in spite of the constant jabbing and almost adolescent urgency in the man before him. His perfect uniform gleamed with honors and decorations earned over a long and distinguished naval career--the Iron Cross, The Order of the Red Eagle, The Cross of Honor, the Order of the Rising Sun, and now the Knight's Cross. He had worked and sailed his way through every rank in the service, from lowly SeeKadett in 1895, through Oberleutnent, Kapitanleutnant, Kapitan zur See in 1919, and on through every rank of Admiral until he assumed his current post as the Grand Admiral of the entire German fleet this very year. He was the first man to hold that rank since the great von Tirpitz himself. He had fought at Dogger Bank, and at Jutland. He had stood face to face with the best that the Royal Navy could sail, his ship's guns blackened with the anger of their fire in the heat of battle.

A tall, handsome man with intelligent eyes, he commanded respect effortlessly, his deportment and carriage the perfect image of the command officer. He had labored for years to restore the tarnished honor of the *Reichsmarine*, slowly rebuilding the fleet within the confining restraints of the Treaty of Versailles, but Hitler wanted more. He repudiated that treaty with an incisive and even belligerent speech.

This conference today was the end result of that repudiation, and the humiliation Germany had been forced to endure at the end of the

Great War. The German Navy was to undergo a new rebirth, becoming a force capable of regaining the honor at sea that had been lost in the clash of arms in Europe. It was the Army that had lost the war, or so Raeder believed. It was lost amid the gas ridden trenches and barbed wire of France, under the thunder of artillery, not on the high seas. The result had been depression, hyperinflation and crushing unemployment.

Raeder had little doubt that Hitler would soon be putting all those millions of unemployed to some nefarious use. But how could he impose economic reason on this man? How could he tell him that Germany was still struggling to rebuild herself as a nation, and that all dreams must have limits, see careful and well timed planning, build slowly and surely over the years, and be backed by well governed policy and sustainable economics? Germany needed steel. She needed oil. She had only a few working shipyards worth the name, all land locked in the Baltic Sea or accessed via the narrow and shallow Kiel Canal. Yet the Fuhrer seemed to envision the *Reichsmarine* as a vast global force, plying seas the world over, insurmountable. He wanted nothing less than absolute supremacy.

Raeder cleared his throat, quietly opening the folio he had carried to this meeting, and seeing Hitler's eyes immediately gleam with renewed interest.

"Your battleships, my Fuhrer," the Admiral said in a low, measured voice. "You are already familiar with our *Scharnhorst* Class battlecruisers." He gestured at the line drawings briefly, and flipped the page. "Here we have the next evolution of that design, and both ships will soon be ready for commissioning, the *Bismarck* and *Tirpitz.*"

The sleek lines of the ship diagrams had just the effect Raeder had hoped for, quieting Hitler for a moment as he stared at the documents. Yet a moment later the Fuehrer spoke again, with that same restless urgency in his voice.

"The guns?" Hitler pointed at the turrets in the carefully drawn schematics.

"Eight 38 centimeter guns, fifteen inches in diameter, arranged two each on the four heavy turrets. These ships will displace over 50,000 tons, nearly 20,000 tons beyond what we have now in *Scharnhorst* and *Gneisenau*, and they will be almost as fast at 30 knots, with a range of over 10,000 miles. These are true battleships, fast, well armored, and very powerful. They will stand with anything the Royal Navy has. In fact, they will make the entire British fleet obsolete the very day they sail."

As if he had heard nothing that was said, the Fuhrer looked blankly at Raeder and said: "Only two?"

"We have plans to improve upon this class with further designs," said Raeder quickly. "This next design will interest you even more... *Schlachtschiff H.*"

He turned another page, rotating the folio so Hitler could take in the full sweep of the diagrams before him. In design and form it was much like the *Bismarck*, only bigger, with a second smokestack and more powerfully drawn turrets.

"These ships will displace 55,500 long tons or more, and we have improved the main batteries to 40.6 centimeters--a full sixteen inches."

"The British have such guns. Why not twenty inches?"

"Twenty inches? My Fuehrer, the extra weight would require a ship of some 90,000 tons minimum, and we have no harbor that could accommodate a vessel of that size, nor could they transit the Kiel Canal. The draft would exceed the maximum depth there. If ever built, they would have to be kept at off shore anchorages, making supply, maintenance, and repair work very difficult and slow. Nor could they dock safely at most foreign ports likely to come under our control."

"And yet they would outclass everything in the Royal Navy by a wide measure," said Hitler waving his hand. "They would not dare to challenge such a ship, with even two of their existing battleships, eh?"

"That may be said this very moment of *Bismarck* and *Tirpitz*," said Raeder, convinced of the power of his latest additions to the fleet. "And it will be even more applicable to *Schlachtschiff H*. Their keels have been constructed from transverse, longitudinal steel frames, and she will have twenty one interior watertight compartments." He ran his finger along the hull schematic as he spoke. "The design will be immune to torpedo attacks, if a destroyer ever dared to try as much, and this hull design will make *Hindenburg* virtually unsinkable."

Hitler loved the technical details of steel weight, tensile strength, yet all he heard was the name. "*Hindenburg*?" he said. "Not Hitler?" He smiled.

"We thought to name this class after the *Helgoland* series from the last war. One of the ships in that class was the *Oldenburg*, but as this was to be our H series design, we thought *Hindenburg* might be appropriate, followed by *Brandenburg*, *Oldenburg*, and so forth."

Hitler thought for a moment. He had reservations about allowing a ship to have a name too closely associated with the Reich. What if it should be sunk? For the moment however, he was focused on the guns. "Yes, yes, leave it at that. But the guns. Can they be bigger? I want guns that will break the back of a British battleship in one blow."

"We have designs for seventeen and nineteen inch guns as well, but the key concept here, my Fuhrer is to mount a gun best fitting the size of the ship. It's a consideration of weight versus speed. What we want to achieve here is both speed and power. She will have a top speed of 30 knots. Anything that can catch us will surely be outclassed, given the protection we are building into this ship—strong horizontal protection with face hardened Krupp steel belt armor to 320 millimeters, 350 on the command tower, and 385 on the main guns. She will also get better deck armor, 200 millimeters thick, and we've added this new feature, six submerged torpedo tubes. They may be useful against convoys as well."

"Do not speak to me of armor. I assume as much. It is the guns that interest me. These ships should have guns in the range of twenty inches."

Raeder had anticipated this from the Fuehrer, but was unwilling to become bogged down now in a argument over gun size. "My Fuehrer, I have appointed Admiral Fuchs to make a detailed study of this very issue, and he will meet with you to report on his findings in short order." Raeder had press ganged Fuchs into the battle, wanting him to try and convince Hitler that 16 inch guns would be more than adequate.

"Very well," said Hitler flipping the page. "And these?"

Raeder had detailed out six ships, designs H through M, each with modified armament, armor, engine plants, and other minor details. "Let us consider all these as elements of the H class we are proposing," he explained. "Six ships in all. These will form the heart of our main battle fleet. The fast *Panzerschiff* cruisers I mentioned earlier will be excellent as escorts on the initial breakout, and fine commerce raiders in their own rite. We envision a concept of one or two powerful ships operating in conjunction with the *Panzerschiff* and squadrons of U-boats. The entire task force will be refueled from tankers at sea and remain capable of extended operations in the Atlantic—up to two months if necessary."

"It will most certainly be necessary," said Hitler. "And the British know as much. They will guard their convoys with battleships, and they will outnumber us in that category and every other category as well. But think bigger, Raeder. This navy must be strong enough to stand against anything the British have. How soon can these ships be built?"

"Two keels have already been laid—"

"Build them all," the Fuehrer said briskly. "Have them at sea in three years—four at the most. We will have to start with what we have now, but these ships will make fine additions."

Raeder heard something dark and ominous in that. Start what? He knew the answer to that question even before he asked it. Another war was coming, of that much he was certain. It was January of 1936, and he wondered if they would reach the end of this decade without conflict erupting again. The only question now was time. How long did he have to get the fleet in shape for battle at sea? He decided to ask for a realistic interval, knowing full well what it would take to build the ships Hitler wanted.

"Give me at least six years, my Fuehrer, and I will deliver a fleet that the nation will be proud of and one that every other nation on earth will learn to fear and respect."

"Six years? I built the entire Third Reich in six years, Raeder. You will have to do better than that. Surely you can build me these ships in far less time."

Raeder smiled, wondering if even one of the new battleships would ever be commissioned, but he could not say this to the Fuehrer.

"I will do my utmost," he said firmly.

Hitler looked at him, the well of those dark eyes opening, as if to devour his very soul in their inky blackness. "See that you do," he said in a low voice. "See that you do."

Part III

Glorious

"Remember not only to say the right thing in the right place, but far more difficult still, to leave unsaid the wrong thing at the tempting moment."

— Benjamin Franklin

Chapter 7

HMS Glorious: 16:20 Hrs – 8 June, 1940

Lieutenant Commander Christopher Hayward Wells leaned on the weather deck gunwale staring at the sea, clear and calm, and almost too placid for these waters. There was something wrong here, he thought. The Norwegian Sea was a tempestuous place, cold, unforgiving, cruel at times, but not today. Today it was smiling and fair, with visibility near maximum, though still cold at just a few degrees above freezing even in the mid-day sun. Yet it was a smile that seemed a cold smirk to him, the twisted grin of fate, and as if on instinct he still kept his gloved hands sheltered in his pockets, collar up against the slightest breeze. He was always cold, it seemed, and he would never be warm enough in spite of his great coat and a good felt lining he had snuck in beneath his cap.

Yet there was more than the cold on his mind that day. Wells could not seem to quiet the odd feeling of presentiment in his mind. Perhaps it was that gruel of a porridge at the morning mess, he thought. Maybe it was that lump in my bunk last night, and too few hours asleep. Nothing to be concerned about. Yet there *was* something to be concerned about. He could feel it the moment he emerged from his quarters and stepped on deck, though he could not see what it might be.

HMS *Glorious* rode easily in the calm seas, her pace a sedate 17 knots, and steaming on only 12 of her 18 boilers. She was going home, with an easy careless stride, her work done for the moment. The operation she supported was finished, a fight lost, another retreat, just one step back. That was the first thing wrong, thought Wells. Now there is nowhere left to go. Those are the hard coiled ropes reddening the skin of our backs now. We came out fighting at the opening bell and we've taken a bloody drubbing. Yet look at *Glorious* now! You wouldn't think there's a war on at all. When you feel those ropes at your back the last thing you do is drop your guard. What's the Captain doing? We've no air cover up!

HMS *Glorious* was an odd ship with an odd history, first conceived in the fertile mind of Admiral of the Fleet Jackie Fisher as a fast battlecruiser meant for operations in the Baltic along with her sister ship *Courageous*. Heavily gunned and with virtually no armor, they were designed as fast bombardment ships to support planned amphibious invasions, and soon became the laughing stock of the fleet, dubbed *Uproarious* and *Outrageous* on the docks and quays wherever they berthed. They couldn't really stand with any decent battleship, and what good was a fighting ship if all it could do was use its speed to run away from the fight? That idea was soon scrapped after the hard experience of Jutland, and both ships were refitted as aircraft carriers, which did little to bolster their standing as proper naval fighting ships. To many is seemed like they were putting on a dress.

When he first learned of his assignment to *Glorious*, Wells was crestfallen, his hopes for a position on one of the real battleships dashed. How did I ever end up here, he thought, on this strange mutant of a ship, a hybrid of cruiser and aircraft carrier, with an ex-submariner for a Captain who didn't seem to have the first idea of what he should do with the planes assigned to the ship? They had just picked up 20 RAF *Hurricane* fighters from Norway and had another 15 planes already assigned to the ship for self-protection, but they were all sitting below decks in the hangers that morning.

They aren't doing us any good there, thought Wells. Though the carrier had two destroyers with her in escort, not a single plane was up on combat air patrol for reconnaissance or defense. Nothing was even spotted on deck in the event of any emergency.

Wells shook his head inwardly, noting the creamy white wakes of the two destroyers a couple cables off the port and starboard bow of the carrier. Neither one had radar, so why were they in so close to the ship, he thought? You would think one might at least be out in the van as a scout ship under these circumstances. The Captain had the ship in a zig-zag- pattern, so he must be more worried about the U-boat threat than anything else.

His eyes strayed to the main mast above the island. He had a very odd feeling about it, as though something were amiss, yet everything looked in order. Then he realized that it was what he did *not* see that set off those inner alarm bells. There was no watch posted there this morning! What in the world was the Captain thinking? Perhaps he was still below decks, or on the hanger deck dressing down the airmen again.

Glorious was an unhappy ship, he knew, and it was going to stay that way unless they could find a Captain with more sense and some rudimentary understanding of how an aircraft carrier was supposed to operate. The ship had spent some time in the Med in the early years of the war, and had lately come from Malta where Wells had the opportunity to meet the commander of the 7th Cruiser Squadron, Rear Admiral John Tovey. Now there was an officer, he thought, full of dash, yet upright, never brash, commanding respect of the men under him without reference to his rank. That's the sort we need here, he thought sullenly.

The longer he stared at the empty crow's nest the more unsettled he became. We aren't ready, he knew. Not just this cockamamie ship, but the whole of the Royal Navy. It's been hit and miss in the early going. All the Germans have thrown at us were a few sorties by those pocket battleships, which we handled well enough. But they have a good deal more in the cupboard, and one day soon they'll be pouring a very bitter tea. The U-boat threat is one thing, but we'll get worse if I'm not mistaken. Here they've gone and run us right out of Harstad and with it all of Norway. We'll have no bases of any note in those seas now, and they will have all those ports to serve as replenishment stations for anything they slip out of the Baltic. Something tells me they've a good deal more to throw at us than the *Graf Spee.*

Wells was not privy to the real intelligence on the Kriegsmarine, but he had heard the rumors. The Germans had been building feverishly since 1936 when they repudiated the limitations of the Treaty of Versailles and launched hulls in rapid succession. It was said they were building better commerce raiders, faster than the *Deutschland* class ships the Royal Navy had sparred with, and better armored and gunned. It was said they were building battleships as well, aiming to pose a real challenge to the heavy units of the British fleet. It was said they were even building aircraft carriers. That was one advantage the Royal Navy possessed at the moment, carriers that could put eyes in the sky over their battle fleets, and even sting enemy ships with the torpedoes off their *Swordfish* biplanes.

Well, maybe the Germans will throw one in the soup, he thought. This one here wasn't doing any good for the fleet at the moment. HMS *Glorious* had been teamed with *Ark Royal* to provide cover for Operation Alphabet, the final evacuation of Norway. Half way out Captain D'Oyly-Hughes, known as D-H in the ranks, had requested permission to steam independently for Scapa Flow where he was eager to get on with the court martial of a senior airman who had refused his orders to fly a mission against land targets on the grounds his planes were unsuited for it and his crews untrained in such operations.

The man was correct. *Swordfish* were so named for a reason. Dubbed the "old stringbags" by the airmen who flew them, they were lumbering, slow, yet surprisingly durable as a good deal of the ack ack fire they took would go right through the canvass portions of the plane, leaving the structure largely intact. But for land attack missions they were quite out of their element, particularly if the Germans had any BF-109s about.

It had been quite a row between Air Commander Heath and the Captain. Heath was all but accused of mutiny and put off the ship. Now the Admiralty had ordered *Glorious* to return as soon as possible, eager to shuffle her crew off to Plymouth for a long overdue leave and then settle the matter between D-H and Heath. That was the rumor passing round the hammocks and bouncing from one bulkhead to another below decks, but the only part that mattered to most of the men was that they were going home.

As he looked for the ladder up he was pleased to see his friend Lieutenant Robert Woodfield heading down to take some air. The two men had come up together, though Wells tested better and was a step up in rank now, though he never lorded it over his friend, even in jest. "Hello Bob," he said. "Fair day, isn't it?"

"Fair out here," said Woodfield. "A bit thick up on the bridge if you're heading that way."

"What is it this time, Woody?"

"What else? D-H is still ranting over the placement of those RAF *Hurricanes* below decks. Ever since Air Commander Heath was put off the ship the Captain has made it his personal endeavor to visit the flight deck daily and roust about down there."

"What's his problem today?"

"He says the *Hurricanes* are not properly arrayed and cabled off below decks."

"Yes? Well those RAF boys are damn lucky they're even here at all. Landing on the deck as they did without arrestor hooks was a fairly good bit of flying yesterday. I half expected to see most of them overshoot the deck or go right off into the sea."

"After Commander Heath crossed him the Captain seems to think every airman aboard has it in for him now. I think he fancies the thought that he's cleaning house down there and setting everything all prim and proper."

"We'll he'd do better to have some of those planes in the air instead of worrying over how they're cabled off below decks. We've no top cover and look there, Woody," he pointed to the vacant crow's nest on the main mast. "Nobody assigned to the watch either."

"Well, I raised this point with Captain Hughes at noon. He says the five planes below decks on ten minute notice for takeoff are more than sufficient with visibility this good."

"I suppose it might be more than sufficient if we were a submarine and could scoot beneath the sea on a hostile sighting. Well, with visibility this good why have we no lookouts?"

"The Captain explained he has two destroyers cruising on our forward arc that would most certainly sight anything of note, or so he put it."

"What? Those destroyers are no more than 400 meters off our bow. Our mainmast is twice the height of those ships. They would have to be well out ahead of us if they hope to sight anything before we could with a pair of good eyes and a field glass up there. Mark my words, Woody. We're all alone out here and virtually blind as a bat while those planes are still below decks. I intend to strongly recommend we at least spot the ten minute flight on deck if the Captain refuses to launch."

"Good luck with that, Mister Wells. I tried that with the Captain as well. He explained that to launch aircraft we would have to turn about into the wind. We were ordered to maintain an average speed of at least sixteen knots and the time required to launch and get our nose pointed south again would require the ship to burn more fuel at high speed in order to make up for the loss. It's obvious that is his only concern is the U-boat threat. No aircraft had ever sunk a submarine or ever would. Those were his exact words to me. That's why we've been in a zig-zag pattern the last three hours."

"Well the Germans may have more than U-boats out there! Who cares about the bloody fuel?"

"The Captain cares, that's who. We've standing orders to maintain a full 33% in bunker at all times and we're running low. That's the explanation I was given, and from the look on the Captain's face he wanted no more questions about it."

"Let them top us off after we make port! That fuel reserve is for contingencies of just this sort. In my opinion the security of the ship and crew should supersede concerns over fuel."

"The Captain apparently believes otherwise. He's even ordered two-thirds on the boilers. That's how concerned he is about the fuel. We've 18 good boilers down below and only twelve are fired at the moment."

"Good god," said Wells. "Then we've even lost our legs. If anything happened upon us we couldn't even make a run for it. It would take us nearly half an hour to work up those other six boilers."

"Yes, well old D-H will say you're too worked up yourself, and over nothing, which is exactly what he said to me when I pointed out we had no one assigned to mainmast watch. Damn sloppy, if you want to know what I really think."

"Agreed," said Wells, yet he took no comfort or consolation in having another confederate soul to commiserate with here. "Perhaps if a few of the other senior officers would concur we might move the Captain on this."

"Perhaps," said Woodfield, "but the Captain would likely interpret that as another mutiny given his present state of mind."

"Mutiny? Nonsense. It's any senior officer's right to speak his mind on a matter like this."

"You might think as much, but line up three of us in the same hot minute and I'll guarantee you that D-H will go off like a clock and chime on it the whole rest of the way home. Touchy fellow, that man. Thinks he can do anything he wishes. Word was he got off scot-free when he ran the nose of his submarine into another ship before they sent him here. Some think he has the Prime Minister's ear."

"Well I wish he had more sense," said Wells, looking off the port bow. Then he saw what he knew he had been fearing all along, the dark smear of smoke on the horizon.

"Say... Look there, Woody. What do you make of that?"

"My god! Those can't be ours, can they? Everything we've got out here is heading south by southwest as we are."

"I'm off to the bridge to see about it. Good luck, Woody. Let's hope those are friendly ships after all."

But they were not friendly ships, as Lieutenant Commander Wells was soon to learn. The destroyer *Ardent* off the port bow had apparently seen the contact as well, and was now peeling off to investigate, her search lights flashing a challenge as she did so. It was not long before heavy shells came hurtling back in response.

When Wells arrived on the bridge, breathless from the climb up several ladders, he saw the Captain leaning over a voice tube and heard the order to ready the *Swordfish* of 823 Squadron for takeoff.

"Squadron to be ranged on the flight deck at once, Mister Stevens," said the Captain, an edge of impatience obvious in his tone. "Helm, increase speed. Ahead full."

"Sir, we haven't the steam up. Six boilers are down!"

"Well then send down and bloody well get them up!" The Captain spied Wells just as he came onto the bridge. "You there, Mister Wells. Get to the W/T room and send a sighting report. Two battlecruisers bearing 308 degrees, distance 15 miles, on a course of zero-three-zero. We'll send the same on the remote. Be sure we send our position."

"Aye sir...Shall the ship come to action stations?" He had heard no general alarm, and for all he knew the ship's crew were lolling about on routine duty and unaware of the grave danger they were in now.

"Get on with it, Mister Wells, and kindly leave the ship's condition to *me*, if you please, sir."

Wells felt the sting and knew he had best get moving at once. Yet even as he ran for the hatch he knew it was all wrong. The ship was still on its original course. The Captain should have turned away from the sighted contact at once. What was he doing? He paused, wanting to point this out, along with the lack of a watch on the mainmast, the lack of planes overhead, and all the rest, hesitating for a few brief seconds with all that had been said between himself and Lieutenant Woodfield still rankling in his mind. He knew he would be in the right if he spoke now, but he also knew the Captain would likely go into a rage and take his head off, so he mastered himself, knowing there would come a better time to speak his mind and focusing on the moment at hand. The sighting report was vital. *Ark Royal* was out there somewhere, as was the cruiser *Devonshire*. Surely they could lend a hand if they knew what was happening here.

So he turned and ran aft for the Wireless Telegraphy room, one deck below, not knowing that those few seconds of hesitation, a brief moment of restraint, were going to make all the difference in the world—not just for him, but for the ship itself and the lives of every man aboard.

When he reach the W/T signals room the operator there handed him a message right off the wire. "It's *Ardent*, sir. They say the contact is presumed hostile and they are attacking." It was acting Chief Barrow on the main W/T duty that afternoon.

"Right, Mister Barrow, well send this sighting report straight away." He gave the man the information he had been told to relay, then turned to get himself back to the bridge as soon as possible.

"Send it Billy," said the Chief.

"On Home Wave or Fleet Wave, sir?"

"On whatever we're set for, man! Be quick about it!"

Telegraphist William Barron began keying his message when Al Rose at the next station looked over at the Chief. "I thought we were still supposed to be on Narvik Wave at 7.3 MzH? Nobody was supposed to spin the dial until we cross 65 degrees north, sir."

"We tested on that last night. The power pack is dodgy and we couldn't raise a soul, so we switched to Home Wave early. Who's listening at Narvik anyway?"

"Sort it all out, Chief," said Wells. "Send on both waves." Even as he started away he had the very odd feeling that he was late for something very important. He had to get back to the bridge!

He *was* late. Just those few seconds late, though they would soon change everything, at least insofar as his own fate and that of the ship was concerned. It was one of those tides in the affairs of men that Shakespeare had written of, and he was about to take it at the flood.

Chapter 8

BC Scharnhorst ~ 16:46 Hours, June 8, 1940

The lookout squinted into his field glasses, certain now of what he was seeing. It was no cloud, not on a day like this with visibility so good. Midshipman Goos leaned out to his mate, two tiers below him on the high mast and shouted out the contact.

"Smoke on the horizon, Schulte, starboard side, bearing east at sixty degrees true!"

The word soon rippled down to the bridge of the battlecruiser *Scharnhorst*, welcome news to the ears of her Kapitan Kurt 'Caesar' Hoffmann. Holder of the Iron Cross and Cross of Honor from the last war, his temperament was well suited to his position, cool, hard, calculating and with an iron will. His peers simply called him 'the praetorian' after his middle name 'Caesar,' a handle he accepted with a wry grin.

After the war began in September of 1939, Hoffmann left the light cruiser *Konigsberg* to assume his post as Kapitan of *Scharnhorst*, and achieved immediate success in his first major sortie with *Gneisenau* by finding and sinking the auxiliary cruiser *Rawalpindi*. It was a great mismatch, with the two German ships badly outgunning the British ship, an old passenger ship that had been hastily converted to a cruiser with 6-inch guns of WWI vintage. Hoffmann gave the British commander every opportunity to surrender his ship, ordering him to abandon the ship three times. To his amazement, all he received in answer were salvos of fire.

The niceties over, he promptly returned fire. In that action the ship and crew exhibited the remarkable skill in gunnery that would aid them throughout the many trials ahead. Within three minutes they had obtained the range and struck the hapless cruiser full on the bridge, killing the ship's Captain and most senior officers there.

Minutes later another salvo literally broke the recalcitrant cruiser in two.

A few months later the Kapitan and his ship had been less fortunate and unable to engage when the twin battlecruisers were boldly attacked by HMS *Renown*. It was a battle Hoffmann thought the Germans should have won, with eighteen eleven inch guns between the two ships against only six 15-inch guns on *Renown*. The German ships also had twice the armor protection of Renown, with 350mm at the belt against only 150mm for the British battlecruiser.

Yet, unable to range on the enemy effectively in the tempestuous seas, her radar malfunctioning, Hoffmann realized the best course would be to use their speed to break off and fight again another day. Leaving the scene in heavy seas and at high speed, the ship took on water, which swamped her bow and put the forward turret out of action. The water was literally flooding in through the range finder equipment and cartridge ejection scuttles! It was a problem that would plague both battlecruisers in heavy seas, as their "Atlantic" bow installed after completion still proved inadequate in keeping the sea at bay.

He was still galled by the thought that the Kriegsmarine should have logged a victory that day. Yet the war was only just beginning. His ships were just the first to find and duel with the heavier British units, and they were still working out the defects that had been hampering operations at the outset of the war. Problems with metal fatigue, heating tubes in the boilers and performance in heavy seas were all to be addressed in lengthy refits as the Twins wintered in Wilhelmshaven. He knew that Germany had more might to darken these waters in the days ahead. *Bismarck* and *Tirpitz* had been working out together, ready for action any day now, and behind them were even more powerful ships.

He had not had a look at her yet, the ship Germany now placed so much faith in, mighty *Hindenburg*. While the two *Bismarck* class battleships mounted eight 38cm 15-inch guns, *Hindenburg* would finally match the best naval arms of their adversary with eight 16-inch guns, and 380mm belt armor for protection. Behind her would come *Oldenburg*, but after that he doubted if any of the other ships planned for the war would ever be built. We are lucky to have so many battleships in the fleet now, he thought, enough to give the British a real fight this time. Doenitz was arguing that the steel needed for a single battleship could build ten U-boats, and he was correct. If that were true then it meant his ship would have to do far better than the likes of *Rawalpindi*.

They needed a kill, and now "the Twins" were prowling the waters west of the Norwegian coast like two dark panthers looking for prey. The ships were hoping to interrupt the British supply effort for Norway, but word had just come over from Admiral Wilhelm Marschall aboard the division flag *Gneisenau* that the British were evacuating.

It seems we will have little to do now, thought Hoffmann before a sudden call from the watch sent him to the view port to study the horizon. Where there was smoke, there was fire. Something was out there, and he might get a ship or two before the operation was called off after all.

"Notify Admiral Marschall of the sighting," Hoffmann said coolly as he studied the smoke through his field glasses. "Let's see what we have." He thought it might be transports, but if this were the edge of a distant convoy there would be escorts. It was not long before he spotted the faint wink of a light beneath the smoke, and the silhouette of a small ship that could only be a destroyer.

A bridge messenger was quick to the Kapitan's side. "Sir," he said, "signal return from *Gneisenau*. We are to work up speed and turn to engage."

"Ahead full," said Hoffmann. "The ship will come to action stations."

The alarm sent men moving in all directions, but Hoffmann was the still point on the bridge, his eyes fixed on the distant contact. He noted his watch, seeing it was just after 17:00 hours. A lucky time, he thought. We hit *Rawalpindi* at 17:06. Maybe we'll get lucky here as well.

"Helm come hard to starboard and steady on zero-three-zero."

"Hard to starboard, sir!"

Scharnhorst was in the lead, but her boilers had been giving her trouble again and Hoffmann doubted he would get full speed. He leaned out, looking for *Gneisenau* behind him, seeing the other ship following smartly in his long white wake.

Fregatten Kapitan Lowisch, was an artillery officer up on the foretop firing control station. He soon called out again, with new sighting information.

"Kapitan Hoffmann," he said. "I've a better look now. Thick funnel and mainmast amidships, sir, and what looks to be a flight deck. I' think we've found a carrier!"

"A carrier? Out here all alone with nothing more than those two destroyers?" Hoffmann was watching one of the escorts making a brave charge. The other was aft of the main contact, running in the carrier's wake.

"Helm, come about to zero-seven-zero."

"Sir," said Lowisch again. "It's definitely a carrier. Perhaps *Ark Royal.* I can make out deck cranes, elevators, and that leading destroyer is getting nosey."

Ark Royal... One of the best they have, thought Hoffmann. They certainly know we're here and will be reporting our position at this very moment. If they get planes up and after us it could be a rough ride home. Why haven't they turned away if they've seen us?

"Helm. Starboard again. Come round to one-five-zero." The Germans were making their final approach turn, and now he saw that the destroyer near the main contact was beginning to make smoke.

Very strange that a carrier would be here this way. Was there something over the horizon that they had not yet seen?

The ship's chief gunnery officer, Schubert was now at the Kapitan's side. "Sir, that destroyer looks to be making a torpedo run on us."

"You may begin training on targets, Schubert. Use your secondary batteries on the destroyer. The main guns will target the carrier."

The action had finally begun, and they saw that *Gneisenau* was already firing at the intrepid British destroyer. He had to admire the British pluck and courage given the circumstances. That destroyer Captain clearly knows he's got two large capital ships in front of him, at least heavy cruiser size or better, yet here he comes.

There was an immediate explosion on the enemy destroyer, and Hoffmann raised his binoculars to have a closer look. That must have hit the boiler room, he knew when he saw the ship's speed fall off dramatically. Yet it was also making heavy smoke now, and zigzagging forward so it was difficult to assess the real damage.

"Torpedoes ahead!" came the call from the upper watch. That was the real threat here. The destroyer was firing its deck gun, but they had no more than a 4.7 inch battery there, and it would not pose any real threat to *Scharnhorst* with her heavy armor. But a torpedo was another thing altogether, and nothing to be trifled with.

"What is our speed?" Hoffmann knew he might soon have to maneuver if those fish were well aimed.

"Sir, we are ahead full, and now making 29 knots."

And that was all we are likely to make, thought the Kapitan, noting that *Gneisenau* was gaining on their position, probably running full out at over 30 knots to do so now.

"Torpedoes passing close ahead!"

"Steady," said Hoffmann. This first salvo was going to miss. "Target ranges?" He sized up his prospects now.

"Sir, destroyer at 14,500 meters bearing one-two-zero. Main contact at 26,000 meters."

A long shot if ever there was one. The secondary batteries would deal with this destroyer easily enough, but no battleship he had ever heard of had managed to hit anything at 26,000 meters. They would begin ranging on the target, but most likely have to close considerably to do any real damage. Would he have the speed? The British carriers were very fast.

"Let's not have *Gneisenau* get all the dark meat on that turkey," he said to Schubert. "Fire secondary batteries!"

The twin 5.7-inch guns echoed his order in response, even as Witte, the bridge messenger rushed to the Kapitan's side again with orders to direct main batteries on the carrier.

Where else, thought Hoffmann with a half smile? Herr Marschall wanted a real feast today, not just the trimmings with these destroyers. He passed the order to Schubert, who was only too eager to comply. The big 11-inch batteries were already well trained on the target, and soon darkened the bow of the ship with their opening salvo. Hoffmann could immediately see that the 5.9-inch guns, also mounted forward above the two main turrets, were going to interfere with his main batteries. The bigger guns were firing much farther and they would have to elevate their barrels into the blast wave of the secondary guns, so he instructed his fire control officer to cease fire with the smaller guns. The British destroyer was running for its own smoke screen now, though he had little doubt it would continue to do everything possible to save its charge.

"Salvo short," called Schubert. "Adjusting range now."

Hoffmann could see the first shells splashing in the water near the carrier, good on bearing, but obviously short. He was still amazed that they had seen no planes launch and could not imagine why.

"Sir, Admiral Marschall sends that we may deploy shipboard aircraft as needed."

Hoffmann nodded at that, though he did not believe the deployment would be necessary, and Schubert concurred. The smoke screens would hamper them in time, but they already had the range and they would soon close for the kill.

The main guns boomed again, but minutes later he saw the rounds fall long, well over the carrier. "That's the frame," he said to Schubert. "Now paint me the picture."

His gunnery officer was quick to respond. He heard the deep throated order to fire, and the guns roared again. The sighting call was 24,175 meters, still very long, but they obviously had the range now. Then, to his amazement, he saw bright fire on the forward deck of the distant carrier, and a second hit right on the island!

"Hit!" said Schubert, beaming with the news. "My god, what a shot!"

The bridge crew gave a cheer, and Hoffmann smiled, well pleased. That is one for the record books, he thought, and right on that forward deck! Now let them try to launch anything. His real worry, that he might soon be facing a gaggle of British *Swordfish* torpedo bombers, was now far less of a shadow on his mind. Behind him he saw *Gneisenau* hastening up on his starboard side, her guns also trained on the enemy carrier and eager to carve the turkey as he had it in his mind. They were firing.

"Alarm!" called the watch. "Torpedoes at 330 degrees!"

That damn destroyer had fired a second salvo, and now he had to make a speedy maneuver, bringing the helm hard to port and then back again on 170 degrees to avoid the deadly attack. If that were not enough, the British destroyer was still impudently firing her deck gun, and he felt the chink of a small caliber hit. A third torpedo alert followed soon after.

"That little demon is going to be trouble today," he said aloud. The destroyer was dancing in and out of its own smoke screen and barking like a wild hunting dog at a bear. Well, this bear has already shown it has teeth, so beware. The British carrier had been foolishly holding to its course. Why didn't it run?

No sooner had he thought that when he saw the carrier's silhouette narrow in the distance, and he knew it had turned. Someone has come to his senses, he thought. They should have turned on 120 or 130 long ago, and that looks to be exactly what they are doing now, right into that smoke with the wind at their backs. Now it will ride with them for some time.

"Pound that damn destroyer, Schubert! It might get lucky with one of those torpedoes."

"Aye sir, redirecting secondary batteries now."

Chapter 9

Aboard HMS *Glorious* Lieutenant Commander Wells heard the first rounds strike the ship and felt their jarring impact. He was up the ladder to the deck above, and soon shocked to see nothing but smoke and fire. If he had spoken his mind earlier, voicing his concerns about the lack of air cover, and the shamefully absent watch on the mainmast, he had little doubt that he would be right there on the deck where he could now see the bodies of the Captain and almost every senior officer, struck dead by that fated salvo the German ship had fired at extreme long range.

That hit was supposed to have struck only the forward deck in one recording of this history, yet this time it was more than the hesitation and restraint of Wells that was amiss. Something more had happened that no man then alive could see or know. It had served to guide that salvo unerringly to its target with even better accuracy. Instead of one 11-inch shell through the foredeck, two of the six rounds fired found their mark, and the second struck here, where Wells should have been himself, lying dead, but for his inner tussle that saw him delay his trip to the W/T signals room just long enough to matter.

That and the confusion over what signal wavelength to use had kept him there, safe from harm, for just long enough. Now he was back, seeing the bridge crew dead or stunned senseless, and Executive Officer Lovell there among them, alive but wounded on the deck. He ran to his side, only to hear his rasping voice telling him to take command.

"The ship is yours, Mister Wells. God save us…" He slumped unconscious, and Wells stood up, eyes wide, his face ashen white. There was no time for hesitation now. He had to act, and that quickly, or the ship would surely be lost. They were still steering 180, due south, and he knew their only chance in hell was to turn and put the wind at their backs, along with those pursuing German ships.

"Helm! Come to one-two-zero and all ahead flank!"

No one answered and he ran to the wheel himself, seeing the helmsman down and bleeding on the deck. One-two-zero it is, he said to himself, wrenching the wheel over and hoping their speed would hold up now.

The turn would take him right into the thick smoke screen that had been laid by destroyer *Acasta*, still in dutiful attendance out in front of the carrier. Brave *Ardent* had charged in alone, guns and torpedoes firing, making smoke and doggedly doing everything possible to buy the carrier the time it needed to get up those last six boilers and make speed for a getaway run.

One look at the forward deck told Wells that there was no chance to launch any planes. Yet the crews had managed to bring up two of the *Swordfish* there, albeit with ASW bombs mounted on one instead of torpedoes. That was all they would be able to spot, for he could see by the smoke from the hole in the flight deck that there was obviously a fire below in the hanger.

Yet hole in the deck or not, Lt. Commander Charles Stevens was not about to wait. He had his co-pilot Basil Wise get up several men from the RAF ground crews and put them to man-handling a single *Swordfish* around the damaged section of the deck and pointed aft! He was going to try and take off using the long, undamaged section of the deck behind him, and with little more than hope and the plucky nature of the aircraft itself for any chance at getting aloft.

The engine sputtered to life as Wells watched, spellbound. He saw Stevens leap aboard the plane, quickly settling into his harness and giving a thumbs up. Then he set the engine roaring and the plane began to move, lumbering down the deck, the wheels scudding over debris as it went. Every man on deck cheered him on and, by god, he pulled back on the yoke and got the nose of the plane up just as he ran out of runway. It howled in protest, very near a stall, but managed to pull through and get aloft.

Three things had now happened to set history off on a decidedly different course. A moment of doubt and restraint that saved the life of Christopher Hayward Wells, who then set the ship's course on the only one that offered any hope of escape for the ill fated *Glorious*. Then came the narrowing of fate's focus on that third salvo from *Scharnhorst*, bettering it to smash the bridge and place the ship into his able hands. The third was Lt. Commander Charles Stevens' pluck and courage in getting his plane aloft, which was soon spotted by the watchmen aboard *Scharnhorst* and *Gneisenau*, and became an omen that changed their thinking about the battle at hand.

The Twins were still steering 170 when *Glorious* turned from within the heavily effective smoke screen that *Acasta* had laid for her. Hoffmann picked up the course change to 120, and he thought both German ships should have turned on that same heading in pursuit. As it now happened, they continued to run almost due south, and with her boilers now running full out, *Glorious* began to get up speed. If the Germans had turned with her the two sleek panthers had both the speed and the range to take down the gazelle, but they did *not* turn, and each passing minute opened the range until it was again beyond 26,000 meters.

All the while brave *Ardent* was still fitfully firing torpedoes at the oncoming German ships until *Scharnhorst* riddled the destroyer with numerous hits from its secondary batteries. Yet the hand of fate moved with the second hand of the clock that day, with each second slowly wedging a lever in time and setting events of the war off another course, even as *Glorious* had come about in that fitful moment of smoke and fire on the bridge. Wells saw the *Swordfish* wheel about and gain altitude, coming round to make an attack run at the German ships. There was a chance, a fleeting chance now, that the ship might be saved, and Wells yelled to the signalman to get off yet another frantic message in the hope someone would hear and come to their aid.

* * *

That message was received by Senior Telegraphist T. Jenkins, who was in charge of the W/T Remote control office aboard HMS *Devonshire*, a cruiser steaming little more than 40 miles to the west northwest of *Glorious* at that very moment. He did not know it then, but the two German ships were even closer, no more than 24 miles away between *Devonshire* and the carrier. The flagship of Vice Admiral J. Cunningham, *Devonshire* was on a very guarded mission that day, transporting King Haakon and the Norwegian Royal Family, cabinet ministers, a trove of documents, and a considerable store of gold bullion as well.

When the sighting report was handed to Jenkins it looked like a long string of unintelligible characters:

VE MTA V OW2 O-U 2BC 308 15 030 154GQOX 11 BT 1615 IMI.

To Jenkin's trained eye, however, the message was plain as the fair day around them. It read: "To Scapa W/T from *Glorious* – Most Immediate - Two Battle Cruisers, Bearing 308° - 15 miles, course 030." The bearing to reference grid point GQOX followed that with the final request to repeat the message if received. It was sent up to the bridge in the raw where it soon caused quite a stir.

Vice Admiral Cunningham, turned quietly to a warrant officer and asked that the location of the sighting be plotted, and minutes later a young Midshipman named Corkhill showed the plot to the senior officers. The Admiral's eyes darkened as he studied it, a squall of trouble there. It was very close, so very close that the probable position of the German ships was just over the horizon.

Cunningham ran his hand over his chin, thinking deeply. Thirty points to port and he might be on the scene within minutes, but what would he do when he got there? He had good speed, but the notation of two battlecruisers was most troubling. Which battlecruisers, certainly not *Lutzow* and the *Admiral Scheer?* He was privy to knowledge of their position and knew the *Admiral Scheer* was in for refit and now being reclassified as a heavy cruiser. *Lutzow* had her stern nearly blown off by the Royal Navy Submarine HMS *Spearfish* and was laid up for at least a full year. Neither ship could be anywhere near the action, though it could be a sighting of the *Admiral Hipper,* known to be operating in these waters, but the report designated two ships.

Two battlecruisers…He knew what this meant, and also knew of the warnings made by a staffer at Bletchley Park regarding the possibility of German heavy units moving to interdict this very operation. It had not been confirmed but here it was…two battlecruisers. This could only be the Twins, and that would mean *Devonshire* would be facing eighteen 11-inch guns to her eight 8-inchers if he turned the ship now.

"Anything further? Nothing from *Ardent* or *Acasta?*"

"No sir, just this one message."

Sighing heavily, the Admiral knew his current charge was vital and that he had to see it safely home. "Mister Hughes," he said to a staff Flag Lieutenant. "Kindly go to the W/T room and collect all copies of this message and the operator's logbook, if you please. I want to have a closer look at them."

"Very good, sir." Hughes saluted and was off as directed. Then Cunningham gave the order for engines all ahead full, with the ship's main guns to stand ready, but no change of course followed. The eyes of the bridge crew were on him, yet none dared to meet his gaze directly. He knew what they were waiting for, but there were charges laid on him now that were as heavy as the gold in the lower holds of the ship.

The message was unintelligible, he said to himself, knowing otherwise. Yet that would have to be the official report. Would it be heard by any other ship in the region? *Ark Royal* was behind him to the north with a good air wing and an escort of cruisers and destroyers. With 8000 men at arms in the convoy she was covering, there would be no way the carrier could intervene. Her charge was heavy as well.

"Sir," came a report from another watchstander. "Top lookout reports two mast heads to the east."

"Very well," said Cunningham. "Go Below, Mister Owens, and see to the condition of the boilers. Tell them we'll have need of all the speed we can make shortly."

"Shall I send that over the voice pipes, sir?"

"No, Mister Owens, see to it personally. That will be all."

The man gave him an surprised look, then saluted and went below as ordered, thinking the ship would soon be hot in the chase and riding to the rescue. Two battlecruisers were more than the Admiral could risk now, though he hated what he had to do just then, knowing the speed he was counting on would take his ship away from the fight that must now surely be underway with *Glorious* and her light escort of only two destroyers. He wondered if his decision might sign the death certificates of hundreds of men that day.

* * *

Aboard *Scharnhorst*, Kapitan Hoffmann received a message from *Gneisenau* with another smile. It read simply: 'Congratulations for having sunk the destroyer north.' The dogged British destroyer *Ardent* was now listing over and slipping beneath the sea. But where was the carrier? It was still lost in the thick smoke and well ahead. We should turn on 130 he thought, but with those boilers acting up below I won't get any closer than I am now unless we hit this carrier again. The main guns of both ships had been silent for some time, unable to sight their target in the thick smoke.

Then he received the report of enemy aircraft aloft and on a bearing to attack, and that was the news that changed his mind. One destroyer was down, but it fired six or seven salvos of torpedoes and I had to dance like a clown to avoid them. Now here comes the second destroyer, and the carrier is launching torpedo planes as well. This is no longer a good situation.

"Signal Admiral Marschall," he said quietly. "Advise him we are having boiler problems and cannot stay in the chase."

"Very good, sir."

There was nothing wrong with the engines on *Gneisenau*. What would the Admiral do? The Kapitan was aware that he had orders to avoid action with British surface units and seek only unescorted transports and supply ships. Yet this qualified as a good potential target. Thus far there had been no cost for this engagement. A single British destroyer had put a scratch on his ship with a 4.7 inch gun, but paid with its life. A single *Swordfish* came at them like a mad hornet and put its torpedo in the water before being chopped to pieces by the ship's anti-aircraft guns.

When the word came back to steer for Trondheim he found himself in agreement. There was no longer any point in risking the ships in action against a British operation that had already failed. So Hoffman ordered the ship to fly its flag at half mast, knowing he could not stop to rescue any of the men he put in the sea off that British destroyer. Brave men, he thought. We'll lower our flag and tip our hats to them this time around. Because the next time it may be my men in the water. This war is only beginning.

* * *

HMS *Glorious* slipped away that day, speeding southeast and then eventually south to escape her fate. Almost 1500 other men were spared a watery death that day as well, and they would be much needed in the months and years ahead. One of those men was Lieutenant Commander Wells, still on the bridge of the embattled carrier and lucky to be alive. He would bring the ship from the edge of almost certain destruction and sail her home, gaining considerable laurels for his action in the heat of combat.

Lieutenant Woodfield found him some time after at Scapa Flow when the ship was safely at anchor. "See here, Wells," he said extending a hand to his friend. "Look what I've got!" He handed Wells the morning paper, beaming. "You've been mentioned in dispatches, my man!"

"What? Me?"

"Right there, mate…" Woodfield pointed, reading. "Lieutenant Commander Christopher Hayward Wells, R.N. has been mentioned in dispatches for seamanship, bravery and good leadership and his name appears on the Honors List for June. It's all right there, Welly. Your gallant and selfless effort in the face of enemy fire to assume command of the embattled HMS *Glorious* and steer her safely home under the most arduous circumstances. And there she sits." He pointed to the carrier where it rode at anchor, safely home in Scapa Flow. "Good show, Wells. Bit of a broken nose, she's got, eh? But otherwise all in one piece."

"Lucky to have only that," said Wells, his eyes glued to the newspaper, a smile on his lips.

"You were right after all, Welly," said Woodfield. "The Germans did have more out there than a few U-boats."

"It's not the first we've seen of their surface fleet," Wells warned him, "and by god, it will not be the last either. Those were just a pair of battlecruisers. Word is they've got *Bismarck* and *Tirpitz* ready now—real battleships."

"RAF has been hot to get a look at them."

"That they have. The Twins were bad enough out there, Woody. Put *Bismarck* and *Tirpitz* together and then we've a real nightmare on our hands."

"You may be right, Wells. Say, have you heard about Cunningham?"

"What of him?"

"He's to be mentioned in dispatches and then sent off to Africa."

"Africa?"

"Well more likely Gibraltar first. Things are not exactly going our way on the continent, my friend. The Germans have given us the boot! We're pulling the last of everything we have out and using ports from Cherbourg to Bayonne. That will mean the Germans will get them all in due course."

"My god, the Germans with all those French ports?"

"That's about the size of it. We're finished in France, Wells. We won't get back there for a good long while."

Wells shrugged, disheartened with the news. "Kicked out of Norway and France in less than a year. It's damned embarrassing."

"Certainly," said Woodfield. "But we're still masters of the sea. This *Bismarck* and *Tirpitz* haven't pushed their bows into deep water yet like we have, and winter will make a skating rink of the Baltic soon. I think things should quiet down for a while."

Wells looked at the gaping hole in the flight deck of HMS *Glorious*, a bad feeling coming over him as he stared at it. Something about the moment haunted him for years after. It was as if he did not belong there, Woodfield too, and not even the ship.

"We damn near lost her, Woody," he said at last.

Woodfield was going to say something more, but the look on his friend's face was enough to quiet him.

Now that France and Norway were secured, the Germans could get on with plans for even more ambitious operations in the deep water Woodfield had spoken of, thought Wells. We very nearly went into it today...And I tell you what I think, the Germans won't be content to spar with us in the Norwegian Sea for very much longer. They have their minds set on the Atlantic, and something tells me I'm going to be in the thick of it—right up to my hatband in no time at all.

Part IV

Resurrection

"Nations, like stars, are entitled to eclipse. All is well, provided the light returns and the eclipse does not become endless night. Dawn and resurrection are synonymous. The reappearance of the light is the same as the survival of the soul."

— Victor Hugo

Chapter 10

21 June 1919 ~ Scapa Flow

21 Years earlier, another ship named *Hindenburg* rode at anchor in Scapa Flow, one of seven capital ships tethered off between Cava and Risa Islands. The whole of the German High Seas Fleet was there, safely imprisoned under the watchful eyes of the Royal Navy. The ships had been taken as ransom in exchange for the lifting of the allied naval blockade of Germany after the Great War. Britain wanted to be sure that they would never again pose a threat to the North Sea or any other waters sailed by the Royal Navy. It was a demeaning and humiliating interment for what had once been a proud battle fleet.

Elsewhere in the Flow, all the lighter cruisers and destroyers were also ignominiously moored in long grim lines. Germany had been defanged insofar as her ambitions as a naval power were concerned. Her ships were still manned by skeleton crews, but otherwise they were no more than hostages, bereft of ammunition and fuel, and each day that passed further emasculated the Kaiser's once proud navy.

Hindenburg was a latecomer to that fleet, ordered in 1912, laid down a year later and finally commissioned in May of 1917. She had seen little action in the Great War. A battlecruiser by design, she was part of Scouting Group I in a few indecisive sorties, but all the major fighting at sea had already been concluded by the time she began her brief service career. Her last hope of glory at sea, and perhaps a fitting death, had been the plan by Admiral Scheer to sally out and confront the British Fleet one last time, inflicting as much damage as possible so as to push the scales of the post war negotiations more in Germany's favor. *Hindenburg* was to have boldly sailed upon the Thames estuary to challenge anything she found there, but when a mutiny began at Wilhelmshaven, and mass desertions began, the planned "death ride" of the High seas fleet was aborted.

Now, on that quiet day in June of 1919, a light mist hung over the nearby islands, and the long days light had painted the calm sea a pale shade of green. Gulls wafted aimlessly over the tall masts and superstructures of the big grey ships, but there came a sudden stirring, and a flight of startled birds launched themselves from *Hindenburg's* main mast and fluttered away. Off in the distance, the battleship *Emden* was the first ship to settle low at the stern as water began flooding her interior compartments. Unbeknownst to the British, the Germans had conspired to scuttle the whole fleet, right under their noses. One by one the ships settled deeper in the water, some keeling over, creaking and rattling as the cold ocean rushed in to their bellies, others seeming to dive like U-boats, slowly submerging into the green waters of the Flow.

Hindenburg was the last to suffer this shameful fate, a ship come of age too late to fight for her nation, and now lost to the hungry sea, as the whole of the High Seas Fleet died that day. All the fire and smoke and ire of Dogger Bank and Jutland died with them. Never again would their iron bows plow the heavy seas, or their turrets turn and range on distant enemy dreadnoughts.

Years later, a curious man named Cox would invest the whole of his personal fortune to purchase the ships from the British Admiralty and raise them for salvage. To the Germans it seemed an unseemly and distasteful enterprise, and a desecration.

The old battlecruiser *Hindenburg* was dragged from her grave by using a 40,000 ton floating dock, also surrendered by Germany after the war. Her tall mast and stacks soon reappeared, and the sallow grey of her a barnacle infested superstructure rose up out of the Flow. Yet it was not a resurrection, just the final throes of her death that now awaited. Eventually the whole of the ship, and many others, were raised and dragged off for scrapping at Rosythe, with some of the steel even resold to the Royal Navy again for use in their own building programs. It was a last bitter and ironic twist of fate for the once proud German High Seas Fleet.

* * *

Long years passed before the name *Hindenburg* was again on the lips of men eager for the sea. Admiral Raeder had been diligent and resourceful in his charge. He had fought stubbornly to secure the necessary materials and particularly the steel required to rebuild the new *Reichsmarine*. In doing so he had often jousted with Goering, commander of the Luftwaffe, who had equal designs on building the air force for the war that was soon to come.

Raeder's greatest fears had been realized when Germany invaded Poland just a few years after his fateful meeting with Hitler. He had asked for six years, but the work on many of the ships he had promised was far more advanced than he let on in that January session of 1936. The first two ships worthy of the name battleship had already been completed by late 1940. *Bismarck* and *Tirpitz* were fitted out and had finished sea trials that very year. He had worked tirelessly to make sure they would both be commissioned together, sailed together at trials, and be ready for joint action as a formidable heavy unit, the first real menace ready for action at sea in the war that was slowly heating up to the low boil.

Poland had fallen in 30 days in September of 1939. Then came the long "phony war," a blessed interval of five to seven months until May of 1940 when the German Army again surged across their borders in an operation much like that of the old Von Schlieffen Plan from the Great War. This time there were no trenches, and barbed wire, nor the nightmare pounding of artillery and gas. This time it was lightning quick advances by Guderian's armor, a real *Blitzkrieg* that had shocked and defeated the Anglo French and allied forces with equal ease.

France was overrun as easily as Poland, and soon the German army was securing vital ports on the coast of the Atlantic. Raeder was eager to put them to good use! Up until that time, the war at sea had been nothing more than intermittent raiding sorties by the impudent Deutschland Class "Pocket Battleships," three in all, the *Deutschland, Graff Spee,* and *Admiral Scheer.* Joining the fleet in 1936, they were not really worthy of the name battleship, being nothing more than well armed heavy cruisers. They displaced only 16,000 tons and carried only six 11-inch guns, heavier in caliber than most other heavy cruisers, but far less firepower and armor than any real battleship in the Royal Navy.

That said, they had nonetheless managed to raise hell in the Atlantic, though *Graff Spee* had been finally holed up in an Argentinean port and scuttled when cornered by a squadron of British cruisers. She had given a good account of herself, using both guns and guile to confound the enemy while she steamed over 30,000 miles, sinking one merchant ship after another. At one point she had even erected a false turret and second wooden smoke stack to alter her profile and fool pursuing vessels. She clawed the enemy in battle, damaging several British cruisers, herding the captured sea masters and captains of the merchantmen she sunk into her storerooms, but could not escape unscathed, finally putting in to Montevideo for repairs. Unable to complete them in a timely manner, she sailed out to scuttle herself instead when faced with a superior battle fleet.

The sortie had thrilled the German people, and the professional officers of the newly named *Kreigsmarine,* but the ship's fate being scuttled in the face of the enemy had a sour, hollow ring. The purgatory of Scapa Flow, and the demise of the High Seas Fleet there, were still bitter memories. The incident was a reflection of that event, as well as a harbinger of what might come. The picture painted of

German fighting ships being scuttled under the eyes of their British masters rankled, and Raeder gave orders that no ship of the German Navy would ever again be scuttled until she had fought to the last gun. Then he continued forging those guns with great fervor, intent on filling out as many of the ships he had promised the Fuehrer as possible, and building a fleet that could be of some real use in the war.

For now however he did not put his real battleships in the shop window, unwilling to commit his heavier vessels to any significant action at sea. Instead he contented himself with jabbing raids by these lighter pocket battleships in early 1940, keeping the Royal Navy off balance as much as possible, testing their reactions and tactics at sea.

Admiral Sheer, had an equally brilliant sortie, lancing deep into the Atlantic and even into the Indian Ocean, and sinking well over 115,000 tons of enemy shipping, the best record of any ship to date. Then he had put his newer battlecruisers to the test with mixed results. The made a credible showing in the Norwegian Sea, but had no real laurels to claim. On one occasion they had brushed up against HMS *Renown*, and broke off without much of a fight. That said, *Scharnhorst* and *Gneisenau* had effectively supported Germany's occupation of Norway, which provided valuable ports on the Norwegian Sea and better access to the Atlantic.

As a young staff officer to the famous Admiral Hipper, Raeder had been exposed to Hipper's novel plans for dramatic commerce warfare in the Atlantic involving major elements of the German fleet. We cannot stand toe to toe with the Royal Navy, thought Raeder. No, we will have to dance and jab, yet we can still punch hard now that *Bismarck* and *Tirpitz* are ready. It might be better to wait for *Hindenburg* as well, but we have the power to act now if we choose...If I choose.

He was planning a new operation, much bigger than anything that came before. Admiral Lütjens was eager to get sea. He could send him out with *Scharnhorst* and *Gneisenau*, or he could send Hoffmann and give Lütjens something even bigger. If Hoffmann could punch through the British screen near Iceland, and get into the Atlantic to threaten the convoys, it would certainly draw off Royal Navy assets. He would give him orders to sink what he could, and then take his raiders to the French Port of Brest if the army was wise enough to quickly seize the dockyards there. Would the port be ready and waiting to harbor the tired German raiders when they came running home from the hotly contested campaigns in the Atlantic?

I can set those two two panthers on the prowl, he thought, and then surprise the British with another pair of tigers. *Bismarck* and *Tirpitz* were fueling and taking on ammunition for their first joint sortie into the fray. The British will not expect much for the rest of this year, which is why we will surprise them. Soon they will be obsessed with trying to neutralize the French Fleet! They will be greedy to get their hands on those ships, and keep them from our grasp. Well, I do not need the French fleet. I could not provision the ships, nor could I fuel them, and I certainly would not give them to the Italians! Perhaps we might pick the carcass and find a few ships we can put to use. For the moment, however, the French provide a nice additional distraction for the British.

Scharnhorst and *Gneisenau* are out harassing the British evacuation from Norway. I will send those panthers out again, only this time for a run to the Atlantic. With any luck the tigers will find them at sea when they break out, and then let the British try to deal with four raiders of considerable power in the Atlantic at one time.

Yet the best was still ahead, he thought. The real dreadnaughts of the fleet were almost ready to take their place on the board. The battlecruisers were merely knights, posted now to key squares in the opening of the chess game he was playing. *Bismarck* and *Tirpitz* were strong rooks finally ready to strike along an open file into the Atlantic, but soon the queen would make her appearance. The first ship in the long promised H class had already been fitted out and was running in secret night action trials in the Baltic.

Rumors of this fearsome vessel had undoubtedly reached the British Admiralty. They had tried, unsuccessfully, to get good aerial photographs of her. Raeder smiled to think that they would soon have more than enough time to study her powerful lines and awesome guns. The *Hindenburg* had been raised up yet again, not the old battlecruiser whose bones were picked over by a profit seeking British entrepreneur. No, this was an entirely new ship, over two hundred feet longer and twice as heavy as her old WWI namesake.

He still remembered the smile in Hitler's eyes when he attended he launching ceremony. She was an awesome ship when finally completed, measuring over 900 feet in length, with a beam of 128 feet making her the widest ship in that category and providing her with exceptional stability at sea. Raeder's fighting falcon, Admiral Fuchs had finally won Hitler's grudging approval for the installation of 16 inch gun turrets, four in all, and then only by demonstrating that anything bigger would delay the construction of the ship for at least two more years. *Hindenburg's* guns could be the equal of anything in the Royal Navy, today, he argued, or they could wait another few years to field something stronger.

Raeder was pleased with the outcome, believing anything larger than the massive 16 inch batteries was nothing more than a wasteful addition of excess weight. In his last meeting with Hitler on the matter, the Admiral had seconded Fuchs' argument, and reminded Hitler that he should be mindful of the fact that these were *German* 16 inch guns, not the pop guns the British were putting on their newest ships, the 14 inch guns of the KGV class battleships.

And better yet, the ship was actually completed! She was ready to put to sea in a matter of days to begin her trials in the Baltic, and she would not be alone. A second massive ship in the H class was already well advanced on the shipyard building program, the *Oldenburg*. She would not be ready for some months yet, as the foundries were still spinning out her massive 16 inch gun barrels, but she would have more than enough company when she finally did join the fleet, and *Hindenburg* would not be alone when she sailed. I will soon have two more lions in waiting, he thought.

Raeder had also resurrected one of the O-Class battlecruiser designs from Plan Z. Originally intended to replace the *Deutschland* class raiders that had been so successful. They were moved forward in production when *Graf Spee* and *Admiral Sheer* had demonstrated what a smaller ship could do, even when alone at sea, if she was given the right, combination of speed firepower and armor. The designers were keen create an up-gunned version of the *Deutschland* series, faster and more powerful. Where *Graf Spee* had carried six 11 inch guns at 28 knots, the sleek new O-Class battlecruiser, named *Kaiser*, would carry six 15 inch guns, two each in three of the very same turrets that had been mounted on the *Bismarck*, and the *Kaiser* was the fastest capital ship in the fleet, capable of 36 knots in early trials with her new hybrid steam and diesel engines. She was given only 190 millimeters of belt armor to achieve that speed, enough to counter the heaviest armed 8 inch gun cruisers of the Royal Navy, and she would be faster than anything carrying bigger guns.

Beyond this, a pair of fast new *Panzerschiff* armored cruisers would be ready to steam with her as well, bearing proud names of German provincial regions: *Rhineland*, and *Westfalen*. These were basically re-workings of the *Deutschland* class, with the same 11 inch quick firing guns in two turrets of three guns each. They would be faster at 33 knots, and protected with armor to 120 millimeters. While twelve were planned, only two had been completed, and other ship designs had caused all subsequent ships in the class to be cancelled.

Along with these the aircraft carrier *Graf Zeppelin* was also fitted out and ready for operations, the brainchild of naval architect Wilhelm Hadeler. It would carry modified versions of BF-109Es and

Stuka dive bombers as the primary armament, 38 fighting planes in all, with a detachment of 4 *Arado* 196 seaplanes as well. Raeder had also worked hard to build the *Seydiltz*, renamed *Peter Strasser* when commissioned, and that ship would be ready soon too. These additions, combined with the fleet's best new radar, made the carriers excellent scouting ships. Steaming as part of a task force, they would provide added anti-aircraft defense and extended air search capability to the fleet, not to mention the considerable striking power of their *Stuka* dive bombers.

Raeder had promised the Fuehrer six new battleships before the war had started, a fantasy in the time allotted. He knew as much even as he flipped through the various designs back in January of 1936, but instead he had delivered six exceptional new designs that strongly augmented the power of the *Kriegsmarine*, making it a fleet at last worthy of the name. It might not be able to deliver the dream of Admiral Tirpitz when he advocated a world navy, or *Weltmachtflotte*, but it would be enough to pose a credible challenge to the one navy which could claim that title, the Royal Navy of Great Britain.

Together these ships were all the Admiral could muster in the time he had been given, and even completing this much had put a great strain on the nation's resources. The *Oldenburg* would be the last that would come out of the German shipyards for some time, though the keel and hull was complete for *Brandenburg*, the third H class battleship in the series.

Taken as a whole, he now had another mailed fist to bring to the fight with the Royal Navy, fast, powerful new ships that Germany would not have available if he had not been so diligent, or had the favor of a Fuehrer intent upon building a credible navy. The speed of his ships relative to the bulk of the Royal Navy heavy capital ship classes was a decided advantage, and he also had tremendous operational range. The only problem would be finding the oil to keep the fleet in service.

On paper at least, Admiral Raeder's fleet looked much more promising. It wasn't the massive heavy fleet the Fuehrer wanted in the end, but it was twice as strong as it might have otherwise been, and would be further augmented by a large fleet of U-boats as soon as production ramped up. Now, he thought, we will put this navy to the test and see what we can do. God help any ship that comes under our guns…help them to the deepest regions of hell!

In due course I will add the *Oldenburg* and *Brandenburg* to that list, thought Raeder, but now he contemplated what he hoped would be the greatest naval operation of the entire war. Its aims were far grander than anything the old fleet had ever attempted, its most notable operation being the support rendered to the invasion of Norway. That accomplished, the Germans now planned a real offensive operation aimed at the convoy lifeline that sustained the British war effort.

We will take them by the throat this time, he thought. Four big ships at once, and *Graf Zeppelin* along with them!

Chapter 11

June, 12, 1940 ~ CiC, Home Fleet, Scapa Flow

They were called mystery ships, decoy ships, or simply Q-boats, armed merchantmen disguised as humble tramp steamers or cargo vessels and intended to lure in unsuspecting German U-boats. If they sighted a periscope the crews were trained to stage a "panic party" on deck, running this way and that so as to entice the U-boat to surface and use its deck gun as opposed to the limited and more expensive torpedo in an attack. Then, when the enemy was up and out manning its gun, the Q-ship would raise its skirts and reveal a row of three pounders, all ready to blast the submarine to pieces.

That morning the mystery on Admiral Tovey's desk was the strange report from Q-ship *Prunella* concerning an unidentified ship that had set off a bit of a panic party at the Admiralty right in the middle of Operation Juno, the evacuation of Norway. It had come on the heels of another warning from Convoy HX-49 out of Halifax about a large warship sighted off Cape Farewell. It seems the navy was seeing ghosts and mystery ships everywhere.

Tovey shook his head, bothered as he read that no further sighting could substantiate the report from *Prunella*, though it had caused quite a row and sent off the battlecruisers *Renown* and *Repulse*, with two cruisers and five destroyers on a wild goose chase to look for these ships. RAF reconnaissance later verified that the Twins were still at Trondheim, so it was all for naught.

That left the evacuation convoys dangerously exposed, and was, in part, one reason why the Germans very nearly sunk their teeth into HMS *Glorious*. There had been only two destroyers available to escort her home, and only one came back. In fact they did take a good bite out of *Glorious*, hitting the ship twice and killing most of the bridge crew. Were it not for the actions of a junior officer, who arrived on the bridge at a crucial moment and took command, the carrier would certainly have been lost.

He pinched the bridge of his nose, chasing a headache as the memory of a similar incident in his own career returned to him. Then he was a young Lieutenant, newly arrived at the British China Station in the Pacific at Weihaiwei and lucky to be posted to the squadron flagship, HMS *King Alfred*. He remembered it now, a distant look in his eyes. There had been another panic party underway in the Tsushima Strait, and another mystery ship as well. A Russian dreadnaught had been raiding Japanese shipping and threatened to impose a naval quarantine on the whole region, which was preposterous in itself, as a single ship could not hope to live up to such a boast.

Yet this ship was a real mystery indeed. It fought and won several engagements with elements of the Imperial Japanese Fleet, the very same fleet that had so devastated the whole Russian navy just a few years earlier in the famous battle of Tsushima Straits. And then it bore relentlessly down on the narrow channel there where Admiral Togo had sortied again with the Japanese Fleet to intercept the rogue. There was another battle there, he thought, still shivering inwardly as he remembered the distant shadow of the Russian ship, enormous and threatening on the sea ahead as it rounded the headlands of several small islets south of Iki Island.

King Alfred was leading in the entire squadron of six cruisers to support the Japanese, the Captain and First Officer out on the weather bridge. Tovey had been with them there, but was sent in by the Captain to make a course correction. That order had saved his life, for just seconds after he left the weather bridge where he had been posted as First Officer of the Watch, a shell from the Russian ship struck there and killed both the Captain and First Officer. *King Alfred* was at the edge of battle, leaderless, and Tovey took command.

It was the first real battle at sea he had ever seen, and now he was in the thick of it. He had always had ideas about how he would fight, and here was a chance to prove himself. So he pointed the bow of *King Alfred* right at the enemy and forged ahead, intending to close the range as quickly as possible before ordering a turn hard to port to bring the whole squadron behind him around and concentrate their firepower in broadside.

He could still see it all in his mind, hear the sharp crack of the enemy guns, amazingly accurate. But he held steady, and then made his turn, giving the order to fire. What he saw next was a memory that haunted him to this very day. The shells were falling very near the dark silhouette of the enemy ship, some finding the mark with bright fire and smoke that soon masked the scene in cinder grey. Then there came a shimmering glow, as though a pale moon was shining through heavy mist, rippling with St. Elmo's fire.

He remembered looking away to check his compass heading, then back again…and the Russian ship was gone! What had happened, he wondered. It was there, bristling with fire just a moment ago, and then it was simply gone! Had it been struck by the heavy weight of shot and shell his squadron was throwing, or by fire from the Japanese? Was it an unseen torpedo that had struck home, fired by one of those brave Japanese destroyers that had charged boldly forward through the gauntlet of the Russian ship's deck gun fire? Was it a hidden mine? He did recall that explosion forward of the ship…

Tovey closed his eyes, lingering on the memory, and the mystery of that seminal moment in his career, and then letting it go. He had more to concern him that day, much more.

It's all coming apart at the seams, he thought. I'm here to sort things out. Forbes was a good man, the former CiC here, but they've given Home Fleet to me now, along with those extra stripes on my cuff there, and much earlier than I ever thought I would see them. Tovey had been quickly recalled from the Med where he had been commanding the 7th Cruiser Squadron. They could have picked anyone else. Why me? Was it because Cunningham was heading for Gibraltar to plan an operation aimed at securing Dakar and denying the Vichy French Navy any use of that port? North and Somerfield are already there and waiting for ships to build Force H. So it's all in my lap now, the whole of Home Fleet, right here in this pile of reports and dispatches. But thank god for Daddy Brind. There's a clear head and steady hand as Chief of Staff.

Now he looked at the stack of reports again, taking heart to read the dispatch concerning the young Lieutenant Commander who had taken command and brought HMS *Glorious* safely home. There is hope, he thought as Brind stepped briskly through the door after a quiet knock. The two men were going to see what they could do about the mess up north where the Twins, *Scharnhorst* and *Gneisenau*, were causing so much trouble.

Brind arrived his cheeks red with the morning air, a fistful of cable intercepts in his hand and a determined look on his face. Wizened and grey, Brind was nonetheless a vital and energetic man, and perfect for the role he now found himself in.

"Good morning, Admiral. I hope I'm not disturbing you, but this is about our little hunting expedition with Force F," he said. "*Rodney* and *Renown* are heading for Trondheim with *Ark Royal*. Word came in that *Gneisenau* and the cruiser *Admiral Hipper* were out to sea there. With any luck we just might get lucky and catch those brigands but we have more than *Scharnhorst* and *Gneisenau* to worry about now. We've just received word that *Bismarck* and *Tirpitz* have left Kiel and they were spotted in the Kattegat at 18:00 hours last evening with a number of merchantmen. We got a Beaufort reconnaissance flight in a few hours later. Cloud deck was too thick to confirm the report, but there's an awful lot of activity shaping up south of Kristiansand as well. It looks like the Germans may be planning to another sortie."

Brind turned to the wall map fingering the position of the sighting. "Coastwatchers report *Graf Zeppelin* and a few of their new destroyers were working up steam off Bremen even as we speak. Then we got this latest report concerning *Bismarck* moving up through the Kattegat, and I'm willing to bet they are heading for Kristiansand, sir, which would give the Germans two strong battle groups to sortie into the Norwegian Sea at a moment's notice."

"Any word on the *Hindenburg?*" Tovey asked.

"Nothing yet, sir. It's still in the shipyards fitting out, though we haven't any recent photography. There's bad weather over the whole region and damn near down to ground level in places. But we don't think that ship is ready, sir. How could it be?"

"Let's pray to god it is *not* ready," said Tovey "Obviously the Germans are taking advantage of our situation to move some heavy units."

"This has all the markings of a major operation," said Brind. Radio traffic is off the scale, sir. What do you make of it, sir?"

Tovey was very quiet, thinking. "Now here we are with *Rodney* and *Renown* out after the foxes and a pair of real wolves shows up."

"It looks that way, sir."

"This is the last thing we need now. They aren't giving us a moment to breathe. Kicked out of France and Norway, this news of Italy formally joining the war in the Med, and now they tee up another operation."

"Italy was no surprise, sir."

Six days ago intelligence from the Med had revealed the fact that large numbers of Italian submarines were leaving ports from La Spezia to Taranto and heading out to designated patrol positions. So the Admiralty knew that it was only a matter of time before Italy entered the conflict, and ordered similar preliminary moves with their fleet units in Alexandria.

"If they throw *Bismarck* and *Tirpitz* at us now we've a real nightmare on our hands," said Tovey. God only knows what they're up to with the rest of the fleet. Intelligence has been rather spotty from the Admiralty in recent days."

"Do you really think they would risk this many capital ships in a major operation at this time, sir?"

"The movement of *Graf Zeppelin* is somewhat disturbing," said the Admiral. "It's their only carrier of any note, and with it they can provide good air cover over the Norwegian coast or anywhere else for that matter. It's even a threat to the fleet here, though I think RAF and FAA would hand them their hat if they dared."

"They could be running these ships up to Kristiansand just to thumb their nose at us while they slip the Twins out to sea," Brind suggested. "They know Home Fleet will have to stay put here is they do that."

"Possibly, but if I were going to make a run for the Atlantic with the battleships I'd certainly want the carrier along as well. Coastwatchers must have had an eye full."

"That they did, sir."

"In light of all these movements this business with the Twins could also be aimed at drawing us up north. It's a real shell game here. Given this news I think we must immediately recall the *Rodney* group. We can't have them up near Trondheim with *Bismarck* and *Tirpitz* holding knives at their back off Kristiansand."

"Agreed, sir, but it would put them in an interesting position if the Germans do head west with an eye towards breaking out."

"Yes, and it might be an uncomfortable position as well. I think we better have a look at our cards, Brind. What's our situation with the convoys?"

"A good number are at risk now, sir. We've seven inbound long haul convoys at sea at the moment, three from Halifax, two from Freetown and two from Gibraltar. Then we have three outbound convoys out of Liverpool heading for Gibraltar. That's 350 merchantmen to look after. A troop ship is scheduled to leave Halifax tomorrow, and at least ten more long haul convoys scheduled before month's end."

That reminded Tovey of the odd sighting by the escort ship *Ausonia*, and he asked Brind about it. "Anything further from HX-49?"

"You mean the sighting report we received? No sir, all's quiet there. It was most likely a Canadian ship returning to Halifax. If it was a German raider they had a real feast in front of them and there wasn't much *Ausonia* was going to do to stop them."

"Probably true, but just the same I think we'd better confirm that assumption with the Canadians. Well…A lot on our plate today. Where's that report on current fleet dispositions?"

"I have it here, sir." Brind handed the Admiral a folder, and he opened it slowly, deliberately, indeed like a poker player sliding his hand open in a crucial game:

HOME FLEET:
2nd Battleship Squadron: *Resolution, Rodney, Valiant*
Under Repair: *Nelson, Barham*
Working up on sea trials: *King George V, Prince of Wales*
Battlecruiser Squadron: *Invincible* (G3 Class), *Renown, Repulse*
Under repair: *Hood* (at Greenock)
Aircraft Carriers: *Ark Royal* (at sea), *Furious* at the Clyde
Under Repair: *Glorious,* Working up: *Illustrious*
Carrier Cruiser Escorts under repair: *Cairo, Enterprise*
1st Cruiser Squadron: *Devonshire, Sussex, Norfolk, Suffolk*
Under repair: *Berwick*
2nd Cruiser Squadron: Galatea, Arethusa, (at Sheerness)
Under Repair: *Aurora, Penelope*

18th Cruiser Squadron: *Southampton, Birmingham, Manchester, Sheffield* (in the Humber), *York* (at Rosythe), *Newcastle* (in the Tyne)
Under repair: *Glascow*
36 Destroyers (16 of these under repair)

He looked at the suggested assignments for the new Force H being assembled for Admiral Somerville at Gibraltar.

"Well," he said after some time. We've given *Valiant* a facelift, but old *Barham* is still wearing grease paint from the last war. She's scheduled to head for the Med for the buildup at Gibraltar. If we send *Hood* and *Resolution* along with them that won't leave us much here at all if the Germans do sortie."

"We have *Invincible* ready again, sir. They just fitted her with the new radar sets for fire control."

HMS *Invincible* was conceived in the early 1920s as an answer to the growing naval might of both the United States and Japan. At the time the design was revolutionary in that it proposed a ship combining incredible firepower, speed and armor protection. They were approved on 12 August, 1921 with orders for four ships placed soon after. When the Washington Naval Conference met that same year to negotiate fleet size and ship specification limits, the Royal Navy was faced with the prospect of having to cancel all four planned ships. Instead they chose to eliminate two older dreadnoughts then in service, scrapping them to make room for at least one new G3 class ship as a trial of the concept. *Invincible* was the result of that wise decision.

She was 856 feet long with a beam of 106 feet, much like the previous design of HMS *Hood*, but the gun placement and superstructure and funnel arrangement was quite different. 16 inch guns were chosen for the design, the same as those slated to be used in the *Nelson* Class ships, in three triple gun turrets, but with a very unusual arrangement. Two turrets were mounted forward of the main superstructure and conning tower, which got 203mm of armor. The turrets themselves were among the best protected in the navy, with 432mm armor. The third was mounted amidships, between the conning tower and twin funnels just aft of these guns. This unique arrangement saw the main turrets and barbettes and magazines grouped closer together, which meant the heavy side armor and bulkhead length could be shortened to reduce weight.

The result was amazing speed, with powerful engines that could drive the ship to 32 knots, and range exceeding any other battleship in the fleet. *Invincible* was the pride of the Navy, still state-of-the-art twenty years after she was conceived, and Tovey found himself regretting that the Admiralty had been forced to cancel the last three ships slated for that class.

They were scuttled by the Washington Naval Treaty, he thought, and thank god for the clause we managed to negotiate that allowed us to retain this one ship. We should have built more G3s, Tovey knew. Instead they fuddled about with the *Nelson* class trying to use the work done for the N3 battleship designs, after scaling it down to meet the requirements of the treaty. What we got was too slow for the war that we find ourselves in now. As it happened, both the Americans and Japanese were busy building new designs that violated the treaty. We were snookered and lost our chance to have all four G3s at sea today. But by god, at least we've got *Invincible.*

Just as HMS *Hood* had been the only one of four ships planned for the *Admiral* Class battlecruisers, *Invincible* was an only son born of the G3 class design proposals. Really a fast battleship, it was nonetheless decided that the ship would form the flag of the speedy Battlecruiser Squadron, which is where Tovey planned to be if things heated up, replacing Admiral Whitworth who was taking the position of Second Sea Lord.

"How is she working out, Brind?"

"Very good, sir. New ears for the old girl, and better anti-aircraft protection. Gunnery trials were entirely satisfactory after the new 4.7 Dual purpose guns were refitted. Engines and propulsion are still top drawer."

"Good to hear it, as I intend to place my flag there tomorrow."

"You're going to sea, sir? Tomorrow?"

"Mister Brind, where else would an Admiral of the Home Fleet better dispose himself than at sea with his ships? Tomorrow will do quite nicely. We'll settle in for a day and depart on the 14th. That will give *Rodney* time to get south and stand a watch closer to home. As for *Renown* I want to her within arm's reach in 48 hours."

"I understand, sir."

"Now then…We'd better have a good look at everything else. Something tells me the Germans are up to something big here, and we had best be prepared for it."

Tovey's nose for battle was serving him well.

Chapter 12

Doenitz leaned heavily over the map, his eyes scanning it with misgiving. "Too soon," he muttered. "We are not yet ready for major operations in the Atlantic."

"Well it seems Herr Hitler is," said Raeder. "These plans were drawn up specifically to satisfy that man. You most certainly read the Fuhrer Directive."

Doenitz shook his head. "Of course I have read it, but that does not mean we should commit the bulk of the fleet like this—all our newest designs.."

"Not all. I'm keeping Kaiser, Rhineland and Westfalen in the pen. What else can I do? Hitler specifically ordered this planning be given the highest priority."

"You insisted on building these ships, Raeder, so now don't be surprised when the Fuhrer asks you to use them."

Raeder folded his arms, thinking. "We've sat on our thumbs for all of a year, with little more than the *Graf Spee* and *Admiral Sheer* to challenge the enemy. Now we are waiting for *Hindenburg* to rig out and run through trials. The ship is almost ready, and so are *Bismarck* and *Tirpitz*."

"Well if you had left me a little steel in the bin, and if we could keep fat Goering's hand out of the purse, then I might have more to support you. As it stands, we've no more than a hundred U-boats ready now, a third of what we need for this war, and many of those are early Type VII boats, not suited for operations in the Atlantic."

"Well how many boats can you commit?"

"I can give you one or two wolfpacks for the Atlantic by pulling in most of the units I have there now. But they will have to operate in the east. All the boats are coming out of Wilhelmshaven, swinging north of the UK and then loitering southwest of Ireland. That's where the real pickings are at the moment. The rest will have to operate along the French and Spanish coast, or in the Med."

"That will have to do then." Raeder was equally concerned, but in spite of his reservations there was still the thrum of a thrill within him over the operation. It was truly grand, truly dangerous. Can we risk it, he wondered? The heart of the fleet? Of what use are the ships if we simply leave them riding at anchor in the Baltic Sea or building up layers of frost in the fiords up north? Winter is coming, and it may be a hard one if the Allies regain their balance. We have knocked them back on their heels. Yet what of the fuel situation? We'll burn off virtually every drop of oil we have in an operation of this size. It could take us months to recover to a level where we could function normally again.

"Do you really propose to operate on this scale?" Doenitz voiced the same basic question, seeming to read his mind, fully aware of the risks and difficulties involved.

"I know, Admiral," said Raeder. "I have had nightmares about it for months. But we will not sail out in one great sortie to seek battle with the British Home Fleet. That would be foolish. The bands will play, the crews will stand in dress whites on the decks and then it is out of our hands. How much will come back? That is the question I keep asking myself. No. The virtue of the ships we have built still lies in the unique combination of speed, power and endurance. We will accomplish our aims with maneuver, not a set piece battle. To do this we have deployed tankers that will allow at sea replenishment for our capital ships in the Atlantic. Our *Trosschiff* fleet support ships are as important as any of the battleships. We have six deployed to support the battlecruiser operation at this very moment."

"And what about Norway?" said Doenitz. "If you send out all your warships who will watch the coast? The garrisons will be isolated, without replenishment by sea."

"We have a supply convoy scheduled to go with *Bismarck* and *Tirpitz*. In fact, this is part of the cover plan for the operation as a whole. If I can convince the Royal Navy that these initial movements are aimed at reinforcing Norway, then we might not raise enough suspicion to prompt a major response from their home fleet."

"I would not count on that," Doenitz shook his head again. "The British have been masters of the seas for generations. They will know trouble when they see it, and act accordingly."

"That may be, but the plan is sound. *Scharnhorst* and *Gneisenau* will soon head for the Atlantic. They'll be looking to draw in as many British heavy units as possible, and I think the English will oblige us. We already have a Condor report showing the movement of two battleships and a carrier."

"Be careful what you wish for," Doenitz cautioned.

"True, but this sortie with the battlecruisers will force the British to assign capital units to look for them. Yes, there is always the chance they may find them, but thirty-two knots is a good speed if they have to avoid engagement."

"Those ships have had teething problems, Raeder. They ship too much water over the bow. Get them into heavy seas and you could find you've lost your forward turret without firing a shot. And as for the superheating tubes on the boilers, *Scharnhorst* will be lucky to average 28 knots in the Atlantic."

"Yes, well remember, the battlecruisers are only a feint, a shadow on the sea to cause alarm. Then comes *Bismarck* and *Tirpitz* escorting the convoy north to Bergen and Tromso from Kristiansand. That is the theater. Operation Valkyrie follows. The British will watch that with great interest, and perhaps even commit more units to the Norwegian Sea to keep an eye on us there. We'll scoot them up the coast, then turn west for the Denmark Strait."

"And *Hindenburg?*"

"It will not be ready in time, but it will stand as fleet reserve. If the other units draw off the hounds as I suspect, then *Hindenburg* may be able to show a mailed fist and force the British to retain heavy units at Scapa Flow. The weather is very good for us now, all socked in, so the RAF will see nothing. Each group will be more than enough to defend itself, and a nightmare for the British at the same time."

"Would it not be better to combine the entire force into one powerful surface wolfpack?"

"You think like a submariner, Doenitz. The Fuhrer might warm to such an idea, but that will result in nothing more than a major tactical engagement that will achieve nothing. We cannot trade the British battleship for battleship. My idea is to disperse the fleet to pose a wide ranging threat at many points."

"But then you will dribble your force away, a ship here, a ship there, and the hounds would run the foxes down one by one. Would it not be better to concentrate the fleet?"

"No, Doenitz, dynamic dispersal. What we do, the enemy must also do. If we concentrate, so will they, and they outnumber our battleships more than two to one. But if we disperse the fleet we force the enemy to also dilute his forces in trying to run these foxes down, and if they do they will see the fox may be a wolf instead! The idea is to break through to the Atlantic, disperse, and then we dance with the convoys. The *Graf Spee* and *Admiral Sheer* have proved that concept. Now I turn *Scharnhorst* and *Gneisenau* loose. Just when they mass their forces to oppose that, the battleships sortie. The convoys are the prize, my friend. They are the real reason for sea control and interdiction."

"Something tells me that will be my task in the end," said Doenitz darkly. "And this is what will decide this war, not these surface engagements. If you want my opinion it is all a waste of steel and petrol. Even if you do attempt this dynamic dispersal as you call it, the British have enough forces to still overmatch you."

"Perhaps, but they are spread thin as matters stand. Their battleships are old and slow. They play nursemaid to the merchantmen half the time and have but a handful of ships with the speed to catch our forces if we break out into the Atlantic, and some of those are their older battlecruisers—no match for a ship like *Bismarck*, let alone *Hindenburg*."

"Don't be so sure, Raeder." Doenitz wagged a finger at him now. "A 15-inch shell is a 15-inch shell, and if it hits one of your nice new shiny ships it will explode just the same."

"That is the risk we take any time we sail," Raeder reminded him. "It would be nice if my battleships could slink out beneath the surface like your U-boats, Doenitz, but that is not the case. We may have to fight to break out, yes, this I know. Yet we will hurt the enemy as well, for every hit they score. You must have faith in that."

Doenitz smiled. "Well, my friend, you realize that we could both be out of a job if this plan fails. Who do we send? Who commands the task groups at sea?

"Lütjens, he's the only man for the job. I'm giving the battlecruisers to Hoffmann and putting Lütjens aboard *Hindenburg*. Lindemann will command the *Bismarck* class units."

"Lindemann? He's a Captain. We have Admirals to spare."

"I want fighting men." Raeder was not going to turn the operation over to desk Admirals. Let them sit at home as they were accustomed. This was a job for men who knew the sea, and the ships they fought on.

"What about Marschall? He won't like losing *Scharnhorst* and *Gneisenau*."

"Hoffmann fights, Marschall worries about ammunition and fuel expenditure."

"And what about Thiele?"

"A good leader, but he's a cruiser man. I'll leave him there with the heavy cruisers. That's where he does the best job."

There it was, the map, the tiny models of the massive ships sitting there, the men waiting, ready, filled with urgency, and the silence now as the two Admirals reached an end to their meeting. In that silence many things grew, germinated by the memories of that last war. Jellicoe had been waiting for Scheer with the whole Grand Fleet at Jutland the last time the German Navy sortied in earnest. This plan might lead to the largest clash at sea since that time. It could either be a decisive moment that broke the back of the Royal Navy and changed the whole character of the war, or it could be the death ride of the *Kriegsmarine*, skewered just as it was being born. Neither man could see the outcome, but both men would live with it, one way or another.

"Well, Doenitz, gather your U-boats into a nice tight fist for me when they swing through the Faeroes gap." Raeder placed his finger on the map, fingering a spot in the Atlantic. "I'll want them here."

* * *

"**Any** idea when we might see *Prince of Wales?*" Admiral Tovey was also running down his fleet list, checking on every ship he might have available.

"She'll be a good while, sir," said Brind. "We've only just completed fitting her out. Captain Leach is optimistic that he can resume trials in a few weeks."

"I'll want him working out by week's end."

"Week's end sir? They'd have to put to sea with a hundred workmen aboard."

"Then do so. We'll need that ship sooner than we may think. Thank God they came off the docks a little early and we even have them this close."

The *King George V* Class had been proposed before the 1936 expiration of the Washington Naval Treaty. At that time Britain was attempting to negotiate reduced caliber gun sizes, and proposed a 14-inch maximum for new construction to lead the way. These guns were subsequently ordered and built before Japan and other nations refused to sign on to the idea, and so the ships were under gunned, and with turrets that were overly complex and unreliable. To compensate, however, they were among the best protected battleship designs in the world, with 374mm of new cemented belt armor and excellent anti-torpedo bulwarks and magazine protection. The first two ships in the new class were ready earlier than expected, but still making adjustments and running trials.

"Now… what about *Nelson?*" Tovey asked about the ships the Navy had built when the much better G3 orders were cancelled after *Invincible*. They were smaller with a length of only 660 feet, but crowded three triple 16-inch gun turrets forward giving them the heaviest throw weight of any ship in the fleet. Well armored, they were slow as molasses compared to modern ship designs, and capable of only 23 knots.

"*Nelson* is presently at Greenock completing her refit. They're running out that new Type 282 radar for trials."

"Didn't she get the Type 279?"

"She did sir, and all her other major repairs have been completed at Portsmouth before Jerry bombers made it a little too hot there. So we moved her to Greenock for this last bit of work."

"Cancel it. *Nelson* is to make ready to rejoin the fleet here at once. We'll pair her with *Rodney*, and the two of them can watch the Shetlands passage. As for *Hood*, what wrong with the old girl now? Didn't she just get new tube condensers?"

"That she did, sir. They have her down at Gladstone Dock, Liverpool, with crew just returning from leave. At the moment they are running anti-aircraft and armament drills on the new 4-inch guns that were added, and splashing a bit of paint about. There's also a plumbing problem aboard, sir."

"Plumbing?"

"Well it seems the condenser refit damaged a few feeder pipes and they have no working toilet facilities aboard."

Tovey's eyes narrowed. "What? See that it is corrected at once. Recall the crew from leave if they aren't back yet and lay in a fresh stock of ammunition. When they see the lads all lined up at the gangways they'll bloody well get the toilets fixed. I want *Hood* back here in 48 hours."

"But sir... She was scheduled to cover that ANZAC troop convoy, US3, and then after that she's bound for Gibraltar and the Dakar Operation. We mustn't forget the French fleet."

"I'll need *Hood* here, Mister Brind. We're already sending *Barham, Resolution* and *Valiant,* and that is all we can spare for the moment."

"I see... Shall I inform Admiral Somerville, sir? He was set to place his flag aboard *Hood* at month's end and is also expecting *Ark Royal* for Force H."

"I'm afraid all of that is up in the wind now. I may be biting off more than I can chew, but they've handed me the biscuit here and it's time I take charge. With both *Bismarck* and *Tirpitz* near Kristiansand there is simply no way I can release *Ark Royal* and *Hood* at this time. I'll need them both here. In fact I'm inclined to hold that new carrier in home waters as well."

"*Illustrious?* She was also nominated for service in the Med, sir."

"Yes, well I've already discussed it with Admiral Pound. With *Glorious* laid up, fleet air cover is rather thin. He's agreed to allow *Illustrious* to hang on here for a spell. Tell Admiral Somerville we'll send *Hermes* in the short run and then *Glorious* after they patch her up. Along with *Eagle* that should fill the bill."

"*Illustrious* has taken on aircraft, but she's still working up at trials, sir."

"Good enough, but she stays here. *Hermes* will simply have to do for Force H at the moment. The disposition of the French Fleet has yet to be decided. We still have time to build that force up further, if need be, pending the outcome of that situation."

That reminded him of something, and he shifted to his dispatches. "See here, Brind. This Lieutenant Commander that brought *Glorious* home safely, is he still aboard the ship?"

"I believe so, sir. That crew was overdue for leave and they were sent out to Devonport yesterday, but the officers will remain until next weekend."

"Send for the man. I'd like to speak with him. We'll need good men like that in the days ahead. How long for those repairs?"

"A week to ten days, dir. The bridge needs work, but the real damage was to the forward flight deck. They can't use the elevators effectively until that's cleared and patched, and there may be some structural work required there."

Tovey tapped the desk with his pen, thinking. "The jig is up, Daddy. I can feel it. This time the Germans mean business, and a dirty business it will be. The fleet is to cease lolling about and any ship under repair for any routine maintenance is to be immediately recalled to active duty. Home Fleet will be going to sea. It's time we give Admiral Raeder something to think about as well."

"Aye, sir," said Brind. "The crews are ready. They're spoiling for a good fight—ship to ship—every man jack among them."

"Yes, well get word out to Admiral Holland on the *Hood* and get him moving north as soon as possible. These German ships are fast. *Hood*, *Renown* and *Repulse* are the fastest ships in the fleet along with *Invincible* and I intend to get them into the hunt."

"I'll see the orders go out, Admiral."

Part V

Encounters

"I don't believe in accidents. There are only encounters in history. There are no accidents."

— Pablo Picasso

Chapter 13

The young officer stood before the Admiral's desk, saluting. "Lieutenant Commander Wells reporting as ordered, sir."

"At ease Mister Wells. In fact please be seated. I understand you were instrumental in saving *Glorious* from more serious harm, and you are to be commended."

"Thank you, sir, but it was all in the line of duty."

Tovey was looking through a folder as he spoke. "I've read the reports, and the statement of the ship's executive officer as well. A bit of a run in with the Twins…A sticky spot for a carrier with no escort to speak of. I cannot help but wonder why the German ships were not sighted earlier. How was it the ship found itself under those guns, in your opinion?"

Wells started to speak, then checked himself, thinking of the implications of anything he might say here. Captain D'Oyly–Hughes had lost his life in that encounter, and would not be there to present any other side of the story. In spite of what he thought of the man, Wells felt he owed him an easy rest now.

"May I ask if this is this a formal inquiry, sir?"

"The Admiralty will certainly convene such a hearing, but at the moment I should like to get to the bottom of this before all that shuffle and bother. If you feel uncomfortable speaking about it I will understand, however any light you might shed on the incident would be appreciated."

"I understand, sir. Well… to put it simply, the ship was in a low state of readiness insofar as any potential surface contacts as a threat. The Captain was steaming in a zig-zag pattern, but with six boilers down, sir. Our speed was no more than 16 or 17 knots."

"You believe the Captain was worried about a U-boat attack?"

"That seemed to be the only precaution he took, sir—the zig-zag pattern, with five point turns every ten minutes."

"D'Oyly-Hughes was a submariner, and a good one, so I can understand his appreciation of the threat posed by U-boats. What I cannot understand, however, was how he allowed his ship, a carrier of some value, to come upon a pair of German battlecruisers. There were two destroyers present. Where were they posted?"

"About two cables off the bow, to port and starboard, sir. In fact I was on a lower weather bridge when we first sighted the enemy smoke on the horizon."

"You heard the alarm from the mainmast?"

"No sir, there was no alarm. In fact there was no watch posted on the mainmast at all, sir."

"No watch?"

"No sir, and we had no air cover up, and nothing spotted on deck either. Planes were on ten minute standby on the hanger deck, however."

"Yet nothing on the flight deck?"

"No sir."

Tovey raised an eyebrow at that. "Well then…It's fairly clear how you came to be under the guns on this one. I've read the weather log for the day—clear and unlimited visibility, yet that works both ways, for friend and foe alike. A carrier with light escort and destroyers improperly posted, no air cover, no mainmast watch, six boilers down and no planes ready for immediate launch is a recipe for disaster, and that is what we nearly had there. Were it not for the gallantry of Lieutenant Commander Barker aboard *Ardent*, and your timely arrival on the bridge after that first hit was scored, we might have lost a very valuable ship and a good many lives. How was it you came to the bridge at that moment?"

"Sir, I saw that smoke on the horizon and was concerned. No alarm was raised, though *Ardent* saw it too and was making challenge with her search light. I thought I would see what might be done on the bridge."

"What might be done? Do you mean to say you went there on your own initiative? You were not a scheduled watch stander?"

"No sir, I was not posted at the time, but with no action stations sounded I became concerned."

"I see…Did you see the Captain before the action opened and the bridge was struck?"

"I did, sir. He was ordering 823 Squadron up when I arrived on the Bridge, and then immediately ordered me get to the main W/T room and report the sighting."

"As he should have."

"Correct, sir. It was just by chance that I was off the bridge when they took that hit."

Yes, thought Tovey, by chance or fate, a glint in his eye. It was just as it had happened to him aboard *King Alfred*. "Do go on, Lieutenant Commander."

"Well sir, I passed on the sighting information, then started back to the bridge, arriving to find virtually every man down and the whole bridge enveloped in smoke. It was then I saw Mister Louvell, and he urged me to take command."

"What was your order then, if I may ask?"

"Sir? Well the bridge crew was pretty badly shaken up, Admiral. I could see that our only chance was to make a run for it. The Captain had been steering 220, but the ship was at 180 from what I could see. I gave the order to steer 120 and ahead full."

"Away from the German ships?"

"Yes, sir, by the most direct route possible. *Acasta* was out in front laying a good smoke screen and I wanted to take every advantage of that. The wind would also be at our backs with that turn, so the smoke would ride with us as well, and I thought we might make a go of it."

"Thank god the helm answered smartly, Mister Wells."

"Actually...No one answered that order, Admiral. The Helmsman was down, so I took the wheel myself."

Just as I did, thought Tovey...yes...Well this is a man I can use. He looked at Wells for some moments, then put the folder he had been reviewing down on the desk.

"Mister Wells," he began. "You are not carrier man by training. In fact your file shows you to be well schooled in cruiser operations."

"Yes sir. I was only just posted to *Glorious* three weeks ago to relieve a man down with illness."

"I see you've tested well in gunnery, and even trained on the new Type 279 and 284 Radars."

"Yes sir."

"*Glorious* is going to be in repair for some time, but I have need of good men at sea right now. I should like to transfer you to HMS *Invincible*, unless you have objection."

"Objection? Why...No sir. None at all." This was not the time for a moment's hesitation. "I should be honored to serve in any capacity." Wells was elated. A battleship! Not just any battleship. This was HMS *Invincible*, the finest ship in the fleet and truly one of a kind.

"Good then. We'll see how you train out in surface operations. You may report to Captain Bennett aboard *Invincible* tomorrow morning. I understand you and other officers aboard *Glorious* were awaiting leave, and if this upsets any plans you may have had..." He raised an eyebrow, waiting.

"I am entirely at your service, Admiral."

"Good. Good. Mister Brind will see to the paperwork. Good day, Mister Wells. That will be all."

* * *

The fleet left Scapa Flow the next day on the 14th of June with the battlecruiser squadron in the van. Admiral Tovey led the way aboard HMS *Invincible*. They would sail all day to reach a point south of Iceland by dawn on the 15th, and there Tovey hovered while he waited on other fleet elements to catch up. *Ark Royal* had refueled at Scapa Flow and was hastening out to join him, and Admiral Holland had roused *Hood* from its nap at Liverpool and got her out to sea with *Repulse,* and was still some 300 miles to the south. The slower battleships *Nelson* and *Rodney* were not with the fleet. Instead they were to assume patrol duty east of the Faeroes.

Tovey had seen to it that the young Lieutenant Commander Wells was included in his Flag Staff for seasoning. "Watch and learn," he had told him, "but like any good officer, feel free to speak your mind if you have one. Don't be bothered by these stripes, or even the raw temper I have at times, Mister Wells. I want officers who can take initiative and keep cool, yet critical minds under pressure."

Wells promised he would do his very best, but to be there on the bridge of the flagship of the fleet, with the Admiral of that fleet ever present, was an eye opener for him at the outset. He soon saw that Admiral Tovey's command style was much different than that of Captain D'Oyly-Hughes. Where Hughes had been somewhat irascible and prone to hound the officers and crew, Tovey exhibited that same calm, professional manner that he expected of all those around him.

He was assigned to work with the Flag Lieutenant, an honorary title given to Commander James Villers, a new man on Tovey's hastily assembled staff.

"Ready to flog the sea a bit, Mister Wells?" said Villers.

"I am, sir, and lucky to be here."

Villers was a dark haired, blue-eyed man, tall and aristocratic in bearing, with a stiff posture and a penchant for folding his arms behind his back, as many senior officers often did. Wells never adopted the habit, though his old friend Woodfield said it was a good way to avoid putting one's hands into his pockets, which was frowned upon.

"Good show aboard *Glorious*," said Villers. "The fleet needs every ship we have now, what with Italy jumping in, the French sitting on the fence, and now Jerry rattling swords again up north. So we'll go and have a look to see if they really want to mix thing up with the Royal Navy."

"They'll be sorry if they do, sir."

"That they will, Wells. That's the spirit, and you'll be right in the thick of things here. You're to be my messenger to the Admiral."

"Admiral Tovey, sir?"

"There's only one aboard, Mister Wells."

"Of course, sir."

"Yes, well I'll be spending a good deal of time in the plotting room pouring over charts and maps. You'll be my voice to the bridge and also serve as my liaison to the W/T room."

That brought back the memory of that day on *Glorious* just before she was hit. Wells had been sent as a messenger to the W/T room with the Captain's sighting order, and that order saved not only his life, but by extension, the life of the ship itself. He hoped nothing of the sort would repeat itself here, though the thought that he would take the wheel of HMS *Invincible* and lead her in battle briefly crossed his mind. He was wise enough to know that he had a good deal to learn before he should ever contemplate a thing like that, and this was a posting any Lieutenant Commander would lust for, right on the bridge level and in the know. He would see how the ship was maneuvered, and why. He would be privy to every signal and contact made. It was going to be grand.

"There's been a good deal of rumor circulating round the mess decks, Wells," said Villers. "In your position you learn more than most on this ship, but I wouldn't throw logs on any of those fires, or even set yourself to quash them. The business of the Flag Bridge should be kept under your hat."

"I understand, sir."

"We'll be making a rendezvous with *Ark Royal* shortly with Admiral Wells. Any relation?"

"No sir, it's just coincidence."

"Well perhaps you'll make Admiral one day yourself. Let's step into the Flag Plot Room."

The two men moved aft to the open hatch where several charts were pinned to the walls and a large central table held a general map depicting the region from Scapa Flow to Greenland. They were surprised to see Admiral Tovey present.

"Good day, Admiral. I wasn't aware you were here yet, sir."

Villers saluted, with Wells following suit, and Tovey looked up from the chart he had been studying. "A bit musty below in the wardroom, Mister Villers. Ah, I see you have our young Lieutenant Commander there. Step over here, Mister Wells, and we'll have a look at our situation."

"I was just going to brief Mister Wells, sir."

"I'll do the honors." Tovey handed his Flag Lieutenant an Admiralty message decrypt. "Have a look at that, if you please."

Villers read the message quickly, raising a single eyebrow as he did. "The Twins, sir? Out to sea from Trondheim…Well I can't say as it surprises me."

"And the Germans will know that we are out to sea as well the next time they have a look at the Flow. So, gentlemen, here's where things stand. I'm posting *Nelson* and *Rodney* as you see here." He pointed to the situation map where two small wooden models indicated the battleships, held in place on the metal tabletop with embedded magnets.

"*Rodney* will watch the passage between the Flow and the Faeroes. *Nelson* to backstop the cruiser patrol in the Iceland-Faeroes

Gap. That leaves us with the Battlecruiser division, the fast hounds. I intend to take up a position here about 200 kilometers south of Reykjavik. From there we can move to interdict the Denmark Strait easily enough, or return to the Iceland-Faeroes passage if needed."

"This message doesn't indicate any sailing date for *Scharnhorst* and *Gneisenau*, sir."

"It does not, and that means the we cannot yet plot their farthest on. Unless we back-date to their last known sighting, and I'm afraid that was over 48 hours ago. So this is where *Ark Royal* will come in handy. It was set to pay a visit to Trondheim, but I recalled it two days ago. The carrier should join us soon." He looked at the Lieutenant Commander now. "Where would you post your air search, Mister Wells?"

Stepping up to the table, Wells took a long look. "If I recall correctly, sir, *Ark Royal* will be carrying a mix of *Swordfish* and Blackburn *Skuas*. I'd want planes in the air an hour before we reached our expected cruising station and flying a twelve plane fan approximately here, sir." He indicated a section of the Denmark Strait as it approached the ragged icy coast of Greenland. "The ice floes peaked in April and have been thinning for weeks now. That gives the Germans a decent channel."

"A reasonable deployment, Mister Wells. We shall have to see what your namesake on the *Ark Royal* decides, but I may just pass along the recommendation." He gave Wells a wink, turning to receive another dispatch from the W/T room.

"It seems the Admiralty is wanting to keep me well read today," said Tovey. "Carry on, gentlemen. I mean to visit Captain Bennett for a moment."

As it happened the advice of his new staff officer was in accord with that of the Vice Admiral, Fleet Aircraft Carriers, and this particular search was going to troll up much more in the net than any of them expected.

Chapter 14

The news from Chief Dobrynin was not encouraging. Beyond the difficulty he experienced in handling the new control rods he was starting to see a basic problem in the reactor itself. Now he was meeting with the Admiral and Fedorov to discuss the situation. Kamenski was invited, but he had not yet arrived. Knowing he was going to be the bearer of bad news, Dobrynin began his briefing.

"Something in the makeup of the materials in this latest control rod is not harmonizing well with the reactor, sir," he began. "I made a close inspection of this new control rod after the procedure was concluded, and I began to see signs of unusual wear, micro-fissures, tiny cracks. It is very unusual for a new rod to exhibit these conditions. Apparently that last attempt to displace in time placed a great deal of stress on both the reactor and the control rod."

"The fact that we moved in space rather than time was rather alarming," said Fedorov. "We did move in time, but only for the briefest moment."

"Yes, I could hear it," said Dobrynin. "On all previous shifts the sound moved in the direction of our displacement. If we were shifting forward into the future there was always a rising chorus, and for shifts into the past it always descended. This may sound strange to you, but it is a very subtle harmonic that I can hear in the system as it operates."

"Those ears of your served us well," said Volsky.

"Yet not this time, Admiral. The sound attempted to rise, but it was as if it struck a barrier of some kind. The sound just quavered in a long, steady timbre. Then it simply faded."

"This does not sound good," said Fedorov. "Given the possibility that this could happen again, and the ship could find itself marooned on dry land, I would not advise we attempt to use this control rod again until we know what is happening."

"I am in agreement," said Volsky. "We have not given much thought to how these time displacements have affected the structural integrity of the ship itself. Beyond that, we are still bearing the scars of many engagements. I spoke with chief Byko to get a comprehensive report on the ship's condition. We have no battle bridge, damage to the fantail, the hull is patched amidships, we have damage on our main mast, and now we have lost the Horse Jaw sonar system. Byko believes we need an extended time in port, a week or ten days so that he can complete repairs to the hull. In this light, damage to the main reactor system is the last thing we need. I cannot risk this."

"It's not serious at the moment, sir," said Dobrynin. "I noted unusual flux readings in the core, and they were not easy to control this time. The rod is doing something it was not designed for, and it did not seem to bear up well under the stress. If this rod were tested in a live reactor after production, I believe it would have been discarded and destroyed."

"Inspector General Kapustin has told me that that these last two control rods have a much higher quantity of the material mined along the stony Tunguska River. It could be that the effects we experienced with Rod-25 require a very precise measure of this material in order to work."

"That's the problem, sir," said Fedorov. "We really don't know what we're dealing with here. We don't know what this material is, we don't know where it came from, and we don't really know how to control it in spite of chief Dobrynin's best effort. It's a miracle we have been able to move in time as we have, but that may have largely been the work of the unique properties of Rod-25."

"So it is fair to say that our first live field test of these additional rods has failed." The Admiral rubbed a cramp from his neck, stretching to ease the fatigue in his shoulders. "We could try the third rod, but something tells me it may produce similar effects. Our situation here is far from certain, and we could have the whole Royal

Navy after us again in a few days for all I know. It would be good to know we could leave this war, but who knows where we might end up if we try this again."

"Agreed, sir. Perhaps we could do some testing under reduced power. But I would like to give the reactors a full inspection before we initiate this procedure again."

Volsky nodded, thinking the situation over. "Now here we are in the North Atlantic of 1940, and if experience is any guide we are likely to come into conflict with someone here, the Americans, the British, even the Germans. Our problem remains as it was. There are no friendly ports in this world for us, and any ship we meet at sea could be an enemy. The ship is broken and needs repair, and the world we sail in now is also broken. I'm afraid it may be beyond our capacity to do anything about that, Mister Fedorov. Karpov thought he could shape the days ahead to his liking, that he was invincible, but the world is much bigger than anything he could hold in his arms. It may be all we can do to survive here, and to do so we are going to have to change enemies into friends. What have you learned about the geopolitical situation here, Fedorov?"

"You are correct sir, this is not the same world we left. Russia is fragmented into at least three major states, and two of those are at war with one another. Soviet Russia, centered on Moscow, is presently engaged in conflict with the Orenburg Republic in the heartland. Apparently the Siberian state remains neutral, and all three states are still neutral in so far as the war is concerned, but that may change."

"What have you learned about these three Russian states? Who controls them?"

"Something very shocking has happened, sir, and I must now confess that I believe I may be responsible for it."

"You are responsible? What do you mean, Mister Fedorov?"

"Admiral, the Soviet Union is now being led by Sergei Kirov, not Josef Stalin." He left that out there seeing the reaction on all their faces.

"You have confirmed this?"

"Kirov was mentioned by name in several news feeds, so he was not assassinated in 1934, and he apparently prevailed in the power struggle against Stalin and took control of the Red Faction in the civil war. I have no hard information on that yet. In fact I have found no reference to Stalin whatsoever in the radio intercepts we've been monitoring. It is as if he never lived."

"That would indeed make a colossal difference. But how could you be responsible for that?"

"Remember, Admiral, I met Sergei Kirov as a young man in 1908. I foolishly told him to be wary of Stalin. In fact I even whispered the month and year of his assassination and told him to beware. I don't know what I was thinking to do such a stupid thing. Perhaps it was that I always admired him, and wondered what the Soviet state might have become under his rule and free from the shadow of Stalin."

"You are suggesting Kirov had something to do with Stalin's demise?"

"Quite possibly, sir. It does appear obvious that Kirov won the power struggle between him and Stalin, and that alone is quite remarkable."

"What about this Orenburg Federation you speak of?"

"It seems to have initially formed around Denikin and the White Russian movement that opposed the Bolsheviks, but from what I can gather Denikin is not empowered there either. A man named Volkov is controlling that government, and his name is mentioned prominently in almost every newsfeed we get."

The Admiral raised an eyebrow at that. "Volkov? I have heard this name... Yes, that was the name of the intelligence officer that accompanied the Inspector General. Probably coincidence."

"Yes, I remember now, sir. But he should be safely lost in the year 2021 and of no concern to us."

"That may not be the case," came a voice, and they turned to see Pavel Kamenski at the door of the briefing room. "Forgive my tardiness, Admiral, but I have just come from a little chat with your radio operator. I was equally curious about the state of our homeland, as you all are, and thought I would listen in briefly to Radio Moscow. Mister Fedorov is correct. Most of the news concerning Orenburg does seem to revolve around this nebulous figure known as Volkov. It may be a coincidence as you suggest, Admiral, but I must tell you that in order to remove the man as a potential threat to your operation at the Primorskiy Engineering Center, I sent this Volkov off on a little wild goose chase. When you disappeared, Mister Fedorov, there were only so many ways one could leave Vladivostok. We had men watching the airports and harbors, and that left the railroad. So, Admiral, just to get him out of the way I ordered this Volkov to search the entire route of the Siberian rail line to look for your Mister Fedorov. Of course I knew he would find nothing, because I already suspected there was another dimension to this secret operation of yours. In time I decided to reach an accommodation with you to see if I could help sort things out. So I sent the Inspector General to meet with you, Admiral, and here we are, one big happy family now. Yet after this amazing revelation concerning that back stairway in the railway inn at Ilanskiy, I now begin to hear more than I wish to in the name Volkov."

Fedorov stood in stunned silence for a moment, then he spoke, his voice laden with alarm. "Do you believe he may have found that stairway and moved into the past?"

"The thought has crossed my mind." Kamenski came in, closing the door behind him, and took a seat. "From what you have described that fissure in time connected 1908 with the year 1942. What we do not know, however, is whether that fissure continues on into the future. It could be that someone coming up those stairs could move beyond the year 1942, or even that someone coming down those stairs from the year 2021 would find himself in a most unusual place."

"I had never considered that," said Fedorov. "The fact that I was able to move back and forth as I did was astounding enough. I did often wonder who else may have come up or down those stairs over the decades, and whether that stairway still opened a strange portal to the past, even in our day."

"This may be all speculation," said Kamenski, "but they called this man a prophet, at least on the news I heard. It was said he had an uncanny knack for predicting the future. Now I must tell you one more thing. Before I came to see you at naval headquarters Fokino, Admiral, I received the report from the squad of security men that were traveling with Volkov. Apparently he disappeared without a trace.... At Ilanskiy. I did not know of this peculiar stairway at the time, and thought he may have simply gone under cover. But his men said they searched the entire facility, and I imagine they would have found those back stairs, but nothing seems to have happened to any of them."

"I did find that the effects were not consistent," said Fedorov. "When I first went missing, Sergeant Troyak and Zykov searched for me as well. Troyak tells me he went down those stairs, even as I did, but nothing happened to him. Yet I ended up in 1908!"

"Almost like a door swinging in the wind, sometimes open, sometimes closed." Kamenski tapped his fingernail on the table as he considered this. "God help us if Volkov found it open. He may have gone down those steps as well, and who knows how far down he went. He may have found himself in 1942, or even 1908. This is what I fear, and if that is so then Karpov was not the only gopher in the Devil's Garden. Volkov is a bit of a devil at heart himself."

"This is all most disturbing," said Volsky, "much more so than any problem we might have with our reactors. Look at all the trouble we went to over Orlov. To think that a man like Volkov has been at large in the past all this time, with knowledge of every twist and turn in the history… Why this is truly chilling. I can see how he might be able to position himself and become a very powerful man indeed."

"We do not know that this has indeed happened," said Kamenski, "but I feel the same chill, Admiral, and if we should discover this to be true, then we are faced with the question of what to do about it."

"What could we do about it?" Volsky seemed completely nonplussed. "We cannot sail *Kirov* Orenburg. It is deep in the heartland, and we could not even reach that place with a helicopter from the Black Sea. And don't get any ideas about going to fetch him, Mister Fedorov. If Volkov is in power there he will be well protected and completely beyond our reach."

"If this is true, Admiral, he remains locked in a power struggle with Sergei Kirov. Russia remains at war with itself, sir, and I cannot escape the feeling that we are responsible, that *I* am responsible. If I had not insisted on this crazy plan to search for Orlov none of this would have happened."

"Do not blame yourself, Fedorov. You did only what you thought was right. You have worked tirelessly to protect the integrity of the history, but that may be beyond our power now. That said, we are Russians too. If our nation remains torn in Civil War, it may be that we, too, must choose a side. I do not have to think too long about this before I know who I would choose and support in this conflict. This ship bears his name."

Kamenski rubbed his forehead, thinking. "Are you suggesting we use the power at our disposal to influence the outcome of the events underway here, Admiral?"

"I begin to sound much like Karpov, do I not? As far as possible I would like to avoid any conflict here and see to the repairs on the ship and the wellbeing of the crew. But the fact remains that we are here, and perhaps here for a reason. This barrier you spoke of, Chief. That got me thinking. What if neither of these control rods can move us forward in time again? Unless we wish to risk another shift and accept the consequences of a catastrophic failure, we may be here for a long while. In that event we must find friends here, or all the world will become our enemy. If I had to find one man alive here I might embrace, it would be Sergei Kirov. Yet the Royal Navy is likely to be our first challenge. Perhaps I could have another chat with this Admiral Tovey. Yes, you tell me he will have no recollection of that meeting, but I got a strong sense of the man when we met. He may be one we could make a friend instead of an enemy. We reached an accommodation before, and perhaps we can do so again. Find out all you can about this, Mister Fedorov. We have much to consider."

"Right sir, and to begin with perhaps we should decide our present course. We have been hovering off Cape Farewell, and we have already been sighted by that convoy. Chances are we will soon arouse more interest or suspicion if we stay here."

"I suppose I should also sort out the ship's command structure before we proceed. Karpov is gone and we have no acting Captain. How do you feel about assuming that role again, Mister Fedorov?"

"I would be honored, sir."

"Very well, then I designate you acting Captain, with Rodenko as your *Starpom*. Gentlemen…if we cannot get home with one of these control rods, then home is where we find ourselves. As much as my tooth hates the weather there, the cold waters of the north are also our home. We could head north again, just the way we came, or we could turn south and seek to linger in the warmer waters of the South Atlantic."

"I've done some thinking about this, Admiral. From our present position we are about 3500 kilometers from Severomorsk by way of the Denmark Strait, north of Jan Mayan, and then east above Norway. That is just under four days at 20 knots and three days if we can increase speed."

"Old familiar waters," said Volsky. "And our route south?"

"That depends on how far south, but if we were to seek neutral waters off the southern coast of Brazil we are looking at five to six days sailing at 20 knots."

"My heart tells me to go south and find a nice warm island somewhere as before. My head tells me that fantasy will be short lived, and that we must eventually come to grips with the world we have helped bring into being here. We cannot hide from it any longer. So we will go north, and you may get another chance to meet the man you inadvertently helped put in power, Fedorov. We will go pay a little visit to Sergie Kirov, if he will have us."

Chapter 15

The weather was threatening, and Admiral Volsky was concerned about the bow in heavy seas. He gave orders for the ship to ease away from the convoy lane and come to all stop to allow Byko to get divers in the water again and do what they could to reinforce the hull. There they lingered for a long 48 hours before concluding undersea welds and repairs and turning north as planned.

It was not long before the history began to take notice that a burglar might be in the warehouse. Rodenko was on the bridge standing the command watch when radar reported airborne contacts to the northeast. As a precaution he sounded air alert two, and put the ship on a guarded watch. Fedorov had been resting below but he came to the bridge the minute he heard the alert.

"What do we have, Rodenko?"

"Two aircraft, sir, low and slow bearing 40 degrees northeast about 50 kilometers out and cruising at about 300 KPH. That puts them a little more than ten minutes out if they have us, but they don't look to be on an intercept course at the moment."

"It's much too fast for a *Swordfish*. It has to be a *Skua* off a carrier. The British had nothing that fast on Iceland either."

"This has an odd feel to it, eh Fedorov?" It was much like that first plane that sighted the ship when they appeared in the Norwegian Sea of 1941 so long ago. The memory of that moment when the plane overflew the ship and Fedorov ran out the side hatch to the weather bridge was still crisp in his mind, but now it seemed a hollow echo.

"They may not have us on radar yet," said Fedorov. "If they even have radar."

"Do you want me to set up some jamming signatures?"

"That would be wise at this point. I would prefer to remain anonymous as long as possible, and I don't want to have to be put in a situation where we have to fire on those planes. Not unless that is absolutely necessary."

"Aye sir." Rodenko could not help but appreciate the vast difference between Fedorov and Karpov. He knew that if Karpov were here now the ship would be at air alert one and tracking with SAMs already, and that he would not hesitate in the slightest to shoot down anything he deemed a potential threat. The only thing that had ever stayed his hand was the inevitable depletion of ammunition, except for that one time, just when he was ready to fire on the American Submarine in the Pacific, the *Key West*. That seemed like a lifetime ago, he thought, and perhaps it was.

Rodenko was able to retrieve the jamming signatures they had used before, and so he quickly set up a program and began broadband interference on the channels most likely used by any planes in this timeframe.

15 June, 1940

Captain Richard Thomas Partridge was up with his squadron of *Skua* fighters for reconnaissance that day. In another writing of these events he would have been far to the north leading in six *Skuas* against the German battlecruisers where they fled to Trondheim after the attack on HMS *Glorious*. Out for blood and an equal measure of revenge for the loss of the carrier, the six pilots would bore in with a relentless dive bomber attack, losing four of six planes while 803 Squadron also lost four of nine. Partridge himself would have his plane shot from the sky that day, the second time he would lose a *Skua* over Norway, and be taken as a POW.

A little over a month earlier he and two other planes had come across a stray Heinkel-111 over Norway in the mountains north of Bergen and he made a run at the bomber, exchanging fire which ended in a draw. Both planes were hit and damaged. Partridge found his engine had stopped and he was soon forced to make a very chancy landing, wheels up in the ice and snow. Amazingly, he made it down safely that day and, after using his flare gun to fire the remaining petrol in his plane to destroy it, he and his radio telegraphist, Lt. Robert Bostock, set out on foot looking for shelter and food.

A few miles away the Heinkel had made an equally dangerous crash landing, and the surviving crew of that plane was also out looking for shelter. As chance would have it, they came to the very same shed that the British flyers had found, entering to what could have become a very dangerous, if not deadly situation. Whether it was something in the man's character or simply a realization that enemies could become friends in the service of their own survival as human beings, Partridge, simply offered his hand, the time honored gesture of good will. The Germans recognized it for what it was, and the embers of war, still a young fire in the world in mid-1940, did not consume that sheltering shed that day.

The Germans had mistaken Partridge and his mates for *Spitfires* when the attack came in, so Partridge, managing some broken German and sign language, played out the story that he and his radio man were from a downed *Wellington* bomber. After huddling in the shed for the night, strange bedfellows all, the British and Germans eventually started for a nearby village and were soon encountered by a Norwegian ski patrol. Partridge and Bostock were repatriated to British forces, and it was the German aircrew that ended up as POWs.

This time, however, Captain Partridge was not over Trondheim trying to dive bomb the Twins. All that had changed. HMS *Glorious* was attacked as it was before, but not sunk. The Twins did flee to Trondheim, but *Ark Royal's* mission to attack them there was suddenly called off by the newly arrived CiC Home fleet, Admiral John Tovey.

Instead *Ark Royal* hastened south through the Faeroes Gap to join up with HMS *Invincible* and provide air cover for operations aimed at interdicting the Denmark Strait. So this day it was an area recon mission out in front of the fleet flagship's advance, and dull, easy work compared to the gallant charge he might have made that day, yet the encounter he would soon have was laden with the heavy weight of fate.

The sea was interminable, a wide grey slate with occasional whitecaps from wind-stirred waves. It was to be a simple out and back, more for security of the fleet than any real attempt to cover the Strait of Denmark. That work would begin the following day, as the *Ark Royal* was still too far east. It was then that he saw something on his radar set, and let his radio telegraphist, Lt. Robert Bostock, in on the news.

"Something winked at me just now," he said. "See anything at two-twenty?"

Bostock looked left and scanned the sea ahead, but could see nothing of any note. Partridge noted his radar signal now seemed erratic. He thought he had a clear reading, but now it was suddenly lost in a backwash of interference. Another man might have written it all off to a dodgy antenna or faulty equipment, but there just seemed to be something else out of whack in the moment, some unaccountable magnetism was pulling at him, and without thinking or knowing why, he simply turned on 220 to investigate. Call it a hunch, a reflex, a suspicion, but he was going to have a look.

"Mister Bostok," he said. "Notify Fleet Air Arm that I am investigating a possible contact bearing 220 from our present position."

"Got an itch, Captain?"

"We'll have a scratch and see."

* * *

On the bridge of *Kirov* Rodenko was disheartened to see the contact turn on an intercept heading. "Someone is getting curious, Captain," he said. "They must have had a reading on us before we jammed. In another eight minutes that plane will have us in visual range. Recommend air alert one, sir."

Fedorov scratched his temple, frowning. "Not just yet," he said, thinking hard. The last thing they needed now was open hostilities, another plane chased by a missile or riddled with 30mm shells; another dead aircrew missing from the rolls of history. It always starts this way, he thought, with notions of humanity and the consequences of taking down a single plane. Then it ends with the holocaust of a nuclear warhead...well, not on my watch.

"Sir," said Rodenko. "Five minutes."

Fedorov found himself staring out the forward view panes, watching the wounded bow of *Kirov* still slicing cleanly through the sea at 20 knots. He walked slowly to the ship's intercom, and punched up the code for the mainmast watch. A pair of human eyes with field glasses perched beneath the spinning rotation of the dual panel Fregat Radar system seemed a redundancy, but he had something on his mind that needed human hands at the moment.

"Mainmast watch," he said quietly. "Raise the naval ensign."

"Raise the ensign, sir?"

"That is correct. Do it now, please, and be quick about it."

"Aye sir. Raise the ensign."

"Captain Fedorov," said Rodenko. "I thought the Admiral wanted all recognition marks stowed, sir."

Fedorov said nothing, his eyes set, still scanning the distant horizon. "The ship will come to air alert one," he said quietly. "Mister Samsonov, *Kashtan* system please. Lock on the target but do *not* engage. Understood?"

At three minutes out Fedorov knew the incoming plane already had the ship in visual range, and he also knew that it was likely to make as close a pass as the pilot deemed advisable under the circumstances. The two sides had stumbled upon one another in the muddled uncertainty of war, and as the Russian naval ensign was raised high on the top mast above the spinning radar set, Fedorov had extended one arm with an open hand, even though he still held a knife quietly behind his back if his gambit failed.

This was a reconnaissance flight, he reasoned. They will not be carrying heavy ordnance. The ship could endure a strafing run if this plane attacked, but he would not fire first—not this time. The raising of that flag was a handshake in thought, and whether it was by chance or design, it was seen by the one man who needed to see it that day, and recognize in it the gesture he himself had made to those three German airmen when they came stumbling in out of the cold.

* * *

"Mister Bostock," said Captain Partridge. "What do you make of that?" He gestured to the left, banking the plane slightly so both men could have a better look at the sea. There was a ship, large and formidable in shape and design, a dark threatening wedge of steel scoring the gunmetal sea.

"It's big!" Bostock was duly impressed. "Signaling ship sighted," he said breathlessly.

"What's that up top, Bobby? Look, it's flying a blue cross on white!"

"Norwegian or Danish?" said Bostock.

"Don't be daft, man. That's a Russian naval ensign."

"Russian? Down here?"

"Get a good look with your field glasses, will you, and verify what I'm seeing. I'll hold the range and circle."

He banked into a turn, knowing better than to bore straight in with this unknown sighting. The ship was enormous! He was a veteran of many operations in these waters, some flying air cover over the fleet with ships like the mighty *Hood* and *Invincible* in attendance, two of the largest warships afloat in 1940. This ship was easily the length and breadth of *Hood*, though now that he looked closely he could not make out any large caliber gun turrets, only secondary batteries mounted fore and aft. What was that spinning about on the mainmast beneath the ensign?

"Get that signal off to *Ark Royal*," he said with just a little more urgency. "Large warship, heavy cruiser or battlecruiser in size and flying Russian colors. They look to be steering zero-five-zero. Estimate speed twenty from that wake and bow wave."

Partridge was very good at his job.

* * *

Fedorov watched the plane bank and angle off to one side, the wings dipped so he could clearly see the insignia of the Fleet Air Arm on the wings. The plane had turned and that was a very good sign. They were looking them over now, and they would certainly be keying off an urgent signal. He glanced at Nikolin, who gestured that he was picking up the signal and decoding the Morse. At that moment Admiral Volsky stepped through the main hatch to the citadel, huffing from the climb up the last ladder and stair.

"Admiral on the bridge," said Rodenko, coming to attention.

"As you were, gentlemen," said Volsky. "I heard the alarm, and now I see we have company. He walked slowly to Fedorov's side, hands clasped together under leather gloves.

"Reconnaissance flight, sir," Fedorov reported.

"You elected to hold your missiles in hand, Mister Fedorov. I hope no one is shooting at us for a change."

"I thought I would try something else, sir. I have raised the naval ensign. I know I have rescinded the order you gave to strike the colors, but that was in the Pacific before we shifted here, and I felt this situation was different. From what we have been able to determine, Soviet Russia is still neutral, and in our own history it was eventually an ally of Great Britain in this war. I believed showing the flag and holding fire was the wiser course. An open hand might be the better way to start here, Admiral."

Volsky gave him a long look, then smiled. "Agreed," he said calmly. "What are we looking at?" He pointed at the plane, knowing he was likely to get more information here than he needed.

"Blackburn *Skua* fighter, sir, an early carrier based aircraft in service for the British before they began to introduce the *Fulmars*—that was the plane type that spotted us the first time we were discovered in the Norwegian Sea."

"Yes, the plane you said you saw in a museum—the plane that should have *been* in a museum when we first laid eyes on it." The Admiral remembered how he had also held fire and allowed the plane to overfly the ship in spite of Karpov's urging him to shoot it down. This time he had another cool head on the bridge, and he was glad of that, though he knew that if they could not find a way to displace again in time he might miss Karpov one day. This was the Second World War, and they had seen entirely too much of it in recent months, with the ship and crew still bearing the scars of that trauma.

"I think I will one up your open hand, Mister Fedorov." The Admiral turned to Nikolin now at the communications station. "Mister Nikolin, you are undoubtedly monitoring that plane's sighting signal. Can you send on that same channel?"

"Of course, sir."

"Good. Then send our call sign and ship's name please. It's time we introduced ourselves with our voice instead of a missile or a shell from the forward deck guns. Send it in English, if you please: BCG *Kirov* bound for Severomorsk, and leave it at that."

Volsky turned to Fedorov and smiled. "And what will they think of that, Mister Fedorov?"

"I'd have to think about that, Admiral. BCG will give them a puzzle, but there was a ship by that name in the Russian Navy during this war, Project 26 cruiser, the first of its class. The ship had three turrets with 180mm guns, even as we have three gun mounts close to that caliber. They just might buy it, sir, though that *Kirov* served in the Baltic Fleet and was trapped there when Germany finally attacked the Soviet Union. But things may have changed."

Volsky laughed. "You really do love this history! Well then, my little salutation is likely to raise a few eyebrows in the British Admiralty...perhaps it will raise the brows on a certain Admiral as well. We shall see. For now, however, that flag and the name *Kirov* may buy us more time and security than silence or gunfire. This situation is about to get very interesting."

Part VI

Deja Vu

"There's an opposite to déjà vu. They call it 'jamais vu.' It's when you meet the same people or visit places, again and again, but each time is the first. Everybody is always a stranger. Nothing is ever familiar."

— Chuck Palahniuk, Choke

Chapter 16

"**Good** day, Captain. Good of you to get wet and come over in the launch." Admiral Tovey returned the man's crisp salute and gestured to the chair by his desk in the Admiral's office aboard HMS *Invincible.*

"No bother, sir."

"Yes, well I've received your sighting report, but thought I'd get it right from the horse's mouth, if you will." Tovey held up the message transcript, glancing at it briefly before he folded his hands on the desk and fixed Captain Partridge with a steady gaze. "Ship sighted. Well we heard their signal as plain as you did, I suppose. BCG *Kirov* bound for Severomorsk. Very odd, wouldn't you say?"

"It was somewhat surprising, sir."

"I'm not sure of that leading designation, but *Kirov* is a registered ship in the Soviet navy. That's well known enough. The mystery, however, is what the ship was doing out here. All the information we have leads us to think it was still assigned to the Soviet Baltic Sea Fleet."

"Indeed, sir. I wasn't aware of that."

"You had a good look at this ship, Captain?"

"I did, sir. Picked up the contact initially on radar and then lost it in interference. But I got curious and took a look down that bearing just in case. This one's a big fellow, sir."

"You say it was a cruiser or battlecruiser?"

"Yes sir, and unless my eyes deceived me I thought it to be just about the size of *Hood.*"

Tovey took note of that. "Certainly not a simple cruiser at that size, Captain." *Hood* at 47,000 tons was more than four times the displacement of a typical County Class Heavy Cruiser, and well over 200 feet longer.

"No sir. And I've been up over the fleet on air cover for some good time now. This ship was big, Admiral, clearly a warship in every angle and line of her, yet lightly armed, or so I thought. I made out no more than three secondary batteries, and no main gun turrets on the foredeck. In fact the deck seemed relatively swept clean, sir. But she had good battlements, and some odd equipment up top side."

Tovey's eyes had narrowed as he listened, and he felt a haunting recollection rising in the back of his mind, of that strange encounter from his days at the China Station as a young Lieutenant. "Do go on, Captain."

"Well sir, it was like a pair of window screens, spinning round and round, lights were winking up at me...I saw just a very few gun mounts that looked to be Ack-Ack batteries in the range of twenty or thirty millimeters. Yet no other visible weapons. It was quite extraordinary, Admiral."

Yes quite extraordinary, thought Tovey, and heading our way from that last sighting report. He had a mind to send over a request for another air sortie to keep the ship under observation, and decided this would be the wisest course at the moment.

"Captain, you are welcome to a spot of tea before you hit the launch again. I think we'd better have another look at this ship. Your description does arouse some interest, and I'd like to keep an eye on this one."

"I'd be happy to go up again, sir."

"We'll leave that to the Vice Admiral."

At that moment there was a quiet knock on the door and Tovey looked up to see the young Lieutenant Commander Wells there.

"Excuse me, Admiral. Flag Lieutenant Villers has sent over this message, sir." He saluted, handing off the message and starting to withdraw.

"Oh Mister Wells. See the Captain here to a good spot of tea, will you? He has a long wet ride back over to *Ark Royal* ahead of him."

"Aye sir."

"Thank you, Captain Partridge. You've given me just what I was needing, a good sharp eye. Please give my regards to the Vice Admiral."

Both men knew enough to make a quiet exit and Tovey was left with the message in hand and some very troubled thoughts. He had heard of this Captain Partridge, and knew him to be a very steady hand, well experienced, and a combat veteran. His description of this supposed Russian ship was nonetheless quite odd, and equally disturbing.

Might he have misjudged the size of the ship? Yet he seemed to rivet that point more than once, and put in for his own credibility with that line about flying air cover over the fleet. I suppose it was no boast. Yet there isn't anything the Russians could float to in any way measure up to HMS *Hood*. That remark about the equipment spinning up on the mainmast suddenly triggered a memory of those last moments with Captain Baker on *King Alfred*, and the whole scene flooded in, as fresh as a morning biscuit out of the oven.

"Have a look at that, Mister Tovey," he said to his First Lieutenant of the watch. "Do you see any main armament forward?"

"Can't see a thing, sir. Nothing more than those secondary batteries winking at the Japanese, but they can't be anything more than six inchers, sir."

"Indeed... Well then what is all the brouhaha concerning this ship? It looks to be no more than three twin turrets from the fire I've observed... What in blazes is that whirling about on her mainmast?"

What indeed? The description offered by Captain Partridge was chilling now in the cold light of Tovey's recollection. He found himself immediately heading for the bridge to see Captain Bennett but diverted to the Flag Plotting Room to look at the map first. There he found his Flag Lieutenant still reviewing a chart of the Cape Farewell area.

"Mister Villers," he said quickly. "Do you recall a sighting reported by HX-49 in recent days?"

"It must be in the message stack, Admiral."

"Find it, please." He was immediately at the latest map plot, seeing *Ark Royal's* position as it was arriving, and *Hood* and *Repulse* farther south. Given the last reported heading of the contact seen by Captain Partridge, his ships were perfectly arrayed in a wide dispersal to net this fish.

"You have the sighting report from the air search as well. Kindly plot those two points, connect them, and then give me an intercept course for *Invincible* and *Renown*. I want to have a look at this Russian cruiser."

Villers looked at the map. "If I recall, sir, *Ark Royal* made the sighting about here." He moved a green neutral marker onto the map. "I'll send all the information over to the navigator, but I should think if we stay right on 300 for the time being we can work into a reasonable intercept easily enough."

"Good then."

"What do you make of that last message, sir?"

"Message? Oh yes." Tovey realized Wells had handed him the latest note from the Admiralty just before he led Captain Partridge out. He had been so completely absorbed with his muse on this Russian cruiser that he had almost completely forgotten about it. He looked down at the message in his hand, reading quickly.

"More fish in the kettle," he breathed. "The Twins sighted that far east of Trondheim? And the *Hipper* has gone missing as well. This is getting very interesting."

"Do you think they mean to make a run for the Atlantic, sir?"

"That is why we are here, Mister Villers. But this says nothing about *Bismarck* and *Tirpitz*."

"No news on them yet, sir. Still socked in from Bremen to Kristiansand."

"Which makes for just the perfect weather to move those ships. Let me know the moment anything comes in." He looked at the clock, seeing it had just slipped past midnight and was now the 16th of June. "It looks like another 24 hours will make for a very interesting day."

* * *

With the knowledge that a British aircraft carrier was close at hand, Rodenko and Chief Byko had been working feverishly to get new equipment installed to improve the ship's situational awareness. The replacement Fregat system that had been installed at Vladivostok had good coverage against an airborne target out to 230 kilometers and missiles out to 50 kilometers, but being a line of site radar system, it was limited to between 26 to 30 kilometers on surface contacts. They had been relying on the KA-40 helos with *Oko* long range radar panels, but now they had only one aboard, and if it were to be lost or damaged the ship would lose valuable long range radar.

The *Starpom*, an old radar man by training and experience, had requested a Mineral-ME surface search radar set. With all that had happened, there had been no time to install the radar, but Byko had men up working on it now and the system was slowly being integrated into the ship's formidable sensor suite. Once ready it would provide passive over the horizon radar coverage utilizing ionospheric reflection out to 450 kilometers, and an active search mode that could range out 180 kilometers. It was not as precise as the 3D Fregat system, but it could at least provide bearing and contact data for detection, and coordinate setting of surface targets. Several hours later it was the Fregat system, however, that again detected the approach of aircraft, this time at higher elevation.

"Three contacts this time," he said. "And look at their bearing, Fedorov. I would guess that carrier is somewhere here." Rodenko tapped the electronic map display with a light pen."

"That last plane was a Blackburn *Skua*," said Fedorov. "They can range out about 700 kilometers, so that puts the carrier inside 350 klicks from our present position. I would guess it is probably 200 klicks out."

"We could pop up the KA-40 for a quick look," Rodenko suggested. "Once we get that fix for the carrier's course and speed, we can then use predictive plotting to estimate its position."

"In due course, but I don't want the helo up with incoming fighters. We can't afford to lose the KA-40. For the moment this looks like nothing more than a follow-up search on the contact they made earlier. I think we should just stand pat. But if you can get that over the horizon system up any time soon I would rest a bit easier."

Rodenko nodded, then asked the question that had been on his mind for some time. Fedorov obviously had different ideas about how they should handle the ship now, a relief after Karpov's brazen and arrogant style.

"That carrier won't be alone, Fedorov. What's our plan?"

"We haven't really decided. The Admiral seems quite willing to try and seek accommodation rather than confrontation here. But you are correct, there will be cruisers and possibly a battleship with that carrier. Once we get clear skies I think we will use the KA-40 to nail that down. In any case, the clock is ticking. They know where we are, and have to be wondering about us. We can get some sense of how close they are by the loiter time on this next group of planes. The longer they hang around, the closer that carrier is."

"So what will we do if they intercept?"

"We'll certainly see them coming, but given the situation with the bow, the ship is best left at no more than ahead two thirds. The Admiral is right, Rodenko. We need friends here now, not enemies. We can't risk another shift attempt unless Dobrynin can sort out why this control rod failed, so we may be here a long while."

"Strange that we even expected it to work like Rod-25," Rodenko had a good point.

"True enough. We grew accustomed to the magic, and now we taste what it is like to be mere mortals again, still moving into the future, but only one day at a time."

"We've at least proven that we can handle ourselves here. Karpov consistently overplayed his hand. We didn't have to confront the Americans in 1945. I know we had to fight when we first sortied, and the Captain was superb in that confrontation with the US carrier battlegroup, but remember, we had the whole fleet there, and help from naval bombers and a good submarine bastion as well. When that volcano went off and we found ourselves back here again, Karpov was a fool to try and take on the entire American Pacific Fleet in 1945."

"Pride goeth before the fall," said Fedorov.

"Indeed. Well, finding ourselves in 1908 was quite a shock. We could not understand how it happened without Rod-25, but it really tempted Karpov. He simply could not see any way he could fail to defeat the forces of that day, though I cautioned him many times that our power was limited to the ammunition we carried."

"I think he believed he could work a decisive intervention before he ran out of missiles, and from the look of things now, perhaps he did. Yet I may be as much to blame for what we've discovered here."

"Don't carry that too long, Fedorov. The world is a vast and complex thing. Who knows what really happened? And what if Kamenski is right and this is an altogether different world?"

"Then we get right to your question, Rodenko. With the history this badly fractured what does it matter what we do to the unseen future now? I think Admiral Volsky is beginning to see things this way. If it turns out we can't shift forward again, then what do we do? Our situation is a bit like that of the French now."

"The French?"

"France will capitulate and sign a surrender and armistice with Germany in just a few days if that part of the history remains intact. The French fleet was the odd man out. It was left under nominal control of the Vichy French Government, and in about two weeks the British confronted the French Fleet at Mers-El-Kebir, Oran, where a good part of it was anchored. They gave them several choices. One was to join them and fight Nazi Germany together. The others were not so palatable—either sail to a British or neutral port and be demilitarized, or scuttle in place. The thing is…we may get those same alternatives handed to us if the Admiral tries to get cozy with the British here. The Royal Navy is about all Great Britain has at the moment, and the wolves are at the door. Their very survival depends on control of the seas, and they will want every square on the board well covered."

"We could be quite a stone in their shoe," Rodenko put in.

"Exactly, but I don't think the Admiral could accept any internment situation that might allow the British access to our weapons and technology."

"He accepted internment on St. Helena."

"Yes, but insisted the ship remain fully militarized and under our control with freedom of movement should that become necessary. All he gave Tovey was his word to stay out of things if left alone. The British would not give the French that latitude, and I doubt they will give it to us now either. Our only real card to play here is that naval ensign flying on our mainmast. Soviet Russia is a neutral state, and we must hope the British respect that."

Chapter 17

The speculation by Fedorov and Rodenko soon proved a stark reality. The carrier was not alone, and the long loiter time of the three planes that again found the ship that day told them it was within 200 kilometers. The aircraft observed them at some distance. At one point a single plane made a closer approach, but otherwise the encounter was without incident. Eventually the planes turned for home, and Fedorov immediately took advantage of the situation to get the KA-40 up just as Rodenko had advised. The long-range radar returns soon painted the picture of what they were facing, and so they thought it best to summon Admiral Volsky to the bridge.

"The main body is here, sir," said Fedorov. "Rodenko notes three strong returns and these four smaller contacts, probably destroyers. Then there are two more strong contacts coming up from the south. They undoubtedly intend to intercept, sir, as they just made a five point turn to 315 and that will put them off our starboard bow right about here in seven hours."

"And what are these contacts you have noted to the north?"

"Unknown at this time, sir, but if I had to guess I would say these are most likely British cruisers assigned to patrol the Denmark Strait."

"Is there any ongoing operation that we should be concerned about this time, Mister Fedorov?"

"In the history I know, sir, *Scharnhorst* and *Gneisenau* would be at Trondheim now. *Scharnhorst* was supposed to have taken a torpedo during the attack that sank the British aircraft carrier *Glorious* a few days ago. The two ships returned to Trondheim for repairs and were attacked there by British Hudson bombers and planes like those we have just witnessed off an aircraft carrier. If that's the case, sir, I wonder what ship this carrier is. Aside from *Glorious* there was only *Ark Royal* and *Furious* available to the Home Fleet at this time, and *Furious* was laid up in a refit operation."

"Then this would have to be *Ark Royal*."

"It would seem so, sir, but that would mean the attack that took place yesterday at Trondheim never took place."

"So there is a crack in your mirror, Mister Fedorov. This history is not playing out as you expect. I don't see why we should think that it would if our entire nation is broken in pieces."

"That is probably true, sir, but what this means is that I can no longer accurately predict what we may be facing in the days and months ahead. All I know is that this carrier should not be here."

"And if this aircraft carrier is not alone, why are all these ships here?"

"The British must have intelligence on some enemy movement that prompted them to muster this fleet."

"At the moment it looks like they have intelligence on us! Could we be the reason?"

"We were spotted by that convoy on June 12th, Admiral. I calculated the distance from this fleet's position to their probable home base at Scapa Flow. It is about 1500 kilometers. Assuming a cruising speed of twenty knots, the ships had to leave Scapa Flow no later than the 14th in order to be here now."

"That is some fairly fancy footwork. Do you think Home Fleet would've reacted in this manner?"

"They would've known we were not one of their ships, sir, and soon after that they could've learned we were not a Canadian or American ship either. That quickly narrows down the possibilities."

"Didn't they already know where these German battlecruisers were?"

"That's the odd thing. Yes, they also knew where the cruiser *Admiral Hipper* was operating. I don't see why they would conclude we would be a German raider, or what would prompt such a sortie of capital ships to investigate."

"Then something else must be going on that we do not know about, Fedorov. Keep a wary eye on that situation map. We're about to enter the Denmark Strait and I think we will soon have company."

That gave Fedorov an idea, and the Admiral knew him well enough to know what that light kindling in his eyes meant. Fedorov walked quickly to the navigation station and pulled the pad device from his bookshelf there. He was busy with that for some time before he returned, a smile on his face as if he had just struck gold.

"Admiral! I just realized I had a complete enigma code simulator and decoding application. I can even determine rotor settings and plugboard positions from research data I have on the subject and interpret the entire German naval enigma code! If Nikolin can pick up the signal I'll be able to read German Navy high command orders to all their fleet units. This means we will be able to learn about any operation long before it begins."

Admiral Volsky gave him an astonished look. "You have broken this code, Mister Fedorov?"

"Not me, sir. It was broken by Alan Turing and other analysts at Hut Four in Bletchley Park. In fact they're working on it now but there a lot of missing pieces to the puzzle and it will be some time, at least a year before they can interpret it with any reliability. But I've had this application for several years now. The entire code is well known in our day and all I have to do is key the correct date and time and it is very likely that I can read the code almost verbatim."

"You never cease to amaze me, Fedorov. This is a very interesting development. Information was as powerful a weapon in this war as anything else, and here you are telling me you have the key to unlock the entire German naval code. This will be very useful. See what Mister Nikolin can do. Is there any chance he can intercept the signals?"

"Of course, sir. U-boats, for example, received and transmitted messages in encrypted Morse code. I can research the exact wavelength and equipment they used and I'm sure we'll be able to pick up the signals."

"Excellent, Fedorov. This is sounding better and better every minute. Devote yourself to this task in the next few hours, please. We need more information about what is happening. I feel like a poker player who is been dealt a bad hand, but I think you have just passed me and Ace and King!"

It was not even three hours before Fedorov had something in hand. He was able to research the common German shore to ship transmission frequencies, and Nikolin spent a good long while listening in. They fished for some time before he picked up a signal that had an odd structure. There were sets of ciphers, five characters each, and Fedorov immediately knew these had to correspond to typical formats used with enigma code messaging. He went to the Admiral immediately, showing him the signal they had harvested, a look of real satisfaction on his face now.

"Have a look at this, sir. We isolated it from a stream of encrypted Morse code just an hour ago."

To Volsky it was no more than a series of random letters, and he could see no meaning in them all: LKGIF FTIFK IBGQA UEUCX OWWCM HYPHX PGZQQ, and on it went. But Fedorov tapped the screen of his pad device and soon a complete translation of the five character phrases appeared in their place. He looked up at the Admiral, a fire in his eyes, and read the message aloud.

"*Bismarck* and *Tirpitz* will proceed to breakout point as planned, to arrive by 1800 hours, 16 June. That's all the message we were able pickup, sir, but we got the essence of it."

"*Bismarck*? This is one of their battleships, a very famous battleship."

"Yes sir, both ships in the same class, but here is another anomaly. Neither ship should be ready at this time in the war. In fact, *Bismarck* did not make its maiden voyage for almost another year, and *Tirpitz* was not yet ready to join her at that time. The fact that both these ships are operational now means that things changed well before the war. The Germans must have been building up their fleet from the mid-nineteen thirties in order to have these capital ships ready for action now. If the British were in any way aware of these ships planning an imminent operation, we have our reason why home fleet is all in a tither. It was all they could do the hunt down and sink just one of these ships. If both sortie together they would represent a grave challenge to the Royal Navy at this time."

"What if they fail to do so, Fedorov? What might have happened?"

"I think it was inevitable that they would eventually get both ships, sir, but their presence in the German Navy order of battle exerted a strong magnetism on the Admiralty, and posed a constant threat. As it was, *Bismarck* did not go to her grave alone. They took the biggest ship in the Royal Navy with them in that campaign, HMS *Hood*. These are powerful, dangerous ships, Admiral, and if they are planning a sortie now, it is very likely that they will get their pound of flesh, no matter what the Royal Navy throws at them."

* * *

"**Message** from Admiralty, sir." Wells had just come from the W/T room and found Admiral Tovey in the Flag Plot Room near the situation map. He saluted, handing off the paper and waiting in the event the Admiral had further instructions.

"Thank you, Mister Wells." Tovey read the decrypted message and Wells could quickly see the concern in his eyes. Even the decrypted message was a code within a code: *Most Immediate – FAA HMS Sparrowhawk has flown. Otto and friend have left Birmingham for Holyhead – 06:00 GMT this day.* HMS *Sparrowhawk* was the Fleet Air Arm designation for the important Hatston airfield just north of

Kirkwall on the main Orkney Island near Scapa Flow. The time was obvious, and Birmingham was the code word for Bergen, Norway, with the heading determined by the destination point of Holyhead. The travelers, Otto and friend, were what caused that thrum of anxiety. Otto was, of course, Otto von Bismarck and the ship that bore his name. His friend was the *Tirpitz*.

Tovey looked at the plotting board, seeing his position just southeast of Reykjavik, with *Hood* and *Repulse* still well south. *Ark Royal* was finally steaming with his flagship and he was all set to investigate this unusual sighting of the Russian cruiser. But now all bets were off. With two fast battleships heading east from Bergen, he would now be forced to turn about and support *Rodney* and *Nelson* in Force F. They were entirely too slow to get into a chase in the Faeroes region. That was a job for his fast battlecruisers. The Germans might be heading further east with the aim of getting up around Iceland for a run through the Denmark Strait, but something told him that was where the Twins were headed. He would order *Hood* to continue north to backstop his two cruisers there, and possibly investigate this Russian ship, but *Invincible* would have to turn about.

"Things are about to get interesting, Mister Wells. I would like nothing more than to see about this Russian ship we've been shadowing, but it seems *Bismarck* and *Tirpitz* have left Bergen and they are our first order of business. Please inform Captain Bennett that I would like the fleet to come about to zero-nine-two. Then get to the W/T room and have them signal *Ark Royal* that the air search west will have to be cancelled. I'll want them ready to search the Iceland-Faeroes Gap in four hours."

"Very good, sir." Wells was elated. *Bismarck* and *Tirpitz!* They were really hunting big game now, and with any luck he was likely to see a major sea action soon with the finest ships on earth. Even as he thought that, a warning note sounded in his mind. Be careful what you wish for…

"Oh… There was one more note, sir. This one a verbal directive from Mister Villers. He says Admiralty is of the opinion that this Russian cruiser sighting may be bogus—at least insofar as its identity. They got it straight from Bletchley Park. They have confirmed that the cruiser *Kirov* is presently in the Baltic. They believe it may be a German oiler planning to rendezvous with anything they might be pushing through the Denmark Strait."

"I see…" That took just a bit of the sting off his disappointment. "Bletchley Park, you say? That will be Mister Turing's watch. Have the gentlemen at Whitehall seen the report given by Captain Partridge? Have they seen our subsequent sighting reports?"

"I'm not certain, sir, but I can see that they are forwarded."

"Please do so. Opinions are like noses, Mister Wells. Everybody seems to have one, but this is certainly no oiler. Make sure Mister Villers clarifies this for the Admiralty, and Bletchley Park as well."

"Of course, sir." Wells started to salute again but Tovey simply smiled.

"Mister Wells, things will be getting quite busy in the hours ahead and you will be bouncing about like a badly hit cricket ball in due course. I think we can leave off the formalities of a salute every time you see me."

"As you wish, sir." Wells was on his way, more excited than ever now. A mystery on top of a battle! What good luck. If the real cruiser *Kirov* was still in the Baltic, then who was out there wearing its hat and overcoat? First things first. He had to get that course heading change to Captain Bennett.

When Wells had gone Tovey folded his arms, looking at the plotting board again. Still in the Baltic… That information was more likely fact than opinion. What was going on here? There was an odd feeling about this whole scenario, as if he had lived through this situation before, a kind of *Déjà vu* that he attributed to his memories of that brief, violent encounter aboard *King Alfred*. Now, more than ever, he wanted to stay the course and find out first hand with his own eyes just what this ship was. But if wishes were horses....*Bismarck* and *Tirpitz* were a known quantity, and would demand the whole of his attention for the moment.

Rodney and *Nelson* might give them a good fight, he thought, but they'll never be able to finish it. The Germans can break off at their whim. So I'll keep the two old girls close to the Shetlands, and cover the Iceland passage with *Invincible* and company. Let the Germans try to slip out of the theater on my watch. Not bloody likely.

Chapter 18

Carrier Graf Zeppelin ~ Norwegian Sea ~ June 16, 1940

The sighting made by Fleet Air Arm out of Hatston airfield was only half of the story, frightening as it was. Sailing some twenty nautical miles behind the two big German battleships, only now emerging from the edge of the thick cloud deck that hung low over the sea, was the sole operational German aircraft carrier at this point in the war, *Graf Zeppelin*. Commanded by the former first officer of the *Admiral Scheer*, Kapitan zur See Kurt Böhmer, the carrier would bring up to 42 aircraft to sea, that would make it the equal of any of Britain's fleet carriers of the day with the added edge that the aircraft carried were far more capable than those fielded by the British.

Graf Zeppelin would carry modified versions of 12 BF-109Es and up to 26 *Stuka* dive bombers as the primary armament, with a detachment of four *Arado* seaplanes to make 42 planes in all. The Messerschmitt fighters were faster and much more agile than the *Skuas* aboard *Ark Royal*, and even better than the new Fairey *Fulmars* just starting to come off the production lines.

This formidable new addition to the German fleet was accompanied by the Schwere Kreuzer *Prinz Eugen* and three unique new ocean going destroyers, actually called Spähkreuzers under Raeder's Plan Z. Originally conceived in the 1930s under the name Zerstörer 1938A/Ac, these 'Atlantik' type destroyers were further modified to produce the equivalent of light anti-aircraft cruisers. At 6,500 tons they were bigger than typical destroyers of the day, with a combination of diesel and turbine engines to extend their blue water performance. Armed with twelve 4.7-inch dual purpose guns and a suite of lighter 20mm guns, they were ideal for both AA and ASW defense. In true Nordic tradition the three new hounds bore the names *Beowulf, Siegfeied* and *Heimdal*. Kapitän zur See Helmuth

Brinkmann was in command of this detachment, with his flag aboard the cruiser *Prinz Eugen.*

Kapitan Böhmer was eager to get back into battle. The time he had spent aboard the *Admiral Scheer* had convinced him that the new Kriegsmarine was now a force to be reckoned with, and this operation was more ambitious than any mounted since Jutland. His first fighting air patrol was already spotted on deck as the task force sailed for the breakout point, three BF-109 fighters and two *Stukas.* He would get them out in front of the two battleships in short order, and give the next British recon plane a nasty surprise. Hauptmann Marco Ritter would lead the flight, an experienced airman recruited from the Luftwaffe to join the elite carrier unit.

"Send to Ritter that he is cleared for takeoff," said Böhmer. "He is to overfly *Bismarck* and *Tirpitz*, but let them know we are coming. The only thing they have ever seen in the skies above them are British planes, and all that is about to change."

The young midshipman hurried to pass on the order while Böhmer watched from the island bridge. Ritter was out on deck. He knew him by the crimson scarf he would always tuck into this flight jacket. As if sensing the Kapitan was watching, he turned and held up a fist, pumping three times as he prepared to mount his Messerschmitt fighter. Then he climbed confidently into the open cockpit, settling into his harness and sliding the canopy closed.

These planes will make all the difference, thought Böhmer. With *Graf Zeppelin* in attendance we can hold the snooping British *Skuas* at bay, and chop them to pieces if they get too pushy. And as for the *Swordfish*, let them try their luck against my Messerschmitts. Then comes the real fun—sending a couple dozen *Stukas* into battle over their battleships. Yes, this changes everything.

The order he had given was received on the flight deck, and now Ritter was the first to turn over his engine, and would be the first to take off from the deck of a German aircraft carrier on a combat mission, an historic moment. The long nose of the Messerschmitt growled as the prop spun up to a blur. Then the chalks were removed and the Flugdeck flagman began his ritual, finally saluting and then pointing the way with his flag. The plane roared to life, began to gain speed, and then howled into the sky, wings wagging in salutation.

"There you go Marco," said Böhmer under his breath with a smile. "Good hunting."

He watched as the remaining two fighters followed Ritter into the sky, then the two *Stukas* like great black crows, fat wings bent and squared off at their thinning tips. They were ready to follow just in case anything was found that might need their attention. The mission was to scour the skies in the immediate van of the route planned by the battleships.

Minutes later Hauptmann Ritter saw the white wake of the trailing ship *Tirpitz* ahead, took in its broad beam and trim fighting lines. Just ahead he could see the flagship *Bismarck* proudly knifing through the grey seas. He led his three fighters down in formation, and, as they flew over the battleships, he could see men on the grey steel platforms and weather decks waving as he tipped his wings again in greeting.

The three fighters flashed overhead, followed closely by the two *Stukas*, and then all five planes climbed, the fighters fanning out to begin their search sweep to the south. From that moment on they left friendly waters and entered the realm that had formerly been the sole domain of the Royal Navy. It was always their convoys and battlegroups that would ply these waters, their aircraft carriers that would overshadow the fleets with watchful eyes.

Ritter flew on ahead, glad to have clearing skies for his search sweep. He would see no British aircraft up that day, a bit of a disappointment as he had hoped to log a kill on his first sortie. What he did see an hour later and nearly 400 kilometers west southwest of his carrier was the telltale formation of a small task force north of the

Faeroes Islands. As he approached he realized he was looking at the two 'bookends,' as the Germans called them *Nelson* and *Rodney*. The unmistakable configuration of their three big gun turrets all forward of the bridge was easy to spot. There they were, moving ponderously forward in the sea, with what looked to be a cruiser out in front, and three destroyers in attendance.

Not wanting to be seen just yet, he noted the position and quickly climbed for an overhead bank of clouds. He would signal this first sighting at sea, the opening action of the campaign that was now unfolding. Then, his fuel tanks nearing the point of no return, he banked and turned for home, making sure his initial heading was well away from the real position of the German fleet, just in case he had been spotted.

Böhmer received the news with some elation, and quickly passed in on to Brinkmann and then Lindemann ahead of him in *Bismarck*. At last, he thought. We have the one thing the Kriegsmarine never had before when facing the British—situational awareness. No more waiting on the U-boats to search and scout for us. Now we have eyes in the sky…As long as I can keep this ship afloat. Well, before anything can get within arm's reach of *Graf Zeppelin*, they will first have to run the gauntlet of my 26 *Stukas*, and then face down *Bismarck* and *Tirpitz*.

He was feeling very confident that morning, but there was one factor left out of his war equation that no man alive that day could have possibly considered or planned for, a fate that was wholly unaccountable, and yet one that would be decisive in the balance of the scales of time. The mirror of history had indeed cracked, and something had come through that fissure that would soon change everything.

* * *

"**Those** British ships have turned," said Rodenko. "In fact they are now moving east on a heading to the Iceland-Faeroes Gap."

"Perhaps they got wind of the same message Mister Fedorov intercepted."

"Not likely, Admiral," said Fedorov, "though the British had other means of intelligence at their disposal. They could have simply sighted the Germans battleships by air search."

"We do not yet know what this breakout point is, do we Fedorov?"

"No sir, but it does not surprise me the British are turning east. Their first order of business will be to make sure nothing gets through the Iceland-Faeroes Gap. That accomplished, the Germans would have only one route to the Atlantic, and that would be the body of water directly ahead of us, the Denmark Strait."

"So it looks as though we will not have our close encounter of the third kind with the Royal Navy just yet."

"There are still two ships to the south maintaining their original heading, sir," Rodenko warned.

"They may be dividing their force and sending a reinforcement east," said Fedorov, realizing that he had to guess and conjecture now, and could no longer read the answer in his books. "That will mean they will most likely move the aircraft carrier out of this sector for the time being."

"Then we will simply continue on this heading, move north, and keep to our plans for a visit to Severomorsk. It is somewhat strange, sailing home like this, is it not? The last time we passed through this strait I was having an extended stay in the sick bay and Karpov was in command. Now the Captain is dead and we are finally heading home, the only hitch is that we're eighty years early!"

Fedorov seemed restless and bothered as Volsky watched him. The Admiral realized what must be running through his young ex-Navigator's mind. "I know what you are feeling now, Fedorov. None of this is written in your history books. We have hit a crack in your mirror. In fact, perhaps our very presence here has cracked it even further. The British will soon find out that we are not the cruiser we claimed to be, and they will be very curious. For the moment, however, something to the east is of much greater concern to them, and your clever Enigma code application has told you what it was. So do not look so forlorn. You see, in that way you can still read the history, and in other ways we may find that simply sitting back and reading it may no longer be a luxury we have here. We may have to *make* our own history here soon—at least this is what my instincts begin to tell me."

Fedorov gave him a half hearted smile, understanding what he was trying to tell him, but still feeling somewhat adrift. "You are very wise, Admiral," he said. "I do feel like I have lost my compass, and for a Navigator that is a very serious matter."

"But even if that is so you could still use your eyes and head to navigate by the stars, yes? Like the British, you have other means of intelligence at your disposal."

"I suppose I could, sir."

"Then that is what you must do here. Just use that good head of yours, all the knowledge you have stored away up there, and use the eyes in your head to find your way now. I have every confidence in you, books or no books. You have never steered us wrong."

"Thank you, sir." He felt better hearing that from the Admiral. They were no longer Gods at sea with omniscient knowledge of all the events to come in a sure and certain order. This was a new world now, strangely familiar, recognizable in so many ways, yet entirely new. It was a kind of déjà vu, feeling like he had been here so many times before in his mind, in the quiet reading he would do each night, lost in days of yore. Yet now he was *living* in them, and the cold light of reality was more challenging than anything he could possibly have imagined when he thought to place himself in the history he read about so often.

Yes, it was challenging, but also exciting in many ways. He wasn't reading it now, or watching it like a movie. He was living it! Before he had labored always to keep some impassable barrier between himself and the history, so as not to tamper with it, or contaminate it, tainting it with his greed or wanton actions as Karpov had. He thought he could preserve it, as a kind of sacred ground, inviolate, unchanged, like the reflection of the room as he peered into a mirror, always there, but untouchable. Yet now he knew that was no longer possible, if indeed it had ever been possible. Now he knew what Karpov had embraced from the very first—that if this was the life they found themselves in, they had the power to act and strut boldly onto that stage, and take up their role in the play.

Karpov always wanted to steal the lead, he thought. Was he the villain or the hero? I suppose only time will tell. And what role do I play here now? We have two choices, to flee from the events of these days and cloister ourselves away on some deserted island, hoping the world never finds or bothers us, or to take our role here, as any man alive today might. Yes! That was what he finally understood now. Any man alive today, from the highest to the lowest, always had one thing that Fedorov had denied himself, the power to act, the right to exercise his will and take a stand, one way or another.

I wanted to do that all along, he knew. What was I doing at the railway confronting Surinov and his NKVD thugs? What did I do with that whisper in Mironov's ear?

He sighed, letting the trouble in his mind go. He could not save the world, nor hold back the tide of fate and inevitable change, and it was beyond his power to ever put this broken world back together again as it was. All he could do was look at this world with the eyes in his head and accept it as it was. He was no different than any other man alive now, a mere mortal after all and not a titan adrift in time.

Other men faced the cracks in the mirror of their lives, did they not? Now he knew what that mirror was—a reflection of the world as he *wished* it could be. Yes, all men carried that, and then came loss, failure, pain, illness, divorce and they shattered the mirror and forever changed the reflection of the world they hoped to live in. To be alive was to be able to face that reality and still act and live, unfettered by the lost hopes and the wish to live in the world he may have inwardly desired.

Yes, he realized. Suffering is not the affliction of pain and loss. No, *it is wanting things to be other than the way they are!* Now he smiled, keenly aware of this new realization and feeling strangely light. No man's mirror was perfect. They were all cracked, and the happy men in this world were the ones that knew that, accepting it without regret and living on as best they could.

So here he was. Here they all were, sailing for Severomorsk with the whole of history to live over again in this eternal *déjà vu*. Now he knew that at least a part of that history was his to determine and shape. Yes, he could *make* history instead of simply reading about it now. The Admiral, God bless him, was correct.

I have been standing there looking into the mirror to see the reflection of the world around me, he thought, seeing it there but thinking I could not touch it, that it was forever beyond my reach. Now I suddenly realize that I am standing right in the middle of it, the whole of it, and anything is possible.

A bit of an Anglophile all his life, the words of one of his favorite poems, a rhyme by John Masefield, resounded in his heart and soul now.

> 'I must go down to the seas again
> to the lonely sea and sky
> And all I ask is a tall ship
> and a star to steer her by...

Yes, now he answered the call of the running tide, wild and clear. Now his was the gull's way, the whale's way, a vagrant gypsy life. He breathed in deeply, and the air seemed sweet and cool, fresh and unburdened with his worry and fear. They were here, and yes they just might change things, and that was fine. There would come a day, just a little more than a year on now, when they would have to face the impossible prospect of being here at the very moment the ship was supposed to appear in late July of 1941. At that moment they might face their own annihilation in the all consuming maw of paradox— but that was not today. He suddenly had 'the wheel's kick and the wind's song' in his heart again, and it felt grand.

Part VII

Intervention

"...Destiny's interventions can sometimes be read as invitation for us to address and even surmount our biggest fears. It doesn't take a great genius to recognize that when you are pushed by circumstance to do the one thing you have always most specifically loathed and feared, this can be, at the very least, an interesting growth opportunity."

— Elizabeth Gilbert

Chapter 19

Iceland was only recently occupied ground for the British in June of 1940. They had stuck a fork in it just a month earlier in "Operation Fork," which saw the landing of Royal Marines at key airfields and port facilities. Meeting no real resistance from the local population, they quickly rounded up any vestige of German citizenry and braced themselves for a possible counterattack that was really quite impossible at that moment. There were plans drawn up by Germany, dubbed "Fall Ikarus" for the occupation of Iceland, but it was not deemed possible for several months time, and by then winter would be seizing the island in its icy grip, making further operations there impractical.

It was not likely the Germans would then attempt an invasion by sea, and it was too far to contemplate an air drop by Falschirmjaegers that would eventually have to be supported and supplied by sea. First they had to control those seas, and that was not likely to occur in 1940, or so the British believed.

Yet in those dark days, caution still ruled the day, and the British prepared, weathered the inevitable protest voiced by the Icelandic government over this 'flagrant violation' of their neutrality, and began to dig in for the long haul. When the first Marines reached Reykjavik, they seized the post office to put up a flyer asking for local cooperation, then went to the German Consulate, knocking politely.

"What is the meaning of this?" said Colsul Gerlach, an indignant look on his face, eyes wide and laden with recrimination. "Iceland is a neutral state!"

The Royal Marine officer saluted politely and spoke in a quiet voice: "May I remind you, sir, that Denmark was also a neutral state. Would you care to cable Berlin and kindly ask the Wehrmacht to withdraw? If so I would be happy to round up my Marines and be off home as well."

His point was well made. Just 746 Marines has seized this valuable prize, soon to be reinforced by 4000 Army troops from the 147th Brigade of the 49th West Riding Infantry Division a week later, with the occupation force eventually growing to just over 25,000 men. There they would sit in a long, lonesome watch until the duty would be handed off to the United States a year later. In the meantime, all they would have to comfort them for such a bleak posting were the bolstering words of the new Prime Minister, Winston Churchill:

'Possibly the most trying circumstances in which an army can be placed are those where it is isolated from home and friends in a rigorous climate and confined to the monotonous role of watching and waiting. His Majesty's Government are thoroughly aware that Iceland Force is so placed and is fulfilling its role with fortitude and cheerfulness. The security of Iceland is of the first importance and I am confident that it is placed in trusty hands.'

At that moment, on the 16th of June, more trusty hands were arriving on the former liner *Empress of Australia* in Reykjavik Harbor as elements of the Canadian Royal Regiment of Canada arrived. Known as "Z Force," this first element was commanded by Brigadier General L. F. Page, and his force had sailed from Halifax, arriving right in the wake of *Kirov's* passage north. In fact, they had spotted what looked to be a large cruiser the previous day, steering north into the Denmark Strait, and passed the word on to the British.

Another pair of trusty hands that day belonged to Lieutenant Bonnell, who had welcomed the Canadians ashore and tried to accommodate them as best he could. Word of the cruiser sighting was somewhat disturbing, and so he quickly passed the word to the modest air detachment, which consisted of no more than a single big *Sunderland* four engine flying boat and a smaller single engine bi-plane *Walrus*. These two planes were the first elements of the Fleet Air Arm's 701 Squadron, that would later be replaced by 98 Squadron RAF with eighteen planes.

For the moment, however, those two planes were all the British had, and they got the *Sunderland* up to have a look around. It made what it thought was a periscope sighting and quickly alerted the Canadians, prompting them to quickly offload their forces from the *Empress of Australia*. Then the big plane lumbered north into the Denmark Strait, and soon found the ship in question, shadowing it briefly and sending the new position and heading up the newly forged chain of command.

So it was the Admiral Lancelot Holland aboard HMS *Hood* was informed three hours later in a message from the Fleet Flagship. *"Regret that we must be on our way. Please investigate contact information to follow."*

He read the message with routine purview, one of twenty he might get this day, but took a brief moment to visit his navigator and have the sighting plotted.

"It's well up north and heading into the Denmark Strait, sir," said the young Warrant officer.

"Just how far off would that be?"

"I make it a good 330 nautical miles, sir."

"Good lord, that's eleven hours off even at our best speed, and that is assuming the ship is standing still."

Holland turned to Captain Glennie, folding his arms as he considered the situation. An old hand with battleships, Holland had served aboard HMS *Revenge* and HMS *Resolution* before moving to command the 7th Cruiser Squadron. That duty was handed off to Tovey briefly and Holland was recalled to take over the Battlecruiser Squadron. He was somewhat surprised when Tovey was subsequently recalled from the Med to replace Admiral Forbes at the helm of Home Fleet, and then equally surprised when Tovey decided to plant his flag in the Battlecruiser Squadron aboard HMS *Invincible*. To ease the sting he was still made the nominal commander of that squadron, and second in command of Home Fleet.

Now Tovey was heading off east to see about that sighting of *Bismarck* and *Tirpitz*, he thought, and so the Denmark Strait is left to me. He had taken passing notice of the initial sighting of what was described as a Russian cruiser up north, but now he was being asked to have a closer look.

"Well it's not bloody likely that we'll catch up to this ship, but just to please the new Fleet Commander, lets nudge it up to 26 knots, shall we?"

"Very well, sir. We might also get word out to *Manchester* and *Birmingham*. That's their watch and they'll be well north of that ship's last reported position."

"Indeed, and with eyes puckered north for any sign of the Germans. Now we'll have to tell them to watch their back side as well. I suppose it can't be helped. Have the message sent, Captain."

"Right away, sir."

* * *

The Denmark Strait ranged from 300 to 500 kilometers wide, and with ice year round off the Greenland coast, though by June it receded somewhat, giving ships a little more open sea for passage. It was still a lot of sea room for a pair of light cruisers to cover, but *Manchester* and *Birmingham* had been on patrol for several days, with little to see but an occasional wide ranging gull or ghostly bergs looming like broken ships amid scattered floes of lighter ice.

The two ships had served ably in the Norwegian campaign and they were paired up again for invasion watch duty in the Humber before being sent out to sea again on this watch. At 32 knots they had good speed, but even with twelve 6-inch guns each, they were no match for what was now heading their way. The *Sunderland* that had made that sighting of the Russian cruiser to spur Holland on his way was now busy with more pressing matters and scouring the seas at the north of the Denmark Strait. They made another lucky sighting at 15:00 hours and soon tapped out the warning in Morse code.

'MOST IMMEDIATE - RKS 1 - SIGHTED TWO HVY CRUISERS, ONE DESTROYER – 67.49,-27.02 APP BEARING 312 ISA – SPEED 24'

Birmingham was Daddy Brind's last command before he was hastily moved to his current position as Chief of Staff, Home Fleet in early March of 1940. Now the ship was captained by Alexander Madden, destined to rise to command of the battleship *Anson* later in the war and to eventually hold the lofty position of Second Sea Lord. Now, however, he was a light cruiser Captain, huddled in the cold upper bridge in spite of the milder temperatures at this time of year.

The real chill, however was that sighting report which was just called down from the top watch. Two cruisers and a destroyer? More like two battlecruisers and a cruiser, he knew. The Germans won't have any destroyers out here, so those two bigger ships will be Salmon and Gluckstein, the Twins, or possibly two of the pocket battleships. Either way you slice it we had best be sharp eyed and ready. The ship is scheduled to get the new Type 286 radar in just a few months time, but we'll have to rely on the old fashioned methods until then, a man on the mainmast and four eyes on the bridge.

By the time they saw what was coming it was almost too late. The *Sunderland* seaplane had reported a contact and now the pallid horizon seemed to darken with a smudge of charcoal at one point. Captain Madden was experienced enough to take a good long look with his field glasses. Those were ships ahead, and now he was in a most uncomfortable position.

"Signal *Manchester* and see what they find at about fifteen degrees north," he said quietly to his senior officer of the watch.

Time passed and the runner from the W/T room was up with the news. "*Manchester* confirms our sighting, sir. Three ships."

"Then get that off to Home Fleet on the double, and signal Captain Packer that I want to stay on this heading as long as possible to try and confirm the sighting. I doubt if these are cruisers as the *Sunderland* had it. The ship will come to action stations."

"Aye sir. Action stations!" The bells clanged right after sending booted feet thumping on every deck of the ship. Men were quickly donning life jackets, anti-flash aprons, steel helmets, gas masks. The fire parties were rolling out the hoses, ready ammunition was being fed to the guns and the turrets were soon training on the distant targets.

The weather was lowering, ragged clouds sweeping up from the east where far off Greenland sat in white ice-encrusted silence. Bold of them to come barreling right down the strait, thought Madden. They can see us now, plain enough. But with this weather closing in they won't see us for long, nor we them. In twenty minutes it's going to be thick out there.

Visibility was already falling off, though the converging courses had closed the range to shape the distant shadows into tall battlements of steel. Then the grey mist shrouded the sun for a time and they darkened again.

"Range, Bobby?" Captain Madden shouted the question to his Senior Watch Officer, Lieutenant Robert Ward.

"I make it a whisker over 21,000 yards, sir."

'Too far for any gunnery with this weather coming in."

"Aye sir."

The 6-inch guns on the two light cruisers weren't going to hit anything at much over 15,000 yards, even though the guns could range further. The barrels would have to elevate past 13 degrees to fire even that far, which began to slow the rate of fire, as they had to be lowered again below twelve degrees to be reloaded.

"Let's come ten points to starboard. Signal *Manchester* to follow."

He was heading east, away from the weather to keep eyes on the sighting for as long as possible, but it was a decision he would come to regret, for it kept the enemy eyes on him as well. The wink of light from the squarish shadows at the edge of the sea told him their visitors had fired. Ward saw it, looking over his shoulder, field glasses in hand.

"Incoming fire, sir."

"Noted." Captain Madden knew it would be nearly a minute before those shells would fall, and he did not expect them to have the range, but he was wrong. Three waterspouts bloomed up off his port bow, short but uncomfortably close. He looked over his shoulder to see shells fall near *Manchester* as well.

"Bloody good shooting for the range," he said aloud. "Starboard ten again." He was moving the ship to a new heading, just in case, but *Manchester* was slow to correct their course and follow. Cold fingers laid out the signal on the lamps even as lights winked again from the distant shadows. They heard a dull rumble of thunder, but it was not the weather. A second salvo of 11 inch shells were in the air and heading their way.

"Midships and ahead full," Madden called.

"Ahead full, sir!"

The forty seconds from fire to shell fall seemed interminable, but the gouts of water were soon in his foaming wake, and had the ship been there a moment longer, it might have been hit.

"Well gentlemen," said Madden. "The better part of valor here is to put some range between us and those ships. Their optics seem to be well polished today. Make smoke and turn on zero-nine-zero. Signal *Manchester* the same."

"Sir, make smoke and come to zero-nine-zero, aye."

But *Manchester* would not get the message in time. Instead she would get an 11-inch shell right amidships, between her two funnels, and it would sheer off a crane there before plunging into the guts of the ship, through storerooms, mess halls, bulkheads and quarters until it exploded in a broiling fire. Smoke emerged as if from a third funnel, and the ship made a sudden turn to starboard, coming around hard to present her backside to the enemy, still running hard.

Madden saw the maneuver and decided to match it, bringing *Birmingham* around even more as a final salvo came hissing in through the char smudged skies, thankfully short again.

"Well now, we've certainly been handed our hat this time around. Signal *Manchester* and ask if they can still keep up their speed."

The news that came back was not encouraging. The fire had spread to involve the number two boiler room, and Manchester was down to 28 knots, laboring to make even that. Madden decided to steer for the weather, turning both ships full about and then south by southwest, into the edge of the oncoming front. For the moment the enemy fire had abated, and the British cruisers were still well out in front, but now the tables had been suddenly turned and the hunters had become the hunted.

He slowed to 28 knots to keep apace of *Manchester*, knowing that if the Germans wanted to burn the fuel, they could work up to 32 knots and slowly close the range. It was going to be a very dangerous evening.

"How far off were those brigands when they made that hit, Mister Ward?"

"I made the range about 18,600 yards, sir."

"Damn good shooting. Let's let Admiral Holland in on our embarrassment. Tell him we've three wolves on our heels and send our present heading and speed. Any assistance he might render would be much appreciated. And amend that *Sunderland* sighting report. Simply say we are under fire from 11-inch guns. Let the Admiralty decide which ship is firing at us."

Captain Madden looked at his watch. If they come full out, he thought, then they could shave 8000 yards off our lead in an hour. In that event these will be the Twins. The pocket battleships can only make 28 knots and could not close on us if we keep up this speed. We've no radar and visibility will be down to twenty cables or less in another ten minutes from the look of things. But I doubt they'll come full out. As long as *Manchester* can keep up speed we should be safe, and it would be easy to lose them in this weather—but damnit, that wasn't my job! I was here to *find* them, and that I've done. Now how to best get round behind them and become a shadow when they have the speed to turn and engage us at any time?

Let's hope Holland isn't too far off.

Chapter 20

Denmark Strait ~ June 16, 17:30 hrs, 1940

Rodenko saw the action unfold on radar, calling Fedorov to his side so they could plot the positions on the electronic situation map.

"It looks like a pair of British cruisers have run into something to the north," he said. "See these residual signal tracings? Those are gun shells in flight. There's a battle underway."

Fedorov had been reading up on the general situation, knowing that none of that history might matter, but it at least gave him a template of sorts. "My guess is that the Germans are trying to push a couple raiders through," he said. "*Scharnhorst* and *Gneisenau* would have to move quickly to be here after the conclusion of the British evacuation of Norway. Nikolin and I have confirmed that happened roughly on schedule. In that event those two ships would have moved to Trondheim, and *Scharnhorst* was supposed to be meeting up with a repair ship to fix torpedo damage. Yet those details can't be confirmed. They weren't supposed to make their breakout attempt into the Atlantic until January of 1941, so if I am correct then things have changed here. How many contacts north?"

"Three. Two with a little more return integrity than the last."

"Then I'm guessing two battlecruisers and a cruiser, most likely *Admiral Hipper.*"

"Note these two contacts coming up from the south." Rodenko pointed out the position on the map. "They're about 250 kilometers southeast of our position at the moment and making 30 knots."

"Thirty knots? Then they will be fast cruisers or battlecruisers."

"Their return characteristics would argue the latter," said Rodenko.

"The British had *Hood, Renown* and *Repulse* capable of making that speed, but nothing else." He turned to Admiral Volsky now, explaining their analysis and briefing him on the situation ahead.

"It seems we're sailing right into the middle of a battle here, sir."

"What is the situation with those two cruisers?" Volsky was seated in the Captain's bridge chair, and now he swiveled to face the younger officers. Is the fight still underway?"

"I think the gunfire has concluded for the moment according to Rodenko's signal analysis."

"And how far off is that fight?"

"Just under 100 kilometers, sir. The British cruisers are moving on a heading of 260 now, running west towards Greenland, but that will bring them right across our bow if we stay on this heading. The German ships have gained on them slightly, but not by much. As things stand adding our speed and theirs we'll encounter the British in an hour."

"Plot a course to evade that encounter, Mister Fedorov."

"We could run due east, sir. There's plenty of sea room there as we are still at least 300 kilometers from Iceland on a heading of zero-nine-zero."

"Make it so. I think we will watch this one from the gallery for the moment and then see if we can slip out of the theater unnoticed."

"Very good, sir."

The drama unfolding soon took another turn, however. Rodenko noted that the speed of the British cruisers suddenly fell off to 20 knots.

"There's no reason for that," said Fedorov, "other than battle damage."

"It looks that way, sir. At their new speed I calculate the Germans are gaining on them at a rate of 10 knots per hour now. But what is interesting here is that they have just made a course correction to intercept the new British heading."

"In this weather?" Fedorov folded his arms. "Your situation plot shows those cruisers in the thick of that oncoming front."

"Correct. It looked to me as though the British were steering to try and side-slip the Germans and let them pass them by in the storm, but the Germans just came ten points to starboard. They could just be steering to take advantage of the weather front for cover, but something tells my radar nose that—"

"They are tracking them…very strange. The German ships had *Seetakt* radar on the battlecruisers. Both *Scharnhorst* and *Gneisenau* were equipped with two sets of that system on their forward and rear gun directors. They thought its primary use would be for gun ranging, not surface search."

"They may have already put it to good use," said Rodenko. "That initial action was at over 18,000 meters."

"*Seetakt* sets could range from 14 to 25 kilometers depending on conditions."

"If they are tracking them then they'll catch those cruisers in less than an hour at this rate, Fedorov."

"We could balance the scales a bit here and see about jamming that German radar."

Volsky raised an eyebrow at that. "You are suggesting intervention, Mister Fedorov?"

"Well, Admiral. We are here for the short run, and possibly for longer than we may know, and we are right in the middle of the soup. We will have to discuss and decide that question, because I feel it will be decided for us soon if we do not act on our own."

"Probably true," said Volsky. "I would prefer to choose a friend here before one side, or both, make us an enemy. Karpov was of the mind that the British were our real enemy, along with the Americans. He lectured us at length about the cold war and its oppressive effect on Russia."

"On Stalin's Soviet Russia, sir. But we have still not heard a whisper of Stalin's name. remember that now it is Sergei Kirov's Russia." He said that with an enlivened tone, as if he found hope in that prospect that the post war history could play out differently and that Russia and the West could become friends instead of enemies frozen in the chill of the long cold war. If anything that might be the one thing that could prevent the war they found themselves facing in 2021. Perhaps this was the only way to achieve what they hoped all along.

"I will say one thing," said Volsky. "We certainly cannot side with Nazi Germany, so that narrows the decision here somewhat. Do you agree?"

"I would, sir."

"Rodenko?"

"Admiral, if we must intervene in any way I cannot see the ship supporting Germany, particularly if they do attack Russia again in this war."

"And if we are to make friends on these seas the Royal Navy would be a good place to start," Volsky concluded. "Very well. See if we can assist these two cruisers and jam that German radar."

"Any idea what frequencies I should target, Fedorov?"

"Give me a second…" He was already working on his pad device, calling up facts and figures from the war. "Here it is. The *Seetakt* radar operated at 368 megacycles, initially at 14 kW, though the sets were upgraded to operate at 100 kW on the 80 cm wavelength."

"Good enough. They'll be blind in ten minutes. Just let me recalibrate our jamming equipment."

They turned on 090 east and soon found they had broken through the weather front where the British were hiding, though the lowering sun was still masked by the heavy cloud. The rising sea had a dull gleam of polished steel, and the tang of coming rain.

Temperatures were dropping ahead of the front, promising a cold night ahead.

Admiral Volsky was out the weather bridge where he had been watching the sea alone for the last ten minutes. He could still see the stain of dried blood there, and made a mental note to have it cleaned, but the sight of it brought Karpov to mind again.

So, Vladimir, we have made a choice you may not have agreed with here, he thought. You were adamant that the British and Americans were our enemies, and every intervention you made was aimed at trying to defeat them. But as you have seen, these are nations destined to rise on the world stage, and not so easily cowed. Suppose now there is a man in Moscow that Churchill and Roosevelt might trust and not also fear as they did Stalin? Suppose that man is Sergei Kirov, and that he is there because of Fedorov's lucky chance and his quiet whisper to the man at that railway inn? Suppose we save these two British cruisers from harm here and make amends with the Royal Navy? This war does not have to end with an Iron Curtain dividing East from West and fifty years of cold enmity. What if we see that does not happen by making a friend here, and not trying to crush the British as an enemy?

You may have had something to do with this all along—you and Orlov. Something tells me he bore you no good will after that first failed attempt to take the ship. I gave you my forgiveness and a chance to redeem yourself, but Orlov's lot was demotion and a posting to the Marines on the Helo deck. I wonder what really happened on that KA-226? What was Orlov doing there? Was there really a fire, or was he trying to jump ship? One way or another, the dominoes fell. Fedorov went after Orlov and now look at us, and look at the world that resulted from that mission.

He breathed in deeply, smelling the rain coming, the cool texture of the air, a sailor's rain. It would not be a bad storm. His tooth told the tale, and it was not throbbing as it might in a real cruel low pressure zone, with the wintery blast of an icy wind at the leading edge. No, this is around a thousand millibars. Just a typical low coming in from the west. But it will rain tonight, and the air smells fresh and clean, does it not?

The farther north they went, the more the air seemed to carry the scent of home. *Kirov* was like a salmon, swimming upstream again to the place it was spawned, returning home, battered, weary, but home. It was a last brave struggle to fulfill some unseen destiny, just as that salmon came home to spawn again. What will we give rise to if we keep to this course, he wondered?

He passed a moment thinking of his wife, not yet born in this reality, yet somewhere in a future he might never see again, sitting quietly by the fire at home with her tea and a book. We give up so much to go to war, he thought. So very much…

He came in through the hatch, his nose red from the cold, reaching in his pocket for a handkerchief. The bridge crew was quietly at work, selfless, dutiful, yet obviously having thoughts as he might. They, too, had left wives, children, lovers, girlfriends and everything else behind, sailing out to what they thought would be a routine cruise, just a simple live fire exercise and then a long pleasant cruise to Vladivostok. Well, we had to take a few detours along the way. God bless these men, he prayed, and help me keep them from harm.

Fedorov came up to greet him. "We're running on a converging course to those two contacts coming up from the south, Admiral. I suggest we come either east or west to avoid a collision."

"Use your best judgment, Mister Fedorov."

"Then I will turn on 305 degrees, sir. That will take us into the storm and towards Greenland. The chance we might be sighted visually again would be much reduced."

"Do so," said Volsky. "Who might be on those ships of any note, Fedorov?"

"If you'd like to scout them with the KA-40 I could give you a much better answer, sir. They're about a hundred kilometers southeast of us now."

"Do they have radar as well?"

"Possibly, though we don't know what ships we have there yet. If it's one of the battlecruisers, then it may be a little early for them to have anything active in the way of radar. HMS *Hood* fitted out with the Type 279M, installed during refits at Rosyth in early 1941. Same for the Type 284 sets. The former was primarily for detection of aircraft, the latter for gun direction. The rest of the battlecruiser squadron was fitted out in that same time period, if that history holds true."

"So there may be no reason to also jam the British radar."

"I don't believe that is necessary, sir. I think we might just skirt west and slip away here, even if we can only make 26 knots now."

"We'll have to address that condition and get some additional work done on the hull, and soon. I was looking at the map, Fedorov. Do you suppose we could sneak into a fiord near Iceland or Greenland and anchor for a day? It would give Byko some time to put divers down again to check on things."

"There's still a lot of sea ice west, sir, but I'll see if I can find us something."

"Admiral," Rodenko came up. "I think the Germans may have sighted those British cruisers again."

"Sighted them? How can you know this, Rodenko?"

"I'm tracking the arc and fall of gun shells."

* * *

The Germans had found their quarry again. They had been steering 215 southwest and then adjusted ten points to starboard to follow a long range contact on the *Seetakt* radar. A short while after they made that turn their sets were all clouded over with interference, which they attributed to the oncoming storm front.

Kapitan Hoffmann was leading the way in *Scharnhorst*, setting the pace at 30 knots for the last hour. The ship's boilers had been acting up again, with the super heaters doing their work too well, but thus far they had been running at good speed. Their brief encounter with a pair of British cruisers had encouraged them when *Scharnhorst* scored a hit, clearly setting one of the ships afire amidships. Now their blood was up, and they thought they would pursue.

Hoffmann knew his real mission was to evade these cruisers and get into the Atlantic to attack the convoys, but something about the sound of the guns and that beautiful long shot they had scored spurred him on. The British would likely slip away in the weather, he thought, but if I come upon them again, why not sink them?

At 19:00 hours they had turned to run directly into the wind of the oncoming storm, and their speed was down to 28 knots now, but whether it was by chance or fortune, the low clouds ahead seemed to split to offer him a long narrow valley of open sea and sky. The last rays of the falling sun pierced the edge of the clouds and painted the way in liquid gold. He sailed on, the fading light gleaming off the wet steel, the bow awash with the rising sea. Then the lookouts saw something ahead, just a glimpse of what looked to be two ships through a gap in the clouds—two cruisers.

Smiling, he gave orders to open fire with the forward turrets to stick a fork into this quail and see what they had in front of them. The sound and sight of his two triple turrets opening fire was bracing. Good to be in battle on the sea, he thought. Too bad we let that damn carrier slip away in the haze and smoke. Those god cursed super heaters! Something tells me we'll need six months in dry dock to rip them all out and get the boilers right.

Enough of that. Focus on the guns. He imagined the cold metal rammers feeding the next shells into the yawning gun breeches. Soon he saw the barrels elevate again, looking for the range. The blast of the second salvo shook the ship, first Anton, then Bruno, the two turrets firing one after another.

"What do you make the range, Schubert?"

The ship's chief gunnery officer, was quickly at his side. "Another long shot," he said. "17,800 meters," but we are gaining on them. It will only be a matter of time unless these clouds roll in on us and they slip away."

"Good, we'll have a pair of young pheasant for dinner this evening—"

There came a hard thunk, and Hoffman knew enough to realize the ship had just been hit, right on the side armor, but with a small caliber round.

"They are shooting back at this range?"

"Impossible," said the Gunnery Officer.

"That wasn't a gull blown in on the storm, Schubert. And he pointed forward out the weather ports where they could see the spray of two near misses"

"Damage control, Kapitan." A midshipman came in with the message. "A small hit below B turret on the side armor. It did not penetrate, sir. No significant damage."

"So they get their lucky shot as well."

"We're in this open trough between those two cloud formations," Schubert suggested. "They can obviously see us much better than we can see them."

When the next salvo came in spot on target, straddling the bow of the ship with two shells in quick succession, Hoffmann frowned. "They nearly hit us again, but look there, that other salvo of three fell at least three thousand meters short."

"Two ships, two gunnery officers," Schubert said matter of factly.

"Yes, well get to work, Schubert. Get to work!"

Chapter 21

The battle was joined again in spite of every effort by Captain Madden to evade the fast German ships. He had turned into the oncoming storm, seas higher now, wind up, visibility diminishing. There he thought he might work round to the west, then turn north and allow the Germans to sweep past him in the scudding grey clouds, but the raiders had the scent, or at least enough of it before *Kirov's* first tentative intervention in jamming the enemy radar. They had surged up a rift in the front, chasing the falling sun and caught a glimpse of the British cruisers laboring on at just 20 knots.

Manchester had four Admiralty 3-drum boilers, and her number two boiler room was completely down. The fire had finally been put out, fire parties working feverishly for the last hour and a half, but they had lost all steam there cutting speed by a quarter. That and the oncoming weather front with rougher seas had them down to a little over twenty knots when the Germans saw them. Madden was out on the weather bridge, the rain already beginning in short, lashing squalls when he saw the first flash of the enemy guns.

That was a half salvo for bearing, he thought, but if they find the range as quickly as they did before, we can only hope the weather saves us now. Forty seconds later the first three rounds fell, slightly off bearing and well short. It was too far for any chance that his 6-inch guns might find their targets, though he could clearly see the leading German ship bathed in the pale light and last searching rays of the sun above the rising thunderheads. The dark wall of clouds seemed briefly crowned with gold, as if on fire.

He gave the order to fire anyway, the two rear turrets on *Birmingham* barking out their warning as he watched through his field glasses. Then, well before those rounds should have fallen, he saw what looked like a telltale gout of water rising off the bow of the leading German ship, and a second round hit home. Surprised, he looked behind him, thinking *Manchester* had fired the rounds, for he soon saw his own salvo falling well short, as he expected.

"Mister Ward, is *Manchester* firing?"

"No sir, they were waiting on our order." The Lieutenant was at his side now coming out from the armored conning tower into the weather, the collar of his overcoat blown up by the wind, reaching to keep his hat in place and pulling it low on his brow.

"Well then who the devil scored that hit?" The Captain pointed to the thin trail of smoke from the side of the German battlecruiser out in front. Then they saw the guns there glow with fire again, heard the rolling peal of thunder that was echoed and answered soon after by the advancing storm. This time they heard the rounds whistling in and saw them make another close straddle of *Manchester* behind them.

"Never mind for now. Make smoke!" said Madden. "Signal *Manchester* the same." He looked for the thickest segment of the oncoming squall and decided to steer for it. "Port fifteen and into the rain, gentlemen. This is no place to be at the moment."

"Another hit sir!" Ward was pointing now and the Captain's heart leapt, thinking *Manchester* had taken another shell. When he turned, however, he could just barely see the small fire that had broken out amidships on the leading German raider. Yet he could see *Manchester* well enough, and her guns were completely silent, not even sighted on the pursuing enemy. Someone else is out there, he thought suddenly, but who? Could Holland have closed the range this soon? *Hood* is fast, but not that fast. His last reported position was over 100 kilometers to the south.

This was no time for solving mysteries. He started for the open hatch, heading for the wheelhouse to get the ship to safety, thanking his lucky stars that there was an unseen angel at the edge of the storm coming to his aid. Yet in the back of his mind he knew this was not *Hood*. Those were small caliber rounds, and the Germans just shrugged them off. *Hood* would have opened with her main batteries. So someone else is close by, perhaps another cruiser or even a destroyer out of Reykjavik. Good for them.

* * *

They saw the battle forming up on radar, and Fedorov was convinced that it would mean a quick end to one or both British cruisers. At the time *Kirov* had been sailing well south of the action, just over forty kilometers. The jamming may have helped but it looked as though the Germans still had hold of the hind leg of the fleeing British cruisers, and so Admiral Volsky entertained options for further intervention.

"We could easily hit them with a missile, sir," Rodenko had suggested.

"Yes, but that packs a lot of punch, perhaps more than I want to deliver at the moment. I would prefer the deck guns."

"Excuse me, Admiral." Volsky recognized Samsonov's deep voice and turned to regard him.

"Here we have our Combat officer and I am consulting with navigators and radar men. Yes, Mister Samsonov, do you have a suggestion?"

"Sir, we have 200 rounds of special ammunition—rocket assisted 152mm rounds that can range to 50 kilometers. Radar guided, Admiral."

"That sounds like a better solution. Feed Mister Samsonov the targeting data and let's give these rounds a field test. They were scheduled on our initial live fire exercises, but we never got round to those. Time to catch up on old work."

Naval forces had been experimenting with longer range projectiles for many years. The Italian's had a long range 127mm shell in 2021, called the *Vulcano*, but two American programs for an

Extended Range Guided Munition had been cancelled by 2008, with missiles winning the tech battles and the emerging development of rail gun systems starting to soak up scarce budget dollars.

The Russians had extended range rounds for both their 127mm and new 152mm naval guns, and they had proven to be accurate after some teething trouble in the early testing. One enterprising Captain had inadvertently fired a salvo south of Vladivostok, and a shell traveled much further than expected, smashing into the city where the impact broke windows and left a small crater in the pavement outside the nine-storey apartment building! By 2021 the bugs had been worked out of the system, however, and it was fairly reliable.

They fired three salvos from the forward deck gun, six rounds in all, just as *Birmingham* shouted its plaintive protest with a single salvo from her rear 6-inch gun turrets. Two of *Kirov's* six rounds found their target 42 kilometers away, and Volsky began to chuckle quietly, thinking the Germans might now be quite surprised.

"Two hits, sir," Samsonov reported.

"Are the British firing?" Admiral Volsky leaned towards the radar station where Rodenko was supervising the readout.

"It looks like they fired one salvo, sir, then ran for the edge of that storm."

"The range was too long for the guns on those cruisers," said Fedorov.

"Well, they will think they got lucky today and scored a hit." Volsky smiled. "We've tapped him on the shoulder, but when he turns around he will see no one else on the dance floor, just the empty sea and those oncoming storm clouds. So he must conclude the British have some very good gunnery officers aboard. Let us hope those rounds are enough of a distraction to help those cruisers, but in the event the Germans persist, our next field test will be one of the P-900s we received from *Kazan*. I want to be sure they are configured properly."

* * *

Hoffmann felt the second hit, well up in the superstructure and flush against the armored conning tower. A bigger round might have caused real trouble, but as it was the 350mm armor there, all of 14 inches thick, was easily enough to stop this one. Yet the jarring concussion was enough to force every man there to shirk and hunch their shoulders in surprise. The bridge crew took a bit of a knock, but no one was wounded, as there was no interior damage or splintering into the command spaces. *Scharnhorst* has just been hit with a stiff jab. The ship had a bruise on its cheek, but was unharmed and fully functional.

"No significant damage, Kapitan." Leutnant zur See Huber reported. "We took both hits in well protected areas."

The Kapitan shook his head, unwilling to believe the British cruisers could hit him at his range, but they clearly had. Gunnery Officer Schubert had set his mind on answering, and he straddled the trailing British cruiser before they saw both ships make smoke and vanish into the grey edge of the storm. That was a good idea.

"Helm, come round to 320. We'll turn for that squall line to starboard. I think the British will be trying to work round behind us."

A messenger came in from the wireless, handing him the note, and Hoffmann smiled with a nod as he read it. Kapitan Otto Fein aboard *Gneisenau* behind him was perplexed. He wanted to know what they were doing sparring with these cruisers when the route south was now clearly open.

Perhaps he is correct, thought Hoffmann. I am indulging myself here, like a cat playing with a mouse, and I just got bit on the nose for my trouble. I could make this turn and run parallel to the course I think these cruisers have taken, or I could come left and south to the Atlantic. That was the plan, but not before we refuel.

He pulled off his leather gloves, tucking them into his pocket and loosened the upper button of his overcoat as he considered the situation. I could detach *Admiral Hipper* here to chase these cruisers off. That would leave me free to head south unbothered by them again. That was the only reason you engaged here, was it not?

"Helm," he said calmly, resigned. "Belay that last order. Come about to two-two-zero. Make an easy turn, and ahead two thirds. Huber, see that *Gneisenau* is informed of both the course and speed change and ask her to follow. As for *Admiral Hipper*, signal that I want them on three-two-zero to look for those cruisers. They are to report in three hours, and if they do not find them they will meet us at the refueling point."

The German tanker *Altmark* was waiting out near the coast of Greenland, hovering off a misty ice-crusted fiord. Hoffmann was planning to rendezvous with *Altmark* just north of Cape Farewell to refuel his ships before breaking out, and he did not want any British cruisers about to interfere with the operation.

We will hold this new course for three hours, he thought, then turn to meet up with *Altmark*. By then I should know whether *Admiral Hipper* had any luck finding the British. He noted the barometer, seeing rain on the wind shields of the viewports.

An hour later he received a report from *Admiral Hipper*. The British were hiding in the storm. They had seen at least three contacts on radar, but the signals were lost in interference. On a hunch the Kapitan had fired down the bearing of one contact sighting. Hoping to flush his quarry, and he believed the cruisers were dispersing. But now the wireless was silent, and there had been no further reports.

Three contacts…Hoffmann knew of the first two, the pair of hapless British cruisers he had engaged. What was contact three? They were still too far north for *Hipper* to have picked up the *Altmark*. It had to be something else, but what? Could we have a U-boat out here that I am not aware of? That might account for the sudden disappearance of the contact on radar, but it still did not make sense. It could be a tramp steamer, or even a ship involved in the recent British invasion of Iceland. If so that would be fair game here.

"Any signals from Wilhelmshaven?" he asked Huber, thinking they might get some additional intelligence on what was happening on Iceland.

"No sir. Nothing since we entered the strait."

"The British have taken a lease out on Iceland, Huber. That means they might soon have an airbase functional there."

"That may take them some time," Huber suggested. "We should be well out into the Atlantic before we need to worry about planes from Iceland."

"What is the situation with the radar?"

"Still fouled up with interference, sir. It must be the storm."

"Very well. I looked at fuel reports. We did not have time to fill up at Trondheim after chasing that British carrier. That was a mistake. Now we've gone nearly 3000 kilometers and used up half our fuel. "

"But *Altmark* is waiting for us here, Kapitan."

"Yes, and we are lucky for that. We should have had more time at Trondheim, but Raeder was adamant that we put to sea as soon as possible."

He squinted at the weather, feeling ill at ease. Two long shots for a cruiser that should have had no chance to hit his ship, but yet they did. Now a third contact on radar, and then every set down as though…as though they were being jammed.

"The pressure is not too low," he said quietly. "We will push through this front in two hours. In the meantime, make ready for the refueling operation. That is our number one priority now."

"Aye sir."

Hoffmann did not know it then, but his new course was taking him closer to the mysterious antagonist that had flicked those shells at

Scharnhorst, even as it moved closer to the ship that had been dogged by the black hand of fate in an earlier incarnation, *Altmark*...and fate and mystery would soon become fire and steel.

Part VIII

Ride of the Valkyries

*"Now awful it is to be without,
as blood-red rack races overhead;
and the welkin sky is gory with warriors' blood
as we Valkyries war-songs chanted."*

— Njals Saga

Chapter 22

Iceland-Faeroes Gap ~ 17 June, 1940

Admiral Tovey was restless that day, still bothered by his abortive attempt to investigate that Russian cruiser. He did not know why it left him feeling like he had an untied shoe or missing button, but it did. He was a careful, meticulous man, and did not like leaving things unfinished. Yet word from the Admiralty on the movement of *Bismarck* and *Tirpitz* trumped everything else and forced him to turn about south of Reykjavik and head east, then northeast along the coast of Iceland. He had bigger fish to fry.

Now he was in the Flag Plot Room, looking at the map like a butler checking to see if the silverware had been set properly. There were the cruisers *Sussex* and *Southampton* on forward patrol in the center of the Iceland-Faeroes Gap. Coming up on their right flank was Force F with *Nelson* and *Rodney*, the cruiser *Devonshire* and three destroyers.

Nelson had just been pulled out of her refit at Greenock after sustaining serious hull damage the previous December when she ran over a magnetic mine at Loch Ewe. The hull was buckled four feet on her starboard side, sixty bulkheads ruptured and there was flooding over 140 feet of her 710 foot length. Thankfully no one was killed, but the incident was later called "the ball buster" by members of the crew. It seems a good number had been seated on the porcelain throne when the mine went off and the official report read that: "52 suffered lacerating injuries to delicate parts of their anatomies when ceramic toilet pans shattered in the blast." Nelson had taken a hard kick in the pants, and was down for some time.

Most of the repair work was done at Portsmouth before the ship was moved to avoid possible German air attacks. There she was fitted with Type 279 long range air warning radar, and was to have work completed for the Type 282 Gun director radar at Greenock before she was called to action again. The kits were still aboard, with a bevy of workmen to see the work on as she sailed, and there had been no time for her to contemplate or complete working up exercises. The crews were quick running new 16-inch shells aboard over the wooden decks in their shell bogeys, and additional canisters of cordite charges which made up the full charge for firing the guns. They soon had her up to snuff with 100 rounds per gun, 80 being APC and 20 HE with a total of 900 rounds on board. The veteran ship and crew would just have to muddle through, and Tovey had every confidence that they would.

Big slow *Nelson* and *Rodney*, thought Tovey. The Germans had danced around them in the Norwegian campaign, as they could make no more than 23 knots on a good day. Even the guns were slow to hoist, load and fire after the ready ammunition in the turret was used up. The 16-in guns might only average one round per minute compared to twice that for the more common 15-inch guns in the fleet. Aside from *Rodney* and *Nelson*, HMS *Invincible* was the only other ship in the fleet to use the 16-inch guns—good throw weight and range, but not as efficient as the 15-inch.

Force F will be late to the party, he knew. By the time they get up north the Germans will have slipped west. The only question is where will they go? If they turn east of Iceland then it's my watch. If they run further west for the Denmark strait I'll also be in a good position to give chase or possibly cut them off. Then we have a battle, and while I think *Invincible* would give a good account of herself, *Renown* is lightly armored. We'll also be outgunned, but at least we have *Ark Royal* handy with her *Swordfish* and *Skua* bombers. We'll have to see what the Germans do, but the job now is to find them.

He eyed the young Lieutenant Commander Wells, where he was quietly watching him, curious as to what he was thinking. "Your mind looks very active, Mister Wells. Any thoughts?"

"Sir? Oh, I was just thinking about the Germans, sir. They say *Bismarck* is a fairly formidable ship."

"That remains to be seen, but I remind you that you are presently standing on a ship christened HMS *Invincible*."

"Of course, sir."

"Learn nothing from that, Wells. Any ship afloat can be hit and sunk in a battle at sea—even this ship. *Bismarck* is just made of steel and iron as our ship is, and crewed by men of flesh, blood and bone. When it comes down to it, quick thinking and quick shooting decides the hour. You would do well to remember that."

"Yes, sir."

"But unless we find the rascals first none of that matters. Get off to the W/T room and have them signal *Ark Royal* to get a search mounted out ahead of us. 150 mile radius should be sufficient."

"Right away, Admiral."

Wells was off with that message, thinking about the blood and bone he had seen on the bridge of HMS *Glorious* when he returned. Yes, it had been quick thinking on his part that saved the ship, but he had never been on a battleship before, where you deliberately sought to bring yourself under the guns of the enemy so as to deliver your own fire upon him. This was something entirely different, to be seeking the enemy in battle instead of skirting along behind on the carrier, but *Ark Royal* was the eyes of the fleet for the moment.

He could imagine the planes being spotted on deck, up from the elevator and ready to go. And realizing that he was now carrying the word that would send them aloft was somewhat exciting. I'm to give the order that starts this battle! Well, the Admiral's given it, but it is now in my hands until I get to the W/T room—entirely in my hands.

He thought he might take his time getting there, just to let the moment distill a bit in his head, like good Earl Grey, but he soon discarded that notion and let his excitement drive his feet on. Orders were orders and it was, for the moment, all depending on him to get those planes up off the deck and headed north. We will not be caught flat footed out here like *Glorious* was. No sir, not on my watch.

* * *

Far to the north, the foxes those planes would be out hunting were surging west through rising seas. Foxes indeed, they were more like big muscled cats, moving easily in the heavy swell, their wide beam providing exceptional stability, the sharp Atlantic bows easily parting the waves as they sailed at 28 knots. *Bismarck* and *Tirpitz* were an awesome sight together, with the squadron commander Kapitan Lindemann leading aboard *Bismarck*.

Vice Admiral Marschall had bristled at the notion of the operation being handed to a mere Kapitan, but Raeder explained that he wanted to season Lindemann for the Battleship Squadron.

"I want you to meet with Lütjens, Wilhelm," he had said in a placating tone. "I want you aboard *Hindenburg*, the fleet flagship. See to the progress of those sea trials. Put your head together with Lütjens and make *Hindenburg* the finest ship in the fleet when she sails. I want her ready for battle, which is why I send you to see to the details— fuel, munitions loads, lubricants, quartermaster stores. Only you have the mind for such things."

Marschall was still not happy, but the thought of stepping aboard the *Hindenburg* was enticing, and made up for the loss of his Battlecruiser Squadron. It had been enough to deftly move him aside for this operation, and now Raeder was counting on his fighting sea Kapitans, Hoffmann with the battlecruisers, Lindemann with the battleships, Böhmer on *Graf Zeppelin*.

That morning Kurt Böhmer was riding the fading froth of Lindemann's wake in the German carrier, some three kilometers behind the battleships, waiting on news from his scout flights. They had seen a pair of old British battleships earlier, well to the south and in no position to intercept.

Böhmer briefly contemplated paying them a visit with his *Stukas*, his Valkyries as he now called them. But soon discarded the notion. The German fleet could easily evade those ships, and there was no reason to engage them whatsoever. It would be better to get further west before a decision was made on their final breakout course, and Lindemann agreed. If Hoffmann did his job the British would be out in the Denmark Strait, leaving the east coast of Iceland a good place to contemplate a quick breakthrough. So his mission today was to scout that area, and make certain the way was still clear.

It was not long before one of his *Arado* 196 seaplanes emerged from a cloud and spotted a formation of British aircraft heading north. That set alarm bells jangling on the carrier, and Böhmer immediately called down to the hanger deck.

"Ritter! What do you have ready?"

"Anything you need, Kapitan. I have six 109s and twelve Stukas fully armed, two of the fighters are on deck now."

"Get the other four up. We may be having company soon. The *Arados* have spotted British planes."

Something was about to happen that had never occurred in the Atlantic, the first carrier to carrier air duel ever to be fought. The Germans had tangled with the RAF and Fleet Air Arm before, but always with land based planes, and with the British deciding where the action would be fought, their fleet carriers hovering off the coast of Norway. This would be the first German attempt to intercept and stop the FAA carrier planes before they could start buzzing round the fleet like bothersome flies.

Hauptmann Marco Ritter is just the man to do the job, thought Böhmer. He is already and ace many times over, with many confirmed kills in his tally. The rules for German airmen were very strict. The kill had to be filmed or observed by someone in the air, on the ground, or aboard a ship. The mere claim of a kill was not enough. If there was no witness then there was no kill. But Ritter's work was well observed, for he flew with expert skill, lighting fast, and with surgical precision in his dog fights with *Spitfires*. He had six kills there, three on bombers, four more for auxiliary craft, two more *Swordfish* over Norway for fifteen in all. Five more and he would get his Knight's Cross with Iron. Now he was out to make his bones as a carrier airman, Germany's first and best.

So Böhmer watched again as Ritter led his squadron of Messerschmitts up, posting three on continuous patrol over the fleet and taking the remaining three south to the heading reported by the *Arado* 196. The *Stukas* were then brought up and readied for quick takeoff in the event the *Arados* could find the ship those enemy planes had taken off from.

Ritter did not disappoint. He had opened the throttle to lead his fighter section out at good speed, and was soon scanning the low scudding clouds from 18,000 feet. There, down below at an altitude he took to be 11,000 feet, was a lumbering flight of three *Skua* fighter/bombers.

"Hans, Leo, have a look at one o'clock low! We have company. Let's show them the door."

He tipped his wing and leaned over into a dive, and soon the three BF-109s fell on the *Skuas* like hawks.

* * *

Lieutenant Cecil Howard Filmer in Plane 7F was the first to see them. He was immediately on the short range radio to alert the other members of the subflight. These three planes had been kept in a tight fist to respond to any sightings by the four *Swordfish* down below, fanned out in a wide search formation. The occasional He 115 seaplane torpedo bomber might be out here snooping for the

Germans, but now the *Skuas* were being bounced by planes they did not expect to find.

"Bloody hell! Those are Messerschmitts! Get on the rear gun Tommy. Beware the sting, boys!" He was shouting out the squadron motto, their emblem blazoned with a yellow hornet, but the sting they needed to beware was coming from above. Filmer craned his neck at his gunner and signalman, Midshipman Thomas McKee, hoping he was ready.

The *Skua* was a dual purpose plane, with the ability to perform as a fledgling fighter or a light dive bomber, though it accomplished neither role with any real authority. The absence of any German carrier threat at sea had not spurred development of Royal Navy planes. They knew they were fielding interwar models, largely obsolete against a plane like the BF-109, but there was nothing much in the pipeline to redress that issue at the moment. They were stuck with the slow, rugged *Swordfish* as their sole torpedo bomber, and until the *Fulmars* started arriving, the *Skua* was left holding down fighter duty and bombing runs.

"I'm going to jink left, Tommy!"

The rattle of the rear facing .303 Vickers MG punctuated the drone of the *Skua's* engine as Filmer began his evasive maneuver, but the *Skua* was not an agile fighter. It was capable of a maximum speed of only 225 MPH and the 109s were over 120 MPH faster. If one got on your tail that single .303 MG was not enough to bother it unless the gunner was very good, and the Messerschmitt would unload with a pair of MG 131 guns in the wings and a 20mm Motorkanone in the nose. The MGs would rattle their cage, but that 20mm gun would skewer just about any bird it hit.

Ritter got his first kill on plane 7F in that heedless, headlong diving pass. The 109 thundered by, leaving Tommy McKee dead in the rear seat and the plane on fire. Harris and Stevenson in plane 7L fared little better, caught by Hauptmann Hans Frank, who had come over from the newly formed Night Fighter NJG-1 unit to join *Graf Zeppelin*. Only Lieutenant Commander John Casson and his mate Peter Fanshawe escaped. Casson was a bit of a stunt flyer, and he could get maneuvers out of his plane that the designers never thought to put there. He jogged left, scudded into a cloud, then wheeled around hoping to emerge with guns firing, but the BF-109s had flashed past to take down the other two planes in short order.

Outnumbered three to one, Casson knew his only chance was to get into low cloud and make a run for it. "Get the warning off, Pete!" he shouted. "What in bloody hell are these 109s doing out here?"

He knew the worst even as he spoke those words. They were 600 miles northeast of Trondheim, and the 109 had a combat radius of only 310 miles, and that was with drop tanks. If these planes were here, then they had to be off a carrier, and that meant that all the rumors in the hanger deck about the *Graf Zeppelin* were true…It was real, and it was here.

That news was soon in the hand of young Christopher Wells, hastening back from the W/T room with a heavy heart. So you fancy that you carried that order to send those fighters up, do you? Well look what's in your hand now, boyo. Two *Skuas* lost, a *Swordfish* shot to hell, six men dead and the skies swept clean in ten minutes by German BF-109s. Now you can carry that…and he felt the weight of it all the way back, somewhat relieved when he finally reached the Flag Plot Room with the message and handed it off to the Commander Villers as he had been told when entering the room to find both the Admiral and his Flag Lieutenant present.

"There's been an air battle, sir. We've lost three planes!"

Villers took the message in hand reading dispassionately. "Calm yourself, Mister Wells," he said quietly. "If I require your interpretation of a message I shall ask for it." Then he walked slowly to Admiral Tovey. "Confirmed, sir. Two *Skuas* and a *Swordfish* down approximately here." He moved a small model plane out onto the situation map to mark the spot. "BF-109s, sir." The tone in his voice was evident as he placed emphasis on this and it got Tovey's attention.

The Admiral looked at the message briefly, handing it back to Villers. "Confirm the message was also received by the Vice Admiral on *Ark Royal*. I think he'll want the balance of 803 squadron up at once. And signal RAF at Wick to see about support."

Chapter 23

The Junkers JU-87C was adapted from the workhorse of the early Luftwaffe ground attack planes, the very successful JU-87B-1. For carrier operations it had been modified with folding wings, a stronger fuselage, arrestor hook, and ejectable landing gear to permit possible emergency landing in the sea. It was rigged to carry bombs only, as the Fieseler Fi-167 was on the drawing board for a dedicated torpedo bomber on the German carriers, though they were not yet ready. But the *Stukas* were ready, and even as dedicated dive bombers they could still win a race against the British *Skua*, being about 25MPH faster while cruising and almost as well armed with two 7.92mm MGs forward and one MG-17 facing the rear. Their real punch was the 250 KG bomb, over 500 pounds, and four 50kg bombs mounted on the broad vulture-like wings. The 'Jericho Trumpets' were also retained to give the dive bombers that awful screeching noise when they dove on attack. Their one limitation was range, with an effective combat radius of about 300 miles.

Ritter's fighters had disrupted the British search to the north, and one of the *Arado* 196s followed a hunch and pressed on through the low clouds until the pilot was surprised to burst out into a clear patch and find the sea below him crowded with warships. There was a carrier in the distance, ample reason for the seaplane to be quick in its reconnaissance here, but the real find was the sighting of HMS *Invincible* and *Renown* with a pair of destroyers. Elated at the lucky discovery, he skipped into the clouds and turned tail for home, urging his signalman on the wireless to send out the coordinates.

Kapitan Böhmer was equally pleased to hear the news, and immediately notified Lindemann that the British fleet was no more than 125 kilometers southeast of their present position. He asked if he should attack, and Lindemann quickly gave him his blessing. The Valkyries were about to sing in the first German carrier borne air strike of the war. A formation of 18 of his 26 *Stukas* was selected, three squadrons of six planes each, and they were to be escorted by the six reserve BF-109s as soon as Ritter's group could be recovered.

Taking off from a moving carrier at sea was always easier than landing, which was a lesson the Germans were soon to learn when one of the six fighters they had aloft misjudged the approach and came skidding in to lose a wing against the carrier's armored 5.9-inch deck gun turrets. Thankfully the pilot was saved, but the plane was a total loss and had to be pushed overboard, which sent Böhmer pacing on the island bridge. There had been too little time to for training.

It took another half an hour to clear the deck and reset equipment for the launch, and the weather was worsening rapidly. Böhmer looked at the charcoal skies, where the light of the setting sun was glowing blood red, like embers burning in coals. The words of the Nordic poem he had read so often ran though his mind as he smelled the cold air and heard the distant rumble of far off thunder.

> *"Now awful it is to be without,*
> *as blood-red rack races overhead;*
> *and the welkin sky is gory with warriors' blood*
> *as we Valkyries war-songs chanted."*

He briefly considered whether to cancel the mission in these darkening skies, with the wind up and the chances high that his planes would not find anything at all. But war was war, and risks had to be taken. The Valkyries would fly. The strike would send the whole of *Trägergruppe* 186, out to look for the British fleet.

Soon he heard the first growling overture of the opera, as one engine after another sputtered to life and revved up on the flight deck below. The BF-109s took off first, all six forming up over the carrier before the *Stukas* went aloft. One by one the dark crows lifted off the rolling deck. In spite of the heavy swells, *Graf Zeppelin* was a large ship, displacing nearly 34,000 tons with a 118 foot beam, and it provided good stability. The long flight deck, over 800 feet, also gave the pilots plenty of room for takeoff. The *Stukas* were formed up, their engines howling on the flight deck as they waited for final clearance to begin takeoff. Hauptmann Marco Ritter had already returned and was out on the flight deck waiting for the air crews to refuel and rearm his Messerschmitt, eager to get back into the sky. He was counting the planes, seeing that only seventeen had been spotted.

"Where's number eighteen?" he asked an airman.

"Still on the elevator. The pilot is sick and doesn't think he can fly. But seventeen should do the job well enough."

"That's an unlucky number," said Ritter. "Let me go and see about it."

He went below, only to learn that the remaining six *Stuka* pilots were all busy performing pre-flight checks on their planes, which were being armed in the event they were needed later. Frustrated, he spied a lone pilot leaning dejectedly on a bulkhead, enviously watching the crews work on the dark flock of crows.

"You there, what are you doing?"

"Nothing, sir. I have no assignment."

Ritter shook his head. "No assignment? Here I am looking for a pilot and there you are right in front of me. Isn't that a flight jacket you are wearing?"

The Air Maintenance Chief heard the men and yelled at Ritter as he worked on one of the planes. "Don't get excited, Hauptmann Ritter, he's just a recon pilot."

"Recon pilot?"

"Yes, sir," said the Airman. "I fly the *Arado*." The man was the number four *Arado* 196 pilot, still waiting for assignment, listless and brooding below decks. "But I can fly that too," the man pointed at the last *Stuka* on the elevator, a dejected, hungry look on his face.

"You can fly a *Stuka?*" Ritter remembered the man now.

"Yes sir. I trained with *Sturzkampfgeschwader 3* before volunteering for my assignment here."

"Excellent! You're my lucky eighteen."

"Me sir?"

"You can't send him, Ritter," the maintenance Chief protested.

"Mind your spanner, Chief. I am head of air operations on this deck, and if this man can fly a *Stuka* he's as good as any of the others."

Most of the *Stuka* pilots were young and still relatively inexperienced. They had fought briefly in Poland before being drafted into the special units for training with the new carrier based model.

"Just get in the plane," said Ritter. "You can ride it up on the elevator."

Rudel's eyes glowed with thanks. "Right away, sir!" And he leapt for the plane, scrambling up and into the cockpit as the lift started.

"You'll get him killed, Ritter. He's never flown a real combat mission in a *Stuka*, just training."

"Every man gets his first chance, Chief. And nobody lives forever." He watched the young man go, eager, happy to serve, and also noted how he correctly fixed his harness in little time at all. He will have to do, he thought.

Ritter's lucky number eighteen was Hans-Ulrich Rudel, and he had joined the School of Air Warfare right out of high school to learn to fly. There he found the work challenging, and was thought to be ill suited for combat missions by his instructors, which is why they gave him the role of reconnaissance pilot. Determined, he applied himself rigorously, shunning alcohol and cigarettes, and maintaining a rigid discipline in his studies. It was to be a case of sheer will that saw him succeed, and he made numerous requests to be transferred to a fighting unit.

Begging for a more active role, he was sent over to the Kriegsmarine for training on the *Arado* 196 his experience in recon operations saw him assigned to the *Graf Zeppelin* as Number Four pilot in the *Arado Anerkenung* Squadron. Two of his mates were already up there joining in the excitement as they loitered to help vector in the strike wave once it got aloft, but Rudel was sulking below decks when fate, in the form of Marco Ritter, placed a hand on his shoulder.

Ritter took the ladder up, back on the flight deck to watch the *Stukas* take off. When the last plane was ready, he gave Rudel a thumbs up, and a wide smile, remembering his own very first combat mission over Poland. He watched as Rudel's plane roared off the deck, eager for the sky. A nice takeoff, he thought.

Soon the strike wave was up and on its way, only twenty minutes out from the target at their present cruising speed of 225 MPH. They threaded their way through drifts of clouds, moving fast on the wind, and far to the south the alarms were clanging hot and loud on the ships of Tovey's Home Fleet.

* * *

Lieutenant Commander John Casson was back, his *Skua* just landed on the *Ark Royal* as they began to spot the decks with new planes for a hasty takeoff. He leapt out and down from the cockpit, checking on his signalman gunner before he hit the deck. There was a line of bullet holes in his left wing, but it had not caught fire and the low clouds and his acrobatic flying had saved the plane, and undoubtedly his life as well. He spied the Squadron Leader, Captain Richard 'Birdy' Partridge, of Peartree fame on the ship. He was huddling with his gunner's mate Bostock as they made ready to mount their planes.

"Jerry 109s," he said flatly. "Jumped us from above, and had two planes down before we could tip a wing."

"That means they've come off a carrier, Johnny. So we get a crack at *Graf Zeppelin.*"

"Yes, well you had better hop to it! Those planes were no more than fifteen minutes out when they found us. They could be right on my heels."

"Who went down?"

"Filmer and Harris."

Casson patted the chest pocket on his flight jacket where he kept a silver brandy flask given to him by his wife. He could use a swig now, but was only glad to have made it home in one piece.

Squadron navigator Peter 'Hornblower' Fanshaw came running up, breathless as he gathered himself. "I've just got the latest position report. One of the *Swordfish* got clean away and they've spotted the Germans up north."

"Good show, Hornblower. Let's get airborne!" Partridge was keen to get up and about his business, but he could not help but notice the sprig of white heather that Hornblower always liked to set on the dash for good luck. They were going to need it. Every man among them knew their planes were beyond their prime, and no real match for the German BF-109. But in the end the skill of the pilot counted for much in any encounter, and the British were veterans all.

They were sending six *Skua* fighters from 803 Squadron, and another six from 800 Squadron. With no time for loadouts of bombs, the planes were tasked with combat air patrol over the fleet until they could bring up the *Swordfish* for a go at the Germans. Then they would serve as escorts. *Ark Royal* could spot no more than fifteen planes for takeoff at any one time, and the *Skuas* were first up, with Bartlett and Gardiner already climbing into the wind.

Partridge watched all of 803 Squadron go before he ran for his plane. As was customary, the Senior Squadron Leader would be the last to take off. Once aloft he gave the signal to get the *Skuas* up to 11,000 feet while they waited for the *Swordfish*, but they soon had uninvited guests for dinner. The Valkyries had arrived.

Petty Officer Henry Monk saw them first in plane 6C from 800 Squadron. "Trouble at three o'clock he called." He looked to see long, dark lines of planes flying in formation as they broke out of a cottony grey-white cloud. "Look there, boys. Those are *Stukas!*" They were planes they could fight with a good chance of beating them, but Monk had not seen the six BF-109s on overwatch. As the *Skuas* tipped their wings and rolled into action the Messerschmitts suddenly appeared, streaking down from above as before with their wing guns snarling.

The fight was soon on, a dizzy whirl of man and machine in the grey skies, with planes wheeling and firing at one another. The Germans scored a quick kill on Finch-Noyes, but they saw at least one parachute get safely away from his smoking *Skua* as it went down. Partridge, Gallagher and Martin had formed the last sub-flight, and they tore into the *Stuka* formation, riddling two planes with their four wing-mounted .303s A kill went to the Squadron Leader, and he yelled a 'Tally Ho' as he brought his *Skua* around with Gallagher on his right wing in a wide turn.

But the BF-109s had also taken their toll. Riddler was down, his plane a smoking wreck, and no one got out alive. Spurway was hit and had one wing on fire. Partridge came around only to find he was in a fight for his life. A Messerschmitt on his tail had put a round right through his canopy, but it luckily missed, prompting him to kiss his leather glove and pat the sprig of lucky white heather on his dash. He managed to lose the German fighter in the clouds, but when he emerged he could see that the *Stukas* were now tipping over into screaming dives. The fleet was under attack.

* * *

Hans Rudel saw the first two *Stukas* go down, his pulse up, heart pounding as much from excitement as anything else. Combat! At long last he was on a real mission against the enemy. He knew the *Stuka* well enough, having trained with it in France for over six weeks before he came to the carrier disheartened to learn he would be flying an *Arado* seaplane. They do not think I'm any good, he thought, but his iron will was going to prove them all wrong today. Right here, and right now.

As he started his dive he could see the formation of British ships below, and now the skies were puffing up with the sharp muffled explosions of Ack-Ack fire. There were two big ships, and he found himself in a perfect position to line up on the number two vessel in the line. Now he tipped his plane in earnest, pointing the nose down in a near 90 degree dive. He could hear the wail of the Jericho Trumpets as the Valkyries dove to either side. The sound was terrifying, an awful wail of wrath from the welkin sky. The planes ahead of him scored a near miss on the big leading ship, which was now turning in a hasty evasive maneuver.

Rudel could see that his target was forging straight on, and he lined up perfectly on the ship, remembering the bawling cajole of his flight training officer. *'Line up and hold for ten seconds. Don't move a muscle, then let your bomb fly and pull out fast.'* And that was exactly what he did. His hands were like ice on the stick, and flack was exploding all around him, jarring his plane, but he kept in line, heedless of his own personal safety. Then he released the bomb and pulled out of his howling dive, light headed with the G-force of his recovery.

551 pounds of high explosives went careening into the target and blasted up in to the vibrating sky. Rudel got the hit, square amidships on HMS *Renown*, and the bomb went right through the battlecruiser's thin deck armor and exploded three decks down in a boiler room, blowing everything there to hell. *Renown* turned, her speed falling off rapidly, and tall geysers of water falling to port and starboard with another two near misses. A second bomb struck further aft blowing

the *Walrus* seaplane and its lifting crane to pieces and starting a raging fire there from residual fuel in the plane.

Rudel pulled out of his dive to see the billowing smoke and fire amidships. My God, he thought. I hit a battleship! It would not be the last he would have in his sights. Hans-Ulrich Rudel wasn't supposed to even be aboard *Graf Zeppelin* that day, and he certainly wasn't supposed to be aboard that *Stuka*, but the experience would serve him well. He would go on to become one of the most highly decorated combat pilots in history, flying over 2500 missions and stacking up awards and medals encrusted with oak leaves and diamonds throughout the war. No other pilot would match the tally of wreckage he would leave behind him, burning ships, planes, trains and warehouses all to be smashed by the thunder of his *Stuka*.

But all that yet remained to be lived. Now he was just a recon pilot snatched up in a wild minute by Ritter's roving eye. He was just Luck Eighteen, and that was enough.

Chapter 24

Far to the west HMS *Birmingham* was sailing close astride *Manchester* in the midst of the storm. They had sought the shelter of the oncoming front, and now the light cruisers rolled in the heavy swell, and rain lashed the viewports making it almost impossible to see anything. Outside on the weather deck, Captain Madden was braving the elements, his heavy overcoat drenched as he watched for the lamp signals coming from *Manchester*. He could have stayed in the conning tower waiting for the signalmen to bring him the news, but he wanted it fast to make a decision on their present course. The news was not good.

Manchester could not make any more than 15 knots and her Captain Packer was requesting permission to return to Reykjavik. Madden knew he would have to let the cruiser go. There was nothing more they could do in shadowing the German ships, and the wounded cruiser was now a liability. So he reluctantly gave the order to signal farewell and headed for the relative warmth and shelter of the conning tower.

It was then that he heard what he first took to be a distant peal of thunder, but something in the sound rankled his well trained ear. It was gunfire, eight inchers or better. He looked toward the sound, but saw nothing, though well honed instinct had him counting the seconds, as one might wait out the interval between lightning and thunder to measure distance to a storm at sea. Thirty seconds on he heard the whine of shells overhead and was amazed to see water splashes off his starboard bow. They were under attack.

Bloody hell, he thought, racing to the wheelhouse. Here we are sitting at twelve knots in a storm and the Germans have snuck up like a thief in the night.

"Make speed," he shouted. "Ahead full!"

"All ahead full, aye sir."

"Did anyone see the shell flash?"

Lieutenant Robert Ward still had the watch, but they had seen nothing. "We're blind as bats out here, sir. Visibility is down to five cables."

Yes, thought Madden, but bats had their own makeshift radar in the dark, and the Germans had to be tracking him. Their resolution wasn't good enough to get those shells much closer than they were, and thank God for that, but we're on our own now.

"Signal *Manchester* to make their best speed home and we'll try to keep the Germans busy here while they slip away."

A 30 second shell fall time might put that cruiser inside 15,000 yards. It was going to be a long, sleepless night.

* * *

They were huddling near the radio aboard *Kirov*, and Nikolin was translating what he was hearing and recounting a speech given by Churchill that was being broadcast by the BBC. Two days ago France had formally signed the Armistice with Germany and capitulated, leaving Britain alone to face the emerging wrath of the German war machine. In all the history Fedorov knew, Britain's survival was a near run thing, and largely would depend on whether or not the United States would join the war on her side. In that dark hour England's continued existence was in real jeopardy. So they had called the senior officers together one last time to finalize their course of action, and Pavel Kamenski was invited as well.

Nikolin discovered that a segment of what would have been the Soviet Union had now formally declared itself as an ally of Germany—the Orenburg Federation in the central heartland and south into Kazakhstan. *Kirov's* Russia remained neutral, and nothing was heard from the Siberian East. But the news that Orenburg was siding with Hitler was grim indeed.

"From what we have determined," said Fedorov, "the Orenburg Federation comprises all of Kazakhstan, Uzbekistan, Georgia and the Caucasus, and even extends north to the Urals. It is sitting astride the vast oil reserves of Kazakhstan and the Caspian region, and the mineral wealth of the Ural mountains."

"Why not join them?" Orlov spoke up, tentative at first.

"Explain yourself, Mister Orlov." The Admiral invited the Chief to speak his mind.

"As Fedorov says, they have the oil, the resources, and we know those things become essential in the future. Besides, Georgia is my home, and I would feel better fighting for them, if that means anything."

"A good point," said Volsky. "There may be others in the crew who feel the same way, particularly if they hail from those provinces."

"Joining Orenburg means we join with Germany too, and Hitler will be a very unreliable friend," said Fedorov. "Didn't he already prove that?"

"Volkov may be equally unreliable," said Volsky. "What will he do when he learns we are here with this ship? He will welcome us, that is certain, and then I think he will do everything in his power to get control of this ship and the weapons we possess. And I do not think the fact that I once ranked him in the chain of command will matter. Hitler and Volkov…They may prove friends in the short term and be two birds of a feather. In the end, however, only one can remain the dominant power, and Volkov will know this."

"But Hitler cannot get at Orenburg now," said Orlov. "Not without going through Soviet Russia or the Ukraine first. We could sail through the Med and into the Black Sea, and close that southern route if Hitler becomes a problem. I know the way well enough." He smiled as he said that. "I was there in 1942!"

"That is another concern," said Fedorov. "A good number of us were there, Chief. What happens if we do not leave here before late

July of 1941? We have never really determined that. I know that Mister Kamenski suggested things may be different now, but that remains uncertain. Our time here may be limited."

"We still have a long year to decide that," said Kamenski. "Perhaps more information will come to light. Who knows, we may even learn the fate of Captain Gromyko and *Kazan*. Yet for now we cannot become frozen with inaction knowing something may happen to us before the date of the ship's first arrival here anymore than a man refuses to live because one day he must die."

"A good point," said Volsky. So let us look to this day and learn what we may to make a final decision. We have already waded in to the pond by jamming the German radars and firing a few warning shots to try and bother them, but soon I think we must jump in one direction or another."

"Mister Nikolin has some further news to share," said Fedorov.

"Yes sir, I have been monitoring the BBC and following all the news. I recorded a speech today read by a broadcaster on that station and I took a moment to translate it. Shall I read it?"

"What speech is this?"

"Churchill, sir. He was speaking to the British Parliament today."

"Yes," said Fedorov. "Churchill would have only recently been appointed Prime Minister."

The news of that appointment had been received in the House of Lords in near silence, as they had little confidence and less use for the man at the time. But through this dark month of June 1940, the new Prime Minister's voice echoed through the halls of Parliament and rose on the airwaves to stir and bolster the flagging spirits of the nation. He said he had come to the government with "nothing to offer but blood, toil, tears and sweat," but he brought with him his indomitable spirit and a gift for giving it flight in some of the most eloquent and rousing oratory the world has ever heard. Earlier he had vowed that England would fight on in a speech that would echo through the decades ahead when he said: "*We shall go on to the end...we shall defend our island, whatever the cost may be. We shall fight on the beaches, we shall fight on the landing grounds, we shall fight in the fields and in the streets, we shall fight in the hills; we shall never surrender...*"

But this night they heard his declaration to the house of Commons on June 18, 1940, and Nikolin read the translation aloud to the officers all gathered on the Bridge.

"*...The Battle of France is over. I expect that the Battle of Britain is about to begin. Upon this battle depends the survival of Christian civilization. Upon it depends our own British life, and the long continuity of our institutions and our Empire. The whole fury and might of the enemy must very soon be turned on us. Hitler knows that he will have to break us in this island or lose the war. If we can stand up to him, all Europe may be freed and the life of the world may move forward into broad, sunlit uplands.*

But if we fail, then the whole world, including the United States, including all that we have known and cared for, will sink into the abyss of a new dark age made more sinister, and perhaps more protracted, by the lights of perverted science. Let us therefore brace ourselves to our duties, and so bear ourselves, that if the British Empire and its Commonwealth last for a thousand years, men will still say, this was their finest hour."

The broadcast signed off with salutations to the fleet at sea and all men at arms serving the British Empire in her far flung colonies all across the world. There was silence on the bridge for a moment, and then Admiral Volsky spoke.

"An eloquent man," he said "and one I could easily embrace as an ally. Who's side do we choose in this war? Such words make it clear to me that our decision to support Great Britain here is a wise one. The issue is laid bare in this man's words. We all know the British Empire will not last another a thousand years, but I think that if it should fail here in this dark hour as he says, then the Third Reich *might* last a good long while in its place. We all know what Germany will be making ready to do to our homeland soon if that part of the history holds true. Yes, we suffered much in the cold war against the West, but perhaps that can be prevented, and it was nothing compared to the horror the Germans brought in the few years they ravaged our homeland. Perhaps our real mission was never to destroy the West as Karpov desired, but to join it, embrace it, and make it a friend."

"Yes," said Kamenski, "hearing that speech, who could disagree? And that is saying quite a bit coming from my mouth, an ex-Deputy Director of the KGB! I will say that I have learned much of this world in that capacity, perhaps more than I ever wished to know. Yet what we do know now is that we are here in the middle of this decisive era, this great world war, and the outcome may now be as uncertain as the weather appears to be outside as this moment. If I am correct and everything is made new here, then Germany could prevail as the Admiral suggests, and we have in hand the evils of that dark science that Mister Churchill mentioned. We know how this war could end. With Russia divided and perhaps still locked in an internal civil war, the Rodina will not be the great force that eventually beat back the Nazi war machine."

"If I may, sir," said Fedorov. "If Germany does decide to attack Russia, they will most certainly strike as they did against the Soviet state that is presently led by Sergei Kirov, just as Orlov has said. Their long term aim may be to control the oil and natural resources Orenburg controls, but even if Volkov cooperates, getting those resources to Germany is the problem. If Kirov controls the Crimea, then he may also control the Black Sea, so they will not get out that way. The only overland routes lead through Kirov's Soviet state as well. Mark my words—Hitler will attack there soon enough."

"For now the drama is here in the West," said Volsky. "We polled the bridge officers earlier, and it was decided to aid those two British cruisers. Now, however, we must contemplate further intervention. What is the tactical situation, Mister Rodenko?"

Sir, the two German battlecruisers broke of that action and they moved southwest. We turned due west to avoid them in the storm, but they detached a cruiser and it is presently running on a parallel course."

"Then the Germans are ready to make their breakout with the two battlecruisers?"

"Perhaps, sir, but I have picked up another contact off near Greenland, and the battlecruisers have just turned on a heading toward that position."

"Could this be a convoy they wish to attack?"

"No, sir, it is a single ship."

"Admiral," said Fedorov. "My guess is that this is a German oiler. The two ships will want to refuel before heading into the Atlantic, They have broken through here, and probably sent the cruiser *Admiral Hipper* to see that the British cruisers are no further bother. Now they will refuel and then head into the Atlantic."

"So if we wish to stop them, now is the time," said Volsky. "But I think it will take something more than a poke on the nose with the deck guns. These are strong ships, are they not, Fedorov?"

"Yes, sir, and they have very good armor."

"So we are looking at more than one or two missiles to do the job. If our experience is any guide, it may take several well placed hits to disable these ships."

"We have programmed many of the Moskit-IIs to strike at a slightly higher elevation, sir," said Rodenko. "There has been no time to do that with the missiles we received from *Kazan*, but it may be possible. They have a popup maneuver option."

"Yes, it is no good wasting our missiles against the side armor of these ships, eh, Fedorov?"

"*Scharnhorst* class had 350mm belt armor, sir. That tapered forward of her A turret and aft, but that is fourteen inches of Krupp Cemented steel. It was designed to defeat a 16-inch shell at longer ranges. That's the equivalent of a 1000 pound warhead. But I have a one missile solution for you, Admiral."

"We will not contemplate special warheads at this time, Fedorov, I'm surprised you even suggest this."

"No sir, you misunderstand me. Of course I would not suggest nuclear weapons at this time or any other. The missile would simply use a conventional warhead. One of the smaller P-900s from *Kazan*, or even a fast MOS-III should do the job."

"But you just expounded on the virtues of this German armor, Fedorov."

"Neither *Scharnhorst* nor *Gneisenau* will be the targets, Admiral. If I am correct and that last contact Rodenko spotted is a German oiler, then all we have to do is put our missile there, or even some good long range gun fire. Sink that tanker and the Germans will not have the fuel to proceed."

Part IX

Altmark

*"Sacrificial animals think quite differently from those who look on:
but they have never been allowed to have their say."*

— Friedrich Nietzsche

Chapter 25

All over the UK the invasion watch was up, and now the news was filtering in to the Admiralty that the German Navy was at sea in a major operation and had done what no one there had any idea they might ever achieve. HMS *Renown* was attacked from the skies, with planes flown from the deck of a German aircraft carrier, and they pushed right through the veteran fighter cover of the Royal Navy's most experienced and capable fleet defender, the *Ark Royal.*

The British had learned a hard lesson. Their pilots were good, certainly brave and determined, but the plane they were flying was clearly outclassed, and the German fighter pilots were equally hardened by their experience in Poland and France before coming to train for carrier operations. Britain desperately needed a new carrier borne fighter, and the Fairey *Fulmar* was all they had in the pipeline now, with no replacement in sight for the *Swordfish* torpedo bomber either.

The stricken battlecruiser survived the attack, but with twenty of her forty-two water tube boilers destroyed and her speed cut to no more than twelve knots. The ship had to be detached from Admiral Tovey's squadron and sent home with a pair of destroyers cruising to either side for protection against U-boats, and the light cruiser *Southampton* in the van for additional air defense. Darkness and the onset of bad weather aided her getaway, and she would make it safely home, but now Tovey was in a bind. He had lost six big 15-inch guns and thirty-five percent of his squadron's fighting power. With only HMS *Invincible*, the cruiser *Sussex* and two destroyers left in his force, engaging *Bismarck* and *Tirpitz* was now a tall order, particularly if the Germans had more *Stukas* to throw at them.

Tovey paced in the Flag Plot Room, uncertain, yet determined. We took one hell of a beating today, he thought. The mere sight of a British capital ship used to put ice in the veins of a German raider, but not after this. Holland sends that the Twins have blown through our cruiser screen in the Denmark Strait. Now we've lost *Renown* here, and we were damn lucky the Germans had only two *Stuka* pilots that seemed to know how to hit what they were aiming at.

There had been several near misses, but aside from splinter damage, neither *Ark Royal* nor *Invincible* were hit. Tovey decided the wisest course in the short run was to put range between his fleet and the German carrier. Vice Admiral Carriers reported that they had lost six *Skua* fighters in the action and four *Swordfish* trying to find and strike the Germans. Nobody got torpedoes in the water, and now this bloody weather shut the game down. They were just lucky they got most of their planes back safely. Another *Swordfish* was forced to ditch.

"We're going to need more air cover, Mister Villers," he said to his Flag Lieutenant. "Now where can I get it?"

"I can see about *Beaufort* support from Wick, sir. RAF has Number 43 Squadron there with *Hurricanes*, 269 Squadron has the American *Hudsons* we've received, and then we have 42 Squadron with *Beauforts*. No torpedoes yet, but they can rig out as bombers."

"*Beauforts* have the range to get out here, but not the *Hurricanes*, and fighters are what we really need now. We can't very well fight the German fighters with torpedo bombers."

Villers hesitated, but ventured to inform Tovey of one other sad fact. "At the moment Wick reports they've received no deliveries of torpedoes for the Beaus, sir, but we can have them armed with bombs."

"No torpedoes? By God, the Germans put BF-109s on the *Graf Zeppelin*, and here we sit on our thumbs and can't even properly arm our aircraft! Admiralty will have to take a very hard look at that."

"The *Fulmars* will be ready soon, sir. And Hawker *Hurricanes* are being considered for modification as catapult launched planes as well."

"Yes, but they aren't here at the moment, are they? No. We'll have to play the cards we have, and I've just lost a jack in HMS *Renown*. The real worry now is that the Germans have a bloody pair of kings out there, and a queen back of them with *Graf Zeppelin*. If we press on and catch up with them, we'll be outgunned two to one as it is. I need Holland and *Hood* now, and he's off chasing the Twins."

"Sir, if I may, we don't have to fight here. We can withdraw and effect a rendezvous with Admiral Holland. We've taken a knock here, but we've done at least one thing. Jerry hasn't turned into the Faeroes Gap. Our last sighting had them moving west. I think they're going to run up over Iceland, Admiral. Perhaps the plan is to join the Twins."

Tovey looked at the map, and thought hard. He had come east to fight and now he had lost *Renown* without ever getting *Bismarck* and *Tirpitz* under his guns! That German carrier out there was changing the rules of the game.

"What do we have at Reykjavik?"

"Sir? Well just two planes, Admiral, a *Sunderland* and a *Walrus*."

"See if we might persuade Wick to send something better. Those Beaus of Four Two Squadron sound enticing, torpedoes or no torpedoes. Damn it, we need air cover, and more than *Ark Royal* can give us at the moment. Make a request for a *Hurricane* squadron to be sent to Iceland at once."

"Most are assigned to homeland defense now, Admiral, but I'll see what we can find."

"You say the *Fulmars* are almost ready? I want them flown out if in any way possible. If they aren't ready for a carrier landing we'll pick them up at Reykjavik."

Then he remembered the aircraft carrier he and Brind had discussed at Scapa Flow before the fleet sailed—*Illustrious!* He had a perfectly good carrier back home working up on trials, and with new aircraft as well, including these *Fulmars*.

"Mister Villers, I hadn't thought to call on her so soon, but I'm afraid we'll have to enlist the services of *Illustrious* as well. I know she's still working up, but the situation appears critical to my eye now, and I want her out to sea and heading our way as soon as possible. And I want those *Beauforts* and *Hurricanes*. I know it may take some doing. The airfields on Iceland will have no equipment or service crews, but we must do whatever we can. The Germans can send their *Stukas* to bomb Iceland all they want, but they won't sink it, eh? Those airfields are essential."

"I'll see to those messages personally, sir."

"So... now we either shadow the Germans under threat of additional air strikes. Or we turn about and head back west to link up with Holland." Tovey folded his arms, chin in hand, considering. "Very well, we turn. Come to 230 degrees. Damn good licking and off we go. We'll turn this watch over to *Nelson* and *Rodney*, and it's down round Iceland for us again. Then we find *Hood* and *Repulse*. It's going to take a heavy fist to win this one, Mister Villers, a heavy fist indeed."

* * *

18 June, 1940 ~ 08:00 Hrs

The German oiler *Altmark* was waiting at the refueling point as ordered. One of five ships in its special class, *Altmark* already had a storied history in the young war, providing able support to the *Graf Spee* on her sortie, and then causing somewhat of an incident on her return leg home. Sailing in neutral Norwegian waters with nearly 300 British merchant sailors captured by the German pocket battleship in February of 1940, the ship was spotted by an RAF Coastal Command Hudson bomber. Elements of the neutral Norwegian Navy boarded *Altmark* the next day, but did not search the hold where the prisoners were being held. So the job was soon handed off to Captain Phillip

Vian aboard the destroyer HMS *Cossack.* The signal from the Admiralty was plain and simple: *"Altmark your objective. Act accordingly."*

Vian did exactly that, hunting down the tanker in Norwegian waters with a small task force of British destroyers and the light cruiser *Arethusa.* In spite of a Norwegian protest over the violation of its neutrality, Vian forced a boarding of the German ship, which ran aground while trying to frustrate that operation with an ill considered attempt to ram the *Cossack.* The British prisoners were found and freed, and *Altmark* was left with a bloody nose, run aground on the rocky coast. Churchill and Lord Halifax had both weighed in on the incident, which caused a bit of a diplomatic row, and also served as fuel for Admiral Raeder's argument that Norway must be invaded.

So the tanker had a way of finding itself in the center of the maelstrom, and finding its way to bad luck as well. It was renamed *Ukermark* and later fated to die in a freak explosion after delivering 5000 tons of gasoline to Yokohama, Japan in 1943. A spark from a cutting tool being used on the dock ignited residual fumes and the ship was nearly blown apart, a total wreck. Thankfully the crew had been ashore at lunch, and only 53 died, but the rest would not escape the bad luck of the renamed ship either. They would be dispatched to France on the German blockade runner *Doggerbank,* another ship that had been renamed, redoubling the bad luck. Crewman Fritz Kürt would later say that he could feel the black hand on the ship all along, and kept having fitful dreams, seeing the numbers 3 and 43 in his mind and by happenstance on the ship itself as they sailed through the wide lonesome stretches of the South Atlantic.

Doggerbank soon suffered the ignominious fate of being mistakenly torpedoed by a friendly German U-boat—three torpedoes from U-43 on the evening of 3 March, 1943, an eerie twist of bad luck and bad numbers. Fate had its bony hand on the throat of *Altmark* and her crew, and only one man of 365 would live to tell the tale. They thought they had escaped a fiery death in that explosion at Yokohama, but all they did now was bring their misfortune to the *Doggerbank*, which went into the sea in the middle of the Atlantic, a thousand miles east of Morocco.

Finally realizing its error, U-43 saw what it thought to be lifeboats, and edged closer to the flotsam of the ship, trying to question the survivors. In the fading light the U-boat could not get through the wreckage and close enough to hear them. So the German submarine turned and left the scene. Days later a single lifeboat was found by a Spanish tanker on March 29th.

There was one man alive there, Fritz Kürt, the last of the crew of *Altmark*, (then named *Ukermark*), who told the sad tale that while fifteen men had made it into the lifeboat, including the Captain of the *Doggerbank*, it capsized and only six were able to scramble back aboard with the ship's dog. Without food and water they drifted for days, trying to reach South America until one by one the parched and desperate survivors were claimed by death and suicide.

The Captain of *Doggerbank* had been trying to navigate by the stars, but lost hope and used his revolver to end his own misery. Fritz Kürt, however, had survived sinkings at sea before, and believed he could beat the odds and the terrible jinx that had dogged the crew of *Altmark*. He resolved to bear the suffering, preferring the last hours of life instead of a quick death. The only man left alive with him was an old sailor named Boywitt, who eventually drank seawater in his agony of thirst when the last of the rainwater ran out. Fritz pleaded with him not to do this, but he could not resist, and was soon delirious and failing fast.

Just after he died the skies burst with rain, providing all the fresh water the men could have needed, but by then it was too late. Only Fritz remained, and a flying fish that landed aboard the lifeboat in a random act of chance provided him with enough nourishment to survive until the Spanish Tanker *Campoamor* saved his life—the last crewman of that cursed ship *Altmark*. After learning of the incident where U-43 had sunk one of their own blockade runners, all pages concerning the episode were ordered ripped from the boat's log and destroyed.

It was an eerie and chilling end to that tale, but that was in another world, and none of it had yet happened. None of it might happen at all this time around. In the altered state of affairs where *Kirov* now sailed, *Altmark* was berthed for repairs for three months and then put to use again as soon as possible.

The Germans were considering renaming the ship to help disguise it now that the British had already made its acquaintance. They almost made the same mistake again but sailors have forever said that renaming a ship was a sure way to bring bad luck. So this time *Altmark* was left with her maiden name intact. As the battle of Norway concluded the ship was provisioned and slipped out to sea again, unnoticed by the British in their frantic effort to complete the evacuation. It would sail to the Denmark Strait and find a nice quiet break in the ice off the ragged coast of Greenland to wait out a humdrum week for Hoffmann's battlecruiser squadron to arrive. Now, on the morning of June 17, it would soon find itself in another storm at sea—a storm of fire and steel.

* * *

After some consideration and a collective decision by all the senior officers it was decided to investigate the lone contact off near Greenland to verify Fedorov's hunch. The weather was still bad, and Admiral Volsky did not want to send the KA-40 for closer observation, but Nikolin had been able to intercept coded messages that named the ship and specified the rendezvous time. Fedorov looked it up, the tanker *Altmark*, and related the strange story of its history to the Admiral.

"This tanker wasn't even supposed to be here. It should still be in repair for another few weeks, but obviously that history has changed. I know we all hesitate to do harm here but, if it is any consolation, this is a fated ship and crew. Only one man aboard will live two years to see 1943. All were fated to die except a man named Fritz Kürt." He described the incident at Yokohama and the strange fate of *Doggerbank* as Volsky listened.

"So he may be out there right now, this man."

"Possibly, sir."

"Bad luck seems to have found this ship again." Volsky sighed, but realized that this alternative was better than directly engaging the German battlecruisers, where much more force might have to be exerted to achieve the result they were hoping for.

"So we will strike this ship, a sacrificial lamb, and become a bit of a wolf here ourselves in the process. I suppose it can't be helped. We will chose your one missile solution, Mister Fedorov, but are there any better attack options? A missile will certainly reveal our position."

"We could use a torpedo, sir. Samsonov tells me we have both Vodopad and UGST Type 53s aboard."

"The Vodopads are a missile torpedo, we could strike with one from this position, but again, we reveal our position with that weapon so I think the Type 53 is the better option here. Those weapons range to 50 kilometers. Get us to the target, Mister Fedorov."

"Aye sir."

For the next hours *Kirov* closed the range, steering 250 on a southwesterly course that eventually brought it a little south of the *Altmark*. The ship's luck was about to run out again. Admiral Volsky finally gave the order to fire on the German tanker, his heart heavy with the thought that he was going to put men in the sea, and most likely take many lives with this action, in spite of Fedorov's consolation.

Chapter 26

The ship rode out the bad weather well enough, and Fritz Kürt was on the aft deck seeing to some hose lines as the skies cleared and the ocean swells began to calm. The weather was breaking up just in time for the refueling operation. That was good. There was nothing more difficult than trying to keep station with a hungry warship in high seas and bad visibility, but now the skies were brightening and the light was fine. He looked east to see the last trailing edge of the passing squalls, off to Iceland now to make rain or snow there, and good riddance, but he knew that this break would not last long. The cool foggy days of June and July were legendary here, where there was cloud cover 90% of the time in those months.

It came out of the storm like a bolt of thunder. The UGST was Russia's most modern standard 533mm torpedo, utilizing a water jet propulsor to travel up to 50 knots and achieve a range up to 50 kilometers. With a wakeless approach, it was very difficult to spot as it homed in on its target to deliver a 300kg warhead, which was 660 pounds of high explosives.

No man saw it, but every man aboard knew what had happened the instant after it exploded. *Altmark* shuddered amidships, where gun munitions had been stored to replenish the battlecruisers if needed. The magazine had been hit dead on and the explosion broke her back in one mighty blow, as though the fist of Poseidon had hammered the keel of the ship. Fritz was thrown from his feet, barely managing to get to his knees when the everything blew amidships. Then he was thrown completely off the ship, scuppered into the sea and flailing to get his hands on anything around him that was thrown into the water with him.

There were 365 men aboard that day, and most were going into the sea with him soon after that explosion…those that were still alive. There was not even time to get off one last plaintive S.O.S. on the wireless for aid before the ship began to sink. A residual of thick black oil was coating the water all about the stricken vessel, some of it already burning and filling the air about the scene with thick, acrid smoke. Fritz knew he had to get as far from it as he could if he wanted to survive.

Torpedo, he thought grimly. Someone noticed us out here and got suspicious. The British have U-boats too. Yes, it had to be a torpedo. Nothing else breaks the back of a ship like that with one hit. Will they surface and turn the machine guns on us? Thank God it's June and the water is not so cold. And thank God the battlecruisers are close by, due in a another three hours. So hold on Fritz, you'll make it through this one. They can sink *Altmark* but they'll never sink Fritz Kürt.

He could still see crews scrambling on the sinking ship, trying to get to any lifeboat they could float, but Fritz was soon glad to be pulling his tired wet body onto a wide section of broken deck plank. The jinx that seemed to follow the ship had struck again, he thought. Well that is the last we'll ever see of *Altmark*. Yes…It must have been a torpedo.

He drifted for some time, shivering with shock and cold, yet knowing all would be well. Some inner sense told him he would live through this, that he had been through much worse before this and survived. Then he saw what looked to be one of the battlecruisers, a dark ship on the horizon coming from the retreating edge of the storm. He smiled, weary and tired, but knowing that rescue was close at hand. But to his chagrin, the ship turned away and slowly slipped beneath the horizon.

What are they doing? He could not believe that their comrades would abandon them like this. Why? Was it fear of the submarine that had attacked them here? That was the grim logic of war. He could see the Kapitan of *Scharnhorst* making such a decision. His ship and crew were all that mattered to him. We are no more than a burden to him now. He passed a moment of quiet despair, then shook himself, bolstering his will to survive. Someone will find us, he knew. I will not die here. He was correct, because the ship he had seen was not one of the German raiders.

Two hours later when Hoffmann arrived on the scene with *Scharnhorst* and *Gneisenau*, he swore quietly under his breath. They had seen the smoke from some distance after they broke through the back edge of the weather front. He did not know what he was looking at then, but he had misgivings at once. The smoke soon became fire, and then they saw the dark stain of oil on the sea, the flotsam of wreckage, and men clinging to floating crates and shards of deck wood. There were three lifeboats afloat, crowded with weary wet survivors, and they were shouting and waving at his battlecruisers as they approached.

And there is my oil, he thought grimly, there it sits, burning on the sea. Now how can I continue south with my belly half empty and the nearest friendly port over 3500 kilometers away? If I make it we'll be running on fumes when we get to the French coast, and there will be no fuel for hunting convoys. Now I must look for another tanker, and this will upset the timetable of the entire operation.

He looked for Huber, his face set, eyes resigned. "Make to Wilhelmshaven. Tell them *Altmark* has been sunk and we have been unable to refuel." See what Raeder thinks of that one, he thought, but for the moment it was his problem, and now he had to decide what to do about it. He was sitting at the point of no return. Sail on and there was no guarantee that he would get his ships to a safe port, though he knew there were other German oilers in the Atlantic for this operation. He would wait two hours, three at the most, to hear from Wilhelmshaven.

The British know we are here, and if one of their submarines sunk *Altmark*, then they will know where we are as well. There will be more than a few cruisers about shortly. The Royal Navy may be gathering like a pack of crows further south.

"And Huber," he said quietly. "Signal *Admiral Hipper* and tell them to come to this point at their best speed. As soon as we get any survivors aboard and get some rum into them we must get out and find some sea room. Post submarine watches on every quarter. Get boats out all along our starboard side and drop the anti-torpedo nets. That British U-boat may still be lurking here."

* * *

Rodenko watched the two German battlecruisers on radar as they reached the rendezvous point with the tanker. *Kirov* was hovering just over the horizon now, the ship Fritz Kürt had seen. He updated the tactical situation board on the electronic map, briefing Fedorov and the Admiral.

"We are here, sir, about 20 kilometers from their refueling point. As we moved to this location the German battlecruisers were on a parallel course to our north, just over the horizon. We're still jamming their radar, so I don't think they will find us unless we show ourselves. Even for a large ship, we are relatively quiet, and they may not even hear us on hydrophones. As for the British, we've lost our track on them for the moment. They would be well to the east, and still in the weather front based on their last position and our predictive plot."

"We could re-acquire the British with the KA-40, Admiral." Fedorov was looking at the map, considering the situation. "They turned in our direction just before we diverted west to make this intervention. If that predictive plot holds true I think it would put them about 200 kilometers east of us now."

"The two cruisers?"

"No sir, I was referring to the stronger contacts we had earlier, most likely capital ships. I believe the cruisers are still well to the northeast."

"And we also have this track here," said Rodenko.

"That will be *Admiral Hipper*," said Fedorov. "It appears to be steering to rejoin the battlecruisers."

"And so what can we deduce from this? Will the Germans proceed into the Atlantic even without refueling here as they planned?"

"That remains to be seen, Admiral. It would be my guess that they are recovering survivors now and possibly awaiting further instructions."

"And if they do proceed? What then, gentlemen? In that event we will have wasted a torpedo here and achieved nothing but the addition of a little more misery to this cup of war."

"If they do proceed it will mean they have decided to attempt a refueling rendezvous in the Atlantic."

"So then we either leave them to the British and head north as planned or we continue this intervention and stop them."

"From their present position I believe they will evade the British and make a successful breakout, sir." Fedorov was all business now, his sharp mind looking at every side of the question.

"If we are to engage," said Rodenko, "we are in a fairly good position now. They will most likely come due south and right across our bow when we spot them."

"Yes, and at first blush they will think they have sighted a British battleship."

"They have shown a tendency to try and avoid such an encounter, sir. When they sunk the British auxiliary cruiser *Rawalpindi* between Iceland and the Faeroes they even ran from the cruiser *Newcastle*, and that was a ship in the same class as the two they just engaged here. In the Norway operation they ran into the battlecruiser *Renown* and choose to run again when engaged."

"But they did not run this time," said Volsky. "It has been my observation that it is that man that runs, not the ship. He is either cautious or aggressive at sea. Perhaps this German squadron has a new commander."

"That is possible, sir."

Hearing mention of *Renown*, Nikolin turned and spoke now. "Excuse me, Admiral, but that ship you are discussing, I intercepted a message half an hour ago. *Renown* was damaged in an engagement off the east coast of Iceland and is now returning to Scapa Flow."

"A sea engagement?" Fedorov was surprised to hear this.

"No, the signal mentioned an air attack."

"Air attack? That is fairly far from the Norwegian coast to have German planes make a successful attack. Very strange."

"Thank you, Mister Nikolin," said Volsky. "Keep listening with those sharp ears of yours, but we are still left with the question of what to do here at the moment. We must either engage or break off and head north as planned, but Fedorov believes the Germans might just have their cake and eat it too, despite our attack on that tanker."

"We can still stop them," said Rodenko, "but if we break off I agree with Fedorov. They will get down into the Atlantic if the British are where we believe them to be."

"At the moment they are still at that rendezvous point," said Fedorov, "probably recovering survivors and waiting on *Hipper*, or else orders from higher up the chain of command. We have jammed their radar. Could we not also jam their communications?"

"What are you thinking, Fedorov?"

"Suppose they are waiting for new orders, and suppose they never receive them?"

Volsky thought about that. "Then I think we will learn the character of man in command there, whether he is cautious or aggressive. Make it so, Mister Nikolin. Jam their communications bands if possible. I want to test the mettle of this German Captain."

"I have another alternative," said Fedorov. "We could contact the British right now and send them the position of the German ships. If they turn soon they may have a chance to cut them off. It all depends on when, or if, the Germans move."

"Contact them?" Volsky smiled. "Well we have already tipped our hat to that plane once. I suppose we could do this. We could say we are that Russian cruiser as before. I like this idea Fedorov! Very well, I hope you've been polishing your English, Nikolin."

* * *

Able Seaman Hubert Witte was standing by in the wireless room aboard *Scharnhorst*, ready to run the next message to the bridge as per his assignment there. But he had a very long wait. The Radio Chief was surly, fussing with his equipment, selecting this band and that, listening, tapping at his headset, and getting more and more unhappy as the time went by.

"This is not the storm," he said finally. "We are being jammed. I have tried three separate communications bands now, and I get the same interference on all three. Get to the Kapitan and inform him, Witte. Tell him if he is waiting for orders from Wilhelmshaven they just might never come. Yes. We're being jammed."

The message was not well received by Kapitan Hoffmann. "Jammed? That would have to mean another ship was very close. Anything on radar, Huber?"

"No sir. They can't shake this interference either. Perhaps that storm has the atmosphere all charged up."

"This is not from the storm, Huber. The front is well past us. Now we can't even receive a goddamned radio message." He wondered if that British submarine was still out there somewhere, surfaced, unseen on some quarter and operating new British jamming equipment. Suddenly the cool air after the storm seemed hot at his neck, and he frowned, deciding.

"Anything on the hydrophones?"

"Nothing, sir."

"Well, we are sitting ducks here. Have the last of the survivors been taken aboard?"

"They have, sir."

"Then we're heading south as planned."

"But Kapitan, what about the fuel situation?"

"What about it? You think this was the only tanker assigned to this operation? We'll find something in the Atlantic if I can get off a message to inform Wilhelmshaven of this development. The British got to *Altmark* before we did. Now that submarine is out there radioing our coordinates and jamming us, by God! We leave *now*. Helm, come to one-eight-zero south and ahead two thirds. Signal *Gneisenau* to follow. *Hipper* will have to either find us or fend for itself."

They snookered us good on this one, he thought. Two damn cruisers and a good submarine Captain. Well, at least I put a heavy round into that cruiser. But the scales have not yet been balanced. If they thought sinking *Altmark* was going to cancel this operation then they will now get the bad news.

He went to his Flag Bridge, sitting down at a small desk there and removing a plain brown leather folio from the drawer. There were his original orders, to be destroyed should the ship ever be placed in a compromising position.

By now Kapitan Lindemann will have pushed his nose towards the Iceland-Faeroes Gap to see what the British have waiting for him there. He is either running the gap as I sit here, or perhaps shifting further west to take the Denmark Strait on our heels.

He flipped ahead to his support schedule. There it was: *Altmark - 0:600 hours, June 18.* Too bad we were just a little late. Running his finger down the page he looked for his alternate refueling point. *Nordmark, DHRX – Discretionary – Currently holding: diesel, lubricants, armament stores, victuals. On station through 21-6-40 before moving to grid location 3C.*

He noted the planned operations zone of the ship, somewhat discouraged. It would require him to backtrack to the north if he wanted fuel now. Otherwise it could be three or four days before he could find another tanker in the Atlantic. He would keep *Nordmark* in his back pocket. It was a long way back to Trondheim. Even if *Bismarck* and *Tirpitz* do get through, they will be hungry as well when they get into the Atlantic. That was the one thing Hitler and Raeder should have thought a little more about when they built the fleet—the goddamned fuel! Where do we get the fuel to keep all these ships at sea? The Russians are sitting on top of half the oil, and the British in Persia have the other half. Yes, Orenburg has declared itself and joined Germany this week, but getting any oil from them will be no easy matter.

The ship was already turning, moving, the powerful engines building up speed. He did not like the feeling settling in his gut now. Something was not right here. That engagement with the British cruisers still galled him, and he had the lingering suspicion that there had been a third ship nearby when that action was fought. No cruiser he had ever heard of could score two direct hits like that at over 18,000 meters in bad visibility. Something else hit them, hidden, unseen in the concealing mist and fog. Then there was the strange interference affecting the radars and now even his ship to shore transmissions. And was that attack on *Altmark* just a chance occurrence, the fortunes of war, or was there something more sinister behind it?

Settle down, he told himself. You are tired, cold, hungry now. A man never thinks right when he's hungry. What you need now is a good cup of coffee and a little food. That will set your mind right. …But why do I have the strange feeling that someone is watching me, reading me like a book, gauging my every move?

Chapter 27

When the message came in Admiral Holland did not know quite what to make of it. Now he was conferring with Captain Glennie when a midshipman handed off a note. The W/T room had received a message: 'SIGHTED TWO LARGE WARSHIPS, BELIEVED GERMAN BATTLECRUISERS, POSITION 67.14,-31.27 – COURSE 180 – SPEED 20 – SS KRV'

"SS KRV? What ship is that?"

"I'm told that is the call sign for the Russian cruiser *Kirov*, sir. Convoy HX–49, sighted it some days ago heading northeast for the Denmark Strait."

"Nothing more from *Birmingham*?"

"Not since we were last notified of *Manchester's* departure for Reykjavík. We may run into her soon if we stay on this course. It seems they had a run in with the Twins, and thought the better of trading with them."

Holland took a look at the map, laying out his rulers to cross index those coordinates. "That would put this sighting about 120 nautical miles west of us, and now heading south at 20 knots. If this is so the Germans have certainly shaken off our cruisers."

"Yet *Birmingham* signaled they were engaged again, and believe the ship was firing 8-inch rounds."

"That would be the *Hipper*," Holland concluded. "Most likely detached to keep our boys busy while the Twins made a run for it. But what are they doing so far west off Greenland?"

"They could be meeting a tanker, sir. It's a long way from Trondheim, and it also puts them in a very good position to get by us, and out into the Atlantic. We would have to turn immediately to have any chance of staying with them. Look here…" He laid out a pair of rulers, one to mark the contact's course south at 20 knots, and the other to plot an intercept. *Hood* would have to travel the long edge of the triangle.

"They'll travel a 100 nautical miles in the next five hours if they are moving as this sighting report suggests. To catch them now we'll have to cover 160 miles, and run up at 30 knots the whole way."

"Yes, but on the word of a Russian cruiser? Wasn't this ship being regarded with some suspicion by the Admiralty? Cruiser *Kirov?* All the information we have placed this ship in the Baltic. What do you make of this, Captain Glennie?"

"We know *Scharnhorst* and *Gneisenau* are out there, sir. The hole they put in *Manchester* is ample evidence of that. This position sighting would correspond to their last known heading after that engagement."

"Damn, what's happening with *Birmingham?* Why haven't we heard anything further?"

"Last word we had she was still under fire. There's been nothing since."

"I can't say as I like the sound of that." Holland leaned heavily on the map table considering what to do. He was noting position of convoy traffic out of Halifax, his eyes dark and concerned.

"TC-5 left on 11 June with a full brigade on troop ships."

"They should be well east and out of the threat zone by now, sir."

"Yes, but have a look at HX-50. Forty-eight ships, and a good number carrying fuel oil, petrol, gasoline, crude, even benzene. They'll be four days out now and the Commodore's report on sailing was that there were eleven neutrals in the sailing order, very slow, most unable to make even nine knots in fair weather and calm seas At that speed they would be about 100 miles south of Cape Farewell by now, and a fairly ripe tree for the picking. Captain Glennie, I think we must turn southeast and see about this sighting, yet I want this contact verified before we go running off into the blue. We have orders to link up with Admiral Tovey, but if this report holds water, then the Twins will sink their teeth into HX-50 and raise havoc. The only escort presently with the convoy is the armed merchant cruiser *Voltaire*—just a former passenger ship with a few 6-inch deck guns."

"Nothing that will bother the Twins, sir."

"Indeed. Contact *Repulse*. As soon as this weather breaks I want them to get a *Fairey III* up and search out ahead of us to look for the Germans."

The *Fairey III* was a three-seat spotter-reconnaissance biplane adopted by the Fleet Air Arm for use on large ships and carriers. It was small enough to be launched by catapult from a ship like *Repulse*, which was carrying two planes at the moment. *Hood* had her catapult, crane, and turret-mounted flying off platforms removed some time ago when they were deemed too wet for suitable use.

"If we do spot them," said Holland "then we'll go full out and attempt to engage. For now we turn on 230 and increase to 28 knots. At the very least we may be able to get close enough to protect this convoy."

Captain Glennie nodded. "Shall I look into this business concerning the Russian cruiser, sir?"

"See what more Admiralty has on it. Events are stacking up like dirty dishes here, Captain. Tovey ran into a hornet's nest east of Iceland. Jerry put a couple of 500 pounders into *Renown*—Stukas! Now Home Fleet is heading back our way. It looks like *Bismarck* and *Tirpitz* are swinging up north of Iceland, and they obviously have *Graf Zeppelin* with them."

"That's a rough go for Tovey now, sir. Without *Renown* he's badly outgunned."

"Which is why he's consolidating with us. We had better pass this sighting on to him as well, and I can tell you now he won't like it. Tell him we're investigating the contact but will remain in a good position to effect a link-up with Home Fleet at his discretion. If we don't act on this information now the Germans could slip right out into the Atlantic and raise hell. HX-51 was supposed to have left Halifax today. That's another thirty-five ships on our watch. If nothing turns up in the air search we can always swing back east if need be, but we can't leave these convoys exposed like this."

"Very good, sir."

* * *

Kapitan Hoffmann was below decks, checking on the condition of the super-heaters in the boiler rooms. *Scharnhorst* had difficulty with them for some time, most recently in her encounter with the British carrier that managed to slip away, in part because the ship's speed fell off at a crucial time and she could not pursue effectively. The Kapitan did not want anything of the sort to plague him out here. To conserve fuel and keep the pressure on the heating tubes reasonable, he had kept speed to 20 knots. They would need nothing more unless the ship had to go into action.

He spoke with Rolf Zanger in the number one boiler room, and all seemed well.

"How are our new recruits faring, Kapitan," asked Zangler.

"You mean the men off *Altmark*? Still drying out with a belly full of rum. Half of them will be scrubbing the oil off their backs for days."

"We had one man in here an hour ago looking for work. He told quite a tale, sir. Said he thought he spotted us to the east, and that we were going to leave them in the water. Says we sailed right off, sir."

"That's nonsense. We were north of *Altmark* when we came on the scene. The man was obviously disoriented."

"Could be, sir, but he seemed fit and ready for work, an old salt. That sort knows a compass heading well enough."

"Who was this man?"

"Called himself Fritz, sir. I told him to rest and come back tomorrow."

"Alright, Rolf. Keep my boilers in line. I may need speed in the hours ahead."

"You can count on us, Kapitan."

Hoffmann headed forward, thinking about what Zanger had told him. It dangled in his mind with all the other odd threads that had been bothering him ever since they first engaged those two British cruisers. The man says he saw another ship out east…It was probably nothing, but with the radar still down we're blind as a bat out here. It's time we got an *Arado* up and had a look around. I've learned more than once to follow a hunch when it won't leave me alone.

He resolved to get two search planes up at once, one from his ship to have a look out east, just in case this survivor's report was more than his wishful thinking, and a second from *Gneisenau* to have a look north and see about *Hipper* and the British cruisers.

* * *

"Well, Mister Fedorov, it seems our plan has achieved mixed results." Volsky was looking at the latest long range radar plots, clearly not happy. "The Germans are moving south in spite of our intervention. We apparently have a man with considerable backbone in command of that squadron, and though our message to the British seems to have prompted them to turn as well, it does not look like they will intercept any time soon. What is the predictive plot on this, Rodenko?"

"If both contacts hold present course and speed they will sight each other in five hours, and the Germans be on our horizon in less than an hour if we remain here. They'll pass just west of our present position, very near the horizon."

The ship had been hovering, describing a wide circle about twenty-five kilometers from the scene of their torpedo strike on *Altmark*. Now Volsky had to decide their next course.

"Five hours. That would be a sight to see, eh Fedorov?"

"Under other circumstances I might agree, sir, but after dueling with *Rodney* and *Nelson*, and then hammering it out with *Yamato*, I think I'd prefer to keep as far from a hostile battleship as possible."

"Agreed."

A call from the intercom interrupted them, and Rodenko flipped the switch. The voice of Chief Dobrynin was on the line, and he sounded bothered and very concerned. *"Admiral, we have a problem."*

"What kind of problem, Chief?"

"I'm getting those unusual flux levels in the core of number one reactor—that's the system we used in this last shift, sir. I don't like it, and I want to cut power there immediately to have a closer look and see what is going on."

"What will that mean, Chief? We may have company soon."

"You'll have fifty percent power until I bring that reactor back up, and it could be several hours."

"How serious is it? Can the procedure wait?"

"I would not advise it, sir. I'm not happy about these flux levels. If they get any higher we could get a reactor scram, and I have had to lock out our special control rod."

"What does this mean, Chief?"

"If a scram occurs all the unused control rods are immediately inserted into the core to stop the reaction, sir. But I've locked out the special rod in the number 25 position. We won't get a complete shutdown in an emergency and I could be forced to use a boron injection. That could contaminate the fuel cladding. In that event restart is much more complex and could take a good long while."

Volsky folded his arms. This was not good. The ship was already hobbled by the hull damage to the bow, and now to have the reactors acting up was even worse. They had superb situational awareness, able to see any potential threat on radar long before it could close with them, but without the speed to evade contact, they could find themselves in a very uncomfortable situation.

"Very well, Mister Dobrynin. I'll need power for at least an hour. Can you hold things together that long?"

"I will monitor it closely, Admiral."

"Keep us informed if the situation worsens."

"Aye, sir."

Volsky looked at his senior officers. "Not a very satisfactory situation. Plot a safe course to evade the Germans as they come south, Mister Fedorov. The last thing we need now is a pair of German battlecruisers darkening our horizon."

They turned east at twenty knots, chasing the last squall lines as they fled towards Iceland. Rodenko was keeping a watchful eye near the radar station when he was surprised to suddenly pick up airborne contacts. He started to report, then stopped himself, realizing how he had been hovering over Kalinichev there, and assuming his duty. So he tapped the man on the shoulder. "Make your report, Kalinichev. I'll update the situation map."

Kalinichev nodded. "Con, Radar. I have two airborne contacts. One bearing two-eight-zero, very close at 22,000 meters. Designate Alpha one. The second bearing one-one-five, range 150, flying low and slow. It just came on my scope, sir."

"They have to be seaplanes off the capital ships," said Fedorov. "The German battlecruisers carried the *Arado* 196."

"So we have jammed their radar and they want to have a look around," said Volsky. "I assume the British are doing the very same thing."

"The weather is clearing, sir. This is a logical deployment."

"Very well…We've already been sighted once by British search planes without incident. The Germans are another matter. Are these planes armed?"

"They could carry 250 kilograms of bombs, but I doubt they will be configured that way for a simple search operation. It's unlikely they would attack if they sight us, sir."

"But they would reveal our position to this German Captain out there. How fast are his ships?"

"Both were rated for thirty-two knots, Admiral."

"And Dobrynin is asking us to reduce to fifteen. Well that cannot happen any time soon now. If we hold this speed we may just be able to ease off to the east, but if those German ships get curious?"

He raised his thick grey brows, a warning in his eyes.

* * *

Schulman saw the ship plain as day. He had been flying the *Arado* for three years now, and was well experienced. The Kapitan had told him to have a look out east, and lo and behold, what was this hovering just over the horizon? It was big, a large warship to be sure, and every line and angle of the ship looked threatening. There was power there. He immediately notified his signalman to send off a message.

"Let's hope they hear us," the man returned. "The ship's communications were all fouled up, from what I heard."

"Send it anyway. This ship is very close. If need be I can turn around and get back to *Scharnhorst* in a few minutes."

Even as he said that he knew that it was the wisest course. That had to be a British warship out there, a battleship, he thought. It was just his luck that he came upon it as *Kirov* was still cruising west, ready to make its turn to evade any possible conflict here. But the course change came too late. Schulman had seen enough to be justifiably worried. In his mind the ship was bearing down on his comrades and he set his mind to make sure they were warned.

"Has *Scharnhorst* confirmed receipt of our signal?"

"Not yet, Leutnant."

"Then we go and deliver the mail ourselves. That ship is not far over their horizon and it looks to be trouble."

He banked away, feeding power to his engines and turning for *Scharnhorst* again. It was the easiest search patrol he had ever flown.

Part X

Shadow of Death

*"Yea, though I walk through the valley of the shadow of death,
I will fear no evil: for thou art with me; thy rod and thy staff
they comfort me..."*

— Psalms 23:4

Chapter 28

Kapitan Hoffman had just settled into a chair in his ready room for much needed coffee when the lookouts spotted the plane returning. They called the air warning, sending the ship to battle stations and quickly ending his anticipated rest. He was up on his feet again at once, and out onto the weather bridge.

"What is it?"

"There, Kapitan." Huber pointed low on the horizon where a plane was bearing down on them. "Someone is curious."

Hoffmann took a pair of field glasses from the rack and raised them to his tired eyes. A minute later he smiled. "Secure from battle stations," he said quietly. "What's wrong with your eyes today, Huber? That's our *Arado*."

He handed Huber the glasses, and the other man looked again. "So it is, sir. I thought it was a *Swordfish*. What are they doing back here already? They just took off fifteen minutes ago."

"Most likely engine trouble," said Hoffmann. "I'll be in my ready room off the bridge, and my coffee better not be cold, Leutnant."

"I'm sorry, sir."

The Kapitan's coffee was still warm, but he soon learned there was nothing wrong with the seaplane's engines. The plane circled, fluttered off the starboard side and landed on the sea, the long green pontoons scudding through the waves as it thrummed its way toward the ship. *Scharnhorst* slowed as the plane came along side and they signaled *Gneisenau* by lamp to take the van. It was not long before Huber was in the Kapitan's ready room again.

"Schulmann has come back to report a sighting, Kapitan, south east over the horizon. Very close!"

"What's wrong with his damn radio? We have to slow to five knots to recover his plane and that submarine could still be out there."

"The interference, sir. He says he sent the message but received no confirmation, so he came back himself, and lucky for us. He reports a large warship—heavy cruiser or battleship!"

"Battleship?" That got Hoffmann's attention, and all he could think of was that odd story Rolf Zanger had told him in the boiler room. There *was* another ship close by. Like an itch that had just been scratched he nodded with a self-satisfied half smile on his face.

"Tell Schulmann to get back in his plane and take off again. Come to thirty knots and turn on the reported heading. Signal *Gneisenau* and see that they are informed."

"Aye, sir."

"Any news yet on the whereabouts of *Hipper?*"

"Nothing yet, sir. But the wireless—"

"Yes, the damn wireless is still all fouled up."

Another ship, thought Hoffmann. This could be the ship that has been jamming us. There may have been a third cruiser out here working with the others, or perhaps a battleship.

"What was the contact's course and speed?"

"Two-three-zero and cruising at about fifteen knots."

"In no hurry…" But that heading would put it off his port bow in little time. "The ship will come to battle stations. Raise flags for *Gneisenau.*"

"We are going to fight here, Kapitan?"

"I want to have a look at this ship. If it is a cruiser, then it was probably shadowing us for some time and with the radar jammed we could not see it. In that event we will see how they like our guns. If it is a battleship, then we will show them our wake. If they pursue and manage to keep station that will say much as to what this ship is. Only a fast battlecruiser like *Hood* could keep up with us."

"And if it is *Hood*, sir?"

Hoffmann gave him a long look. "Why then things get very interesting, don't they, Huber. Go! Get to the bridge with those orders. I'll be there in a moment."

* * *

"We've been seen, but the plane has turned away, Admiral." Rodenko saw that it had already slipped back over the horizon. "It appears to be returning to the German battlecruisers."

"The tattletale runs home," said Volsky. "I don't suppose it would have done us any good to shoot that plane down. The missile fire and explosion would have been seen by those ships. We are too close, and now we are sitting here like a big fat goose in a pond. How long before the reactors can give us normal power again?"

During the sighting they had another call from Chief Dobrynin. The flux levels were too high. They were very near a critical state on the number one reactor that would soon require a complete shutdown if not mitigated. He wanted permission to begin scaling down that reaction to see what was happening, but it meant that the ship had to reduce power for a time. *Kirov* slowed to just ten knots, and there was a noticeable rise in the tension on the bridge.

Rodenko kept a wary eye on the radar with Kalinichev, soon seeing what he feared most. "They are turning, Admiral. And their speed is up near thirty knots now. They should break the horizon in a few minutes off our aft port quarter."

"And what will they think of us here," Volsky thought aloud.

"We won't give away much from that perspective," said Fedorov. "But if we come around and give them our full silhouette, we might put the fear of the lord into them when they see our size."

"You are suggesting they may break off if they see us as a threat?"

"It's a possibility, sir. Their real intent is to get into the Atlantic and attack the convoys. All we are is an obstacle. If they think we are a cruiser trying to shadow them, we could be in jeopardy here. But if they think we are something more…"

"There they are, sir!" A forward lookout had seen something on the horizon.

"Activate the Tin Man. Let us have a closer look."

All eyes were fixed on the overhead screen as the high powered cameras in the Tin Man focused and resolved on the contact. First one, then a second ship appeared, their battlements tall and dark against the horizon. Admiral Volsky glanced at Fedorov.

"That will be *Scharnhorst* and *Gneisenau*, sir. No doubt about it now. The British called them the Twins."

"Beautiful ships."

"Beautiful but deadly, Admiral. They will be carrying nine 11-inch guns each and will have the range in five minutes."

Volsky raised an eyebrow at that. "Helm come left to three-thirty. Let's show them our full silhouette as Mister Fedorov suggests." It was as if a pair of gunfighters were slowly squaring off a fifty paces, and *Kirov* was reaching to move aside its overcoat, and reveal the gun on her hip. They wanted to look every bit as threatening as the distant ships closing on them.

"The ship will come to full battle stations," Volsky said quietly, his eyes fixed on the Tin Man display, watching the other gunfighter's hands very closely for the slightest twitch or indication that he was ready to draw.

"Mister Samsonov, what is our present SSM missile inventory?"

"Sir, nine missiles on each of the three primary systems."

"Then ready on the MOS-III system. Target the lead ship."

The Admiral looked at Fedorov. "In for a penny, in for a pound, Fedorov. If those ships fire I'm going to show them who they are dealing with, and in no uncertain terms…before they demonstrate that famous German marksmanship and end our little journey in a most uncomfortable way."

Fedorov said nothing.

* * *

Hoffmann was on the weather bridge, eyes glued to his field glasses and standing like another tin man, his posture stiff and straight. He saw the dark shade stain the horizon and had an eerie feeling, as if he were looking at the shadow of death itself. It slowly fattened and extend and he knew the ship was turning. The squadron was at battle stations, running fast, their bows white with sea spray. He saw the big turrets turn, barrels elevating, and looked again.

"What do we have here?" he said aloud to himself. "That is no cruiser…" No. It was much too big, its bow high and the long foredeck strangely clean and empty. Then the superstructure rose, tier after tier to a high mast where something gleamed in the grey light, a blur of motion there. But he could see no guns, nothing more than a few secondary batteries. He thought this might be a large liner, another British auxiliary cruiser impressed into the ranks and forced to wear war paint, but it did not look like any passenger ship he had ever set eyes on.

This is a battleship…*Look* at it. It has an evil aspect, imposing, menacing. Look at its size! The bow is high and proud, and the bridge and main mast is well back. The ship looks fast, but they can't be making any more than ten or fifteen knots, as if they had all the time in the world, heedless…or fearless…but where are the guns? There's nothing on that long forward deck at all.

It was not *Nelson* or *Rodney*. This ship was much longer than either of those ships, by at least a third. It was easily as big as *Hood*, though it looked nothing like that ship. Could it be the British G# battlecruiser? But no, that ship had two prominent stacks. There were no stacks here. This ship is not making smoke at all, just sitting there, turning like some grey behemoth that has slowly taken notice of intruders, with bad intent.

There was a high standard on a mast amidships, but he could not make it out at this distance. It fluttered like a black ghost above the ship, indiscernible. They can clearly see us, but yet they do not fire, he thought. Perhaps this is some strange commercial ship, a big toothless tanker rigged out to look like more than it is.

The Germans had played tricks of their own like that. Their commerce raiders like *Orion, Thor* and *Komet* would carry false stacks, wooden and canvass facades to mimic new funnels, gun turrets, and change the ship's superstructure and silhouette. Deception was as much a part of war as anything else, but this was the most mysterious looking ship Hoffmann had ever seen. It was time to break the impasse and send greetings and salutations. If the radio was jammed then he would do it the old fashioned way. If this ship was his dark and nefarious shadow, the source of the jamming that had confounded his radar and communications, then he would soon find out. There was nothing else in the sea around them that would be deemed a friendly vessel, except the *Hipper*, and he could recognize that ship's silhouette easily.

He passed a brief moment of hesitation. What if this is a neutral ship, an American warship of some kind? So he decided to begin with a warning shot, the proverbial shot across the bow.

"Huber! Signal *Gneisenau* to hold fire for the moment. We will say hello with Anton and see what comes back."

Anton was, of course, the forward "A" turret on the ship. He looked over his shoulder, craning his neck as the battle flags rose to communicate his message. *Gneisenau* winked her aft lamps to indicate they had received and understood the order. Satisfied, Hoffmann settled his cap firmly on his head and slowly raised his field glasses. 'The praetorian' was going to announce himself.

"Warning shot off the bow. Lead them, but make it close."

The triple turret slowly rotated, three barrels elevating, wet with sea spray. Then they fired, the bright flash followed by a deafening roar, and heavy black smoke rolled out to port. It had begun.

Hoffmann watched the long fall of the shells, waiting for the geysers to mark the shot. He saw them plunge into the sea thirty seconds later, tall and white.

"Range?" He called in to Schubert, his gunnery officer.

"19,500 and closing. Those warning shots were short, but we'll have the range soon enough."

The Kapitan waited, observing the distant ship closely. They had not returned fire, but yet they were not running, still cruising sedately along as if they had no care in the world. Then he saw what looked like an explosion on the forward deck, and for the barest instant he thought one of the rounds had been under charged and was coming in late, hitting the ship square on the foredeck.

He could even see what looked to be a fragment of the deck thrown up into the air, then it exploded again, or so he believed until he saw something come hurtling toward them, soaring up and then diving for the sea.

The MOS-III was the fastest missile in the Russian inventory, *Zvezdnyy ogon'*, the *Starfire*. It had a range of 160 kilometers, and could cross that distance at 1.7 kilometers per second after a ten second acceleration burn, five times the speed of sound. To Hoffmann as he watched it seemed as though the thin white stream stretching out behind the object was a javelin shaft of lightning.

The bright fire of its engine cast an evil glow on the sea as it raced in, right for *Gneisenau*, low over the wave tops. Then at the last it leapt like a flying fish in a programmed popup maneuver and smashed into the heart of the ship, right above the gunwales. There was a violent explosion as the missile delivered its 300 kilogram warhead, the same size as the UGST torpedo that had broken the back of *Altmark* earlier. The roar of the missile's engines still followed, finally catching up just after it thundered against the ship.

Hoffmann gaped at the scene, seeing *Gneisenau* roll with the heavy punch, the broiling smoke and fire amidships burning fiercely hot from the excess fuel left in the missile. A secondary anti-aircraft battery was completely immolated. The missile had struck very near the funnel, just above the number four boiler room. The lifeboat there was completely devoured, and the blow had penetrated deeply into the ship, gutting mess halls, quarters, repair shops , storage areas and very nearly blasting its way out the starboard side of the superstructure. Everything in its fiery path was destroyed. The smoke towered up, heavy and black, three times the height of the ship.

"Mein Gott!" Hoffmann was stunned by the sudden lethal violence returned by the distant intruder. This was a battleship, most certainly, but what in the world had it fired at them? Rockets! He knew that Germany was hard at work on them even now, but apparently the British were too! One shot, one hit, and look at the fire on *Gneisenau!*

"Huber! Give them both turrets and then hard to starboard and ahead full. We have the devil to pay!"

It was his transgression, he thought, but *Gneisenau* paid the price so far. *Scharnhorst* fired, guns belching retribution, and then the ship wheeled hard right, churning up the sea with the violence of the turn.

Curiosity killed the cat. The Kapitan was heading for the armored citadel, his face drawn and set. The smoke from the fire on *Gneisenau* was lying heavy on the sea, the black smoky blood of a stricken steel ship. They had managed to see his turn, and now turned with him, but not before they let off a salvo from their aft turret.

The two ships were now racing away from the enemy, and quickly opening the range. *Gneisenau's* speed was slightly off, which meant the fires amidships may have gotten to one of the boiler rooms. Hoffmann wanted no part of this mysterious British battleship. His only consolation was that the enemy seemed to have no speed. It could not follow and slowly receded, disappearing over the horizon.

If we hadn't slowed to recover that *Arado* we would have been in the van and it would be my ship burning now, he thought grimly, my men charred in that fire. One thought seared his mind now, the dark smoke clouding his soul: this was something altogether unexpected. What was it? Why did we hear nothing of British naval rocket weapons? How many ships carried them? Were they all so accurate, so terribly fast?

"Come about and swing north as soon as we get over the horizon and out of sight. There is more here than we can chew right on now. With *Gneisenau* burning it's no good heading south into the Atlantic to look for another tanker. The British will see us twenty miles away. We will have to find *Nordmark* instead. So as long as we have speed we must use it now to get north to find fuel. Notify Lindemann."

Now he knew what had devoured *Altmark* in one swift blow as the survivors had told the story.

This will change everything...

Chapter 29

Denmark Strait ~ 17 June, 22:00 hours

The *Fairey III* spotter-reconnaissance plane had been flying for some time on a southwesterly course, seeing nothing. Then the rear .303 Lewis gun operator noted a column of smoke on the far horizon behind them, fisting up into the sky like a black thunderhead. For a moment he thought it was only weather, but then he remembered the evening forecast, clear with good visibility west all the way to Greenland.

"Something at five o'clock," he reported, and the pilot craned his neck to see enough there to prompt him to bank right.

"That's trouble," he said. "Something burning, but it's well off to the west. Probably a steamer that ran afoul of a Jerry U-boat. Signal *Hood* and ask if they want us to have a look."

Holland was curious that day, so he vectored the plane off its intended search pattern, and had it work its way northwest to see what it could find. As they approached, it became evident that a ship was burning in the distance, and a second contact was spotted nearby.

"Have a look there at three o'clock, sir, another ship!"

"Can't say I like the looks of that one. Could that be the *Bismarck*? Get off the sighting report and we'd better head home. The fog is rolling in and we won't see a thing in ten minutes."

Holland soon had the puzzle to solve. Three ships, two heading north at high speed, one burning and trailing heavy smoke, and a third ship about twenty kilometers to the west. All three looked to be fighting ships. Could one be the cruiser Fleet Air Arm had spotted earlier? The first two ships were undoubtedly the Twins. The third could have been *Hipper*. He decided as such, and then, realizing he was now heading in the wrong direction, he quickly came about and assumed a course to the northwest. Home Fleet was informed of the development at once.

* * *

Even while Holland had been laboring north through the storm the previous day, Tovey had acted decisively, withdrawing the whole of his force and swinging back along the rocky coast of Iceland. There he lingered for some time, waiting for the new carrier *Illustrious* to arrive with the heavy cruiser *Devonshire* and three more destroyers.

By the time *Kirov* had put its missile into *Gneisenau* and sent the Twins off north, Tovey's Home Fleet was consolidated off the cape near Vir south of the Katla Volcano and ready to continue west at high speed to effect the link-up with Admiral Holland.

The Admiralty had not been entirely happy with Tovey's decision to withdraw, and the Prime Minister seemed to be exerting considerable pressure on the situation in the form of his eloquent displeasure. The fact that the newly appointed commander of the Home Fleet was sending them home HMS *Renown* with considerable damage from two 500 lb bombs did not go unnoticed. A message was sent expressing some obvious discontent over the incident, particularly on the part of First Sea Lord Dudley Pound.

'*We have sent you to find and sink German ships,*' came the cable, '*not to send our own home for the repair yards. The Prime Minister is of the opinion that you have shirked your duty to vigorously pursue and engage the enemy.*'

Tovey read the message with some dismay, and a rising anger. He knew enough about the musty halls of the Admiralty to know that Their Lordships were now in some heated discussion as to his eventual fate. Yet for the moment the timely dispatch of HMS *Illustrious* with much need air support and another heavy cruiser gave him hope that someone there was still pulling for him. He did not know who, but suspected that it might be Third Sea Lord Admiral

Bruce Fraser. The two men had seen eye to eye before concerning fleet dispositions in the Med and there was much mutual respect between them. Tovey had great faith in the man.

Yet the Admiral was ill tempered that day, and when young Lieutenant Commander Wells came in with a dispatch he was hastily dismissed.

"Not now, Mister Wells!"

Tall and stocky of frame, Tovey was an imposing figure in his wrath, and his temper was legendary. It was said his anger could melt a candle ay thirty paces when he really let it fly, and his displeasure had cowed and skewered more than one blundering officer in the past. Yet he was a fair man, aware of his own intemperate moods at times, and one to quickly set right any wrong unjustly delivered. He composed himself, looked up at Wells, seeing the man wilt a bit under his gaze, and spoke again.

"There you stand only recently mentioned in dispatches for gallantry, Wells, and here I sit under suspicion of being a shirker and slacker at the helm. Don't you mind my bluster one bit. I tend to blow off steam on occasion, and sometimes I deliver a broadside at an undeserving soul simply because he comes within range. Now then… what have you for me ?" He eyed the dispatch in Wells' hands.

"Pardon the interruption, sir. Mister Villers sends that *Scharnhorst* and *Gneisenau* have turned north and appear to be withdrawing."

"Withdrawing? Well that is news. Don't you ever belay it in the face of my bad manners again, young man. Here, let me have a look."

Tovey took the dispatch with interest now, more than surprised with what he saw there. "Apparent damage? Is Holland saying there's been an engagement?" He got up from his desk and went to the situation map, waving Wells to his side.

"Here, Mister Wells. Kindly update the board for me with these new positions, if you please."

"Sir…" Wells took back the dispatch, eying the coordinates and trying to remember his map work. The last thing he could do here would be to misplace a marker and set the whole damn strategy off on the wrong foot. He was justifiably nervous, but forced himself to think. Find a base latitude, my man, he thought. Then tick off the boxes and find your square on the grid. It's right there in front of your nose, just read the coordinates, you dolt.

He reached for the wooden marker representing the Twins, the naval ensign of the Kriegsmarine displayed prominently on the attached flag. "I would place them about here, sir, given the time elapsed since this sighting and their last reported heading and speed. I've placed a spot on the actual sighting coordinate here. Then we have *Manchester* withdrawing on Reykjavik here, and Admiral Holland with *Hood* and *Repulse* has turned and is presently about…here, perhaps 150 miles southwest of the Twins. He is at reduced speed to effect a rendezvous with us at your discretion, sir. As for *Birmingham*, we've heard nothing, Admiral, not since *Manchester* left her." He picked up one last marker, uncertain about what he could say about it.

"From the look of these postings," said Tovey, "Holland never got anywhere near the Twins. Yet that report states one of the ships appeared damaged and was still on fire."

"Mister Villers has spoken with the pilot off *Repulse*, sir, and the man claims the smoke was visible for fifty miles. It's how they first spotted them, then low fog and haze obscured the scene and forced them to turn and end the search."

"I wonder if they had a run in with *Birmingham*? It would do me well to learn she took a good bite out of one of those ships. Then again, her silence is most disconcerting. Well… you haven't finished. What's that in your hand?"

Wells reflexively looked at the green marker, usually used to indicate a neutral ship. "This was the marker that was set for the

Russian contact, sir. Yet from that dispatch I'm not exactly sure how to color it now. Mister Villers indicated the pilot off *Repulse* seemed convinced he was looking at a very large warship. The dispatch is suggesting *Admiral Hipper.*"

"Indeed...Set the marker, Mister Wells. You can leave it green for the moment until we sort things out. We'll be hell bent for leather the next nine hours getting west and up into the Denmark Strait. I was set to have a close look at that ship earlier, if it is that Russian cruiser, and to be honest I'm surprised it remains in the vicinity at all. When we do get there I intend to solve this little mystery if the situation permits."

Wells waited, still just a tad discomfited in the Admiral's presence, then ventured a remark. "A bad throw for *Renown*, sir."

"It certainly was. Jerry slipped one in on us and played a good face card, Mister Wells. *Graf Zeppelin* has changed the game a bit here, which is why I have been forced to draw a new card with *Illustrious*. But you know what the old farmer said: who knows what is good or bad."

"Sir?"

"Just an old tale I heard once, Wells. A farmer had a good plow horse to get in his crop, but just before the harvest it bolted in a storm and ran off on him. The neighbor commiserated with him, of course, and lamented that he and his son would not get much of their crop in without that horse. The farmer, stoic old chap that he was, simply said 'who knows what is good or bad.' Then, three days on, lo and behold if the old mare doesn't return with a lusty wild stallion on her tail. This changed everything, at least in the neighbor's mind, and he rushed over to laud the farmer for his good fortune. Now, with two horses, he told him, you will get the harvest in before anyone else!"

Wells had heard the story, and though he thought he might be stealing the Admiral's thunder he chanced a response. "But who knows what is good or bad, sir?"

"Exactly. One never does know, does he? Sure enough the Farmer's son broke his leg the next day trying to tame that horse, and the neighbor was quick to point out that without his son there to help him…Well, you can see where this is going, eh, Wells?"

"I do, sir."

Tovey smiled. "So we've lost a horse in *Renown*, and it looks like the dog went with it now that *Brimingham* is missing, but who knows what is good or bad? It's simply the situation now and we'll deal with it as best we can. In the meantime, tomorrow morning things will start getting very dicey again. You may want to see about a good night's rest, though there won't be much of the night in these latitudes."

"I will, sir."

"Good enough. Dismissed, Mister Wells. My regards to the Flag Lieutenant, and you may inform Captain Bennett that with *Illustrious* in hand now we'll be on our way. Destroyers are to make for Reykjavik for refueling. The rest of us go without."

* * *

When the Twins received the hard shock Admiral Volsky had sent their way on the tip of a MOS-III missile, *Kirov* turned east into the void between the Germans and the British force that had been stalking them. They noted the approach of the British seaplane, saying and doing nothing in the fading light of June 17. The plane seemed to take a distant look at them, then turned away.

Rodenko watched the Germans withdrawing on radar and, soon after, he saw the British relent with their southerly pursuit course and turn about as well. Now both groups were heading northeast at about 24 knots each, but separated by about 100 miles of ocean and with the British well to the south. He passed a brief moment realizing that from their present position *Kirov* could engage and easily destroy either one of these groups, remaining unseen and well beyond the range of any reprisal. Such was the power at their disposal, even crippled and hobbled as the ship presently was.

If Karpov were here he had little doubt that he would have attacked all these ships by now. Admiral Volsky has been threading a needle here with his measured response to the situation. Yet if we continue on to the northeast something tells me we may run into a good deal more trouble than we expect. The decrypt from Fedorov's Enigma program was somewhat ominous. What if the Germans have another strong battlegroup heading this way?

He held the first night watch thinking on all that had happened to them, how Karpov had tried to take the ship and failed, and then how it had been given to him in trust, only to be lost again when he lost the trust of the men who served under him. He thought of all the harm they had done, all the lives they had taken, the brazen way they would sail into any situation confident in their ability to prevail.

But what were they sailing into now? What had really happened with that new control rod? Were they trapped here if Chief Dobrynin could not discover how to make it work again? And what about Fedorov's fear that they were now a candle burning low, and that time would be faced with an insoluble problem a year on when *Kirov* was supposed to arrive, like a patron at a theater finding someone else in his seat—himself!

It was all too much for him to contemplate. There was only one thing to do in the situation now, and that was to keep faith with the men and protect the ship as best he could. It was clear, however that the Admiral had made a choice in this broken version of the events now underway. Fedorov seemed troubled about it in the beginning, but something had happened to him, he seemed to be looking at the situation with new eyes now, imbued with some newfound energy that was aimed at building something new, and no longer struggling to protect the sandcastle world from the inevitable sea. Yet he still exercised caution, a reasoned moderation. He did not want to engage those German ships, which is why he suggested that tanker was a better plan.

One way or another, men went into the sea, and it was strange what he said—that they were all fated to die; that none would live to see 1943 but one. Is that man still alive out there somewhere? Did he make it off the ship this time? And were any of us any different? We are all fated to die.

All these thoughts ran through his mind as he looked out the forward viewport. It would not be dark long. The sun had barely dipped beneath the horizon in this high northern latitude, leaving a pale gray wash over the sea, streaked by the glimmering reflection of the moon, fat and near full. *Kirov* was the darkest thing in the sea, a ghostly shadow adrift on the swells. It was the land of the midnight sun up here, and daybreak would come just a few minutes after the witching hour, very close now. There was no real darkness here, no place to hide and rest in the quiet, only this vast open liquid palette of grey, the ghostly specter of the moon, and a longing for sleep.

What were they doing here, he wondered? Why had this happened to them? Would they ever know any other life but this endless vigilant watch on the sea?

The words of that poem the Admiral had read to them still haunted him…*there are wanderers o're eternity, whose bark drives on and on, and anchored ne'er shall be.* He had asked the Admiral about it, and Volsky had given him the book, though he had kept it in his jacket pocket with no time to read. Now he took it out again, opening to the place the Admiral had marked, his tired eyes scanning down the long thin column of poetry…

'*All heaven and earth are still—though not in sleep,*
But breathless, as we grow when feeling most;
And silent, as we stand in thoughts too deep —'

He looked out, seeing the moon, the quiet sea, feeling the breathless time before the return of the sun and the heralding of another day in these uncertain waters. Fog seemed to be forming in thin, spectral vapors over the water. It was already past the midnight hour, and he could see the horizon glowing with the coming of a new day, just as this man must have seen it once, and labored to put his feeling to words that morning…

'The morn is up again, the dewy morn,
With breath all incense, and with cheek all bloom,
Laughing the clouds away with playful scorn,
And living as if earth contained no tomb,
And glowing into day: we may resume
The march of our existence…'

Chapter 30

Kapitan Otto Ernst Lindemann stood on the bridge of the *Bismarck*, staring at the message he had just been handed, his beady eyes narrowing, lips taut to give him a bird like, hawkish aspect. Tall and thin, his ears jutted out like a pair of gun directors on the main mast of the ship.

Enamored of the sea ever since he heard the stories of steamers on the wide Pacific that his uncle would tell, Lindemann was fortunate to come from a family that could afford the steep tuition for his years in the naval academy. Academically gifted, he was somewhat slight physically, and was almost disqualified from active service due to troublesome lungs from a bout with pneumonia as a youth. The condition meant that service on a U-boat was out of the question for him, but when World War One came he was gratified to be assigned to the battleship *Lothringen* commanded by the famous Admiral Reinhard Scheer.

Assigned to patrol duties, the ship saw little combat, and Lindemann's position as a Wireless Telegraphy Officer seemed inglorious enough to him in any case. But his luck soon saw him drawing high cards where ship assignments were concerned. He moved to the newly commissioned battleship *Bayern* in 1916, then the most powerful ship in the fleet, and he stayed with her through the sad end of the war, one of the last 175 crewmen to sail with her during the ignominious surrender and internment of the German High Seas Fleet at Scapa Flow in 1919.

His heart was heavy as they sailed, and he was glad that he had been ordered back to Germany before the final end, when the entire fleet was scuttled right under the noses of the British. When he got word the ships were gone, however, he had to fight off the tears. "*Hindenburg* was the last to go," a friend had told him, and it left him feeling bereft and sallow inside.

He stayed with the new Kriegsmarine, one of only 15,000 men allowed in the service by treaty until Hitler tore it up and began to rebuild the navy. At one point he served on the Staff of Admiral Raeder, and came to know the man and appreciate his mind for strategy on the high seas. "The German Navy may never again be large enough to seek open battle with the British," Raeder had told him, "but we can build ships that will teach them to fear us, fierce raiders that can ravage their convoys if war should come again. So work hard, Lindemann. One day you may find yourself on one of them, a real battleship again!"

So Lindemann left off staff work and telegraphy and studied naval gunnery, eventually lecturing on the subject at the Naval Gunnery School in Kiel. Soon he did find his way onto one of the new ships, as First Gunnery Officer of the pocket battleship *Admiral Scheer*, one of the fast raiders the Admiral had spoken about. The ship served briefly in the Spanish Civil War, and they even showed it off to the British at Gibraltar. Having been educated in England as a youth, Lindemann was able to speak English, and jousted with the British Admiral Somerville there.

"They call it a pocket battleship," he said, "and it will give your heavy cruisers fits, Admiral. Yes?"

"That it might," Somerville had said diplomatically, "though I don't think you would bother a real battleship with those guns. Touché." Somerville smiled at him, but Lindemann had taken his point well enough. A *real* battleship… That was what he found himself standing on now. What would Admiral Somerville say if I should sail *Bismarck* into the harbor at Gibraltar to pay him another visit?

The British were fond of queens and ladies of the sea. All their ships were old women, he thought. Well *Bismarck* will be referred to as "he," and that will make the difference plain enough. When he got the ship as his first real command at sea he swelled with pride. As

Germany's most experienced gunnery expert, he was eager to see what the new 15 inch guns could do, and show the British what a real battleship truly was. It was a miracle that Raeder managed to get these ships in fighting trim in time for the outbreak of war. We have dawdled away most of this year, but now we begin.

He felt the sheer, raw power beneath his feet as they plowed through the storm in the vanguard of the fleet. The ship was riding the heavy seas well, and they had sailed right into the face of an oncoming weather front late on the 17th of June. The viewports were thick with rain, however, and the inclement weather had grounded all operations from *Graf Zeppelin*. Visibility was so low that *Bismarck* and *Tirpitz* had to turn on their search lights, aiming them at each other to allow for safe station keeping and prevent an untimely collision.

Yet Lindemann had heard the forecast earlier from the weather officer. The storm would be brief and they would soon break through to clearing weather, with cold white clouds drifting like vagrant seafarers low on the water. The weather ship posted to that area had sent that heavy fog was forming behind the front, typical for this time of year.

Hoffmann had been out of contact for some time, then the message came, confounding him when he received it. Now he was huddling with his personal adjutant, signals officer Second Leutnant Wolfgang Reiner and Fregattenkapitän Paul Ascher, a staff officer assigned to bridge operations on the battleship. Asher was another gunnery officer, having served aboard the *Graf Spee* during her spectacular but ill-fated sortie. He had personally directed the gunfire that damaged the British cruisers *Exeter* and *Ajax* at the Battle of the River Plate, and had escaped internment to return to Germany.

"What is the meaning of this? Hoffman has withdrawn north?"

"Apparently, sir," said Reiner. "They broke through a British cruiser screen and attempted a rendezvous with the *Altmark*. When they got there they found the ship had been sunk."

"Sunk? There were no details?"

"No sir, only that it was believed to be a torpedo. Then Hoffmann's group was engaged by a battleship or battlecruiser and *Gneisenau* sustained damage amidships with speed down to 24 knots. Hoffmann broke off and turned to find *Nordmark*."

"Was the enemy ship identified?"

"No sir. And there was one other detail. I don't know quite what to make of it—something about naval rockets."

Lindemann turned his head, a disgusted look on his face. "Rockets?"

"That's what the message says, sir. '*Gneisenau* struck by rocket, Severe fire amidships. Number four boiler down. Speed off 8 knots. Proceeding to discretionary rendezvous point to refuel and repair. Beware.'"

"Beware?" That didn't sound like Hoffmann. Lindemann knew the man. Yes, he had orders to evade British capital ships. Lindemann had read them again just that day, realizing that the situation might dictate new orders at any moment.

'The objective of Scharnhorst & Gneisenau is not to defeat enemies of equal strength, but to tie them down in a delaying action, while preserving combat capacity as much as possible, so as to allow Bismarck and Tirpitz to get at the merchant ships in allied convoys. The primary target in this operation is the enemy's merchant shipping; enemy warships will be engaged only when that objective makes it necessary and it can be done without excessive risk.'

Hoffmann obviously found the engagement necessary, but it appears he got more than he expected. Yet Lindemann was bewildered by this notation concerning rocket fire. What was that about? Hoffmann was clearly attempting to warn him, but he could make no sense of it…unless the notation was metaphorical. That did not matter in the end. The reality of the situation was that *Gneisenau* had sustained damage, and Hoffmann's force was now withdrawing north to the discretionary rendezvous point. That would be the tanker *Nordmark*. There had been no sign of pursuit by the British after the successful strike made by *Graf Zeppelin*. Then came the weather front they were still plowing through, which provided him good cover to make his breakaway to the east.

The weather officer had predicted that they would see clearing skies on the morrow, but this was not good. Fog would follow, hopefully by the time he reached the strait. With the sun up all day at this latitude, the lighting will be favorable all night for sighting his ships. If he could not have darkness as a cloak, then heavy fog would do. It would hobble his air units off the carrier, but also hamper the British planes as well.

During their bold attack, the pilots off the *Graf Zeppelin* had indentified two British heavy warships, and one was the *Invincible*, her unique configuration impossible to mistake. A pity the *Stukas* did not put their bombs there. That ship is one of the few I need to respect, he thought.

Subsequent searches indicated the British had broken off and were no longer pursuing him north of Iceland. Now the planes were down with the weather, so the British might still be there, hiding behind the rain squalls like a shadow of death. His-B-Dienst team, a special Marine signals intelligence unit serving aboard battleships to try an intercept and decode enemy communications, had no real information for him yet. The British were being tight lipped. He knew it was Admiral Tovey out there hunting him, new to command, perhaps breaking in new staff as well. Yet he did not know enough about the man to anticipate how he might react to the attack on his force today. It was all just educated guesses at the moment. There was no word from Wilhelmshaven either.

Where were the British now, he wondered? If they are not following, then they certainly know where we are headed and they must have moved south of Iceland. The Royal Navy clearly had cruisers watching the Denmark Strait, and now capital ships from this report. He correctly surmised that the British were now consolidating their battle fleets in an attempt to find and stop him there—in the Denmark Strait.

So what was waiting for them? He had already left the older battleships *Rodney* and *Nelson* behind him, and they were of no concern. That left few candidates in his mind, and he now began to suspect that the British had assigned their faster ships to this operation, *Hood*, *Renown*, *Repulse* and the fleet flagship, *Invincible*. We may have taken one out of the equation with that air strike. That leaves three more to deal with, and the usual entourage of cruisers and destroyers.

Well, I have a substantial force here, and with Hoffmann's flotilla we are more than a match for the British this time around. But those orders from Raeder and Lütjens nagged at him... *The primary target in this operation is the enemy's merchant shipping; enemy warships will be engaged only when that objective makes it necessary and it can be done without excessive risk.'*

I have already violated that mandate when I sent those planes out. Raeder may not be happy about that, but the results should serve as a consolation. Two hits on a British battlecruiser! That may stiffen Raeder's resolve. It is obvious that I cannot fulfill my primary orders unless I first gain the Atlantic. To do so I may have to either face whatever the British oppose me with and prevail, or else evade them completely. Unless we get good concealment in the fog, evasion may be the more difficult thing to accomplish. With *Graf Zeppelin* along I have options that no other German commander at sea has ever exercised, and I have already used them to good effect to put off the initial chase. But the Royal Navy learns quickly...too quickly. They will now do everything possible to neutralize the advantage I have just demonstrated with *Graf Zeppelin*. In many ways that carrier is now the most valuable ship in the Kriegsmarine, and for an old gunnery officer like me to admit that says much.

So I am to attack the convoys, but avoid fighting the British toe to toe in order to get there. Now that our planned diversion by *Scharnhorst* and *Gneisenau* has failed to break out, the Royal Navy will be gathering like a flock of seagulls in the Denmark Strait. Do I fight my way through under these circumstances? Even as he asked himself that question he knew he would have to send to Wilhelmshaven and Naval Group North headquarters for the answer.

"Make to Wilhelmshaven, Leutnant Reiner. They undoubtedly have the message you have just handed me from Hoffmann. Now what do they propose I do? Tell them that I expect the whole of the British Battlecruiser Squadron to be waiting for me in the Denmark Strait. All *Scharnhorst* and *Gneisenau* have done is ring the bell at the police station! If presented with the possibility of a major engagement, what is Admiral's Raeder's pleasure? Does he want his ships to fight here? If not, I welcome his advice on the matter. That is all."

* * *

Hoffman was in his flag ready room, sitting at the table, a cigar in one hand and a ruler in another. His orders folio was open beside him, and he was checking on the position of *Nordmark* and plotting the ship's coordinates. He picked up a compass and pen and quietly stepped off intervals along the lines he had drawn on the map. They had been making 24 knots, which was more than he expected after he saw that rocket strike *Gneisenau* amidships. The fires were out now, no longer marking their presence on the horizon, and that damnable jamming of his radars and communications had finally dissipated once he got north away from the last British contact.

So his instincts had been correct. There *was* another ship in the Denmark Strait, watching, waiting. It wasn't an ice ghost, frigid bergs piled on drifting floes from the glaciers that were often sighted and mistaken for ships in these waters. It wasn't a mirage of hoarfrost or snow swirling over the icy coast. No. It was well out in the center of the strait. He had seen it with his own eyes, taken in the long dangerous lines, felt the odd aura that seemed to be about it, as if it was something wholly unaccountable, beyond his experience and perilous in a way he could not yet comprehend. Then came that flashing attack, precise, deadly, the destructive power and reach of the weapon shocking with its accuracy. A rocket...so well aimed that it bored in unfailingly on the target and seemed to leap at *Gneisenau* like a sea demon, finding the vital superstructure of the ship and not the heavy side armor.

Something told him that this might be some new vessel, a command ship, lurking on the scene, vectoring in the enemy battlecruisers, jamming his communications to leave him blind. It had to be dealt with, and he passed a moment of regret that he did not allow his gunners the time to find the range.

Yet orders were orders. With *Gneisenau* burning, the extent of the damage as yet unknown, the nature of the enemy a mystery itself, his instinct had proven to be the wisest course. Fall back, consolidate, refuel and allow time for *Gneisenau* to effect repairs. Wait for Lindemann.

He took a long drag on his cigar, exhaling slowly, thoughtfully. Then he called in Huber. "Make to *Bismarck* and Lindemann. Request rendezvous and Kapitan's meeting at the alternate refueling point. Tell them we can be there tomorrow by 14:00 hours."

"Very good, Kapitan." Huber hesitated, the hour late, the ship quiet after the long day, yet still with a restless edge about the men as they hastened north. They had seen what happened, and were no doubt wondering what this sudden course change north would mean.

Were they beaten? Was the mission to be called off? Then he turned and asked the question that had been on so many of their minds.

"What was that ship out there, Kapitan?"

Hoffmann took another long drag on his cigar, thinking, his eyes holding a distant look. "I don't know."

That answer seemed heavy with portent, and Huber knew that something had happened that had upset all the careful planning by the naval staff adjutants at Wilhelmshaven…. something big. It seemed as though some dark impending shadow now hovered over them, like the shadow of death, and it brought an unwelcome chill in the silence between the two men.

Huber saluted and started for the wireless room.

Part XI

War Councils

"All wars are planned by old men in council rooms."

— Grantland Rice

Chapter 31

Denmark Strait ~18 June, 1940 ~ 08:00 hrs

"Something up ahead on radar, sir." Kalinichev gave the report matter of factly and Rodenko came to his station to have a look.

"The signal is very weak and somewhat dispersed." Rodenko studied it for some time then went to Fedorov with his report.

"Captain, we have a weak contact ahead, about ten kilometers out now. I believe it is flotsam."

"We had no surface contacts for ships on that heading. Could it be drift ice? "

"More likely a debris field. We're well out in the channel so I don't think this is ice. We could use the helicopter to verify or perhaps the Tin Man could give is a better look ahead."

"Let's keep the KA-40 aboard at the moment. Use the Tin Man."

Moments later they could make out distant shapes on the overhead monitor that appeared to be two lifeboats on the sea, riding the restless swells. In time they encountered a wide oil slick and small fragments of floating debris, spars, deck planks, a section of mast, rigging and canvass. Something had gone down here, and then the bodies in the sea told the tale. *Kirov* slowed to five knots to have a closer look, seeing a lifeless man bobbing in a circular life preserver, and the stenciled name of his ship was now evident. It was HMS *Birmingham.*

"So the British cruisers did not fare well," said Fedorov. "Make for that nearest life raft. And get launches ready to recover survivors."

"You want to bring them aboard?"

"Where else, Rodenko? We can't leave them here, can we? Detail Sergeant Troyak to supervise the recovery operation. I will notify the Admiral."

"Aye, sir."

"Mister Nikolin."

"Sir?"

"Please report to Sergeant Troyak on the launch deck and accompany his operation. I'd go myself but your English is better and it will come in handy. Report on the identity of the survivors by ship's channel radio, please."

When Troyak and a detachment of Marines reached the boats they found the men there hungry and cold, but alive. There were five in one boat, six in the second, where Nikolin reported that the ship's Captain was present, and in need of medical attention.

The Admiral agreed that there was no recourse but to render aid and bring the survivors aboard. The crewmen were given medical attention, a good meal and quartered off the helo hanger deck, their eyes goggling a bit when they first got sight of the KA-40. Fedorov put out a message on the ship's intercom for English speakers to report to Troyak and selected a *Mishman* to serve as a liaison with the British there. Captain Madden was taken to the sick bay for a lacerated arm, and when Admiral Volsky and Fedorov arrived with Nikolin, there he sat next to Doctor Zolkin, the two men both in bandages and chatting amiably in English, as Zolkin had studied in London for some years earlier in his career.

"Ah, Fedorov, Admiral," said Zolkin in Russian. "May I present Captain Alexander Madden, HMS *Birmingham*. Apparently they had a run in with a German heavy cruiser and did not fare so well. The Captain here tells me that they took several hits, and could not flood their forward magazines before they exploded. Most unfortunate."

"Kindly offer the Captain my regrets," said Volsky. "Particularly for heavy loss of life. We have recovered another four men in the flotsam, and I have ordered a further search to see if we can find anyone else out there, but for the moment there are only fifteen survivors"

Zolkin translated, and the Admiral smiled at his old friend, seeing the animated life had returned to his eyes as he first introduced the Admiral and Fedorov. As Zolkin's English seemed quite adequate, Nikolin was able to return to his post on the bridge.

"What ship are you, if I may ask, Admiral?" said Madden, somewhat bedraggled but recovering his strength after I.V. fluids and some good food and coffee.

"We are the cruiser *Kirov*, a Russian ship as you may have deduced."

"Well you are certainly very far from home waters here, Admiral, and in fairly dangerous waters if the fate of my ship is any testimony. We were trying to intercept and shadow a pair of German battlecruisers, but it seems there were three German ships and they got the best of us. They're likely well south by now."

Zolkin translated, and Volsky nodded.

"He's been remarking on the size of our ship, Admiral, and I think he would have many questions."

"As do I," said Volsky. He decided to get round to his real reason for wanting to speak with the British Captain. "Doctor, be so kind as to tell the Captain that we believe there are several British warships south east of our present position, and we could see that he is given safe passage to those ships."

Captain Madden brightened at that news, thanking the Admiral.

"Tell him also that our ship is presently a neutral in this conflict, but I would be most interested in meeting with the commander of those British ships. I wonder if he might be able to make the introductions and smooth the way for such a meeting. Our ship is, indeed far from home and, as you have seen, we present a fairly respectable silhouette. I would not wish to alarm your British friends by making a sudden approach under these circumstances. Would the Captain assist us in making this contact?"

Zolkin translated and Madden looked from one to the other. "I can't think that it would be I any way improper. I clearly saw your naval ensign, and yes, I would be pleased to call ahead on your behalf and eager to do so. We have not been able to communicate with superior officers as to our fate since my ship went down. In fact, we failed to get off anything more than a brief message indicating we were engaged. I believe it was the *Admiral Hipper* that happened on us, just as we sent *Manchester* off. That was our companion cruiser on patrol here. We managed to lead *Hipper* off in a fairly wild run, and she seemed keen on engaging us. I wonder if you've had any word on *Manchester?*"

"We have not encountered the ship," said Volsky, "but I believe it was able to slip away. We saw the action on radar. You succeeded in leading the Germans off, sir, and may have saved your companions from a similar fate by sacrificing your own ship. I ask you to take heart with that thought. The fortunes of war can be cruel and hard, but we must find some way to muddle through. Yes, I think your *Manchester* is safely on her way south."

"That is a great relief. Radar you say? I was not aware that you navy had deployed the devices. If we'd had our sets installed in time I might not be in this position now."

Volsky could see the flash of anxiety in the man's eyes, the weight of responsibility he carried here, and the restrained way in which he held his obvious sorrow over the loss of his ship and most of his crew.

"Well, Captain Madden," he said. "These last days have been very hard. Please get some rest and, when the good Doctor here feels you are fit, I will be pleased to meet with you again and we can contact your comrades."

"Thank you, Admiral," said Zolkin, smiling as he translated. "You are very kind, and your assistance is much appreciated."

"And how is that arm and shoulder, Doctor?" Volsky pointed at Zolkin's bandages.

"Well enough, Admiral. This old bird still has some life in him. Don't worry about me."

As they walked to the bridge Fedorov finally spoke. "So you plan to meet with the British commanders, sir?"

"That has been on my mind, Fedorov. The last meeting went fairly well in the Mediterranean, wouldn't you say? You have seen Nikolin's message intercepts. The British Admiral Tovey is coming to rendezvous with an Admiral Holland. As for the Germans, they appear to have gone off north to refuel. Both sides are huddling, but something tells me they will soon be deploying again, and we are still right in the middle of things here, with a reactor down, damage to the bow and house guests."

"Chief Byko reports he's made good progress on the bow, sir. They have sealed off the sonar bulge, and patched the damaged section from the outside. We've lost the sonar there, but I think we can make way now if the reactor comes back on line soon. Dobrynin says he felt it necessary to remove the special control rod there and mount a spare, sir. He believes he can begin ramping up power in another three hours."

"That is good news.

* * *

Admiral Holland was on the flag plot room of HMS *Hood* when the radio call came in. His Flag Lieutenant, Commander Smith seemed a bit surprised by the call. "Radio message, sir, using our call sign."

"Radio message? Not on the W/T?"

"Radio, sir. Captain Madden off *Birmingham.*"

"Well it's about time we heard something. Where is he?"

"About a hundred kilometers off, sir according to Captain Madden, but he's not on *Birmingham.*"

"I don't understand."

"She ran afoul of the *Hipper*, sir, and got the worst of it. 8-inch shell hit her forward magazine and blew the forecastle sky high. We lost her. Madden made it off alive but there were only fifteen survivors."

"Fifteen? My God...there were over 700 men aboard...Damn bloody business."

"He was picked up by that Russian cruiser that Tovey asked us to investigate."

"All this was transmitted in the clear? What's gotten into Madden's head besides seawater. The man took a hard knock but the security breach is appalling."

"I did mention that, sir. But this ship was not identified in the transmissions. I suppose he hasn't revealed anything the Germans don't already know. A request has been made for a rendezvous, sir. The Russian Admiral wishes to speak with you or Admiral Tovey."

"Admiral? On a cruiser? This is most irregular, Mister Smith."

"Yes sir, but the Russians would like to transfer the survivors off *Birmingham*. Shall we arrange it? The Captain says they can join us in three hours time."

"How in blazes would he be able to say that? The man has no idea where we are."

"That thought crossed my mind as well, sir, but Captain Madden says he can explain later."

"Will he? At least he kept something under his hat."

Holland thought about it. All this in the clear for the German B-Dienst signals teams to intercept. But other than the number of survivors off *Birmingham* nothing of import was revealed.

"Well I can't see any harm in it. Tovey wanted us to investigate this contact earlier, but the Twins set us off on another course. So I suppose we would be following orders to arrange such a meeting. See to it, Mister Smith, but use the W/T please. No radio transmission."

"Of course, sir."

"Were holding in place here to await Home Fleet. See that Admiral Tovey is informed."

"Aye, sir."

* * *

Far to the north another meeting was being arranged, this time in the silent wink of a lamp from the German destroyer *Beowulf* as it made its approach to the rendezvous point with the tanker *Nordmark*. The destroyer was leading in the core of the German fleet, some three kilometers behind in a line of four big ships with another two destroyers keeping station to either side of *Graf Zeppelin*.

Aboard *Bismarck*, Lindemann had received Hoffmann's request and decided the rendezvous would be wise. It would further strengthen his task force, and when they caught sight of *Scharnhorst* looming out of the thick fog to the south, he smiled with the realization that he was now commanding the largest joint task force, and certainly the most powerful one that Germany had put to sea since Jutland. It was an historical moment, but he chided himself for basking in the glow, the sober thought that the British were most likely gathering to the south reminding him that this was not a time for chest thumping.

An hour later Kapitan Hoffmann was in a launch coming across from *Scharnhorst* while repair crews from *Nordmark* shipped over to see how they might assist with the damage control on *Gneisenau*. When the man finally boarded, Lindemann could smell Hoffmann coming as he ascended the stairway up from the lower decks. His cigar was leaving a nice aromatic trail on the cool air. He sat in the chart room with his First Officer, Korvettenkapitan Oels. All the other Kapitans were there, Karl Topp who had come across from *Tirpitz* and Kurt Böhmer off *Graf Zeppelin*. The two "Helmuths,' Brinkmann off *Prinz Eugen* and Heye off the *Hipper* were exchanging notes together. Lastly Otto Fein was over from *Gneisenau*. He had not been scheduled to take command until August, but that was moved up for this mission, and now he was unfortunate to find his was the only ship that had been hit and damaged by the enemy.

"Greetings, Kapitan Hoffmann. I don't suppose you brought one of those cigars for the rest of us?"

"A whole box," said Hoffmann, "and you can split them up any way you like. They were a gift from Kapitan Langsdorff when he returned from South America. Now there was a man who loved a good cigar."

"I suppose the honor of the first pick must go to Kapitan Böhmer," said Lindemann. "His *Stukas* put a couple of dents in HMS *Renown*, or so we now know from Seekriegsleitung. Give the next to Kapitan Heye for sinking that British cruiser, and the third I think you have already smoked, Hoffmann. That is for sending the other cruiser running off home. But it appears the celebration stops there, gentlemen. In exchange the British have sunk *Altmark* and poked a good size hole in *Gneisenau* from the looks of it. Now what is this business about another British warship in the strait and how is it we have repair crews from *Nordmark* all over your ship, Kapitan Fein?"

Fein looked at Hoffmann, a knowing glance, and then spoke. "Damndest thing I ever saw at sea," he said. "We spotted what looked to be a large British warship, very large, but there was something very odd about it."

"Odd is not but half a word for it," said Hoffmann, still puffing on his cigar. "This ship was big, threatening, clearly a warship by design, yet for its size we could see no real guns to speak of. Now I have heard of trying to camouflage your ship to make it appear smaller, a wolf in sheep's clothing, but you do not easily hide guns of the caliber that would normally be mounted on a warship of that size."

"Just how big was this ship?" Lindemann was listening closely, his eyes narrowed, prominent ears vectoring in like radars.

"To be honest, Kapitan, I thought it was the size of HMS *Hood*. In fact at first blush we thought it might be *Hood*, but the silhouette was all wrong."

"It had no stacks as *Hood* should have," Fein put in.

"That was another thing," Hoffmann held out his cigar, letting the thin trails of smoke curl their way up from the ashen tip. "No smoke either. The ship was cruising at probably fifteen knots, but making no visible smoke."

"You engaged this ship?"

"We did. I fired a warning shot across the bow thinking this might be an American ship. That is the last time I act as a gentleman in these waters," said Hoffmann. "But I wasn't quite sure what I had in front of me. It's what came back that we must now discuss, gentlemen." He looked askance at Fein, who waited, a grim expression on his face.

"Your dispatch said something about a rocket. I assumed you were writing poetry, Hoffmann. You say this ship had no big guns but it obviously returned enough fire to blast that hole in *Gneisenau*."

"Oh it returned fire, Kapitan Lindemann, but not with its guns. We were hit by something else, something quite extraordinary, and every man here would be wise to heed my words on this, because if the rest of the British fleet has this weaponry, the entire nature of warfare at sea has just sailed into new waters and we have missed the boat."

Chapter 32

"**We** are taking a bit of a risk here, Admiral," said Fedorov. "I know the British were accommodating before, but our ships were separated by the straits of Gibraltar back then. Now we are under the guns of all these ships, and it is just a bit unnerving."

"I understand how you feel, Fedorov, but a man must have some trust in life. We are prominently flying the Russian naval ensign, the flag of a neutral state in this conflict, and one the British would be wise not to antagonize."

"Well, we are not really affiliated with Soviet Russia here."

"The British will not know that at the moment."

"Yet they will know we are not the cruiser *Kirov* on their current intelligence rolls, sir. There will be questions here. Have we decided how to best answer them? I mean, we cannot tell them the truth."

"No, I suppose we cannot. Well I think we must simply say we are a highly classified secret project of Soviet Russia, out on a training mission to test new weapons. That will hold water long enough for me to accomplish what I am after here."

"What are you after, sir?"

"A meeting of the minds, Fedorov. If Karpov were here he would be arguing that we lay down the law to the British, or else he would have already attacked them. We are not to be excused in that regard, but at least we gave some consideration as to the consequences of our actions in choosing sides here, and I think we chose wisely. Now our task is to persuade the British to chose wisely as well. This Admiral Tovey is here, is he not?"

"Yes, sir. That large ship off the port quarter—but this is another anomaly, sir."

"What do you mean?"

"*Look* at it, Admiral. That is a G3 class battlecruiser! It's configuration is unlike any other ship in the fleet. Note the positioning of the main guns, two triple turrets forward and a third right behind the conning tower and placed amidships. Those are all 16-inch guns, sir. Four of these ships were ordered, and in the world we came from none were ever completed due to the limitations imposed by the Washington Naval Treaty."

"So that is a big crack in your mirror, Fedorov. Are there any other unusual ships present?"

"No sir. That is *Hood* there behind the G3, and that is the battlecruiser *Repulse* if I am not mistaken. Those other two ships are cruisers, and it looks like we have two carriers of to the south as well, most likely *Ark Royal* and *Illustrious*, though that ship is a tad early. Things have changed, Admiral."

"Well don't be so surprised, Mister Fedorov. Look down at your feet and note the ship you are standing on. *Kirov* should not be here either, and we are likely going to raise quite a few eyebrows. I would say that at least a hundred pairs of field glasses are trained on us now, and I am grateful that no gun barrels are so trained."

"Captain Madden spoke well on our behalf, sir."

"Good for him. Now the question is whether we should take a launch over to see Admiral Tovey, or perhaps invite him here."

"I would suggest the former, sir. It may mean fewer questions."

"I understand…but I also think you would give your right arm to step aboard that G3 battleship."

"Battle*cruiser*, sir, though it certainly has the power to stand with any battleship of this era. That said, you may be right, Admiral. I would dearly love to get a look at that ship."

"Then let us conference with Captain Madden and see if we can make the arrangements. Request permission to escort the Captain and the survivors off *Birmingham* to that ship, and a meeting with Admiral Tovey at his discretion."

"Right away, sir."

Fedorov had suddenly lost all his reservations about the meeting, and the lightness in his step brought a grin to Admiral Volsky's face. Well, he thought. I suppose I had better get into my dress uniform. Appearances always matter, especially for the British. They'll look me over as closely as they look over this ship. So now we see if the character of this man John Tovey has changed in this altered reality. This will be very interesting.

The last time I met this man both fear and respect were invited to the conference. He had seen us in combat, knew what we could do. We had driven him off in *King George V*, and bested both *Rodney* and *Nelson* together. We blackened the aircraft carrier *Furious*, and then Karpov unleashed that awful attack against the Americans. He undoubtedly saw the mushroom cloud that day. Fedorov tells me they had a name for us in their code books—*Geronimo*. But it is only 1940 now. None of that has happened yet, and in this world it probably never will. This time we have only mystery to bring with us to the table—no—that is not quite so. We have another guest that I can bring along, and he is right in Fedorov's head: information, intelligence, a full accounting of the situation Tovey now faces should the Germans come south again. Yes, this will be very interesting.

An hour later the word came that the meeting was approved and they were invited to join Admirals Tovey and Holland aboard the HMS *Invincible* for lunch.

"Very well, gentlemen," said Volsky, and they went over in a large launch. Admiral Volsky, Fedorov, Nikolin and Captain Madden were sitting forward with Sergeant Troyak and two Marines to accompany the British survivors off *Birmingham*. Rodenko had the ship, watching them go from the bridge and remembering how Karpov had strutted out the entire Marine honor guard and the ship's band when he went ashore to see the Mayor of Vladivostok in 1908. A pity he could not find a way to parley with Admiral Togo.

Volsky boarded the British battlecruiser up a lowered metal stair, and was duly piped aboard. There he saw a small honor detachment standing at attention, which he saluted.

They were greeted by a young man in smart dress whites. He saluted and stepped forward to extend a hand. "Lieutenant Commander Christopher Wells," he said. "Admiral Tovey sends his compliments and invites you to follow me, sir. Greetings Captain Madden, and welcome back. We've been missing you."

"Thank you, Mister Wells, it seems that you and I have both been through the fire lately. Good show bringing *Glorious* home. Wish I could say the same for my ship."

"I'm sure you did your best, sir, and everything possible under the circumstances."

"Yes, but when a magazine blows…well, that's another story. Lead on, sir."

They made their way along the deck, past the high aft mast where the naval jack of the Royal Navy flew proudly above the fleet flagship. Fedorov' eyes were big, a light of discovery in them, and quiet elation. Once he paused to gape up at the big twin funnels and then stare at the main battery amidships, his eyes sweeping over the massive barrels of steel.

"Come along, Mister Fedorov," said Volsky with a smile. "We mustn't let Admiral Tovey's soup get cold waiting for us."

"Sorry sir." Fedorov quickened his pace. "This is quite a remarkable ship. If built to designed specs, it would have belt armor 14 inches thick, over 17 inches on those gun turrets, and the deck under our feet is all of 8 inches thick in key places."

"Very well protected," said Volsky. "How different we are with *Kirov*, wearing only a helmet and breastplate near the reactor room compared to the full body armor and chain mail of this heavy knight. But while he must charge valiantly in and fight with lance, sword and shield at close quarters, we use the longbow from beyond his reach.

Therein lies our real armor, Fedorov—ranged firepower. It is the reason aircraft carriers were proved so dominant by the end of this war. Yet we even better that weapons platform, in that what we target we hit, and without fail in this era, as they have no SAM systems capable of tracking or hindering our SSMs. If they would ever hit one it would be sheer happenstance."

"Well put, Admiral. And when we add in the fact that we can find the enemy unerringly, see him first and then hit him well over the horizon, it is clear that *Kirov* is the mightiest ship afloat here, but it is strange to think that no more than that intangible element of trust now stands as our only shield sitting this close to those ships. One blast of those 16 inch guns at the moment would blow us sky high."

"Just be sure you do not mention that in these discussions, Fedorov," the Admiral warned him half seriously.

"Of course, sir. Yet for all the power we see assembled here, I fear the German fleet may have the advantage, sir. Nikolin and I have intercepted and decoded a good deal of signals traffic. The Germans Have the carrier *Graf Zeppelin* with their main body. That is a game changer, sir, and it has already made a successful strike on Tovey's squadron, damaging the battlecruiser *Renown* and forcing him to withdraw. That is, in fact why I believe he has chosen to consolidate here."

"I may call on your analysis of this situation, Fedorov. If the opportunity presents, do not hesitate to speak your mind. I think we must find a way to convince the British we are valuable to them as an ally here."

They climbed several levels, which Volsky found somewhat arduous, leaving him a little winded when they reached the Admiral's stateroom high up in the forward conning tower structure. He huffed in to find a row of British officers, in dress whites, all standing to meet him. There he immediately recognized Admiral Tovey's tall stocky frame, the narrow eyes, calm demeanor, and walked directly to him, extending his hand in greeting. Nikolin padded behind, quickly translating what he said.

"I would pay dearly to find a naval architect with a fancy for elevators," he said, which immediately drew a polite laugh from the officers assembled. "I am Admiral Leonid Volsky. A remarkable ship you have here, Admiral Tovey. My Captain Fedorov has been admiring it greatly." Volsky extended an arm, beckoning Fedorov to his side to shake hands with the British officers.

There stood Tovey, with his Flag Lieutenant Villers, then Captain Bennett standing with Admiral Holland off the *Hood*. Vice Admiral Aircraft Carriers had been invited, but *Ark Royal* was busy mounting air patrols at the moment and coordinating her efforts with HMS *Illustrious*. The young staff officer that had escorted them here stood dutifully by the hatch.

As Tovey looked at the man before him he had the sudden and distinct impression that he knew him; that he had met him somewhere before. Was it the way he singled me out as if he, too, knew exactly who I was without counting stripes? I could swear I have spoken with this man before. It was a feeling that had taken root in him the moment he set eyes upon the arriving Russian ship. There was something about it that stirred deep memories, hazy now yet crystal clear in places, where the image of a distant dreadnought lashing out with wrathful fire were still riveted in his mind. That was far away in time, and in the Pacific, but he could not escape the feeling that he had once seen this towering ship, its long raked hull, tall prow, and the strangely open forecastle that was devoid of any heavy armament. Yet that was clearly not possible, and for all his life he could not place any moment where he could recall meeting this man, a high ranking officer in the Soviet Navy.

Now, however, there was the matter of the intelligence he had received from the Admiralty indicating that the Soviet cruiser *Kirov* had been properly accounted for in the Baltic. Yet it was not time for that yet. Courtesy first, then lunch, and business after with gin.

So they all sat down at the table, laid out with white linen and the ships ceremonial silver. The meal was light, but savory, a nice hot soup, cold cuts, fresh bread with butter and sliced cucumber. The staff officer Wells was seated next to Fedorov, surprised that he, too had been invited to the table.

"I'm taking this gentleman under my wing," said Tovey. "He's already saved us an aircraft carrier, and that is a fine start in any man's log as I see things."

"Thank you, sir."

"Thank you, Mister Wells. Though I'm afraid you will have to work quite diligently if you ever hope to top that one." That brought a laugh, and Tovey thought to himself, that's what I've been doing ever since I charged in that day aboard *King Alfred*—trying to grasp that moment in hand and heart again. I suppose it's what every man who's ever found himself at the edge of death in combat does for the rest of his life.

Tovey kept the lunch conversation light, expressing his gratitude for the rescue of *Birmingham's* surviving crew. But he slowly worked in a few points he wanted clarification on. Had the Admiral also seen a convoy further south? He found that this was, indeed, the same cruiser spotted by HX-49 and *Ausonia*, and the same reported to him by Flight Captain Partridge off *Ark Royal.*

As lunch ended his curiosity was overpowering, but he correctly waited for the gin and cigarettes to be offered, noting that none of the Russians seemed to prefer tobacco, but that they warmly received the gin. Then he got round to the business of the day.

"You wished to see me, Admiral Volsky, and I was happy to take this meeting with you here. Yet I wonder if I might clear up one small matter at the outset. Your initial claim some days ago when sighted by our aircraft was that you were the cruiser *Kirov*. Yet my Admiralty tells me that very ship is presently in the Baltic. I must say I forget what ship I'm on at times the way I bounce about the fleet. But might you clarify this for me?"

Volsky thought that he had never been so politely accused of being a liar in his life, though he knew this question was coming. "Well Admiral," he said. "The *Kirov* presently in the Baltic is an older ship, launched in 1936 if I am not mistaken." He looked to Fedorov now.

"That is correct, sir," said Fedorov in passing English. Then he spoke in Russian, with Nikolin translating quickly. "We have a bad habit of often renaming ships in our navy. There were six cruisers in the *Kirov* class, and two of those will be renamed. We are somewhat newer, but graced with the official name *Sergie Kirov* as well, though our ship is of another class entirely, and may not yet be known to your Admiralty or Naval Intelligence."

"We are, in fact, not even well known among our own naval personnel," said Volsky adding a little icing to the cake. "This ship was built under a cloak of considerable secrecy and security. I suppose we will not be the last ship to bear the name *Kirov* either, but for the moment I am happy to share it with our elder brother in the Baltic. I don't think he knows we're stepping on his toes yet."

"I see…A reasonable explanation. Then your mission here is classified as well?"

"It was. We were to test new equipment and conduct exercises. We are presently en route to Murmansk, returning home."

"Well I'm afraid you will find yourself in dangerous waters here," said Tovey. "It is our intelligence that the German Navy is planning a major breakout operation here, which is the reason we have hastened to assemble this battle fleet. It may be wise of you to move south at this time to avoid the action that may soon unfold here. Given your size and silhouette, it would be easy for either side to mistake you for the enemy, and should you proceed north we cannot necessarily guarantee your safety."

Volsky smiled. The low cards have been played, and now the British Admiral led with a spade, hoping to move me out of the theater of operations. But I am an old bridge player, and have a very long suit in spades. Time to play.

"Thank you, Admiral Tovey. But I *can* guarantee our safety as we sail north. In fact I may be able to guarantee yours as well."

Chapter 33

Tovey did not know what to make of Admiral Volsky's last statement. "I'm sorry, Admiral, but I am not quite sure I follow what you mean."

"Forgive me, Admiral. I do not mean to be coy, but we have been well north of your present position, and gained intelligence that you might find valuable. So it was that we came across the wreckage of your cruiser along our route home. I wonder if you are aware that the Germans will have more than this heavy cruiser at sea to the north."

"Which is all the more reason for you to consider safer waters to the south, Admiral."

Volsky took a sip of his gin, then set the glass down. "May I ask Captain Fedorov to speak briefly. He is somewhat of a naval historian, and I think he may be able to shed some light on what I am trying to tell you here. Mister Fedorov?"

Fedorov began to address the officers as if he were lecturing at the academy, looking to Nikolin, who translated skillfully as he spoke.

"From what I have seen, you presently have a strong force assembled. You will be matched, however, by an equally powerful force. Our intelligence indicates the Germans will have *Bismarck* and *Tirpitz*, to put against your flagship here and HMS *Hood*. They will have two battlecruisers *Scharnhorst* and *Gneisenau*, to match *Repulse*, and two heavy cruisers *Prince Eugen* and the *Hipper* to set beside your own cruisers. They, too have carrier support, which is somewhat surprising to me, and I think it was also a surprise to you. We have confirmed this through analysis of signals traffic. And they have also brought three large destroyers, more like light cruisers really. To put it simply, sir, and I mean no disrespect, I do not believe you presently command sufficient force to prevail should it come to a major fleet action here."

Holland raised an eyebrow at that, thinking the Russian Captain seemed a bit too young to be in that position, and here he was telling a pair of Admirals with combined service histories twice his years in age that all their considerable efforts would come to naught. He smiled, politely, but spoke his mind.

"My good man, I should think we will manage well enough if it comes to a fight here."

"I would hope that you would, Admiral Holland, but we believe this flagship and other escorts were east of Iceland some 48 hours ago, and undoubtedly with the same mindset and confidence. Yet here you are, and we are aware that HMS *Renown*, once steaming by your side, is not here."

The boldness of that statement struck through the British officers like a well aimed cricket ball. Flag Lieutenant Villers shifted uncomfortably, but deferred to Admiral Tovey.

"May I ask how you came by this information, Captain?"

"The same way you come by your information, Admiral. We listen to signals traffic just as you and the Germans do, and our ship is highly specialized in general area surveillance. In fact, we can tell you a great many things you may not yet know based on our reconnaissance north earlier today."

"I see... Do go on, Captain. If you have information that would be pertinent and useful, we would certainly welcome it."

Fedorov looked first to Admiral Volsky, something Tovey noted and looked on with approval. The young man seemed confident, knowledgeable, yet correctly deferred to senior authority. He watched the Russian Admiral closely as well, still wrestling inwardly with the impossible notion that he knew this man. Volsky spoke next.

"There is something more I will disclose to you now, and that is a decision I have made personally in this situation in consultation with our senior officers. You have said we cruise in dangerous waters here, and this we came to know, first hand. The German ships responsible for the sinking of your cruiser to the north also encountered us. I believe they were attempting to refuel with a replenishment ship hovering west near the ice floes. In any case, as it happened our course ran afoul of theirs, and there was a disagreement." He folded his arms, watching Tovey to see what effect his words had as Nikolin finished the translation.

"Are you saying you engaged the Germans, sir?"

"Two ships. My Captain here tells me they were battlecruisers, and they did not seem to like the looks of us on their horizon. From our position at the time we were aware of your position as well, Admiral Holland, and it seemed to us that the Germans, after besting your cruiser screen, were now in a very good place to slip by you and gain the Atlantic. I do not have to tell you that would have created a most uncomfortable situation for your merchant marine, as we have also seen the convoy traffic further south. Taking all this into consideration, I made a decision to intervene."

"Intervene?" Holland again has a bemused look on his face. "Now I mean no disrespect either here, Admiral, and please pardon me if I am as frank and direct as your Captain Fedorov. I have had a close look at your ship in the last hour. Your size and silhouette are quite impressive, a marvel of naval architecture, I would say. However how did you propose to 'intervene' with all of six 5.7 inchers on deck? The Twins, that is what we call the two German battlecruisers we are hunting, well…they will outgun you many times over, and I wouldn't think your ship would survive such an encounter. After all, they bested two of our cruisers with twenty-four 6-inch guns between them. That is four times the firepower I saw on your ship." Holland folded his hands.

Soft spoken if a bit smug, thought Volsky, but he understood the man's argument and attitude easily enough. The British cannot see our teeth, and so of course they believe we are toothless. How to convince them otherwise?

"Mister Fedorov, kindly inform these gentlemen as to the decisions we made and relate the action taken."

"Yes sir. Admiral Holland, while it may not appear from a distance that we carry much in the way of armament, appearances can be deceiving. We are, in fact, a prototype design, and considerably well armed with resources beyond the deck guns you have observed and commented on." He noted how Holland folded his arms, his body language closed and clearly somewhat defensive at the moment.

"Some time ago we attempted to dissuade the Germans from attacking your cruisers, but did not apply sufficient force. We were uncertain as to what we should do at the time, so we first tried jamming their radar and communications, but they persisted. We did, however use those 5.7 inchers to prompt the Germans to break off their pursuit of the cruisers, whereupon they turned southwest at high speed."

"You are telling me you drove off the Twins with your deck guns? I find that a bit of a stretch, Captain."

"We were unseen at the time, Admiral, yet we were able to put accurate fire on the lead German ship. I do not think the German commander was driven off as much as he simply decided that bothering with your cruisers, which he believed to be the source of the fire we put on him, was of no further advantage to him. It was our assessment that the Germans were keen to rendezvous with a refueling ship before proceeding south. Though they had clearly broken through your cruiser screen and positioned themselves to evade your capital ships, the need to replenish was, in our estimation, their Achilles heel."

Tovey was taking all this in with equal surprise, but with quite a different reaction. The Russians, a neutral state, had willfully violated their own neutrality to intervene on behalf of embattled Royal Navy units that were clearly overmatched by the enemy. He saw in that a ray of hope, but said nothing for the moment, allowing the young Russian officer to continue.

"On Admiral Volsky's orders, we located their replenishment ship, the *Altmark*, and sunk it, hoping this might dissuade them from continuing south. It seemed we were wrong, for after rendering assistance to *Altmark*, the Germans took a heading due south, and on a course that saw them encounter us while we were performing routine maintenance some hours later. The Twins, as you call them, decided to attack. We suppose they believed us to be one of your ships, but we defended ourselves, engaging and damaging one ship, which we subsequently determined to be the *Gneisenau*. The Germans then broke off their attack and reversed their course. They are now well to the north effecting a rendezvous with the force Admiral Tovey encountered earlier northeast of Iceland."

Fedorov finished, and the British seemed dumbfounded by what he had told them. Holland looked at Tovey, as if to see whether he believed what the Russians were saying here. It was clear that he had real doubts about it as he summed up what Fedorov had said, an edge of incredulity in his voice.

"You are telling us now that you attempted to aid our cruisers, then found and sunk the *Altmark* to prevent the Germans from refueling and beat off an attack by *Scharnhorst* and *Gneisenau* to send them north to look for assistance?"

"That sizes it up fairly well, Admiral Holland."

"You left one thing out, Admiral Holland," said Tovey diplomatically. "They also happened upon the wreckage of *Birmingham* and saved at least fifteen souls there, Captain Madden among them."

"Here, here." Captain Bennett, who had been listening quietly, took it upon himself to raise his glass of gin in a toast.

"Well you have been quite busy, it seems," said Tovey. "I will gladly second your toast, Captain Bennett, and allow me to extend our thanks and appreciation for all these gentlemen have done. You realize, of course, that you have violated the terms of your own neutrality by taking these actions."

"Admiral," said Volsky. "Even though my backside has become much more substantial than I would like at this age, I found it most uncomfortable to sit on the fence in this situation. While we sail under the flag of a neutral country, I do not think there is much time for that luxury in this war. We are all going to have to choose sides here, at one time or another. Our homeland has not as yet made that decision, but you have just lost your only ally in Europe with the fall of France, and I can imagine that prospects look fairly bleak to you just now. So I would like to offer you my hand in friendship here, perhaps a gesture that you might see as having some value. I fear that as soon as Hitler settles himself in the house he had lately broken into, he will not rest there. No, he will quickly turn his greedy eyes on the villas up the street. There are only two directions he might take, and we are both his neighbors now, your country and ours. It seems to me our mutual cooperation and understanding would be a great help to you at this dark hour."

* * *

Lindemann and the others listened as Hoffman and Fein explained what they saw—a rocket, incredibly fast and deadly accurate. It had been fired from a range of at least 18,000 meters and bored in mercilessly, so fast that the eye could barely follow it as it thundered home.

"It maneuvered," said Hoffmann gesturing with his hand to show how the rocket swooped up from the sea. "I could clearly see the exhaust trail in the sky. It arced up from the enemy ship, climbed, and then dove for the sea, skimming right over the wave tops. Then, at the very last minute, it leapt at the ship's vitals above the waterline, as if it was deliberately guided to avoid our heavy side armor. The explosion was terrible to behold."

"The warhead must have been at least 300 kilograms," said Fein "and it penetrated the superstructure amidships easily. Then came the fires. It was as if someone had sprayed gasoline all over the interior compartments and then tossed in a match, but many times worse. The heat was intense. Every compartment involved was completely immolated, and no one in those sections survived. I lost forty three men there."

The testimony of these two experienced officers was sobering, to say the least, and there was no more sentiment of jubilant celebration in the room.

"I know we, ourselves are working on this technology," said Lindemann. "Most of it is top secret and hidden away at the Peenemünde Army Research Centre. There have been proposals for remote controlled aircraft such as Project Erfurt, and men like Goddard in America and our own von Braun have proposed models for rockets as well. They are thinking to send remote controlled aircraft over the channel carrying 1000 kilogram bombs! But it is no more than an idea at the moment, and most senior officers I have spoken with seemed to dismiss it as having no real military applications. How would you control such a plane? A rocket would seem even more daunting. Yes, they have been used for centuries, ever since the discovery of gunpowder, but all current rocket development is unguided and likely to stay that way for some time."

"Not these rockets," said Hoffmann, shaking his head. "Unless the aim was flawless, this rocket seemed to have a mind of its own. Remember, we are not sitting there like a toy in the bathtub! We were cruising near thirty knots. The British hit a ship moving at that speed from over 18,000 meters away, and with accuracy that was more precise than our finest naval gun directors and optics. Now, anyone who wishes to see the result is welcome to visit Otto here aboard

Gneisenau after this little conference, but the question before us now is how do we proceed?"

Silence. All eyes turned to Lindemann, who folded his hand slowly, considering. "We have heard from Wilhelmshaven," he said. "I must tell you, Hoffmann, that Raeder was not happy with your decision to engage that ship. It would have been better if you had kept to the plan and simply ran south for the Atlantic."

"That is what I decided, Lindemann. Then we came upon the ship and thought it was another British cruiser, even though I could not recognize the silhouette."

"Well, perhaps you should have *avoided* engagement. That said, here we are. Raeder was not happy that I engaged the British with our carrier aircraft either—until he received the news concerning *Renown*. Seekriegsleitung made it evident that they believed my decision to elect the Denmark Strait as a breakout point instead of the more open seaways in the Iceland-Faeroes gap was not what they expected. So we are both in the soup together, Kapitan. Now that we have come here to this rendezvous point at your request, we have considerable power at our disposal. It is no longer a question of trying to slip a raider or two out into the Atlantic as I view the situation. In spite of this rocket you speak of, now we have the power to fight our way through."

"Raeder has approved this?"

"I made the request. They are undoubtedly scouring the intelligence to see what we may be up against if we do proceed south now. It is either that, or the whole operation must be postponed, and if we turn for home now it will be a long winter before we see these waters again. This is my belief."

"Then what do you propose, Lindemann?"

"I have conferred with Seekriegsleitung and Lütjens. You all know that he is a careful and cautious man. Yet even he sees the advantage we now have with our present concentration of forces. This was not what Raeder wanted, but choices we have both made have brought us here. So my request was that we refuel now and proceed south by 18:00 hours this evening. What do the rest of you think?"

Karl Topp, the Kapitan of Tirpitz, spoke next. "I'm an old U-boat man, so you may dismiss whatever I say, but I know what the men our ships are named after might advise. Here we have clenched a hard fist. I say we strike south and bludgeon anything in our path. We will have air cover, *Stukas*, and the finest ships in the world. We either use them or continue playing hide and go seek with the Royal Navy. This is what I believe."

That sentiment found immediate support from the two cruiser Kapitans, and Böhmer from *Graf Zeppelin*. "We have two battleships, a pair of battlecruisers, two heavy cruisers and three destroyers," he said. "*Gneisenau* took a hard blow, but there is nothing wrong with the guns, eh Fein? I say we move as Lindemann and Topp suggest."

"One thing, gentlemen," said Lindemann. "If we top off our tanks here we will take every drop of fuel *Nordmark* has. Once in the Atlantic we will be a long way from home, and our control of French ports is tenuous at this point. We have only just occupied Brest, St. Nazaire and La Pallice. Word is that the British took heavy loss at St. Nazaire. We hit a nice fat ocean liner packed to the gills with troops, but it will be some time before the docks and quays, or adequate supplies can be made ready for us there. So we cannot count on those ports being available to accommodate the entire fleet. This means that operations will have to be supported by the tankers remaining in the Atlantic if we push too far south, and we have seen what happened to *Altmark* here. Lose another tanker, or god forbid two, and we could be hung out like fish on a wire."

"Logistics will be uppermost in the minds of Raeder and Lütjens," said Hoffmann. "I will be frank and say that my decision to turn north and refuel was based on this same logic. Yes, we can fight here, but we may need to consider more limited operations."

"Exactly," Lindemann agreed. "I suggested that we fight to secure access to the Halifax-Liverpool convoy route, there are a pair of nice fat convoys within easy reach even as we speak. If we can get south in 48 hours, we will have a hundred ships to feast on. That will make Raeder happy. Then we retire north, and not west to France. This is what I proposed to Wilhelmshaven. Now we wait to see what Raeder and Lütjens have to say about it."

"Have they been informed of the damage to *Gneisenau?*" asked Fein.

"They are aware your ship was hit, but this business about the rocket sits here between us at this table and has gone no further. Frankly I do not know what they would make of it, and so I suggest we do not complicate the matter trying to explain through signals traffic what Hoffmann has told us here."

"But be forewarned," said Hoffmann. "If this ship is spotted again, perhaps your *Stukas* can deal with it Kapitan Böhmer."

"True," said Lindemann. "Perhaps we should assign a code here to alert all the others if we sight this ship."

Hoffman chuckled at that. "No Kapitan Lindemann, we will not need such devices. If this ship appears again you will all see it with your own eyes, plain enough, and believe me, you will never forget it as long as you live."

Part XII

The Witching Hour

*"Tis now the very witching time of night,
When churchyards yawn and hell itself breathes out
Contagion to this world: now could I drink hot blood,
And do such bitter business as the day
Would quake to look on."*

— William Shakespeare ~ Hamlet

Chapter 34

Tovey sat with the latest dispatch from the Admiralty, his mind heavy with foreboding. Operation Ariel, the final evacuation from France had just been dealt a heavy blow. The old Cunard steamship liner *Lancastria* had been crowded with both civilian and service and support troops, one of the last to leave St. Nazaire as the Germans closed in. With a stated capacity of 1300 passengers and 300 crew, the ship had packed in over 8000 souls, ready to sail for England. The Captain of the escorting British destroyer *Havelock* urged them to get out to sea, but a U-boat warning caused her Captain, Rudolph Sharp, to delay. It was a fatal decision.

At a little before 4pm the previous day, June 17th, the Germans sent in the Luftwaffe to attack the desperate flotillas attempting to flee the continent. JU-88s from *Gruppe/Kampfgeschwader 30* scored three direct hits on the lumbering steamship, causing her to list and then quickly turn over. One bomb had penetrated her fuel bunkers, and the sea around the stricken ship was soon black with oil. As if this heavy blow were not enough, the JU-88s made additional strafing runs, killing many as they struggled for life in the water and setting the fuel afire where thousands of desperate men and women were now adrift on the dark oily sea, burned and drowned in an agonizing death of fire and water. It was a brutal act of cruelty masquerading as a wartime operation, the most severe loss at sea ever suffered by a British ship.

"*Most secret – Not to be disclosed or disseminated below flag level,*" he read aloud, then lowered his head, sitting down, his hand covering his eyes. The loss was more than twice that suffered during the sinking of the Titanic, and it would account for a third of all casualties suffered by the British Expeditionary Force on the continent. Fearing news of the disaster would cut home morale to the bone, only the most senior officers were advised, and a blackout concerning the incident was imposed on all press and media.

It was one damn catastrophe after another, thought Tovey. France and Norway gone, the fate of the powerful French fleet still hanging in the balance, the threat of imminent invasion of the homeland, and now this. On top of it all we are now facing this powerful formation of German ships, easily a match for us, and who could foresee such a thing coming to pass? God help us if they do win through the straits and get at those convoys. I must immediately request HX-50 and HX-51 either re-route south or return to Halifax, and there can be no further sailings from that port until this issue is decided. There are ninety ships between those two convoys, and I also have TC-5 to worry about, another nine ships there, with the *Empress of Australia* carrying over 3700 troops. It's another bloody disaster in the waiting, and all that stands between those ships and the bottom of the sea is Home Fleet.

At least that last convoy has some escort. *Revenge* is presently on station with TC-5. There's another eight good 15-inch guns there that I could dearly use right now, but she can make only 23 knots and is too far south and east to matter now. Admiralty has already pulled *Devonshire* off of convoy duty to escort *Illustrious*. There simply isn't anything left, and something tells me the Germans are coming in force this time. We'll just have to face them down with what we have. But if we lose this fight...He did not want to contemplate the consequences.

The offer of friendship and support extended by the Russians seemed more inviting now, though he knew the matter would have to be sent on to the Admiralty first. What could they do, really? He had taken their testimony concerning the engagement with the Twins with a grain of salt. But being diplomatic, he had thanked the Russian Admiral, saying he believed his government would be most interested in further discussions on their mutual cooperation. In the end, however, he had to urged him to remain well south of the action he anticipated soon in the Denmark Strait. Their young Captain seemed troubled, still believing that this was a battle we might not win, but there is little help the Russians could offer us. As imposing as this new ship appeared, Holland was correct to point out it had only half the firepower of a small British light cruiser, in spite of their claims to the contrary. He was of a mind that the Russians had spun out a bit of a bender, stretching the truth concerning their engagement with the Germans.

Yet, as he stood on the weather deck watching the Russian ship haul in its massive anchor and slowly make way, that haunting feeling of *déjà vu* returned to him. He felt certain he had seen this ship before. It was completely irrational. There was no reason why he should feel this way, but he could not deny the clear sense of anxiety he felt to look on the long lines of the cruiser, easily as big as *Hood* or his own flagship.

So he issued his orders. Admiral Holland, with *Hood* and *Repulse* would continue to operate together and take up a position on the right. Tovey would take *Invincible* and the destroyers *Fortune* and *Firedrake* in the center, steaming some 18,000 yards west of Holland's position. Vice Admiral Wells with the two British carriers would hold down the left flank, escorted by the heavy cruisers *Sussex* and *Devonshire*, with destroyers *Tartar*, *Javelin* and *Jackal* in escort, led by the redoubtable Lord Mountbatten aboard *Jackal*. This force would steam west-southwest of Tovey's position, with the cruisers well out in front.

As for *Kirov*, Admiral Volsky offered to take a place in the line, but Tovey politely declined. The Russians were again urged to move off to the south pending developments.

"Well Admiral, we will be on your left should you need us," the Russian had told him. Then he smiled. "I have heard there is good fishing near the ice this time of year. God go with you."

* * *

Far to the north, the German fleet winked goodbye to the tanker *Nordmark* at 18:00 hours as planned. The sun was low on the horizon, but it would not set this day, up to bear full witness to what was now about to transpire. Lindemann had received permission to attempt to force the strait on the condition that he should break off the engagement if any of the capital ships were heavily damaged and in danger of being sunk.

Raeder was keen to preserve the fighting power of his fleet, and he was very pointed on one matter. As Lindemann looked at the final message from Wilhelmshaven, he was in full agreement with the order. *'Under no circumstances is Graf Zeppelin to be placed forward in any position where the ship might be sighted or engaged.'*

The German Fleet commander knew the risk of what he was permitting now. Just days earlier he had lectured Admiral Donitz: *'We will not sail out in one great sortie to seek battle with the British Home Fleet. That would be foolish…No. The virtue of the ships we have built still lies in the unique combination of speed, power and endurance. We will accomplish our aims with maneuver, not a set piece battle.'* Now the situation had changed and Rader was ordering the very thing he feared most—a direct challenge to the Royal Navy with the heart of the German fleet. But he had devised this strategy thinking his navy could never match the might of Britain's fleet. If intelligence was correct on the composition of the enemy force, he now believed he could not only give challenge, but win!

The Germans formed three battlegroups as well. In the east was Group Böhmer with *Graf Zeppelin* and the two destroyers *Beowulf* and *Sigfrid* in escort. The carrier was kept well back, and had the advantage of ample sea room free of ice should it need to run from any pursuing ship. Lindemann set his mind on assuring that would not happen. He was steaming 20,000 meters to the west with *Bismarck, Tirpitz,* and the heavy cruiser *Prince Eugen.* The destroyer *Heimdall* was out in front as an early warning picket so that his heavy ships could not be surprised. An equal measure west, and very near the ice, was group Hoffmann, with *Scharnhorst, Gneisenau,* and *Admiral Hipper.* Fein was given orders that he should steam third in the line of battle, and break off immediately should *Gneisenau* sustain any further damage.

They steamed south, seeing pale floes of ice drifting on the still waters. It was a calm sea, but wisps of fog were forming over the ice and slowly migrating east. A fat gibbous moon rose over the scene, adding its cold light and painting the sea with its glistening 'whale road.' Unless the fog thickened, visibility would be good for battle.

Lindemann had told Hoffmann that if the British managed to concentrate against his main body, he was to detach *Gneisenau* to support the battleships, but if circumstances were favorable, he could take *Scharnhorst* and *Hipper* south and attempt to reach the Atlantic.

Close by the ice shelf, Hoffmann was on the bridge of *Scharnhorst,* cigar in hand, and feeling a cold hand of fate on his neck. There was going to be a battle here, he knew. Both sides are deployed on a front spanning some sixty kilometers. At one place or another, they will meet one another, and then it comes down to steel and blood.

As for that strange ship, let us hope it no longer waits for us to the south. Lindemann did not quite know what to make of my claim about this rocket weapon. He should have seen the damage on *Gneisenau* first hand, as I did. Well, soon we fight our battle, but not before we fill this lurid sky with bats off of *Graf Zeppelin.*

He looked at his watch. The action was about to begin.

* * *

Aboard the carrier *Graf Zeppelin* the last of the bats were spotted on deck and ready for takeoff. The entire contingent of 24 planes would go aloft tonight. One had been shot down in their last engagement with the British, and another crashed on landing. This left two dozen *Stukas*, and one was being flown by Hans-Ulrich Rudel again as a reward for his dramatic first hit on the *Renown*.

"First hit Rudel! That's good luck!" Hauptmann Marco Ritter had been one of the first to congratulate him on his safe return to the carrier.

"Thank you for giving me the chance, sir."

"Thank yourself. It took training, skill and plenty of guts to do what you did. Soon we go for the main event, and you will be right there again, Rudel. No more seaplanes for you!"

Rudel was elated. They were giving him a *Stuka* full time now, and he was eager to get airborne and put it to good use. Tonight they would fly south in a wide formation. The *Arados* were already well out in front, scouting the way. Marco Ritter would lead in the BF-109s, seven of the eleven fighters remaining. He liked those numbers too.

The midnight sun cast an eerie red glow as it dipped low to the horizon, but it would find no rest there this night. Soon they heard from their scout planes ahead: *sighted two large capital ships!* From the heading and bearing information they were steaming on a course to intercept Lindemann's center group. Rudel decided he would pay them a visit first.

The dark shapes of the *Stukas* drifted across the white moon, their fixed landing gear jutting beneath them like the legs of a bird of prey. Rudel looked up to see the fighters accelerating to take the lead. The *Arados* had spotted a squadron of British fighters flying cover, and the fight was on.

Heinrich Jurgen was swiveling his neck in all directions looking for clouds to hide in. The British *Skuas* had seen his *Arado* and two had broken their patrol formation to come after him. The rattle of his rear gunner opening up with his MG-15 broke the silence, the very first rounds fired in anger as the battle began. He was firing at Midshipman R. W. Kearsley in plane 6Q off the *Ark Royal*, but Kearsley would have nothing of it, banking deftly to evade the hot streamers as they whizzed by his plane.

The British pilot opened up with his Browning .303s riddling the *Arado's* tail and send it into a fluttering spiral as it plummeted downward and into the sea. First kill had gone to the British airmen, but Marco Ritter was quick to the scene, leading a sub-fight of three BF-109s in the vanguard of his fighter formation.

"Tommy wants a cracker," he said to his mates on the radio. "Let's see that he pays for it first." He banked his fighter and dove for the *Skua* as it was climbing after its run on the seaplane. The Messerschmitt growled in, wings blazing with fire that took the right wing off plane 6Q and sent Kearsley and his gunner/signalman Eccleshall into the drink to join the Germans. Tit for tat.

The remaining four *Skuas* rumbled into action, but the swift 109s were simply too agile for them. Two were down in short order, but Lieutenant Commander John Casson was wheeling and swerving in the sky, his stunt pilot skills making him the equal of the Germans even though his plane could not match them. He hit his flaps, watched a Messerschmitt flash by, and then quickly lined up on it for a kill.

"There's one for your white heather, Hornblower," he said to his mate in the rear seat. Peter Fanshaw, the squadron navigator had been busy tapping out his contact signal, and now he was on the rear machine gun. It was three *Skuas* to the two BF-109's, which Casson saw as even up. Petty Officer Wallace Crawford was on his right wing, finding him again after losing a German plane in a bank of clouds.

"Tally Ho, Johnny! But watch out above. Jerry's throwing the whole kitchen sink our way."

Casson looked up to see a full squadron of six more 109s and he knew the jig was up. "Signal *Hood* to get her dander up. There's bound to be *Stukas* behind those fighters. Where the hell is 800 Squadron?" He put on all the power he could and started to climb for some heavy gray clouds, looking for cover to try and get into a position to look for the *Stukas*. A wash of rain greeted him, then he broke through to see the dark formation ahead, some two dozen planes.

"Signal the lads, Hornblower. Large formation of enemy planes right off their starboard bow!"

Crawford had tried to follow Casson up. But Marco Ritter found him climbing and made a vicious pass. The heavy rounds shattered his canopy and he was hit in the right shoulder, thrown against the side of the plane as he lost control. He would not make it back to *Ark Royal* that night.

It was nigh on the witching hour and the vampires were on the wing. The *Stukas* looked down to see the same scenario they had been presented with earlier, two battlecruisers, one slightly bigger in the van, and they tipped their wings over and came screaming down like banshees, dark things in the glowing night, shadows on the face of the watching moon.

Below them Holland's battlegroup, with *Hood* in the van and *Repulse* following, threw up everything they could on defense. *Hood's* twin QF 4-inch Mk XVI guns joined with her 2-pounder pom-poms, which began puffing up the sky as the planes came in. But soon the 4-inch guns could simply not elevate high enough, as the *Stukas* could come in at a near vertical dive.

The ship swerved right, beginning a hard zig-zag to try and throw off the enemy's aim. There were three near misses, two other bombs falling wider off her bow as she put on all the speed she had, plowing through the glimmering seas at over 30 knots. Then one bomb caught her flush on B-turret. While the turret face was all of 15-

inches thick, the roof was only five inches and the bomb blasted through, putting two of her eight 15-inch guns out of action. That single blow reduced her standing in any fight at sea quickly from that of a battleship to that of a battlecruiser, now the better of HMS *Repulse* behind her only in stature and reputation.

Repulse took one hit near her fantail, a glancing blow that blew off the gunwale, dented her hull and threw splinters across the deck to kill three unlucky seamen there. There were four other close calls, but the agile battlecruiser was running at 32 knots, determined not to suffer the fate of her sister ship *Renown*. She would escape further damage but the venerable *Hood* would not. The last of the uninvited guests hurtling out of a blood red sky that night was Hans Ulrich-Rudel. He was lined up on the target and put his bomb right down on *Hood's* number two funnel, dead center on the ship. The resulting explosion blew the funnel apart, riddled the forward stack with hot shrapnel and sent an enormous billowing black cloud up as if all her boilers had vented in one mighty belch. He was the thirteenth plane to make the attack, and Rudel's luck was still good. He was now two for two.

The flak defense was good enough to get a pair of *Stukas* that night, and drive three others off, their pilots aborting their runs when the heat was too thick in the sky. Of the six remaining, John Casson got on the tail of one and blew it clean away before dancing off into another cloud. The remaining five had circled wide to look for other targets, but found nothing.

Casson looked to see another squadron of *Skuas* hastening to the scene. 800 squadron was joining the action. "It's about bloody time," he yelled, but one look at *Hood* told him it was already too late.

Chapter 35

Aboard *Kirov*, far to the west, Rodenko was able to use the long range radar to see the action beginning to unfold. He noted the airborne attack underway and the sudden change in speed and direction on the lead British ship told him a hit had been scored there.

"Looks to be some fairly hot action on the British far right," he reported. Volsky and Fedorov were consulting the situation map, and the Admiral did not like how things were shaping up.

"The German center force has just executed a turn to port. They are vectoring in on that same location."

"This Admiral Tovey has a good deal of trouble on his hands now. A pity he did not enlist our aid!" He looked at Fedorov.

"Frankly, I do not think they believed us, Admiral." Fedorov shrugged as he spoke. "They did not see that we could be of any use to them."

"The British center column has turned," said Rodenko as he received the new radar data on the map. "They are heading northwest. There's a battle underway there as well. Looks like a pair of British cruisers have found those battlecruisers we sent packing yesterday."

"This is not good, eh, Fedorov?"

"These are heavy cruisers this time, Admiral. They'll have eight 8-inch guns, enough to stand in a fight, but they'll be overmatched in time by the Germans there."

"Not a very satisfactory situation for the British," said Volsky. "Admiral Tovey is being hit on both flanks, now he must choose which to support with his center column. I think we had better put on speed and get north, gentlemen. The ship will come to 28 knots and steer zero-one-zero."

"We can strike with missiles now, sir," said Fedorov.

"Yes, we have the range, but missiles do funny things at times, Mister Fedorov. We could send in a salvo and find one selects a

British cruiser for its target in a close action like that. No, I think we will see if we can close the range a bit and find a better firing solution. Something tells me that the German center column is where their best ships are, correct, Rodenko?"

"Yes, sir. I read four contacts there, one out in front—most likely a destroyer picket—then a column of three ships about five kilometers behind it, two heavy contacts, one lighter."

"That is the battlegroup that Tovey must concern himself with now. Let us get north and see if we can render assistance."

* * *

Hoffmann lowered his field glasses, smiling. "Look there, Huber, a pair of British cruisers! It looks like they did not learn their lesson earlier, eh?"

"Apparently not," Huber folded his arms. "I make the range about 18,000 meters."

"Let us close to 15,000. If they fire first, however, instruct Schubert that he may answer immediately. Now... Hard to port and come to 100 degrees east southeast. We will get all our guns into the action that way, and move to a conjunction with Lindemann at the same time."

The crews were at the action stations, guns trained in the ruddy light, which presented an eerie setting, with drifts of grey fog over a blood red sea lit by the low crimson sun on one side and then washed over by the cold white moonlight. Here and there ice floes scudded along, some taken head on by the sharp bow of the ship, the shattered fragments clattering along the hull as *Scharnhorst* surged forward. The winds were calm, and it would make for good action by the guns.

Schubert reported all ready and awaiting permission to fire. "Range 16,000," he called down from the upper gun director's position." The British soon obliged him by firing their first ranging salvo, and they could now see the dark shapes of the two cruisers turning east on a near parallel course, unwilling to have their T crossed and not eager to close the range more than it was.

"They will want to get ahead of us if they can," said Hubert. "That way they will put the sun at our backside."

"We have the speed to prevent that. Answer them Schubert. Permission to open fire. Hoffmann gave the order, raising his field glasses to watch the result.

The ripple of fire from the German ship came in three sharp reports, and only from the forward turrets. Schubert had an unusual ranging pattern, firing the centermost barrels of his two forward triple turrets first, then the remaining two barrels of each turret in a second and third salvo, all in rapid succession. In this way he aimed to frame the target quickly, as each salvo of two rounds was set to alternate ranges, plus or minus a hundred meters on the computed target position.

He quickly saw that he had a near straddle on the lead ship, close enough to order fire for effect, and before the minute had ended all nine of *Scharnhorst's* 11-inch guns were ready for action again, the lights winking on in his director tower.

"Ready! Good!" The next salvo added fire to the ochre night, the blast from all nine guns shaking the ship and sending anything unsecured careening to the decks. Seconds later Hoffmann, out on the weather bridge and heedless of the danger there, heard the whoosh and fall of the enemy's second salvo. The shots were short and slightly wide, and he knew the spotters there were rapidly calling in the sighting corrections while crews labored to service the guns.

Schubert's first big salvo fell all around the lead ship now, and bright fire lit up the fantail where Hoffmann saw the first hit of the action. The gunnery officer saw it as well through his powerful optics and made a small correction before giving the order to fire again.

Then the second salvo came in, this time mostly fired by the trailing British cruiser, and Hoffmann heard its incoming wail even louder.

There came a hard knock, the ship shaking with the hit, right amidships on the heavy armor there. Two other rounds dolloped up the sea in a red and white geyser, the water glistening as it reached almost as high as Hoffmann's chin on the upper bridge.

"Starboard fifteen!" he shouted. The score was even, but Schubert was quick to reply. This third full salvo roared in reprisal, and it was quickly followed by the sharp crack of *Admiral Hipper's* 8-inch guns where that ship trailed the lead battlecruiser by about a thousand meters. Hoffmann steadied himself, one leather-gloved hand on the outer hand rail and the other holding his binoculars. Seconds later he saw the sea erupt again near the lead British cruiser, and hits sent up bright fire and smoke, both fore and aft.

Now more smoke, thick and very black enveloped the ship, and he knew it was artificial. The British were turning, ready to run behind a smoke screen if they could. *Hipper* had found the range on the second cruiser with a near straddle, and *Gneisenau* had put a set of three 11-inch rounds right astride its bow, with one hit on the forecastle near the A-turret.

The two cruisers were still firing, and were lucky enough to score yet another hit, this time low on the water line against *Scharnhorst*, where they had both concentrated their effort. They were narrowing the score, yet the difference in this game was not the guns, but the armor. With 14 inches of heavy Krupp Cemented steel that could shrug off a 16 inch shell at any range over 11,000 meters, *Scharnhorst* was invulnerable to hits against her belt armor. With the action running at 14,500 meters, the 8-inch shells fired by the cruisers could simply not penetrate, nor even seriously damage the German ship.

By contrast the bigger rounds being fired by *Scharnhorst* found only 4.5 inches of hull plating, a measly one inch siding on the turrets, and deck armor of only 1.375 inches—and they were doing grave harm anywhere they struck the British ships. *Sussex* in the lead had taken three hits, *Devonshire* following had taken two, though one of these was a lighter 8-inch round from the *Admiral Hipper.*

Though the action was only seven minutes old, it was clear that the British had had enough. They were challenged to face *Scharnhorst* alone, and now found both *Hipper* and *Gneisenau* looming out of the fog, guns blazing. The British cruisers steered hard to starboard, coming around nearly eighty compass points in a churning turn to run south at their best speed before either ship might sustain damage to their engines that would mean certain doom.

Hoffmann lowered his field glasses letting them dangle from the leather cord about his neck as Schubert fired his fifth salvo. He slowly pulled off his leather gloves, stuffing them into his warm greatcoat. Then he reached into his breast pocket and found the cigar he had been saving, lighting it behind his big cupped hand with a smile. He took a long satisfied drag and then gave the order to cease fire.

"Steady on and ahead full," he called as he headed for the conning tower entrance. Now we run east to join Lindemann, he thought. And if he has found the bigger British ships we will show up like Blucher at Waterloo—only this time it is Wellington's flank we turn. He chuckled at that. Victory was sweet.

* * *

Aboard HMS *Invincible* Admiral Tovey was feeling anything but that. The Admiralty was hot for action, wanting news of a victory at sea to bolster the nation's flagging morale, and the dispatches he was now receiving were not promising.

'*Hood under air attack at 19:40 hours, two hits both serious - B turret out of action and speed down to 20 knots. Repulse undamaged and now taking station ahead. Fires under control.*'

No sooner had he read that when Lieutenant Commander Wells arrived with the news of the encounter on his left flank. He had been steering towards the sound of those distant guns, just over the gloaming of the horizon to the northwest. Now the news of two hard blows to Holland's flagship had changed the whole complexion of his deployment. *Sussex* and *Devonshire* were retiring south, hoping to lead the Germans into his path, but spotters up in a *Walrus* reported that they were steady on 100 and heading on a course that might eventually intercept *Hood*. Under any other circumstances he might hope for such an engagement, but now his battlecruisers seemed all too vulnerable. Armor, he thought. Only *Invincible* had the hard steel to really stand in a fight like this. Even *Hood* could be a liability here as much as an asset.

"Mister Wells," he said, the calm in his tone belying the turmoil within him, "Send to *Sussex* and *Devonshire*. They are to run south and then come about and find my wake. And on your way notify Captain Bennett to steer zero-five-zero. It's time we pulled the fleet together into one mailed fist."

"Aye sir." Wells started for the door at a run, but Tovey stopped him, frowning.

"Calmly, Mister Wells, a brisk gait will do. No need to run. And please ask how soon we can expect support from Vice Admiral Aircraft Carriers. Holland certainly isn't covered properly, and where are my fighters?"

"Right away, sir."

There had been too little time. The planes he had begged the Admiralty for were still en-route to Reykjavik. It now appeared evident to Admiral Tovey that the German main body was going to hit Holland hard, and right on the nose. In that instance, *Invincible* needed to be there, and if he turned now, his present position might also allow him to also cut the German battlecruisers off that were running east to join the main body.

Lookouts had reported that the German strike planes, those bloody damn *Stukas*, had turned north, which is just where he expected the German aircraft carrier to be waiting. What he really needed now was support from his own carriers, and he hoped the combined weight of their torpedo squadrons would be enough to get through the BF-109s, which were still circling like vultures over Holland's task force.

Illustrious had received the new prototype *Fulmar* fighter, exactly three to go along with her *Skuas*, which gave him little hope that they could tip the balance in the air duel over the sea. The Messerschmitts were clearly masters of the sky, and the *Skuas* of 800 and 803 Squadrons off *Ark Royal* had again taken heavy losses. It was up to *Illustrious* to bring the weight of her air squadrons to the task, and soon. Between the two carriers they had at least thirty *Swordfish* they could get in the air and, in spite of their antiquated appearance, they had proven to be a fearsomely competent and able warrior when it came to their primary role. The question was, how many could get through those German fighters, and of those how many could get in close enough for a chance at getting a hit?

A strange calm came over the scene now, a dark red gloom seeming to hang over the ocean in rosy fog that was rolling off the ice shelf to the west. It was just after 21:00 hours when he gave the order to make that turn and, as he stared at the plotting board to note the position of the wooden markers on the table, he reluctantly placed a red damage marker on *Hood*. It would likely be another long hour before he could come up to Holland's aid, and it was going to be one of the longest hours of his life.

* * *

Kirov had run north at high speed, working up to thirty knots in spite of the strain on the bow. All the while Rodenko reported on the outcome of the cruiser engagement which did not surprise anyone on the bridge. At 21:30 hours Admiral Volsky brought the ship to battle stations.

"What is likely happening with those German dive bombers, Mister Fedorov?"

"By now they will broken off and returned to their carrier, sir. It will likely take them at least another hour to land, move below decks, and rearm if the Germans are planning a second strike. I would not expect them back in action for another ninety minutes."

"Well if they do come, I am going to extend a SAM umbrella over the British fleet. Mister Samsonov will prepare a barrage of a few S-400s. Once we fire them I believe the shock value alone may be sufficient to break up the enemy strike wave."

"It may, sir. While we were in the Caspian attempting to rescue Orlov the Germans threw several squadrons of *Stuka* dive bombers against the Russian positions on the coast. We had to engage them with all the handheld antiaircraft missiles at our disposal, and they found it most disconcerting."

"Those were no more than needles and pinpricks compared to what we will be throwing at them with the S-400 system. I have little doubt that we can stop this next air attack."

"I agree, sir."

"Then we have the question of what to do about the surface engagement. There is a part of me that wants to let history run its own course here and see what Admiral Tovey can do."

"I understand your feeling exactly, Admiral. Thus far this outcome could have been anticipated, but the real engagement with the action will come when the battleships sight one another."

"One for the history books," said Volsky, "and I wonder what they will write should we light up the skies with our missiles?"

Fedorov thought about that, realizing they were about to reach into the pages of that history and write their name. *Kirov,* battlecruiser of the Russian Federation. How strange it will be to realize no one in that Federation will have the slightest idea of who or what we are? What will be known about us soon if we continue this intervention? What can we reveal here without ripping the lid off of Pandora's jar and bringing havoc and mayhem to the world?

They were walking a fine line again where the desire to do good and work to make for a better world at the end of this crazy chaos of a war might also unleash that one forbidden fruit that could bring it all crashing down again—knowledge. They will see every shot we fire, and my god, what would ever happen if it became known that we were not born to this time and place, that we are strangers on this strange land, interlopers from another time with power beyond the imagination of anyone alive this day?

That thought stopped him…No…not everyone alive was blind to this knowledge. There were at least two other men at large in the world who knew the dreadful secret, and they had both walked the back stairway of the inn at Ilanskiy.

Chapter 36

The last shadow of the German planes swept overhead and turned north. On the bridge of HMS *Hood* Admiral Holland was a stolid totem, a pillar of calm in the tense atmosphere of combat. The pom-poms had fallen silent, and a moment of reserve crossed his thoughts. Inadequate, he thought. Our anti-aircraft suite is simply inadequate. The QF 4-inchers could elevate to 80 degrees, but beyond that there was a cone of silence directly above the ship that could only be filled with the lighter caliber guns. Even the QF-2 pounders had difficulty sighting there. This was where the *Stukas* made their attack runs and the two hits he had taken were the result. The smoke still curling up from B turret was ample evidence of the need, not to mention the armored roof of that turret…Inadequate.

Hood was a paper dragon. He knew that now. Over her long history she had passed through successive upgrades to add protection. It wasn't the main waterline belt. The battlecruiser had a heavy gut that was twelve inches thick there, though it thinned considerably in the middle belt above the waterline to only seven inches and eventually five inches as it approached the deck. It was that deck that he always worried about, averaging only two inches thick in most places. By comparison HMS *Invincible* had six to eight inches of protection there. *Hood* was designed in an era when things like the German *Stuka* were scarcely imagined. And her armor was fitted to protect her at relatively short ranges. She was vulnerable to fire beyond 11,000 meters, when the rounds would plunge at steeper angles and penetrate her the thinner sections of her side armor and decks.

So I have to run into the steely embrace of my enemy to fight him, he thought. This ship was like a boxer that had to get inside, and once there if she could not out punch her foe the ship would be in real jeopardy. Here I am on one of the largest ships in the fleet, he thought, and now with B-turret gone I can't hit any harder than old *Repulse* right behind me.

That was bad enough, but the worst of the damage had been the hit amidships that literally blew half the aft funnel away. The bomb had put several boiler rooms out of action, and the smoke there was intense, though the damage parties had the fires out. The result was a reduction of speed, first to 20 knots, which eventually improved to 24. Now we'd only beat *Nelson* and *Rodney* by a whisker in a race. We've a broken wrist and can no longer dance. Now he had real doubts about the battle looming on his forward horizon. *Bismarck* and *Tirpitz* were thought to be very formidable ships.

Sitting in the Captain's chair on the compass platform, Holland had real misgivings. He had signaled Tovey, advising him of the ship's condition and was ordered to turn on a heading of 330 to effect a rendezvous with *Invincible*. *"Hold on,"* came the reply. *"We're coming."* The only question now was whether the Germans would get to him first. What would they have? Would those *Stukas* be back for another round with 'Sammy' and 'Aunty,' the names given to his last two remaining octuple 2-inch pom-pom guns? He's lost the port gun mount with that dreadful hit amidships.

The ready use ammo had popped off there, round by round, like a fist full of fireworks going off one after another. The screams of the wounded men echoed up through the voice pipes to the bridge, which sound off like the trumpets of the dead. They still clawed at his mind, for he knew more men were going to die here this hour. Where was the Fleet Air Arm now? That yawning sense of vulnerability rose in his chest in an anxious upwelling of adrenaline. Here we are, he thought. The mighty *Hood*, yet we have no business in this fight now, not wounded as we are and outgunned by the Germans.

Then he heard the words he had been dreading from the upper watch. "Alarm starboard green 30! Ship sighted, bearing 350 true…Two ships!"

"Hoist battle ensigns!" said Holland firmly. "Prepare for action. Signal *Repulse* to turn fifteen points to port and we will follow. But if she is seriously hit Captain Tennant is to fall off and take station off our port aft quarter. I want her well back and throwing everything she has at the enemy." The armor on *Repulse* was even thinner, he knew, sizing up the engagement in front of him now.

"The pilot will make the signal report to fleet commander." Captain Glennie was seeing to the necessary details as the ship prepared to enter battle. Tovey would be apprised of their position and situation.

Holland seemed small and quiet in his chair, huddling in his greatcoat, his eyes lost behind the cups of his field glasses. We've twelve 15-inch guns between us, he thought. Enough to beat the Twins, by God, but if that is something more out there...It was something more. The Twins had been confirmed to be well to the west, last reported in action against *Sussex* and *Devonshire*, but they had turned and were now heading his way. He knew what he had in front of him now. The dark silhouettes on the horizon had to be the two German battleships, *Bismarck* and *Tirpitz*. Not much was known of them, but they were soon about to make their acquaintance.

"A-turret ready!" came the call. "Range to targets, eighteen and six pence."

Holland was in a quandary here. His instincts told him that he needed to close the range to at least 11,000, but to do this he would have only his A-turret available for the run in. If he turned now he could bring all six remaining guns to bear, but he would have to accept that damnable vulnerability to the enemy's plunging fire. How good were the German guns? If he tried to get inside how much punishment would the ship take, only to reach a place where the blows might fall on his better armor if they struck?

Well, he thought. We haven't the armor, so we had better damn well use what we do have, and that is the guns. "Port fifteen," he said calmly. "All guns to bear on the leading ship."

"Third ship sighted—looks to be a destroyer or light cruiser sir, well out ahead and thirty points off our starboard bow."

"Engage with secondary battery," said Holland. Then he swiveled to look at Captain Glennie, standing tensely behind him. "Captain, you may begin."

Several observers were heading to the starboard side door, among them Lieutenant Ted Briggs. As he reached the door Commander Warrand was there, gracefully gesturing with an arm to allow him to pass. The simple act of civility was juxtaposed against the act of great violence that was now about to begin. In one telling of these events Briggs would be one of only three men to escape alive from the wreckage of HMS *Hood*, the memory of that simple gesture by Commander Warrand still bringing tears to his eyes sixty years later. But this was an altered reality, and the dice were now rolling again on *Hood's* prospects. Yet as they saw *Bismarck* open fire, and the guns of *Tirpitz* flashing right behind her, the chances of survival seemed slimmer yet.

Captain Glennie wasted no time replying. "Open Fire!" which was quickly repeated by the Gunnery Director. The sound of the warning bell seemed shrill in the still air. Then the roar of *Hood's* opening salvo shook the ship. The big guns had ridden proudly on the fore and aft decks for decades, a symbol of her power and prestige, and yet now they fired in anger at an enemy ship for the very first time.

"Hoist Flag Five," said Holland to send the signal to *Repulse* to fire at will. Fifty seconds later the first whoosh of the German shells came in, and the tall geysers fell off *Hood's* starboard bow, walking ever closer, two, then four, then six rounds fell into the crimson sea. Another set of six rounds fell just off *Repulse*, closer, finding the range but missing the ship itself. The observers off the compass platform saw *Hood's* own fire also falling short of the enemy ships, and that of *Repulse* slightly over.

Holland was watching his brave forward A-turret, seeing the guns had lowered to be serviced and now they trained and elevated yet again. The angry discharge and concussion shook the ship as they fired, the smoke from the blast rolling out thick and dark. It seemed that two demons were heaving brimstone at one another on the lake of hell. Now the German ships were turning to their starboard quarter, their silhouettes lengthening as they maneuvered.

"Fourth ship sighted!" The watchman from above had spotted *Prinz Eugen*, last in line behind the two German behemoths. The ragged shadows of the battleships now rippled with fire, and Holland knew that the Germans had corrected from their spotting salvo and were now firing for effect.

"Quite the pair of dragons," said Captain Glennie, stepping towards the starboard hatch himself for a better look. Then they heard the awful whine of the incoming shells again, as if the rounds were devouring the air as they plummeted down and down until the bright metal tips came careening in, and one struck *Hood* flush on the conning tower with a tremendous explosion.

Holland was flung from the Captain's chair, the blast and concussion nearly deafening him. The glass screening the compass platform was completely shattered and fell like broken shards of razor edged ice all about the deck. Smoke flooded through the shattered viewports and fire licked at the hard armored tower from below. Commanders Davis and Jessel were down. Mister Owens, the Admiral's secretary, was dead. Young Bill Dundas, action midshipman of the watch, had been flung against the back bulkhead. The helmsman was unconscious on the deck, the binnacle still vibrating in its mounting and another a man screaming for help there. Yet the voices seemed distant and muted, and the Admiral instinctively reached for his ear as he pulled himself up to one knee with his other hand, feeling a trickle of blood there. Everyone on the outer deck was gone, the door to the starboard hatch blown completely off and now lying atop the limp body of Captain Glennie.

The Squadron Navigation Officer Warrand had gone back to the chart room to fetch a map and was spared. He emerged to see the chaos on the bridge, and quickly ran to Holland's side.

"Take the wheel, Mister Warrand…" Holland's voice was thin and weak, and Warrand saw a stain on blood at his side where he must have been hit with a splinter. It was only his heavy duffel coat that saved him from more grievous harm.

He was up in a flash, grabbing the long umbilical of a voice tube and calling down for medics. *Take the wheel…* The wheel was the ship, and Warrand knew he had to take command. He reached the station, barely able to see through the choking smoke. *Tovey is west* he thought. *We've got to lead the fight that way,* and he pulled heavily on the wheel, bringing the ship around thirty points. "Ahead full!" He shouted, but there was no answer.

Hood reeled like a drunken fighter, staggering across the ring after taking a right cross flush on the jaw. Warrand was alone. He looked to see that Yeoman Wright was also down near the flag bridge. No voices called from the gun director's station or the watch above. He seemed the only living thing in this chamber of death. Then he felt the ship shake again with yet another hit, this time on her starboard side. The forward battery was silent for a long moment, but now he saw the turret shift and train to the right to compensate for the turn he had made. Then they fired.

The ship surged on, the wind of its own haste finally clearing the smoke, and he saw that he was sailing through a forest of white seawater, vast pillars spouting up from the wave tops, two straddling the bow and four more dead ahead. A rain of water washed over the bow from the two near misses. He pulled the wheel around ten points to starboard, desperately trying to take some evasive maneuver.

Now fresh hands were on the bridge, hastening up from below. Medics were at Holland's side, lifting him onto a stretcher. His head lolled on the pillow, snow white hair stained with blood. Hollow voices called from the standing voice pipe to the forward gun director's position like whispers of ghosts in the chaos on the bridge.

"Hoist Blue 3!" Warrand shouted to the Flag Bridge as the ship turned, hoping someone would answer. Yeoman Wright stirred to life, back on his feet again, his face bleeding where the glass had cut him, but otherwise alive. He relayed the order. They needed to signal *Repulse* by flag, but Warrand knew it was likely the ship would try to match his maneuver in any case. He felt the ship shudder again, but this time it was the two aft turrets firing together. *Hood* was dazed, bludgeoned, but still alive.

Then he looked out the shattered forward screens and saw yet another ship darken the horizon, looming ever larger second by second as it came. A flash of orange erupted from it, another gladiator coming to the arena. Who was there? *Scharnhorst? Gneisenau?* God Help us…

* * *

Lieutenant Commander Wells ran into the plotting room, breathless with the climb and saluted as he handed off the message to Flag Lieutenant Villers. He was not supposed to run, he knew, but could not help himself. The fight was underway.

Villers glanced at the message, reading what looked to be a unintelligible code. 'Y -2 - ADM, C-in-C. H.F., V.B. Cone, IIBS ICH 320-17-67-39°N, 27-79°W, 315-24.' But to a knowing eye it was completely transparent, and he quietly read the message aloud to Admiral Tovey.

"Emergency to Admiralty and C-in-C, Home Fleet. From BC1 - two battleships and one heavy cruiser, bearing 320, distance 17 miles. My position 67-39 north, 27-79 west. My course 315. Speed 24 knots."

Tovey looked up, his eyes squinting at his Flag Lieutenant. Villers read the message again as he walked slowly to the Admiral's side, handing him the signal.

"It appears Holland has a battle on his hands. No further details."

Tovey took a deep breath, but before he could say another word there was a warning gong from above. A signalman hastened in from the bridge. "Alarm Red 20 sir. Two ships sighted."

Tovey nodded and looked at his plotting board. He slowly turned the marker for HMS *Invincible* to the right, pointing it at the damaged *Hood*. Then he reached for the enemy marker that represented *Scharnhorst* and *Gneisenau*.

"So we have company," he said. "Salmon and Gluckstein have come to dinner. Anything coming from that quarter would have to be the Twins."

"Shall we engage, sir? We'll blow them half way to hell in short order."

"No, Mister Villers, we shall not. The ship will come to battle stations, steer steady on and ahead full emergency. Our business is with *Hood*. Let them follow us at their peril." He looked up, lips pursed, eyes alight. The ship's clock wound on, the chime striking out the hour, twelve slow bells to signal midnight, the witching hour.

"Mister Wells," he said, "now you may run."

The Saga Continues...

Altered States ~ Volume II

The first rounds have fallen, heavy shells smashing against the armored conning tower of HMS *Hood*, stunning the ship and its stolid Admiral Holland. Yet *Hood* fights on, her guns raging in reprisal as the pride of two navies meet in the largest naval engagement since Jutland. Even as Admiral Tovey reaches the action, the shadow of Hoffmann's battlegroup looms over his shoulder and the odds stack ever higher against the embattled ships of Home Fleet. Off to the north the *Stukas* rush to re-arm aboard carrier *Graf Zeppelin*, while far to the south another ship hastens north to the scene, from a time and place incomprehensible to the men now locked in a desperate struggle raging on a blood red sea that may decide the fate of England in 1940. Can they engage without shattering the fragile mirror of history yet again?

Learn the outcome and follow *Kirov* north as it heads to home waters, determined to meet the man that may have changed the course of all history, Sergei Kirov. Meanwhile the action moves to the Med where the young Christopher Wells is dispatched to Force H. The British must first prevent the powerful French Fleet from falling into enemy hands and stand against a much more aggressive Regia Marina. With threats on every quarter Britain is faced with the prospect of imminent invasion in Operation Selöwe, when the Admiralty learns of yet another operation that could decisively alter the balance of the war—an attack on the British naval bastion at Gibraltar. The fighting has only just begun as *Altered States* continues the retelling of the naval war at in an exciting second volume.

THE KIROV SERIES ~ BY JOHN SCHETTLER

Kirov

The battlecruiser *Kirov* is the most power surface combatant that ever put to sea. Built from the bones of all four prior *Kirov* Class battlecruisers, she is updated with Russia's most lethal weapons, given back her old name, and commissioned in the year 2020. A year later, with tensions rising to the breaking point between Russia and the West, *Kirov* is completing her final missile trials in the Arctic Sea when a strange accident transports her to another time. With power no ship in the world can match, much less comprehend, she must decide the fate of nations in the most titanic conflict the world has ever seen—WWII.

Kirov II – *Cauldron of Fire*

Kirov crosses the Atlantic to the Mediterranean Sea when she suddenly slips in time again and re-appears a year later, in August of 1942. Beset with enemies on every side and embroiled in one of the largest sea battles of the war, the ship races for Gibraltar and the relatively safe waters of the Atlantic. Meanwhile, the brilliant Alan Turing has begun to unravel the mystery of what this ship could be, but can he convince the Admiralty? Naval action abounds in this fast paced second volume of the *Kirov* series trilogy.

Kirov III - *Pacific Storm*

Admiral Tovey's visit to Bletchley Park soon reaches an astounding conclusion when the battlecruiser *Kirov* vanishes once again to a desolate future. Reaching the Pacific the ship's officers and crew soon learn that *Kirov* has once again moved in time. Now First Officer Anton Fedorov is shocked to learn the true source of the great variation in time that has led to the devastated future they have come from and the demise of civilization itself. They are soon discovered by a Japanese fleet and the ship now faces its most dangerous and determined challenge ever when they are stalked by the Japanese 5th Carrier Division and eventually confronted by a powerful enemy task force led by the battleship Yamato, and an admiral determined to sink this phantom ship, or die trying. In this amazing continuation to the popular *Kirov* series, the most powerful ships ever conceived by two different eras clash in a titanic final battle that could decide the fate of nations and the world itself.

Kirov Saga: *Men Of War ~ Book IV*

Kirov returns home to a changed world in the year 2021, and as the Russian Naval Inspectorate probes the mystery of the ship's disappearance, Anton Fedorov begins to unravel yet another dilemma—the secret of Rod 25. The world is again steering a dangerous course toward the great war that blackened the shores of a distant future glimpsed by the officers and crew. Fedorov has come to believe that time is waiting on the resolution of one crucial unresolved element from their journey to the past—the fate of Gennadi Orlov.

Join Admiral Leonid Volsky, Captain Vladimir Karpov, and Anton Fedorov as they sleuth the mystery of Orlov's fate and launch a mission to the past to find him before the world explodes in the terror and fury of a great air and naval conflict in the Pacific. It is a war that will span the globe from the Gulf of Mexico to the Middle East and through the oil rich heart of Central Asia to the wide Pacific, but somehow one man's life holds the key to its prevention. Yet other men are aware of Orlov's identity as a crewman from the dread raider they came to call *Geronimo*, and they too set their minds on finding him first...in 1942! Men of war from the future and past now join in the hunt while the military forces of Russia, China, and the West maneuver to the great chessboard of impending conflict.

Kirov Saga: *Nine Days Falling, Book V*

As Fedorov launches his daring mission to the past to rescue Orlov, Volsky does not know where or how to find the team, or even if they have safely made the dangerous transition to the 1940s....But other men know, from the dark corners of Whitehall to the KGB. And other men also continue to stalk Orlov in that distant era, led by

Captain John Haselden and the men of 30 Commando. The long journey west is fraught with danger for Fedorov's team when they encounter something bewildering and truly astounding, an incident that leads them deeper into the mystery of Rod-25.

Meanwhile, *Kirov* has put to sea and now forms the heart of a powerful battlegroup commanded by Captain Vladimir Karpov. He is soon confronted by the swift deployment of the American Carrier Strike Group Five out of Yokosuka Japan in a tense standoff at sea that threatens to explode into violence at any moment. The fuse of conflict is lit across the globe, for the dread war has finally begun when the Chinese make good on their threat to secure their long wayward son—Taiwan. From the pulsing bitstream of the Internet, the deep void of outer space, the oil soaked waters of the Persian Gulf and Black Sea, to the riveting naval combat in the Pacific, the world descends in nine grueling days, swept up in the maelstrom and chaos of war.

This is the story of that deadly war to end all wars, and the desperate missions from the future and past to find the one man who can prevent it from ever happening, Gennadi Orlov. Can the mystery of Rod-25 and Orlov be solved before the ICBMs are finally launched?

Kirov Saga: *Fallen Angels ~ Book VI*

The war continues on both land and sea as China invades Taiwan and North Korea joins to launch a devastating attack. Yet *Kirov* and the heart of the Red Banner Pacific Fleet has vanished, blown into the past by the massive wrath of the Demon Volcano. There Captain Karpov finds himself at the dying edge of the last great war, yet his own inner demons now wage war with his conscience as he contemplates another decisive intervention.

After secretly assisting the Soviet invasion of the Kuriles and engaging a small US scouting force in the region, Karpov has drawn the attention of Admiral Halsey's powerful 3rd Fleet. Now Halsey sends one of the toughest fighting Admirals of the war north to investigate, the hero of the Battle off Samar, Ziggy Sprague, and fast and furious sea battles are the order of the day.

Meanwhile tensions rise in the Black Sea as the Russian mission to rescue Fedorov and Orlov has now been expanded to include a way to try and deliver new control rods to *Kirov* from the same batch and lot as the mysterious Rod-25. Will they work? Yet Admiral Volsky learns that the Russian Black Sea Fleet has engaged well escorted units of a British oil conveyor, Fairchild Inc., and the fires of war soon endanger his mission.

All efforts are now focused on a narrow stretch of coastline on the Caspian Sea, where men of war from the future and past are locked in a desperate struggle to decide the outcome of history itself. Naval combat, both future and past, combine with action and intrigue as Volsky's mission is launched and the mystery of Rod-25 and Fedorov's strange experience on the Trans-Siberian Rail is finally revealed. Can they stop the nuclear holocaust of the Third World War in 202,1 or will it begin off the coast of Japan in 1945?

Kirov Saga: *Devil's Garden ~ Book VII*

The stunning continuation to the *Kirov* saga extends the action, both past and present, as the prelude to the Great War moves into its final days. The last remnant of the Red Banner Pacific Fleet has fought its duel with Halsey in the Pacific, resorting to nuclear weapons in the last extreme—but what has happened to *Kirov* and *Orlan?*

Now the many story threads involving Fairchild Inc. and the desperate missions to find Orlov launched by both Haselden and Fedorov all converge in the vortex of time and fate on the shores of the Caspian Sea. Fedorov and Troyak lead an amphibious assault at Makhachkala, right into the teeth of the German advance. Meanwhile, Admiral Volsky and Kamenski read the chronology of events to peek at the outcome and discover the verdict of history. Can it still be changed?

Turn the page with Admiral Volsky and learn the fate of Orlov, Fedorov, Karpov and the world itself. Follow the strange and enigmatic figure of Sir Roger Ames, Duke of Elvington as he reveals a plot, and a plan, older than history itself on the windswept shores of Lindisfarne Castle.

Kirov Saga: Armageddon ~ *Book VIII*

The lines of fate have brought the most powerful ship in the world to a decisive place in history. Driven by his own inner demons, Captain Karpov now believes that with *Kirov* in 1908 he is truly invincible, and his aim is to impose his will on that unsuspecting world and reverse the cold fate of Russian history from 1908 to the 21st century. But it is not just the fate of a single nation at stake now, but that of all the world.

Shocked by Karpov's betrayal, Anton Fedorov plans a mission to stop the Captain before he can do irreversible damage to the cracked mirror of time. Now Admiral Volsky must do everything possible to launch this final mission aboard the nuclear attack submarine *Kazan*. The journey to the Sea of Japan becomes a perilous one when the Americans and Japanese begin to hunt *Kazan* in the dangerous waters of 2021.

Join Anton Fedorov, Admiral Volsky, Chief Dobrynin, and Gennadi Orlov aboard *Kazan* as they launch this last desperate mission to confront the man, and the ship, that now threatens to change all history and unravel the fabric of fate and time itself.

The series continues in the book you now hold: *Altered States*

The Meridian Series (Time Travel / Alternate History)

Book I: *Meridian – A Novel In Time*
ForeWord Magazine's "Book of the Year"
2002 Silver Medal Winner for Science Fiction
The adventure begins on the eve of the greatest experiment ever attempted—time travel. As the project team meets for their final mission briefing, the last member, arriving late, brings startling news. Catastrophe threatens and the fate of the Western World hangs in the balance. But a visitor from another time arrives bearing clues that will carry the hope of countless generations yet to be born, and a desperate plea for help. The team is led to the Jordanian desert during WWI and the exploits of the fabled Lawrence of Arabia. There they struggle to find the needle in the haystack of causality that can prevent the disaster from ever happening.

Book II: *Nexus Point*
The project team members slowly come to the realization that a "Time War" is being waged by unseen adversaries in the future. The quest for an ancient fossil leads to an amazing discovery hidden in the Jordanian desert. A mysterious group of assassins plot to decide the future course of history, just one battle in a devious campaign that will span the Meridians of time, both future and past. Exciting Time travel adventure in the realm of the Crusades!

Book III: *Touchstone*
When Nordhausen follows a hunch and launches a secret time jump mission on his own, he uncovers an operation being run by unknown adversaries from the future. The incident has dramatic repercussions for Kelly Ramer, his place in the time line again threatened by paradox. Kelly's fate is somehow linked to an ancient Egyptian artifact, once famous the world over, and now a forgotten

slab of stone. The result is a harrowing mission to Egypt during the time frame of Napoleon's 1799 invasion.

Book IV: *Anvil of Fate*

The cryptic ending of Touchstone dovetails perfectly into this next volume as Paul insists that Kelly has survived, and is determined to bring him safely home. Only now is the true meaning of the stela unearthed at Rosetta made apparent—a grand scheme to work a catastrophic transformation of the Meridians, so dramatic and profound in its effect that the disaster at Palma was only a precursor. The history leads them to the famous Battle of Tours where Charles Martel strove to stem the tide of the Moorish invaders and save the west from annihilation. Yet more was at stake on the Anvil of Fate than the project team first realized, and they now pursue the mystery of two strange murders that will decide the fate of Western Civilization itself!

Book V: *Golem 7*

Nordhausen is back with new research and his hand on the neck of the new terrorist behind the much feared "Palma Event." Now the project team struggles to discover how and where the Assassins have intervened to restore the chaos of Palma, and their search leads them on one of the greatest naval sagas of modern history—the hunt for the battleship *Bismarck*. For some unaccountable reason the fearsome German battleship was not sunk on its maiden voyage, and now the project team struggles to put the ship back in its watery grave. Meet Admiral John Tovey and Chief of Staff "Daddy" Brind as the Royal Navy begins to receive mysterious intelligence from an agent known only as "Lonesome Dove." Exciting naval action and top notch research characterize this fast paced alternate history of the sinking of the *Bismarck*.

Historical Fiction

Taklamakan ~ *The Land Of No Return*

It was one of those moments on the cusp of time, when Tando Ghazi Khan, a simple trader of tea and spice, leads a caravan to the edge of the great desert, and becomes embroiled in the struggle that will decide the fate of an empire and shake all under heaven and earth. A novel of the Silk Road, the empire of Tibet clashes with T'ang China on the desolate roads that fringe the Taklamakan desert, and one man holds the key to victory in a curious map that guards an ancient secret hidden for centuries.

Khan Tengri ~ *Volume II of Taklamakan*

Learn the fate of Tando, Drekk, and the others in this revised and extended version of Part II of Taklamakan, with a 30,000 word, 7 chapter addition. Tando and his able scouts lead the Tibetan army west to Khotan, but they are soon confronted by a powerful T'ang army, and threatened by treachery and dissention within their own ranks. Their paths join at a mysterious shrine hidden in the heart of the most formidable desert on earth where each one finds more than they imagined, an event that changes their lives forever.

The Dharman Series: Science Fiction

Wild Zone ~ Classic Science Fiction – Volume I

A shadow has fallen over earth's latest and most promising colony prospect in the Dharma system. When a convulsive solar flux event disables communications with the Safe Zone, special agent Timothy Scott Ryan is rushed to the system on a navy frigate to investigate. He soon becomes embroiled in a mystery that threatens the course of evolution itself as a virulent new organism has targeted mankind as a new host. Aided by three robotic aids left in the colony facilities, Ryan struggles to solve the mystery of Dharma VI, and the source of the strange mutation in the life forms of the planet. Book I in a trilogy of riveting classic sci-fi novels.

Mother Heart ~ Sequel to Wild Zone – Volume II
Ensign Lydia Gates is the most important human being alive, for her blood holds the key to synthesizing a vaccine against the awful mutations spawned by the Colony Virus. Ryan and Caruso return to the Wild Zone to find her, discovering more than they bargained for when microbiologist Dr. Elena Chandros is found alive, revealing a mystery deeper than time itself at the heart of the planet, an ancient entity she has come to call "Mother Heart."

Dream Reaper ~ A Mythic Mystery/Horror Novel
There was something under the ice at Steamboat Slough, something lost, buried in the frozen wreckage where the children feared to play. For Daniel Byrne, returning to the old mission site near the Yukon where he taught school a decade past, the wreck of an old steamboat becomes more than a tale told by the village elders. In a mystery weaving the shifting imagery of a dream with modern psychology and ancient myth, Daniel struggles to solve the riddle of the old wreck and free himself from the haunting embrace of a nightmare older than history itself. It has been reported through every culture, in every era of human history, a malevolent entity that comes in the night…and now it has come for him!

For more information on these and other books please visit:
http://www.writingshop.ws or http://www.dharma6.com

Made in the USA
Lexington, KY
16 February 2014